RUNNING OUT OF TIME . . .

Abby was in the bedroom of her Hollywood apartment, sprawled on the floor alongside the bureau, and there was a bad smell in the air. She'd been knocked out. Her last memory was of Hickle.

Looming over her, shotgun in hand.

Had he shot her? She didn't think so. She wasn't aware of any holes in her body, but somehow he'd rendered her unconscious and left her there. And that sour, brackish smell . . .

Gas. The apartment was filling with gas. Gas leaks could be dangerous, could be fatal. Any spark or open flame could ignite an explosion.

Open flame. The furnace pilot light.

She saw it then—exactly what Hickle had planned for her.

"Talk about going out with a bang."

THE
SHADOW
HUNTER

Michael Prescott

A SIGNET BOOK

SIGNET
Published by New American Library, a division of
Penguin Putnam Inc., 375 Hudson Street, New York,
New York 10014, U.S.A.
Penguin Books Ltd, 27 Wrights Lane, London W8 5TZ, England
Penguin Books Australia Ltd, Ringwood, Victoria, Australia
Penguin Books Canada Ltd, 10 Alcorn Avenue,
Toronto, Ontario, Canada M4V 3B2
Penguin Books (N.Z.) Ltd, 182–190 Wairau Road,
Auckland 10, New Zealand

Penguin Books Ltd, Registered Offices:
Harmondsworth, Middlesex, England

First published by Signet, an imprint of New American Library,
a division of Penguin Putnam Inc.

First Printing, June 2000
1 3 5 7 9 10 8 6 4 2

Author's Note

First, I invite readers with Internet access to visit my website at http://michaelprescott.freeservers.com/, where you'll find information on my two previous books, *Comes the Dark* and *Stealing Faces*, as well as updates on my current and future projects.

Second, I want to offer my sincere thanks to everyone who helped me in the writing and publishing of this novel, including Joseph Pittman, senior editor at New American Library; Carolyn Nichols, executive director; Louise Burke, publisher; my literary agent, Jane Dystel, president of Jane Dystel Literary Management; and Miriam Goderich, vice president of JDLM.

Their sensitive comments and strong support made all the difference in guiding *The Shadow Hunter* from a rough synopsis to the finished book you hold in your hands.

Prologue

She had a gun in her purse, and she was ready.

"I hate men," Sheila Rogers said, gulping her daiquiri. "Know what I mean?"

The dark-haired woman nodded. "I know."

"They're pigs, is what they are. They use you and throw you away."

"Sure."

"Like, there was this guy I told you about. What we had was really special, and then all of a sudden it's over, and he won't even talk to me."

"That's rough. Really."

The dark-haired woman had a name, which she had mentioned earlier when they'd met at the Roxbury, a club down the Strip, but Sheila had already forgotten it. She was no damn good with names.

She wondered why the woman was hanging with her, anyway. They'd been club crawling all night, moving from the Rox to the Viper Room, then to Babylon and the Teaszer, and finally to Lizard Maiden at the west end of Sunset Strip. Along the way, Sheila had imbibed a variety of liquid refreshments, settling on daiquiris as her drink of choice. The alcohol had fuzzed up her brain, and she was vaguely aware that she was talking too much. She couldn't seem to stop.

"He was a really great guy," she was saying aimlessly as she leaned on the mahogany bar. "I mean, he was a pig—he turned out to be a pig—but when we were together, it was like magic, you know? Like we were meant for each other."

"Yes."

"Like goddamn destiny. That's what it was. What I thought it was." Sheila shook her head slowly. "I guess I said all this stuff already, huh? Back at the Viper Room or somewhere?"

"It's okay. You can tell me again. Sometimes it helps to talk things out."

"What are you, Mother Teresa?"

"Just a friend."

"Well, shit, I sure can use one of those. Lately . . . I've been kind of messed up."

"How?"

"Over him. He—I don't know, I can't get him out of my mind. It's been two goddamn months. You'd think I'd forget the son of a bitch by now. You'd think . . ."

"Maybe you don't want to forget."

"No. I don't." Sheila leaned closer to the dark-haired woman on the bar stool beside her. "Can I tell you a secret?"

"Sure."

Sheila wanted to whisper, but she couldn't, of course. Lizard Maiden, known to aficionados as the Liz, was not a place for subdued conversation. It was one of the raunchiest clubs on the Strip, a den of flashing lights and thunderous music from the live band, where the dance floor was always packed with swaying, spastic bodies, and along the bar and at the tables lining the walls, patrons leaned close together and shouted to be heard.

"The thing is," Sheila said, "I'm running around

from club to club because I figure if I go to enough places like this, I'll run into him."

"He comes here?"

"Sometimes. Usually on a Friday night, or a Saturday." Tonight was Friday. "I mean, he hangs at all the clubs, so I never know when I might see him. He's a club crawler. I met him down the Strip at the House of Blues." Sheila chuckled wistfully. "Appropriate, right?"

"Even if you do run into him, how will that help?"

Sheila looked away. "It just will, that's all." She shifted her purse in her lap and felt the weight of the pistol inside.

"Maybe if you meet someone else, you'll forget about him. There are other guys out there."

"Not like this one. He wasn't just anybody. He's famous. You've heard of him. Everybody's heard of him."

"So who is he?"

Sheila hesitated, reluctant to reveal much more. She studied her companion. The woman was a few years older than Sheila herself, maybe twenty-seven or twenty-eight, of medium height, slender and self-possessed. Framed by a fall of dark brown hair in a pageboy cut, her face looked pale and angular, her cheekbones high and strong. Her cool hazel eyes betrayed no hint of judgment or reproach.

"Devin Corbal," Sheila said finally. "That's who."

"The actor?"

"I told you he's famous. He's been in, like, six movies. Six. And he's only twenty-three."

"And you went out with him?"

"For two whole weeks." Sheila frowned. "It was

great. Me and Devin were, like, soul mates. For two weeks anyway."

She swallowed the rest of her daiquiri.

"Two weeks," she said again.

The dark-haired woman dismounted her bar stool. "Save my seat for me, okay? I need to use the can."

Sheila nodded, lost in memories of Devin. She barely even noticed as the woman walked away into the surging crowd on the dance floor.

"Need a refill?"

She glanced up and saw the bartender, a guy she knew by sight, though she'd forgotten his name. "What the hell."

The bartender poured another daiquiri. "Who's your friend?"

"Nobody."

"Ain't seen her in here before."

"She's just somebody I've been clubbin' with."

"I remember when you and Dev went clubbing." He handed her the drink. "Get over him yet?"

"What's it to you?" Sheila asked sourly.

"Oh, nothing," the bartender said. "He's here tonight, that's all."

Sheila looked up slowly. "He's here? Devin's here?"

He shrugged. "Just thought you'd like to know."

Lizard Maiden offered a unisex rest room in an alcove near the entrance. The dark-haired woman went past the door, then past a row of pay phones, and stopped at the end of the alcove outside what might have been a supply closet.

No one was around. She reached into her purse, removed a cell phone, and speed-dialed the first number in the phone's memory. The music was not so deafening here, and she could speak in a tone of voice that was almost normal.

"Paul, this is Abby," she said when the call was answered.

"You still at Babylon?" Paul Travis asked.

"No, we've moved on. We've been bouncing from club to club all night. She's starting to open up, finally."

"Talking about the client?"

"Yeah. She's angry, and she could mean business. She keeps touching her purse in a way that makes me think she's got more than mascara inside."

"If she's carrying, you better watch yourself."

Abby smiled. "I always do. Look, I have to get back to her. I'll update you at the next opportunity. Right now we're at a place on the Strip called Lizard Maiden."

"Lizard Maiden?"

"They call it the Liz. It's just west of Bar One—"

"I know where it is. It's where *he* is."

For a moment Abby couldn't process what Travis had said. "What?"

"The client. He's there. At Lizard Maiden. He showed up a half hour ago. He's in the VIP Room, god damn it."

"Bodyguards with him?"

"Two."

"Get them on the phone and tell them we're Code Red. If there's a way to get him out of the club without being seen, have them do it. But don't let them move him into the main room, or Sheila may spot him. Got it?"

"I got it."

"I'll stay close to her. Even if she sees the client, she won't try anything."

"Make sure of it, Abby. Make damn sure."

The call ended. Abby stuffed the phone back into her purse, next to the snub-nosed Smith .38 she carried when on the job.

Naturally Corbal was here. He had to be here, and not in some other club in another part of town.

"Of all the gin joints in all the world," she muttered, leaving the alcove.

Still, it was no big problem. A complication, sure, but as long as she kept Sheila within arm's reach, nothing would happen. Sheila Rogers was twenty-two, anorexically thin, and highly intoxicated—no match for Abby in any kind of fight. If Sheila made a move for the gun in her purse, Abby could drop her simply by closing off the blood flow in the carotid arteries of the neck. She had done that sort of thing before, in similar circumstances.

She skirted the dance floor and approached the bar, and that was when she began to be afraid.

Sheila wasn't there. The stool she had been using was unoccupied.

This was bad.

Abby stood at the bar and signaled to the bartender. He bared his teeth in a predatory smile when he saw her.

"Hey, sweet thing."

She ignored this. "Where's the woman I was sitting with?"

"Sheila?" His smile became a smirk. "I think she went to visit a friend."

Abby's heart sped up. "What friend?"

He leaned close. "Listen, forget about her. She's a

loser anyway. You don't need to hang with her. I just wanted to get rid of her, so maybe you and me could get to know each other."

"So you told her Devin Corbal is here?"

"How'd you know—"

"Never mind. Where's the VIP Room?"

"Sorry, you can't go in there. Celebs only. You know, I get off in a couple hours—"

Abby reached out and grabbed his right wrist, applying painful pressure to the scaphoid bone below the ball of his thumb. "*Where is it?*" she hissed.

The bartender paled. "Around back," he said through gritted teeth. "That way." He jerked his head to the left.

She released his wrist. He rubbed it, gasping.

"Jesus, lady, what the fuck's up with you?"

Abby barely heard him. She was already pushing through the crowded dance floor, praying she was not too late.

Sheila's pulse was roaring in her ears, and her eyes didn't seem to want to blink anymore, and there was a hot, crawling queasiness in her gut.

She knew what she had to do. She had rehearsed it, fantasized it, but in her fantasies she had never been shaking with fear, and her stomach hadn't bubbled like this, and the music hadn't been so loud, the dancing crowd so close and hot.

She had the gun. She was ready. She had to be ready.

He would be in the VIP Room. It was where he always went when he was here. He had taken her to that room one night. She remembered it well—a small room in the rear of the Liz, curtained off. A room with-

7

out windows. A room that would offer no place for him to run or hide.

As she left the dance floor, she reached into her purse and withdrew a Llama .45, fully loaded, the safety off.

The VIP Room was just ahead, unmarked, screened off by a curtained doorway.

She would enter that room and shoot Devin Corbal right in his lying heart. Teach him a lesson for treating her like some whore. Show him she hadn't been kidding around when she warned him he'd be sorry.

Briefly she wished she had time for a hit of coke. She carried an insulin needle in her purse and a small bag of the white powder. She could duck into the rest room, mix the coke with water, draw it into the syringe, and then inject herself in the crook of her arm . . .

But she knew that if she took the time to do that, she would lose her nerve. She had to kill Devin now, before she thought about it too much. It was now or never.

"Now or never," she muttered to herself, boosting her courage.

Go for it.

Sheila took a breath, then pushed through the curtains into the VIP Room, the gun leading her.

The room was empty.

Unfinished drinks were scattered around the tables. Snack foods, still warm, lay on platters. Two chairs had been kicked back from the tables at awkward angles, as if whoever had been in here had departed in haste.

"They cleared him out," Sheila whispered, piecing it

together. "He was in here and . . . they cleared him out."

But he hadn't gone out via the dance floor to the front entrance. She would have seen him.

The back way, then.

She left the VIP Room and looked down the hall. At its far end was a dim, flickering EXIT sign.

Of course.

She ran down the hall, the din of dance music diminishing behind her, and pushed open a metal door. She found herself at the top of a short flight of wooden steps descending into an alley. Her gaze took in the high brick walls, the sloping shoulders of the Hollywood Hills rising to the north, the haze of neon glare and smog that hid the stars, and, ten yards away, moving fast—Devin Corbal.

In the light from a billboard overhead she saw Devin clearly. He was tall and lean, dressed in an open-collared shirt and faded jeans, and he was being hustled out of the alley by two grim-faced men in dark suits who must be his bodyguards.

They hadn't looked back. Hadn't noticed her on the stairs.

From this vantage point she could see Devin's broad back, a perfect target.

Her gun came up. Finger on the trigger.

One of the bodyguards saw her, too late.

Sheila fired once—twice—and then something hit her hard from behind, driving her forward, down the stairs in a tangle of flailing limbs.

She had an impression of dark hair and furious hazel eyes, and then there was an elbow coming up fast to slam the base of her jaw, and she went limp and felt nothing at all.

* * *

Abby clawed Sheila's gun out of her slack fingers and batted it away, then pinned her to the pavement at the bottom of the stairs. She held her down until she was certain that Sheila had blacked out from the blow to her jaw.

Then she looked at Devin Corbal. He lay motionless on the ground. One of his bodyguards performed frantic CPR while the other yelled into a cell phone, "Get the car back here now, *right now!*"

"We need an RA!" the first bodyguard shouted. Rescue ambulance.

"RA'll take too long, we can drive him to the ER ourselves." Into the phone again: *"Where the hell is the car?"*

But the car wouldn't help. An ambulance wouldn't help, nor would an emergency room. Nothing would help. Abby knew that.

She saw the lake of maroon blood that seeped from between Devin's shoulder blades. She saw his eyes, open, staring.

Sheila had fired twice. One shot had gone wild, but the other, by skill or luck, had hit Devin Corbal squarely in the back and killed him instantly.

The bodyguard performing CPR finally reached the same conclusion. He stood slowly, shaking his head.

"We lost him," the man said. "God damn it, we lost him."

No, Abby thought. You didn't lose him.

I did.

1

Hickle watched her as she ran.

Her hair fascinated him. It was long and golden, blown in wild trammels by the sea breeze. It trailed behind her, a comet's tail, a wake of blond fire.

She was crossing directly in front of him now. Instinctively he withdrew a few inches deeper into the overhanging foliage that screened him from view.

She pounded past, plumes of sand bursting under her bare feet. Her long legs pumped, and her slim belly swelled with intakes of air. Even from a distance of twenty yards he could see the glaze of perspiration on her suntanned skin. She glowed.

Months earlier, when he had first seen her, he had wondered if her radiance was a trick of the camera lens. Now that he had observed her in person many times, he knew it was real. She actually did glow, as angels did. She was an ethereal being, tethered lightly to this world.

Soon he would cut the tether, and then she would not be part of the world at all.

He could have done it now, today, if he'd brought the shotgun with him. But there was no hurry. He could kill her at any time.

Besides, he enjoyed watching her.

She continued down the beach, followed by her bodyguard. The bodyguard always accompanied her when she went jogging, and never once had he even glanced into the narrow gap between two beachfront houses, where a trellis of bougainvillea cast a shadow dark enough to conceal a crouching man.

"You shouldn't trust your life to him, Kris," Hickle whispered. "You're not nearly as safe as you think."

There was sun and sea spray and blue sky. There was the momentum of her body, the rhythm of her feet on the sand. There was her breathing, her heart rate.

This was all. Nothing more. Only the moment. One moment detached from the rest of her life, one moment when she did not have to think about threats and security measures, the bodyguard jogging a few paces behind her, the command post in the guest cottage at her house . . .

Damn.

Kris Barwood slowed her pace. The thoughts were back. The mood was broken.

Her daily exercise routine, a four-mile run along the strip of semiprivate beach that bordered Malibu Reserve, had been her one respite from the constant stress of vigilance and fear. The beach had always felt safe to her. It was a special place. People played here with their dogs and flew kites in the salty wind. On one side was the Pacific, studded with wave-battered rocks, and on the other side stood rows of immaculate homes, some boasting the extravagance of swimming pools only steps from the high tide mark. The houses were narrow but deep, extending well back from the strand. Though ridiculously close together, they afforded a curious sense of privacy, and loud parties were rare. Most of the owners worked long hours in intensely competitive fields. They came home to relax, as she used to do—but now there was no relaxation for her anywhere.

"Kris? You okay?" That was Steve Drury, her bodyguard, a pleasant young man with a swimmer's build and a sun-streaked crewcut. When they jogged together, he wore shorts, a T-shirt, and a zippered bellypouch that contained a 9mm Beretta.

She realized she had stopped running entirely. "Fine," she said. "Don't have my usual energy."

"You'll make up for it tomorrow. We'll do two extra miles. Deal?"

She found a smile. "Deal."

They crossed the sand to her house, a three-story modernistic box with wide windows that let in the magical Malibu light. She left Steve at the outdoor shower and entered through the door at the upper deck to avoid disturbing her husband in the game room, where he spent an unhealthy amount of time playing with his expensive toys—pinball machines, model railroads, radio-operated cars, and his favorite, an electronic putting green. Lately, Howard seemed fonder of these acquisitions than he was of her.

The master bedroom was on the third floor, at the rear of the house, with a view of the sea and the curving coastline. Kris stripped, running the shower hot. Under the steaming spray she shampooed and rinsed her long blond hair.

Edward, her hairstylist, had repeatedly suggested that she was reaching the stage of life when it was better to wear her hair short. She had finally told him to quit it. She liked her hair long. Anyway, forty wasn't old. And she could pass for thirty-five in most circumstances. Direct sunlight showed the creases at the corners of her eyes, the gathering tightness around her mouth, the hint of a sag in her cheeks, but while on the air she was lit by diffusion-filtered lights and masked by a layer of makeup that got thicker each year.

She hated to worry about her looks. It was shallow and stupid, and she had other assets, after all. She could shoot tape and record sound, handle every piece of equipment in an editing booth, write copy, extemporize fluently in the coverage of a breaking story. Few of those skills, however, were required in her present position. For better or worse, she had become a celebrity.

Draped in a robe, she dried and brushed her hair in front of the big mirror over the bathroom's marble countertop. The face that looked back at her was strong and Nordic—Kris Andersen had been her maiden name. Her eyes were blue-gray and had the peculiar quality of seeming larger and more intense than ordinary eyes. She had white, perfectly even teeth, and her mouth could execute an impressive variety of smiles, one of many tricks that made her interesting to watch. She knew that if she ever stopped being interesting, she would not be watched for long. Of course there was one viewer whose attention she would gladly do without—

She froze, the hairbrush motionless in her hand.

From the bedroom had come a sound. A rustle of movement, barely audible. It might be Steve or Courtney, the housekeeper, but irrationally she was certain it was *him*.

She heard it again—a whisper of motion, the soft scrape of fabric on fabric.

She turned from the mirror. The hairbrush was her only weapon. Absurdly she raised it like a club, then stepped out of the bathroom, her gaze darting, and there he was by the windows, silhouetted against the vertical blind . . .

"Kris? You okay?"

All the tension leaked out of her, because it was Howard's voice.

She dropped the hairbrush. It thumped on the floor. "Damn," she breathed. "Don't *do* that to me."

"Do what?"

She shook her head, dismissing his question. "I thought you were him," she said simply.

Her husband crossed the room to take her hand in his. "Come on, that's crazy."

"I heard someone out here. I thought it might be— well, it could have been . . ."

"No, it couldn't. Not a chance."

From a strictly rational standpoint Howard was probably correct. But how could she explain to him that rationality played little part in her fears and nightmares, the false alarms and spasms of panic that made her glance over her shoulder at every stray noise and flicker of shadow?

"You're right," she said, feeling empty. "Guess I'm a little overwrought."

He stooped and retrieved her hairbrush, placing it gently in her grasp as if she were a child. "Don't worry about it. Don't worry about anything."

"Good advice. Hard to follow."

He showed her a warm smile that lit up his square, tanned face. After retiring last year at fifty, he had taken to hanging around the house and eating too much. A belt of flab hung around his waist, and his neck had grown thick and loose. "You're no good at taking orders," Howard said. "Me, I'm great at it. Travis told me not to worry, and I haven't."

15

"Your faith is touching."

"Isn't it, though?" His smile faded. "Speaking of Travis, we'll be late for that meeting if we don't leave soon."

"Give me another minute to get dressed."

"Right. See how well I take orders? I'm a natural." He moved toward the hall.

She stopped him. "While you're waiting, could you check the cottage for me?"

"Is that necessary?"

"I want to know if he's called."

"Let's assume he has. How does it help you to find out?"

"I have to know. If you won't check, I will."

"If you worry about it all the time, it defeats the whole purpose of having Travis's people around."

"Their purpose isn't to keep me happy. Their purpose is to keep me alive."

"You're getting worked up again."

His patronizing tone infuriated her. "I have a right to get worked up. It's me he's after. Or is that another thing I'm supposed to not think about?" She turned away, suddenly exhausted. "Check the cottage, all right? I have to get changed."

She returned to the bathroom and finished brushing her hair, performing the task with more vigor than necessary. When she emerged, the bedroom was empty. Howard had gone.

She changed into a pantsuit. At the studio she would put on whatever outfit the clothing coordinator had selected, usually something in blue to bring out her eyes.

Before leaving the bedroom, she went to the windows for another look at the beach. The tide was going out. Seagulls bobbed and weaved on chancy currents of air. She wished she could sit and watch the birds and not deal with this meeting Travis had called or with anything else, ever.

Her life had been easier when she was a twenty-two-year-old radio reporter in Duluth, Minnesota. True, there had been no money for rent or food, but she had been too busy to care. Maybe she should have stayed in Duluth, married the junior manager at the radio station. Sometimes she wished she didn't have this hard-edged ambition inside her, driving her to high-profile assignments, more money, more pressure. But there had always been part of her that felt she would die without fame and recognition and strangers turning their heads. Now she had all of that, and because of it—because of one particular stranger whose head she'd turned—she might die anyway.

Life was a tangle. Her life, at least. Maybe everybody's.

Downstairs she found Courtney dusting the autographed golf balls in Howard's display cabinet. "They're waiting in the Lincoln," Courtney said. "Mr. Drury and Mr. Barwood."

Kris glanced at her watch. She was running late. Having Steve bring the car out of the garage to idle in the driveway was Howard's way of telling her so.

A garden path, bordered by rosebushes, white oleander, and bird-of-paradise, led from the main house to the guest cottage attached to the garage. A gray Lincoln Town Car, the Cartier model, idled in the driveway, Steve Drury at the wheel. The car was her own, but the pleasure of driving it was one more thing Hickle had taken from her.

Steve got out and opened the rear door for her. He

had changed into slacks, a button-down shirt, and a suit jacket that concealed his Beretta. She slipped into the backseat, next to Howard, while Steve slid behind the wheel and adjusted the volume on the Alpine audio system. He was playing a CD of Mozart's *Magic Flute,* her favorite. It soothed her.

The Lincoln pulled out of the driveway and headed down a narrow lane colonnaded with tall eucalyptus trees. At the gate, guards waved the Town Car through, and the sedan accelerated onto Pacific Coast Highway, rushing over the bridge that straddled Malibu Creek. In the lagoon fed by the estuary, a few shore birds lifted themselves into the afternoon sun.

"Did you check?" she asked Howard tonelessly.

He acknowledged her only with a half turn in her direction. "I checked. Nothing serious to report."

"Meaning?"

"He called a couple of times this morning. Not since then. It's been a quiet afternoon. Maybe he's losing interest."

"Sure. Maybe."

But she knew Raymond Hickle would never lose interest in her as long as she was alive.

Hickle sat on the roadside, a hat covering his face, and watched the Town Car pull out of the Malibu Reserve gate. He took a good look at it when it turned onto the coast highway. The car was close; he could see his own reflection in the polished panels of the passenger doors. In the lightly tinted rear window there was the vague outline of a silhouetted figure.

There was no chance that Kris or her driver would spot him. Sitting cross-legged on the curb, the hat pulled low, he was just one of the many faceless derelicts who wandered through Malibu and other towns along the California coast. He could watch Kris come and go, and no one would be the wiser.

His gaze followed the car as it disappeared down the road. He kept staring after it even when it was long gone. Then he got up and retraced his steps to his own car, a Volkswagen Rabbit parked on a side street a mile from Malibu Reserve.

He had no intention of trying to catch up with Kris. Her driver was a security officer trained to spot a pursuing vehicle and take evasive action.

Even so, he expected to arrive at the studio gate well before she did. She had left earlier than usual, and the route she'd taken—southbound on Pacific Coast Highway, heading toward West LA—was not the most direct way to Burbank.

He figured she had an appointment to keep. It would occupy her for a half hour or longer. By the time she reached the studio, he would be positioned near the entrance to the parking lot.

In his car, he had his duffel bag. And in the duffel, he had the shotgun. He imagined holding it now, feeling its sleekness, its smoothness, pumping the action and then the trigger, and the satisfying recoil as the spray of lethal shot fanned wide.

"Blammo," Hickle said. He was smiling.

2

Abby Sinclair was late and walking fast as she came out of the elevator on the eighteenth floor of the Century City high-rise where Travis Protective Services housed its office suite. She had fixed her hair as best she could in the elevator, but in T-shirt, jeans, and Nikes, she wasn't exactly dressed for a business meeting.

At the end of the hall she paused before the double doors emblazoned with the TPS logo. The doors were mirrored, and she was able to ascertain that she looked okay, despite her ensemble. Her reflection stared back at her with cool hazel eyes that revealed little of what she felt inside. Lately, it was just as well that no one knew what she was feeling.

She entered the reception area, passing through a metal detector, then handed a carry-on bag to the security officer at the front desk. "Came straight from the airport. Keep this nice and safe for me, okay?"

The guy frowned at her. "I didn't know you were still working for Travis."

"I've been away for a while. Now I'm back in the saddle."

His frown didn't waver. "Well, ain't that great news."

She wasn't surprised at his hostility or at the cool stares that greeted her as she hurried through the maze of corridors. Only a few people at TPS knew exactly what role she had played in the Devin Corbal disaster, but throughout the firm it was common knowledge that she had been involved somehow, and that her involvement had cost Corbal his life.

She walked past conference rooms, workspaces partitioned into cubicles, and private or semiprivate offices. Roughly half the offices, she noted guiltily, were empty now. TPS was thinning out its staff, making massive cutbacks to stop the hemorrhage of money. Only the most essential employees had been retained, performing the services that were the backbone of the company—threat assessment, personal protection, and investigation. Before long, maybe they would be gone as well, and this office suite would be occupied by insurance salespeople or stockbrokers. She didn't want to think about that.

She reached Travis's corner office and nodded at his assistant, Rose, receiving a squinty glare in return. "You're late," Rose said, her tone implying that this was the least of Abby's sins.

"Just buzz me in."

"Hold on." Rose took her time activating the intercom. "Mr. Travis? Miss Sinclair is here."

Over the cheap speaker, Abby heard Travis's tinny voice grant her admittance.

"Yes, sir." Rose looked at her. "You can go in."

"Thanks a lot."

Abby crossed the anteroom to Travis's door. She was turning the knob when Rose said, "This client's important to us. You might try keeping her alive."

Various rejoinders ran through Abby's mind. She swallowed them all. Sometimes the best thing to say was nothing at all.

She entered Travis's office and found him in conference with a blond woman instantly recognizable as Kris Barwood and a somewhat older, heavyset man who had to be her husband.

"Better late than never," Travis said as he rose from behind his desk.

Et tu, Paul? she thought, but all she said was "My plane was delayed." Her gaze widened to include everyone in the room. "Sorry to keep you all waiting."

Introductions were made. Howard Barwood had a firm handshake of long duration. Kris, no surprise, looked exactly the same in person as she did on TV. Having met a number of celebrities over the past two years, Abby had learned that the beautiful ones really were beautiful. The notion that the camera performed some alchemical transformation of ordinary folks into superstars was a sop to the envious multitudes.

"You just flew in from out of town?" Howard asked.

"Yes—which explains my less than professional attire. I only brought casual clothes with me on the trip."

"I hope we didn't interrupt your vacation."

"No, I was working another case, actually. Got done last night."

"I thought TPS only handled LA clients."

"This wasn't a TPS case. I haven't worked with TPS"—*since Devin Corbal*, she nearly said, but caught herself—"in a few months. I'm an independent consultant. I work with a variety of firms all across the country. Paul left a message on my answering machine yesterday. I got back to him first thing this morning, and he told me a little about the situation you find yourselves in."

"Situation." Kris Barwood leaned forward in her chair, balancing her hands lightly on her knees, a pose she must have learned while doing on-camera interviews. "That's one way of putting it."

"I know it feels like a crisis," Abby said, "but it's nothing we can't handle."

Howard snorted. "Tell that to Devin Corbal."

For a startled moment Abby wondered how they had found out about her involvement in that case. Then she realized Howard had been looking at Travis when he said it.

She and Travis were rescued from any response when Kris cut in smoothly, "When you arrived, Paul was just about to explain what it is you're going to do for me."

"I have kind of an unusual job, Mrs. Barwood."

"Call me Kris." The anchorwoman flashed a smile that ought to have looked artificial but didn't.

"Okay, Kris. I'm Abby."

Howard Barwood spoke up again. "How old are you, Abby, if you don't mind my asking?"

"Twenty-eight."

His eyelids lifted in skeptical appraisal. "Isn't that a little young to be a licensed psychologist?"

"I'm not a licensed psychologist."

"Travis here"—Barwood cocked a thumb in the direction of the desk—"called you a psychological consultant."

"That's one way of describing the work I do. I call myself a dynamic interpersonal risk evaluator. But there's a simpler way of putting it. I'm a pilot fish."

Kris and her husband exchanged a bemused glance.

"A pilot fish," Abby repeated. She tossed her purse on a chair but remained standing. "You know those little fish that swim in the wake of a shark? They gather scraps. So do I. Only, the sharks I swim with are people like Raymond Hickle, and the scraps I gather are scraps of information."

She crossed behind Travis's desk to stand before the wide windows, the panoramic backdrop. "See, when it comes to assessing the threat, personal protection services have to rely on background information and profiling. It would be better to get to know the real man. It can't be done from a distance. It has to be up close and personal."

"How close?" Kris asked. "How personal?"

"If all goes well, I'm going to be Hickle's best friend."

There was a beat of silence, and Kris said, "This man may not have any friends."

"But he wants one. Everybody does. Do you know what people look for in a friend? Someone to talk to. Someone who'll listen." Abby smiled. "I'm a good listener."

"You mean you're going to analyze him without his even knowing it?"

"Not analyze him in a psychological sense. Instead, I need to assess him from a security standpoint. Gauge his intentions, his timetable. And keep an eye on him so if he does decide to act, I'll be there to head him off at the pass."

"And you think you can do all that?"

"I've done it before, many times." And only failed once, she added silently with another twinge of guilt.

Howard straightened in his chair. "Let me get this straight. You're talking about some kind of undercover thing?"

"You can call it that."

"So you meet him, give a phony name, get to be friends. Then it's you and him alone together?"

"Right."

"But you've got armed men stationed outside, radio communication with them in case he turns crazy or sniffs you out?"

"No, it's just me. I carry a cell phone and a gun."

"Just you? Why, for God's sake?"

Travis fielded the question. "Because you're suggesting we attempt virtually round-the-clock surveillance of Raymond Hickle, and that sort of operation almost never works."

"When the police carry out an undercover operation," Kris said, "they have a backup team listening on a radio."

"Yes," Travis said, "for a twenty-minute drug buy. We're talking about installing Abby in Hickle's life for days or weeks. It's not the same. Surveillance requires more than one or two officers sitting in a car outside somebody's home. In a residential neighborhood, that car and its occupants will draw attention within hours. Someone will call the police, there'll be a commotion, and our subject will see it or hear about it."

"Usually men like Hickle are paranoid to begin with," Abby added. "It doesn't take much to push them over the edge."

Howard shook his head. "So don't have them sit in a car. Have them watch Hickle from the building across the street."

"The risk of detection is still too high," Travis said. "A successful stakeout is extremely difficult to pull off over any extended period of time. Somebody will see the binoculars in the window or intercept a radio transmission or wonder about the food deliveries to a vacant apartment or hear something through the wall. Neighbors talk, word gets around, and before you know it, the surveillance team's cover has been blown."

"And if their cover is blown," Abby said, "so is mine."

"There's another factor," Travis said. "You're assuming Hickle stays put. Suppose he and Abby go out together. We'd have to follow. That's not a job that can be done with a single vehicle or even two or three. To keep Hickle in sight at all times without being spotted ourselves, we need a minimum of a half dozen cars rotating in and out of the pursuit, sometimes hanging back in traffic, sometimes moving ahead to intercept him at points where we expect him to go."

"And if he takes me to someplace crowded, like Third Street Promenade on a Saturday night," Abby said, "then TPS would need twenty agents to cover every exit and byway. Hickle could lose the pursuit without even trying, and I wouldn't even know I was unprotected. Besides, in most cases, if things get ugly, it all happens so fast that a backup detail across the street wouldn't reach me in time anyway."

"So things do sometimes . . . get ugly?" Kris asked, sounding more curious than concerned.

Abby flashed on a gunshot in an alley, a voice saying, *We lost him.*

"Now and then," she said evenly, hoping her expression betrayed no emotion. "It comes with the territory."

Howard shook his head. "How exactly do you expect to protect yourself against a psychopath like Hickle?"

"I'm trained in self-defense. If a subject turns violent I know how to respond."

"Abby can take care of herself," Travis said. "She's

one of the most competent people I've ever worked with."

This surprised her. She glanced at Travis with a small, secret nod of appreciation.

"Well," Howard said, "she'd better be." He fixed Abby with a stare. "How many cases have you handled?"

"More than twenty over the past two years."

"I would think you'd want to quit while you're ahead."

"You mean while I'm alive?" She smiled.

Kris was studying her. "How about the Devin Corbal case? Were you in on that one?"

Abby had anticipated this question and was ready with a response. "No, I was in San Francisco at the time, protecting a radio shock jock who'd made too many enemies."

She hated to lie to a client, but if she told the truth, she would be off the Barwood case, and most likely Travis would lose Kris as a client. And she knew that this was a loss he could not afford.

Anyway, no one would be able to prove she'd lied. She had escaped from the vicinity of Lizard Maiden before the police could secure the scene. The TPS bodyguards had said nothing about her. Sheila Rogers, now in custody awaiting trial, had received a concussion during the tumble down the alley stairs and remembered nothing of Abby's assault. The bartender recalled that Sheila had been sitting with a nameless woman friend, but he had not reported his encounter with her, no doubt because he didn't want to admit that he had tipped off Sheila to Devin's whereabouts. In short, there was nothing to link Abby to the case.

Nothing but her conscience, which assailed her

nightly with images of Devin Corbal sprawled on the pavement in a spreading pool of blood.

"Even so"—Howard crossed his arms and looked past Abby at Travis—"I want to go on record as saying I'm against this."

"Your wife is my client," Travis said evenly.

"I know that. It's her safety at stake. Her decision. But if it were up to me . . ." He didn't finish.

"Howard," Abby said, "I appreciate your concern, but this is my job. It's what I do."

"You're a pilot fish. I remember." He looked at her, no amusement in his eyes. "There's just one thing about those fish. Sometimes they get a little too close to the shark they're swimming with. Sometimes they get eaten."

Abby met his gaze. "That's the downside of the metaphor."

The office was silent except for the hum of the air conditioning.

"Kris," Travis asked, "do we have your go-ahead?"

"Yes, you do," Kris said, looking at Abby as she spoke. Howard turned away, arms folded over his chest, hands gripping his biceps in a classic pose of defiance.

Abby nodded at the anchorwoman. "Thank you."

"I should be thanking you," Kris said softly. "You're the one taking all the risks."

3

When the meeting was over and the Barwoods were gone, Abby finally allowed herself to sit. She slumped in an armchair in the corner of Travis's office and asked, "How do you think it went?"

"An unqualified success," Travis said.

"You sure?"

"Absolutely. You dazzled them."

Travis stood and came around his desk. He was a tall man of forty-four with jet-black hair receding from his high forehead. He wore an open-collared dress shirt under a navy jacket, beltless tan slacks, and black loafers. Every item of his ensemble was predictable; he owned a dozen navy jackets, a dozen dress shirts, a dozen pairs of tan slacks and black loafers. He wore the identical outfit every day. It was one of his quirks. He didn't like to waste time pondering what clothes to wear.

"It's good to have you back, Abby," he said.

"I wasn't certain you'd ever want to work with me again after what happened last time. Thanks for telling them how capable I am, by the way."

"I meant it. You've been beating yourself up about Corbal for four months. Let it go."

She looked away. "I shouldn't have let her get away from me."

"You had to call in your location."

29

"I should have found a way to do it while still keeping an eye on her."

Travis sat on the arm of the chair. "A momentary lapse."

"In this business we can't afford any lapses."

"Abby, if you do this kind of work long enough, you're bound to experience a setback now and then."

"A setback? Is that what happened to Corbal?"

"Corbal was a goddamned fool. We didn't want him going into Lizard Maiden or any other club on the Strip. We told him to stay away from all his usual haunts. There was too great a chance that he would run into Sheila Rogers at one of them."

"It was my job to make sure nothing like that would happen."

"My point is, Corbal was headstrong. He wouldn't listen to us. He insisted on taking risks, and he paid for it. Even so, he would have made it out of the building if the VIP Room had been evacuated faster. He had too many friends with him, and it took too long for our people to clear them all out. The friends left via the dance floor, which only cost more time because the club was so damn crowded. Then our staff officers had to get Devin out the back way—"

"Because I recommended using the rear exit."

"It was the right tactical move. And he wouldn't be any less dead if he'd gone out via the front entrance. Sheila would have popped him on the dance floor."

"Maybe not. Maybe in all the confusion she never would have seen him. Or maybe . . . maybe I could've stopped her."

"You nearly did."

"Nearly doesn't cut it."

"You did everything you could. It's not your fault."

Abby didn't answer.

"How'd you get here from LAX?" Travis asked.

She blinked, surprised by the change of subject. "Taxicab."

"Then you'll need a ride home."

"I'll call another taxi."

"No. Let me drive you. On the way over, I can give you a more thorough briefing on the Barwood case. There wasn't time to go into much detail this morning on the phone."

"Okay, Paul. Thanks."

They didn't speak again until they had left the TPS office suite after picking up Abby's carry-on at the reception desk. In the elevator, descending to the underground parking garage, she asked Travis, "How are things going? Business-wise, I mean."

He shrugged. "Could be better. Another client ditched us on Friday. Same old story. He no longer had confidence in TPS."

"Because of Devin Corbal." *Because of me*, she wanted to say.

"It's not so much the incident itself as the ongoing, never-ending media coverage. You'd think they'd come up with something else to talk about. Last week the *Times* ran a hit piece on us—the usual second-guessing and Monday morning quarterbacking. Our clients read something like that, and half of them are ready to jump ship."

"A lot of them already have," she said quietly, thinking of the empty office space, the staff cutbacks. She knew that Travis had always prided himself on keeping his operation small, his services exclusive. There had never been more than fifty names on the TPS client list. It was a policy that had left little margin for error. Now, with clients dropping away month after month, he was facing the end of the business he had founded.

"We've suffered some losses," Travis conceded. "But we'll ride it out. In the end, we'll come back stronger than before."

He seemed to believe it. She wished she could be so confident.

His Mercedes C43 was waiting in the garage. Travis put Abby's bag into the trunk and let her in on the passenger side. Before shutting the door, he leaned in and kissed her, a brief, hard kiss that sped up her heart rate.

He hadn't kissed her in the TPS office suite. One of their rules was that there would be no displays of intimacy in the presence of TPS employees or clients.

Travis kept one hand on the wheel, the other clasping hers, as he guided the sedan into traffic on the Avenue of the Stars. "How does it feel to be back in town?" he asked.

"Not bad at all. It's warm here today." Her window was partially lowered, air rushing at her face.

"In the seventies. Warmer than Jersey, I'll bet."

"I had to buy an overcoat. Used it for a few days and donated it to charity. Couldn't fit in my carry-on."

"What about your gun? How'd you transport that?"

"FedExed it from Newark Airport this morning. Same-day delivery. It should be waiting for me when I get home."

"Who were you working for in Jersey?"

"Gil Harris. He relocated there from San Diego a few months ago. Runs a security firm in Camden. A local manufacturing plant contracted him when they decided their in-house security couldn't handle an ex-employee named Frank Harrington. The guy was making threats against the company. They wanted me to find out if he was serious."

Travis steered the Mercedes onto Santa Monica Boulevard, heading west. "Was he?"

"Darn tootin'. I found his suicide note in the hard drive of his PC. He was planning to ram through the factory gate and open fire with a pair of high-powered rifles modified to fire on full automatic."

"How'd you get to look in his computer?"

"Well, first I let Frank pick me up at a local bar and take me home. We had a nightcap, and I slipped a Rohypnol into his drink. It put him out cold. Then I searched the place, found the note and printed it out, and left it where the police couldn't miss it. Then I called nine-one-one and reported a prowler at Frank's address. He was still asleep when I amscrayed."

"Any close calls?"

"The police got there a little faster than I expected. I had to get out through a rear door. Otherwise, no sweat." She smiled. "Just another day at the office."

"What was the date on the suicide note?"

"Wednesday, March twenty-third."

"Tomorrow."

"Right."

"You stopped him just in time."

"Looks that way."

"You saved a lot of lives, Abby."

"Yeah. Maybe if I save enough of them, I can make up for the one I didn't save." She sighed. "So what's the story, Paul? Tell me all about Mr. Raymond Hickle."

"He's thirty-four, Caucasian, never married. Lives

alone, no pets, low income. Works in Zack's Donut Shack at Pico and Fairfax."

"Behind the counter or in the kitchen?"

"Little of both, but mostly behind the counter."

"Acceptable social skills, then."

"Within limits, yes. He doesn't go around muttering to himself or flashing kids in playgrounds."

"Too bad. If he did, we could get him off the street."

"It won't be that easy. As a matter of fact, he's highly recommended by his previous employers—at least the ones we could track down. There have been quite a few. Those we talked to say Ray Hickle's the best employee they ever had."

"Then why'd they let him go?"

"He quit. Invariably it was his decision."

"Why?"

"Because they offered him a promotion. That seems to be the trigger."

"What kind of promotion?"

"To a supervisory position. The guy is afraid of responsibility, apparently."

Abby shook her head. "No, I don't think so. Tell me about the other jobs he's held."

"Strictly entry-level positions. Car-wash attendant, movie theater ticket taker, dishwasher at a coffee shop, clerk in a photo store, janitor in an office high-rise."

"Common denominator—not much thinking required. You learn the basics, then go through the motions. If you're elevated to supervisor, you have to start thinking."

"I don't believe this guy's dumb."

"Didn't say he was. I'm saying he wants to leave his mind free to think about something other than his job.

Something like Kris Barwood, LA's number-one news anchor . . . and Hickle's one true love."

"And the one client TPS absolutely cannot afford to lose."

"Really? Why?"

"Because right now she's the only media person we've got on our side. Channel Eight hasn't joined the feeding frenzy. She won't let them. She keeps saying the firm has gotten a bum rap. She's said it publicly. If she ditches us, we're cooked."

Abby caught on. "On the other hand, if TPS resolves the situation without incident, and Channel Eight plays it up big . . ."

"It would go a long way toward rebuilding our client list. Yes." He frowned, as if embarrassed to have been drawn out on this subject.

"So give me more details, get me up to speed."

"Hickle started sending Kris personal letters about five months ago. Our screening process intercepted them. At first they raised no alarm. They were fan letters, nothing special."

"Signed?"

"Yes. He's always signed his name. Even included a snapshot of himself, like something you'd submit to a dating service. He's never tried to hide who he is."

"Which doesn't make him any less dangerous." Abby knew that people who stalked celebrities rarely concerned themselves with anonymity. On the contrary, they wanted their famous target to know exactly who they were. And if the time came for a violent attack, they wanted the whole world to know.

"He kept requesting a photo," Travis said, "so we allowed KPTI to send him a color glossy of Kris with a fake autograph, but no inscription. We didn't want to encourage him with anything he might interpret as a personal response."

"Okay." All standard, so far.

"Unfortunately, he didn't go away, as we hoped. Instead, he started writing longer, more in-depth letters, the kind of thing you would send to an intimate friend. They got pretty intense. He sent gifts too."

"What sort of gifts?"

"Jewelry, mostly. Cheap costume stuff. Once he gave her some scented candles because he'd read that she practices aromatherapy."

"What's his history? Any violence?"

"No."

"Ever institutionalized?"

"No."

"Arrests? Police encounters?"

"Can't rule out a run-in with the law, but there's no record of any formal charges against him."

Abby nodded. Early in life, stalkers learned how to hate, but unlike common criminals, they learned self-restraint also. They held their hatred in check. Few of the dangerous ones, the ones with the mind-set of an assassin, got in trouble with the police. They were too cold and careful for that. They bided their time.

"He stopped writing three weeks ago," Travis said, "but he still calls her."

"He's got her number . . ." She'd meant it to be a question, but she wasn't really surprised.

Travis nodded. "Home and business, even though they're unlisted. At first we weren't screening her calls, so he actually got through to her. She made the mistake of trying to talk to him. Of course this only aggravated the situation."

"Sure. Contact is what he wants."

"I explained that to her. And I had her install a second unlisted line at home and screen all calls that came in over the first line with an answering machine, but it didn't work. Somehow he guessed she had a new line and got that number too."

"Persistent little creep."

"And clever." Travis turned onto Westwood Boulevard, heading north. "Kris asked him how he got hold of her address, and he told her. He searched the Internet for her husband's name—Howard Barwood—and found the California Coastal Commission agenda for April of 1999. They post the minutes of all their meetings on the Web. One of the topics discussed in April was a request by Howard Barwood of Malibu to attach a guest cottage to the garage. His address was reported in the application summary."

Abby sighed. No information was private any longer. "Was the application approved?"

"Sure was. In fact, that guest cottage has come in handy. We set up our on-site command post there."

"How often does Hickle call?"

"Six times a day, on average."

"Has he tried to make physical contact?"

"Repeatedly. We're lucky in one way. Kris lives in Malibu Reserve. She moved there for additional security a few years ago, a normal precaution for someone in her position. The Reserve is a pretty tight ship. Hickle has never gotten past the guards at the entrance. Same story at work. KPTI is fenced and gated, and the guards have seen Hickle's photo."

"He's attempted entry at both her home and the studio? How many attempts in all?"

"More than two dozen."

"Escalating frequency?"

"Yes."

"Bad."

At Wilshire Boulevard, Travis turned east. The wide, busy street was colonnaded on both sides by high-rise condominium buildings and a few office towers. Abby lived midway along the corridor.

"You mentioned that Kris Barwood still supports you," Abby said as her building approached. "How did she feel right after the Corbal incident?"

"Scared, upset. Even though she had been with TPS for years, she nearly left us. Howard was ready to tear up the contract, but Kris had the final say. I talked her out of it."

"And now she's your biggest cheerleader. That must have been one hell of a pep talk."

"Let's say I can be persuasive when I have to be."

The Mercedes pulled into the curved driveway in the forecourt of Abby's condominium tower, the Wilshire Royal.

"Want to come up?" Abby asked, keeping her tone casual.

Travis hesitated. "I'd better say no. I've got a lot on my plate today."

"Yeah, I guess I've got my work cut out for me too." She was good at concealing disappointment.

They got out of the car, and Travis unloaded the carry-on bag from the trunk. He opened his briefcase and removed a thick sheaf of papers in a manila envelope. "Your copy of the case file."

"Bedtime reading," Abby said. She stuffed it into her suitcase. "Thanks for the ride, Paul. And—thanks for giving me another chance."

"I've never blamed you, Abby. Never."

"And if TPS goes under, will you still feel that way?"

"It's not going under. Things will turn around soon."

"Sure. I know."

She started to turn away, and then he took her by the shoulders and kissed her—a strong, heady kiss but too brief. When he pulled away, he was frowning. "You know, I may have given you the wrong impression."

She was momentarily confused. Then she realized he was talking about the case, not their relationship. "How so?"

"I've stressed the most ominous aspects of Hickle's behavior, but there's another side to it. He's a reliable employee with no police record, no history of mental illness, no known violent tendencies. He's never issued a clear threat against Kris. I know none of these things are predictive, but when you put them all together, he starts to look less like a crazed killer and more like a harmless eccentric."

"Maybe that's all he is."

"I just don't want you going into this with your mind made up."

"I won't. I have to get to know him. He'll tell me who he really is and what his intentions are. Risk assessment, that's my game. Gather the data, and analyze."

"You make it sound almost prosaic."

She smiled, but it was a sad smile, burdened with wisdom. "It is—when nothing goes wrong."

4

At 3:15 Hickle parked on a side street near the entrance to the Channel Eight studios. From this vantage point he had a clear view of the security gate.

In the backseat of his car lay his duffel bag. He hauled the bag into the front compartment, then unzipped it and removed a twelve-gauge shotgun, fully loaded.

He rested the gun in his lap. The long steel barrel was cool to the touch. He liked running his fingers over it, feeling its smoothness. Sometimes he fantasized about sliding the barrel into Kris Barwood's mouth, feeding her the tube of the gun, watching her eyes above the gleam of metal. Then one pull of the trigger, and no more eyes, no more mouth, no more Kris.

Blammo.

He felt a stir of arousal in his groin. The feeling was nothing new to him. He had been passionate about Kris Barwood since the day he first saw her. Since then, she had been with him constantly, at least in his thoughts. At bedtime he would conjure her in his arms, and the smell of her hair and skin would lull him to sleep. Throughout the day, while at work or doing chores, he would invent conversations with her, magical dialogues in which he was always witty and buoyant, and she sparkled with laughter at his jokes. For many months he had been married to her. She waited for him in his apartment. She shared dinner with him. She looked deep into his eyes.

But in the past few weeks his fantasy had died, exposed as the delusion it had always been. He had maintained the dream as long as he could, until at last reality had broken it into pieces.

She did not love him.

She didn't want to talk to him or read his letters or accept his gifts. He had sent her jewelry with the polite request that she wear it on the air. She never had. He had called her countless times, and on the rare occasions when he'd gotten through, she had been hostile and uncommunicative.

It was so unfair. He deserved her love. No one could have done more for her than he had. Hadn't he dedicated his life to her? Hadn't he built a shrine for her in his heart? He had spent countless hours hunting down the smallest fragments of information in magazine profiles and newspaper clippings, learning her biography, memorizing every detail of her life.

He knew that her parents had sent her to swim camp at age nine after installing a pool in the backyard of their Minneapolis home. He knew she had been the high school prom queen. She'd attended the University of Minnesota, majoring in Journalism, and after graduation she'd secured her first full-time job, an entry-level position at a radio station in Duluth. The next year she'd gotten her first break, a TV reporting job in Fort Wayne, Indiana. He had tracked down a Fort Wayne shop specializing in local memorabilia and had purchased, for thirty-five dollars, a glossy photo of Kris bearing the inscription *Thanks for your support. Keep watching!*

He knew that from Fort Wayne, which ranked 102 among the 210 television markets in the United States, she had gone to Columbia, South Carolina, the number eighty-seven market, and from there to Albuquerque, number fifty-two, and then on to Cincinnati, number thirty. In 1987 she had come to LA. Soon afterward KPTI had started to win accolades and viewers. He knew—*everybody* knew—that Kris was the reason. There was nobody else worth watching on Channel Eight or on any of the other channels, for that matter. There was only Kris. As KPTI racked up Golden Mike Awards and higher ratings, her salary rose. Her first million-dollar contract—1992. Two million for three years—1997. And now her new deal, the richest yet, the richest in the history of LA news broadcasting. "The Six Million Dollar Woman," the *Los Angeles Times* had called her in the headline of a feature story.

He had devoted every minute, hour, day, week, month of his life to Kris Barwood, nee Kris Andersen, born Kristina Ingrid Andersen at Meeker County Memorial Hospital in Litchfield, Minnesota—yes, he even knew the hospital, which was recorded on the copy of her birth certificate he had obtained through the mail for a nominal fee.

She liked skiing (*Redbook,* July 1999) and pasta (*Los Angeles Magazine,* March 1998) and chocolate (extemporaneous on-air remarks, 6:00 News, December 21, 1997 broadcast). She had attended the premiere of *Toy Story* and had enjoyed the movie (*Entertainment Weekly,* November 25, 1995).

He had committed himself to her. He had given his life to Kris Barwood. For a long time he had sustained his hopes that somehow they would be together. Yes, of course she had a husband, Howard Barwood, whom she'd met at a Brentwood fund-raising event for cerebral palsy. Howard Barwood, who had made more than twenty million dollars in Westside real estate by buying old houses on choice lots, tearing them down, and putting up mansions worth three times the original price. All these details had been revealed in an interview with Mr. Barwood in the April 1996 issue of *Success* magazine.

But Howard Barwood was not the man for her. He was merely an accident in her life. Hickle was her destiny.

She should have been able to see this. He had explained it often enough in letters and phone messages. But she refused to be reasonable, refused to treat him with any courtesy or decency whatsoever. She had rebuffed him. She had been rude. She—

Wait.

Down the street came a long gray car. A Lincoln Town Car? Yes.

Kris's car.

It eased forward to the studio gate and stopped, engine idling.

Hickle lifted the gun. His finger fondled the trigger.

Could he kill her at this distance? He wasn't sure. The spray of shot would fan out wide. It would certainly shatter the side windows, but he couldn't be sure of hitting her. She would take cover, and the driver would squeal into reverse and spirit her away . . .

The gate lifted. The car pulled through. Hickle watched it go.

He'd never had any intention of shooting her. Not here. When the time came, as soon it would, he would choose the right place for the ambush. He would make no mistakes.

The Lincoln cruised to the far end of the parking lot, finding Kris Barwood's reserved space near the rear door of Studio A.

Hickle reached into the duffel bag and produced a pair of binoculars. He watched the car through the lenses. The driver got out first. He opened the side door for Kris, who emerged into the sunlight, tall and blond. She was wearing a blue pantsuit, but he knew she would change into another outfit before airtime.

Then someone else climbed out of the sedan's rear compartment. A man. Hickle focused on his face and identified him as Howard Barwood.

He had never seen Howard Barwood in person before. On previous occasions Kris had not been accompanied by her husband when she went to work. Hickle was surprised the man was here today.

He studied Howard, a silver-haired, grinning, thick-necked fool who had won a woman he could not possibly deserve.

Hickle felt a band of tension tighten across his chest. Briefly his hand went to the shotgun again, but the distance was much too great, of course.

Anyway, Howard might have Kris now, but he would not have her for long.

Hickle contented himself with this thought as he watched the bodyguard lead the Barwoods toward the studio door. At the door Howard stopped to say something to Kris, then leaned forward, clasping her by the waist, and kissed her.

Kissed her.

"You fucker," Hickle whispered, his voice hoarse with outrage. "Don't you do that. Don't you even touch her. Don't you *dare*."

The kiss lasted only a moment. Then the door

opened, and the Barwoods went inside. The door swung shut behind them.

Hickle kept the binoculars fixed on the door for a long time. He was not seeing the door. He was not seeing anything at all except the memory of that kiss.

He had watched Kris on TV for months, taping her shows, playing back the tapes frame by frame and freezing on her varied expressions. He had collected images of her from magazines and newspapers. He had watched her jog on the beach and had caught glimpses of her in the windows of her home.

But he had never seen her with her husband. He had never seen him kiss her perfect mouth.

He lowered the binoculars. His hands were shaking. It took him a moment to recognize that what he felt was rage.

Kris belonged to him, whether or not she would acknowledge the fact. She was his, by destiny. She was his, not that other man's. That man had no right to hold her. Had no right to meet her lips with his . . .

Hickle shut his eyes, but it didn't help. Now he saw the two of them in bed together, Mr. and Mrs. Barwood, Kris naked and supine, Howard mounting her, the paired bodies shivering, Howard driving in deeper, rutting like an animal, and Kris liking it, liking what he did to her, asking for more—

His eyes opened. He blinked at sunlight and blue sky. All of a sudden he knew he had to get the hell out of here. And he knew where to go, what to do.

He started the car and drove away, avoiding the studio gate so the guard wouldn't catch sight of his car. He hooked up with the Glendale Freeway and proceeded north to the Angeles National Forest. Near the town of La Cañada Flintridge there was a secluded section of the woods, which he had discovered during an aimless drive last year. A brook whispered through a sunlit glade at the end of a dirt road.

He parked. When he got out of the car, he took the duffel with him.

He marched a hundred yards into the woods, set down the bag, and removed a pair of sound-insulating earmuffs, which he slipped over his ears, and the shotgun and two boxes of shells.

His first shot scared up a flurry of birds. After the second shot there was only stillness and the muffled echo of the shotgun's report.

The gun had a four-shell capacity. He emptied it and reloaded, then repeated the process. Deadfalls of timber and drifts of small stones were his targets. But really he had no targets. A shotgun was not a weapon to aim; it was a weapon to point. The wide spread of shot would wipe out anything in the direction of the blast.

What he sought was not accuracy but familiarity with the weapon. He needed a feel for its range, power, recoil. It must be part of him, an extension of his arm and shoulder. When the time came to use the gun for real, he would get only one opportunity, and he couldn't fail.

5

The Wilshire Royal was one of the more expensive buildings in Westwood, and Abby's mortgage payments were insanely high, especially given how little time she actually spent at home. But the place offered two features she prized: luxury and security.

Luxury was on display in the gushing fountain that ornamented the driveway, the gray marble expanse of the lobby floor, the excellent reproduction of Rodin's *Eve* facing the elevator bank. Security was less obvious. The doorman who greeted her when she headed up the front walkway, toting her carry-on bag, didn't look like a guard, but under his red blazer the bulge of a shoulder holster could be detected by a practiced eye. The two uniformed men at the mahogany sign-in desk wore their sidearms in plain view, but the array of closed-circuit video screens they monitored was hidden below the desktop.

"Hey, Abby," one of them said.

She smiled. "Vince, Gerry, how's it going?"

"Slow day. Have a nice trip?" They thought she was a sales rep for a software firm, on the road a lot.

"Productive." She asked if there was a FedEx Same-Day package for her, and they found it behind the counter. She tucked the box under her arm. It was good to have the gun back. She always felt a little naked without it. "Thanks, guys," she said with a smile and a wave. "See you."

The elevator that carried her to the tenth floor was equipped with a hidden TV camera. The control panel was rigged to set off a silent alarm at the front desk if the elevator was intentionally stopped between floors. There were cameras in the stairwells and in the underground garage, access to which was controlled by a passcard-operated steel gate. The gate, too, was monitored by a surveillance camera. All that was missing was a crocodile-infested moat. She might bring up the idea at the next meeting of the condo board.

She wasn't sure these precautions were necessary. By LA standards Westwood was a safe neighborhood. But she took enough chances in her work. She liked having a refuge to come home to.

Her apartment was number 1015. She opened the door and stepped into her living room, which took up half the floor space in her unit's thousand-square-foot plan. A faint mustiness hung in the air; the place had been closed up for a week. Otherwise, it was just as she'd left it.

She dropped her suitcase and the FedEx package onto the ottoman of an overstuffed armchair. The apartment's furnishings had been chosen primarily for comfort, with no concerns about consistency of style. She liked a chair she could sink into, a sofa softer than a bed. Throw pillows and quilts were tossed here and there, along with the occasional stuffed polar bear and fake macaw, all contributing to a general impression of disorder. Her decorating skills were limited at best, but she had managed to find two paintings that pleased her. Both were prints purchased out of discount bins. One was a late work by Joseph Turner, the landscape dissolving in a bath of light, and the other was one of Edward Hicks's many studies of "The Peaceable Kingdom," predator and prey as bedfellows. The Turner had a spiritual quality that touched a part of her she rarely accessed, and the Hicks, with its naive optimism, simply made her smile.

Briskly she opened the curtains and the glass door to the balcony, airing out the room. Her apartment faced Wilshire; she was high enough to be out of earshot of most traffic noise.

In the kitchen she drank two glasses of water. Flying always left her dehydrated. She found blueberries and peaches in the freezer, defrosted them in the microwave, and dumped them into the blender along with a dollop of vanilla yogurt and some skim milk two days past its expiration date. A few seconds of whirring reduced the blender's contents to a bluish, frothy sludge, which she poured into a tall glass and drank slowly, pausing to swallow assorted vitamin and mineral supplements.

Leaving the kitchen, she changed into a white terry-cloth robe and ran the bathwater. Briefly she considered pouring bath oil into the tub, but ruled against this indulgence. She was about to strip off the robe when the intercom buzzed.

She answered it, irritated. "Yes?"

"Mr. Stevens is here to see you," one of the lobby guards said.

"Okay, Vince. Send him up."

Stevens was the name Travis used when he stopped by. The guards weren't supposed to know that Abby had any connection to the security field, and Travis's name had been well publicized recently.

She waited, wondering why Travis had returned.

When the doorbell chimed, she opened the door, and he stepped inside without a word.

"Hey, Paul. Forget something?"

"Not exactly. I changed my mind."

"About what?"

"The urgency of my return to the office."

She smiled, relaxing and at the same time feeling a rush of pleasant tension. "Did you?"

"What's that they say about all work and no play?" He took a look around the apartment. "Place looks the same as I remember it."

"Hasn't been that long since you were here," Abby said, then realized she was wrong. It had been weeks, and not only because she had been traveling. Even when she was in LA, she had seen less of Travis in the past few months—since the Devin Corbal case.

He circled toward the balcony. "I see your view hasn't improved." Late last year an office tower had been erected across the street, coal-black and butt-ugly and, so far, unoccupied; some financial or legal screw-up had interrupted construction during the finishing stages.

"I'm used to it," Abby said, "though I have to admit, it doesn't do a lot for the neighborhood. All that vacant office space . . ."

She stopped. Both of them were silent for a moment, and she knew Travis was thinking of the empty offices in the TPS suite. She wanted to kick herself.

But when Travis turned away from the balcony, he was smiling. "Do I hear water running?"

"I'm drawing a bath."

"Sounds intriguing."

"I don't think there's room for two."

"Have you ever tested that hypothesis?"

"Actually, no."

"You should. Why don't you see if the water's gotten hot?"

"Why don't I?"

She left him in the living room and retreated down the hall to check the tub. It was half-full and the perfect temperature. The air in the bathroom was sensuously humid, thick with steam. Bath oil didn't seem like a bad idea anymore. When she added it to the water, a lather of white bubbles sprang up, reflecting the overhead light in a bevy of rainbows. She took off the robe, hung it on the back of the door, and lowered herself into the tub. The space was cramped, and she thought pessimistically that she'd been right: there wasn't room for two.

Then he came in. He had left his clothes outside, and she saw him through the steamy haze. He bent over the tub and kissed her, and she felt a small disturbance in the water as he slid his hand into the bath to caress her breast. It was a slow circular caress—the light touch of his fingers, the firmer pressure of his palm— and then with his other hand he was stroking her hair, her neck, the lingering tension in her shoulders.

"I still think you won't fit," she said mischievously.

"We'll see."

Travis reached behind her and turned off the tap, then stroked the lean, toned muscles of her back. The bathwater, leavened with oil, was smooth, supple, some exotic new liquid, not ordinary water at all.

"I've missed you," Travis said.

She was briefly surprised. He was never sentimental.

"I . . ." Why was this so hard for her to say? "I missed you too."

The water rose around her. He entered the tub, straddling her, his knees against her hips, as the water sloshed lazily around them and stray bubbles detached themselves from the lather to burst in small pops. "I'm not sure the circumstances allow for much finesse," Travis said apologetically.

She giggled. "Finesse isn't always essential."

They rocked gently in the water and steam. She let her head fall back, her mop of wet hair cushioning her against the tiled wall. In the ceiling the exhaust fan hummed. The faucet dripped. She heard her heartbeat and Travis's breath.

"Abby," he said.

She shut her eyes.

"Abby."

He was inside her.

"Abby . . ."

Pumping harder. Driving deeper.

Her back arched, lifting her halfway out of the water, and her hair spilled across her face in a dark tangle, and distantly she was aware that she'd banged her head on the damn tiles, but it didn't matter.

He withdrew himself and held her, the two of them entwined amid soapsuds and lacy, dissipating tendrils of steam.

"Told you I'd fit," Travis said.

She couldn't argue.

In late afternoon Abby woke in the familiar half-darkness of her bedroom. She propped herself up on an elbow and looked for Travis, but he was gone, of course. He had returned to the office. She supposed it was considerate of him to have departed without waking her.

Dimly she recalled leaving the bathtub when the water had gotten cold. She and Travis had toweled each other dry, and the vigorous rubbing had segued into more sensual contact, and then they were on top of her bed, and somehow the covers got kicked off and things had proceeded from there. This time the circumstances had allowed for considerable finesse.

She had dozed off afterward. And he had made his exit, gathering his clothes from the living room, where no doubt they had been neatly folded and stacked. He had fit her into his schedule, at least. He had found a slot for her between lunchtime and his afternoon appointments.

She shook her head. Unfair. What had she expected him to do? Cancel everything, spend the day with her? He was trying to salvage a damaged business—and not incidentally, keep some of the most famous people in LA alive.

Anyway, she had never asked for more from him. She liked her space, her freedom. Maybe she liked it too much for her own good.

She got out of bed and threw on a T-shirt and cutoff shorts. Barefoot, she wandered into the kitchen and opened a can of tuna fish. Slathered between thick slabs of date bread, it made a pretty good sandwich. Normally, when eating alone she would watch TV or read, but there was nothing on TV at this hour, and the only immediately available reading matter was Travis's report. She almost got it out of her suitcase, but stopped herself. "All work and no play," she mused.

Travis had said that. He'd been right. She could permit herself a break from work. Even so, she found herself eyeing the suitcase as she ate her sandwich at the dining table.

"You're a workaholic," she chided. "This job's gonna kill you if you don't let go of it once in a while." Unless, of course, it killed her in a more literal fashion first.

A lot of negative energy was in the air all of a sudden. She popped a CD into her audio deck. The disc, selected at random, was a Kid Ory jazz album from way back when. She listened as the Kid launched his trombone into "Muskrat Ramble," but she knew the song too well to fully hear it, and her thoughts drifted to other things. College. A January thunderstorm, and in the rain she broke up with Greg Daly. He was pushing too hard, getting too close. Even then, she'd needed her space. For her, it had always been that way.

She had talked about it with her father once. In memory she could see him clearly, squinting into the Arizona sun, nets of creases edging his calm hazel eyes. She had inherited those eyes, that exact shade, and perhaps the quality of remoteness they conveyed. Her father had been a contemplative man, given to long stillnesses. He ran a horse ranch in the desolate foothills south of Phoenix. One evening she sat with him in the russet tones of a desert sunset, watching massed armies of saguaro cacti raise their spiked arms against the glare, and she asked why the boys in school didn't like her. She was twelve years old.

It's not that they don't like you, her father said. *They're put off a bit. Intimidated, I think.*

This was baffling. *What's intimidating about me?*

Well, I don't know. What do you suppose might be intimidating about a girl who can climb a tree better than they can, or shoe a horse, or aim and shoot a rifle like a pro?

She pointed out that most of them had never seen her do any of those things.

But they see you, Abigail. He always called her that, never Abby, and never Constance, her middle name. *They see how you carry yourself. Anyhow, you don't give them much encouragement, do you? You keep to yourself. You want solitude and privacy.*

She allowed that this was so.

We're a lot alike, Henry Sinclair said. *We get to feeling crowded more easily than most.* She asked him if this was a good thing. *It is,* he said, *if you can make it work in your favor.* When she asked how, he answered, *You'll figure it out.*

Had she? Sixteen years had passed since that conversation. Her father was gone, and her mother too. She was more alone than she had ever been as a child, and still she got to feeling crowded more easily than most.

6

In the evening, after a light supper, Abby went downstairs to the small gym adjacent to the lobby. She used the Stairmaster for a half hour, then left the building and walked into Westwood Village, where she browsed in a bookstore and bought a book on criminal psychopathology and a collection of old *Calvin and Hobbes* comics. She had never quite forgiven Bill Watterson for discontinuing that strip.

Burnout, he'd claimed. She wondered how long he would last at her job.

Mostly her visit to the Village was an excuse to do some people-watching. This was not only her job, it was her hobby. In college she had majored in Psychology because the field suited her temperament. She wanted to observe people and make assessments without being required or even permitted to get close.

Had she continued with her training, she would have been a licensed psychologist by now. But in the summer after her second year of postgraduate studies everything had changed. She had met Travis.

He was giving a lecture in Phoenix at the Arizona Biltmore. His topic: warning signs of violent psychopathology. He was not a psychologist, but as the head of a leading security firm he had the kind of hands-on experience that trumped book learning.

She had read a profile of Travis in the *Arizona Repub-*

lic, which was still delivered to her father's ranch, though her father was no longer there to read it. He had died that June, a week after she earned her master's degree, and had been buried beside her mother in a family plot. Abby had returned to sell the ranch, a job that took longer than expected. Grief and the relentless summer sun had worn her down, and she looked for any excuse to get away. Travis's lecture, open to the public, was the lifeline she seized.

Even without a license, she was enough of a psychologist to know what Dr. Freud would have said about the developments that followed. She had lost her father. She was looking for another. Travis was older, an authority figure, and he came along at the right time.

Whatever her motive, she went to the lecture. Travis was charming. It was not a quality he exhibited with great frequency, but that night he roused himself to eloquence. He told intriguing stories culled from the cases he had handled, mixing humor and suspense, while never allowing his audience to forget that the stakes in his work were life and death.

Afterward she lingered with a group of attendees chatting with Travis. As the ballroom was clearing out, she asked her only question. *You evaluate your subjects on the basis of their letters or phone calls,* she said. *I couldn't do therapy that way. A therapeutic diagnosis requires one-on-one contact, usually over an extended series of sessions.*

The more extended, the better—at least as far as the therapist's bank account is concerned, Travis said with a smile, and several people laughed.

Abby pressed ahead. *So even though your methods seem statistically sound, you can't achieve the same degree of certainty in your evaluation as a working therapist, can you?*

She hadn't meant to sound combative, but Travis

took the question as a challenge and proceeded to defend his approach. He spoke for a long time. When he was done, the group broke up, and Abby headed for the lobby, feeling she had failed somehow or missed an opportunity.

She was unlocking her car in the parking area near one of the city's canals when Travis caught up with her. He came out of the darkness, striding fast, and she thought he was a mugger until the glow of a streetlamp highlighted his face.

That was a good question, he said in a quieter tone than the one he'd used in a public setting. *Truth is, I didn't have a good answer.* She told him he had covered himself well. He laughed, then asked if they could have a cup of coffee together.

They lingered at a coffee bar on Camelback Road until after midnight, and when he said he was staying in town a few more days, she invited him to visit her at the ranch. *It's the real Arizona,* she said. *The Arizona we're losing now.*

I wonder why things always seem most real to us when we lose them, he said softly. He could not have known about her father. Still, it was the uncannily perfect thing to say.

His visit to the ranch the next day lengthened into an overnight stay. She had not had many lovers. There had been Greg Daly and one other young man—no one else, until Travis. And no one like him, ever. He was no college student. At forty he was a man of the world. And yes, he had several of her father's qualities. He could be remote and aloof, even sullen. He could be hard. But where her father had always allowed at least a glimpse of his inner life, Travis kept his deepest self hidden. He was a brisk, uncomplicated man, or so he seemed. But the truth was that she could never be sure just what he was. He puzzled her. Most likely she posed the same mystery to him. Neither of them was good at opening up and revealing too much.

When he returned to LA, they stayed in touch. He flew to Phoenix several times to see her as she concluded the business of selling the ranch. Then it was September, time to pursue her doctoral degree; but strangely, her studies bored her. She had spoken with Travis at length about the advantages of direct, personal contact with the stalkers his agency observed from afar. She had thought of a way to do it. On a trip to LA, over dinner at a seafood restaurant, she broached the subject.

It would be dangerous, Abby, Travis said.

I know.

You'd have to be trained. There's a whole gamut of skills you'd need to acquire.

I have certain skills. Not to mention a master's degree in psychology, a higher than average percentage of fast-twitch muscle fibers, and a winning personality.

Travis smiled, unconvinced. *Why would you do this? You're already qualified as a counselor. Earn your doctorate and your license, then open a private practice and rake in the bucks.*

That's not what I want anymore.

But why?

It lacks excitement.

There are things to be said in favor of a nice, quiet life.

You don't live that way.

When did I ever become your role model?

She didn't answer.

After a long time Travis said, *If you want me to help you, I will. But I won't say I have no misgivings. I don't want to see you hurt.* This was the gentlest thing he ever said to her, before or since.

Her training took two years. She lived in a small apartment in an unfashionable part of LA. The sale of the ranch had given her enough money to support herself, and she took nothing from Travis. Nor did either of them ever suggest that she move in with him. She still wanted her space. She couldn't say what Travis wanted.

He sent her to a self-defense institute specializing in the Israeli street-fighting technique of krav maga. Most martial arts programs were glorified exercise routines blended with elements of dance; their usefulness in actual hand-to-hand struggle was limited. Krav maga was different. There was no beauty in it. It was a brutal skill that aimed at one objective—the immediate, unconditional defeat of one's adversary by any means available. Abby had never used violence against anyone, and the first time she had to deliver kicks and punches to her instructor's padded torso, she did it with trembling reluctance, her vision blurred by tears. After a while she learned not to cry. Inflicting pain was a necessary evil. She could deal with it. She could be tough. Like Travis. Like her father. She took acting lessons in Hollywood. She rode in a private detective's surveillance van, monitoring radio frequencies. She accepted a variety of odd jobs—waitress, cashier, clerical worker, hamburger flipper—partly for extra cash but mainly for a range of experiences to draw on when she went undercover.

Two years ago, at twenty-six, she was ready. Her first assignment had been for Travis Protective Services. More jobs followed. She divided her duties between TPS and other security firms. Keeping her distance, as usual. She prided herself on being an independent contractor. Independent—that was the key word. Nobody owned her. Nobody controlled her. At least, she liked to think so.

When she had paid for the items in the bookstore, she stopped in a bar down the street and ordered a piña colada, her one weakness. Normally she didn't drink alone, but her new assignment with TPS was worth a private celebration.

Midway through the drink, a young man with a fuzzy mustache that barely concealed a rash of acne sat down next to her. He ordered tequila, presenting his driver's license to get it, then glanced at her shopping bag. "Been buying books?"

She didn't answer.

"I'm really into Marcel Proust. You know him?"

Abby ignored the question. She showed him the gun in her purse. "LAPD," she whispered gravely.

He blinked at the gun, unsure whether to be scared or turned on. "You running some kind of plainclothes operation?"

She nodded. "We've heard rumors this bar is selling drinks to UCLA students with fake IDs."

Most of the color left his face. He mumbled something and moved away, leaving his tequila behind. Abby smiled, pleased with herself, and then a voice behind her said, "I could have you arrested."

She turned on her barstool. A man stood a yard away, watching her. He was in his early thirties, wide-shouldered and sandy haired, dressed casually in a dark sweater and cotton pants. "For what?" she asked.

"Impersonating a police officer."

She swiveled away from him and picked up her piña colada. "Go easy on me. It's my first offense."

"I'm not sure I believe that." He took a seat next to

her, resting his hands on the bar. He had blocky fingers and thick, muscular wrists.

She sipped her drink. "Are you saying I'm a criminal?"

"I wouldn't want to jump to conclusions. It might have been an innocent mistake. But I don't think so."

"Why's that?"

"You don't look innocent. But don't be offended. Innocence is boring."

"Well, at least I'm not boring. I would hate to think I was wasting your time."

"You never do, Abby. You never do."

He ordered a draft beer. For a minute they were quiet as he worked on the beer and she finished her drink.

"So," she said, "how's it going, Vic?"

"Could be worse. You?"

"Can't complain. Streets getting any safer?"

"So we're told. Couldn't prove it by me."

Abby had known Vic Wyatt for roughly a year, ever since the Jonathan Bronshard case. Bronshard was a stockbroker who had put up a website with pictures of his family and a description of their happy home, only to become the target of threatening phone calls. He went to Paul Travis. Ordinarily Travis limited his services to celebrity clients, but he made an exception for Bronshard, whose office was down the hall from the TPS suite.

The calls were traced to a pay phone in Hollywood, which TPS officers staked out until the next call was made. They followed the caller home and identified him as Emanuel Barth, a man who'd spent some time in prison for vandalism, breaking and entering, and related offenses. Abby interviewed the patrol sergeant who had supervised the arrest that put Barth away. The sergeant was Vic Wyatt of Hollywood Division.

Mr. Barth, she learned, had a hang-up about upper middle-class families. Friendless, unmarried, chronically unemployed, he took out his frustrations by blaming those who had more than he did. In 1998 he'd broken into an upscale house in Toluca Lake and trashed the place. His fingerprints, on file after a previous arrest, had led police to his shack in Hollywood. A guilty plea had reduced his jail time, and he was now out of prison.

Wyatt had explained all this to Abby, who'd let him think she was merely a researcher under contract to TPS. The information had proven helpful as she went about the business of installing herself in Emanuel Barth's life. Eventually she had found a way to get Barth off the street again, this time for the next three to five years. Wyatt hadn't handled the second arrest; he knew Barth had gone back to prison on a new conviction, but he had never learned of the role Abby played in putting him there. At least she hoped he hadn't.

She had relied on Wyatt several times since. There was a higher concentration of wackos in Hollywood than in most other districts of LA, and as a veteran cop he knew most of them. He might even know Hickle. She considered raising the subject but decided against it. Not tonight.

"You're quiet this evening," Wyatt said.

"Just zoning out. What brings you here, anyway?"

"Some nights I pass the time in Westwood. Nicer ambience than Scum City." His term for Hollywood. "How about you?"

"I live down the street. The Wilshire Royal."

"Fancy digs. Those security firms must pay pretty good for research."

"I survive."

"So far," Wyatt said gravely.

She looked away. She had never told him what she actually did for a living, but he wasn't dumb. He had patrolled the streets for years, and he knew people. He must have guessed some of the truth about her. She knew that if he ever learned the full truth, he might really have to arrest her—no joke.

She steered the conversation in a less dangerous direction. "I'll bet I know what you're here for."

"Do you?"

"You were hoping to pick up a UCLA girl. Some of them might go for a cop."

"I'm past thirty. Too old for them. Anyway, I don't want a girl."

"Your secret's safe with me. Don't ask, don't tell, that's my policy."

"What I meant was, it's a woman I want. A grown woman."

"There are three million of them in the greater LA area."

"Women, yeah. Grown women? I'm not so sure. That's the thing about LA." Wyatt sipped his beer. "People don't have to be adults here. They can be kids forever. Like, I was talking to this grocery checker the other day, and she tells me how her houseplants can read her mind. When she's unhappy, they don't bloom. So to keep them healthy, she only thinks happy thoughts. She beams happy thoughts to her azaleas."

"Future rocket scientist," Abby commented.

"Future nothing. She's thirty-five years old. This is it for her. This is as grown up as she's gonna get."

"She may have other redeeming qualities."

"I don't want somebody with redeeming qualities. I don't want redeeming qualities to be an issue in the first place."

"You have high standards."

"Well, yeah."

"Maybe nobody can meet them."

He looked at her. "Oh, I think somebody can."

This conversational path had turned out to be not so safe after all. "I'd better get going," Abby said.

"Nice to run into you."

She slid off the bar stool and picked up her purse. "I may need to get in touch about something."

"Business related? Don't answer that. It's always business related. Well, you know where to find me— but I was hoping you'd quit that line of work."

She slung the purse over her shoulder. "You mean research?"

"No, not research."

"What, then?"

"That's something I've been trying to figure out. It keeps me up nights."

"Don't lose sleep over me. I'm not worth it."

"I doubt that."

"Night, Vic."

"See you, Abby."

She left the bar and emerged into the whirl of West-wood Village. Two come-ons in a half hour, a new record. Of course, the kid with fake ID had been only— well, only a kid. As for Wyatt, she didn't know quite what to make of him. He was lonely, she guessed. Maybe she was lonely too. Lonely despite Travis. Or because of Travis. Because of the peculiar nature of their relationship, its built-in distance and wariness.

She put the issue out of her mind. It didn't matter. Whatever she was feeling, she could handle it. She could handle anything. She was tough.

Jet lag had never been a problem for her. She dropped off to sleep at midnight and woke refreshed at seven. For breakfast she fried vegetable-protein sausages and an egg-white omelet. She avoided coffee; in her profession it didn't pay to be jumpy. Instead she brewed herbal tea.

Before showering, Abby ran through a workout routine drawn from the *YMCA Fitness Manual*—no-nonsense exercises like sit-ups, bent-knee push-ups, hamstring stretches, and chest rotations. The full program, from warm-up to cool-down, took thirty minutes. On some days she substituted t'ai chi or shadowboxing. There were many ways to stay fit.

Only after she was dressed in fresh clothes, with her hair toweled dry and brushed straight, did she allow herself to look at the case file. Paper-clipped to the back page was an eight-by-ten color glossy. The shot had been taken with a telephoto lens, squashing its subject against an unfocused background smear. It had probably been snapped from a moving car—a drive-by, in the strange parlance of the security business.

The subject was Hickle, of course. He had been caught on film as he emerged from a doorway, perhaps the entrance to his apartment building or the donut shop where he worked. She couldn't tell, and it didn't matter. What mattered was the man himself. He had a thin, suspicious face and small eyes. He was scrawny and looked tall. His black hair was a sloppy, disarranged pile.

She tried to draw a few preliminary conclusions from the photo. Hickle seemed indifferent to personal grooming, often a sign of depression or social alienation. His skin was pale, almost pasty, suggesting he spent most of his time indoors. He wore a shapeless brown sweatshirt and faded jeans, clothes that would not attract attention; he didn't want to stand out. His body language—head lowered, eyes narrowed, lips pursed—conveyed a cagey wariness that reminded her of a mongrel dog that had learned to fend for itself on the street.

Bringing the photo up close, she looked intently at Hickle's face. There was something in his eyes, in the set of his mouth . . .

Anger. Hickle was an angry man. Life had not given him what he thought it owed him, and he was looking for someone to blame.

"Wrong," she said aloud. "He's not looking. He's already found her."

She spent the morning with the file, reading it carefully. When she was done, she returned to the first page, which listed Hickle's address. He lived in an apartment in Hollywood, on Gainford Avenue, south of Santa Monica Boulevard. Unit 420. Fourth floor. Must be a good-sized complex. In that neighborhood the turnover rate among tenants would be high.

The *LA Times* was delivered to her door every morning when she was in town. She studied the classified ads. When she found what she was seeking, she said, "Bingo," just like in the movies.

There were vacancies at the Gainford Avenue address. No apartment numbers were listed, but with any luck, one of the available units would be on the fourth floor. And the units were furnished; she could move in immediately.

By the end of the day, if all went well, she would be Raymond Hickle's new neighbor.

7

The dough was soft and supple like a woman, and George Zachareas's big, callused, age-spotted hands worked it with a lover's touch, pushing and pulling, folding and turning. Gradually he fell into a rhythm, arms and shoulders and upper body thrusting together in a slow, practiced dance. Zachareas—Zack to all who knew him, owner and proprietor of Zack's Donut Shack—found himself smiling, relishing the sheer sensual pleasure of the task.

"I appreciate you staying past your shift," he told the tall young man who stood beside him in a matching red apron and cap, working the same mound of dough.

"No problem," Raymond Hickle said.

Zack was alone with Hickle in the kitchen, having left Susie Parker, a worthless, barely literate high school dropout, on duty at the counter. He figured it was safe to let Susie fly solo at this time of day. Midafternoon was slow; the shop did most of its business in the morning and the late-night hours. Ordinarily Zack didn't come in during the day at all, but Hickle had called him a half hour ago with word that the two hundred pounds of dough made by the baker on the night shift had been used up, and Zack had opted to stop by personally and make an extra fifty-pound batch. It was possible to knead the stuff mechanically, by inserting a dough hook in one of the electric mixers, but Zack preferred to do the job by hand. Hickle had volunteered to help.

"You're a trouper, Ray," Zack said in a voice that approached the decibel level of a divine command. He had been going deaf for years and refused to admit it. "To hang around when you don't have to. After eight hours on the job, you must want out of here pretty bad."

"Not really."

"Any special plans for the evening?"

"No."

"How about the weekend? It's coming up. You got something in mind?"

"I'm working on Saturday, filling in for Emilio."

"Again?"

"I don't mind. It's extra money."

"There's more to life than work, Ray, especially when you work in a place like this."

"I had the day off yesterday."

"Yeah, so you did. Do something fun?"

"Went to the beach."

"Glad to hear it. Look, don't get me wrong. You do a great job, you're the best, but plying dough at a donut store is no life for you. Where's your future?"

"I'm doing all right."

Zack shook his head. At sixty-four he was a tall and vigorous man, but Hickle, three decades younger, was taller still, six foot one, with the potential to develop a boxer's physique if he applied himself. He had a sallow, intense face and thoughtful eyes, and a mop of black hair that was thick and unruly at the top but cropped close at the nape. He could have been handsome, Zack supposed, but he'd missed his chance somehow. His complexion was too pale, his eyes too small and too deeply sunken under his heavy brows, his features slightly out of proportion in a way that was hard to define.

"You could do better," Zack told him. "Hell, you're a smart guy." He lowered his voice to a conspiratorial shout. "Plenty smarter than those clowns I got working the other shifts. Maybe in a couple months we can talk about making you a supervisor—"

"No, thanks."

Zack paused in his labor. "You don't want a promotion?"

"I'm happy doing what I do."

After a moment Zack resumed attacking the dough. He had no way to figure out Raymond Hickle. The guy said he was happy, but how could he be? He had no ambition, no personal life, nothing but eight hours a day spent on menial chores for indifferent customers.

Some of his time was passed behind the counter, making coffee and microwaving muffins and toasting bagels, and some of it was spent in the kitchen amid the stainless steel sinks and the large-capacity appliances and the vat in which sizeable blocks of lard were melted to form a thick soup of grease for deep-frying dough. Hickle had learned to use the donut filler, a conical, hand-operated apparatus that injected jelly into fried donut shells, and he often was called on to clean the blades of the mixers that blended milk and confectioner's sugar into a glaze. As jobs went, it was hardly anybody's dream. Yet Hickle never groused or slacked off, never got sloppy or looked bored. It wasn't natural.

Zack liked Ray Hickle, he really did, and he wanted the younger man to feel good about life. "You know, Ray," he said on impulse, "you're my employee of the month."

Hickle didn't even look up. "I wasn't aware you had an employee of the month."

"Well, I don't, but let's say I do, okay?" He gave Hickle a manly clap on the shoulder, raising a billow of white flour dust. "There's an extra fifty bucks in it for you."

"That's not necessary."

"With all the unpaid overtime you put in, Ray, you deserve it ten times over. I'm adding it to your paycheck on Friday. Don't give me any arguments."

"Okay. Thanks, Zack." There was no enthusiasm in his voice, only empty acceptance.

"So what do you think you'll spend it on?" Zack asked gamely, hoping to spur a more positive response.

Shrug. "Can't say."

"Got a special someone you can buy a present for?"

"Yes, I do."

Zack hadn't realized how much he expected Hickle to say no until he heard the opposite reply. He concealed his surprise behind a smile. "That's good, Ray. Been seeing her long?"

"A few months." Hickle worked the dough with his long-fingered hands. "She's a beautiful woman. We have a spiritual union. It's destiny." The odd thing about this was that he said it so casually, as if such confessions were made every day.

"Well, that's good," Zack said with less certainty. "What's her name?"

"Kris."

"How'd you meet her?"

"It wasn't a meeting, exactly. More of an encounter. I was in Beverly Hills one day, just walking around, and I saw her come out of a store. She didn't see me. Walked right past me, in fact. But I never took my eyes off her. Because in that moment I knew—somehow I just knew—she was the only one for me. I knew we were meant to be together."

"So you went after her?"

"Yes. I went after her. And now I see her all the time."

"Good for you. It shows some moxie, chasing down a girl you like. Hey, next time Kris is in the neighborhood, have her come by for coffee and crullers on the house."

"I'll do that."

There was silence between them as they finished kneading. When the dough was no longer sticky or crumbly, Zack said, "I can take it from here. Why don't you get home to your Kris? She's waiting, I'll bet."

"Oh, yes. She visits me every night. Every weeknight, anyway." Hickle washed the flour dust from his hands in a sink, drying himself with a hand towel. He was pushing open the kitchen door when Zack called to him.

"Hey, Ray, don't tell Kris about the bonus. Buy her another little something and surprise her with it. The ladies love surprises."

"Funny you should say that. As a matter of fact, I've been planning a surprise for Kris." Hickle nodded to himself. "A major surprise."

He disappeared into the front room. Zack stared after him. A strange one, Raymond Hickle. But if he'd found a woman who loved him, then he was luckier than most.

Hickle left the donut shop at 2:45. As always, he scanned the parking lot at the side of the shop for suspicious vehicles. It was possible he was being watched. Kris had security officers in her employ, and they might be monitoring his activities.

He saw nothing. Even so, he raised his middle finger defiantly in the air, turning in a full circle to exhibit his contempt for any hidden observers.

Then he got into his Volkswagen and pulled onto Pico, heading east. After five blocks he changed lanes, then quickly changed lanes again, watching his rearview mirror to see if any vehicle behind him performed the same maneuver. None did. He was pretty sure he wasn't being followed.

At a gas station on Pico he stopped and used the pay phone, calling one of several numbers he had memorized. A message machine answered, as usual. He wouldn't have minded the machine so much if Kris's voice had been recorded on the tape, but it was the voice of a man, presumably her husband.

After the beep Hickle said, "Hi, Kris, it's me. I know you're at work. Just wanted you to know I'm thinking of you. And that yellow blouse you wore yesterday on the air—no offense, but frankly I didn't care for it. Blue is your color. I enjoyed your repartee with Phil, the sports guy, especially that part about the Dodgers. I didn't realize you were a baseball fan. I hope you don't try eating one of those Dodger dogs. Those things'll kill you. Your health is important to me. Bye."

He got back in the car. Two blocks later he stopped at a convenience store and used another pay phone. He felt it was important to call from a variety of locations. To stay on the line too long at any one place might have been dangerous. He wasn't sure why. He just knew he had to stay on the move.

This time he called her work number, reaching her voicemail service. "Hello, Kris. I guess you're busy getting ready for the six o'clock show. I wanted to ask if you got the flowers I sent last week. I hope you liked them. I picked the same arrangement you had on your desk in the *LA Magazine* photo shoot. It was hard to match the bouquet exactly. You should cut off the tips of the stems every few days to keep the flowers fresh. Oh, this is Raymond, in case you couldn't tell. Break a leg."

He drove for another mile, parked at a mini-mall, and used a pay phone outside a submarine sandwich shop. He called the KPTI switchboard. "Kris Barwood, please."

The operator said Ms. Barwood was unavailable. This might have been true, but it was more likely that the woman simply recognized Hickle's voice. He did call the switchboard nearly every day, after all. "May I take a message?" she asked.

"Yes, please tell her Raymond Hickle called. I have some urgent information for her, but I can't convey it through an intermediary. It's important that I speak with Kris directly."

"I'll pass that on," the operator said, sounding bored. He noticed she did not ask him for a number where he could be reached.

He hung up, drove three more blocks, parked at a fast-food restaurant, and used the pay phone, calling Kris's home number again and shifting his weight restlessly until the answering machine beeped. "Kris, hi, it's Raymond. Look, I wanted to tell you this directly, but it looks as if we keep playing telephone tag, so I'll have to leave a message. The thing is, I had a dream about you, and it might have been a prophetic dream. I saw you doing the news, and you were reporting on a murder, one of those drive-by shootings, and then a car came careening right through the wall and into the TV studio, and shots were fired, and you were hit, Kris. You were hit, and there was blood all over. You were a bloody mess. I don't think they caught who did it, either. I thought it was something you should know. Sometimes dreams foretell the future, or so people say. Gotta go now, bye."

He drove a half block, parked at the curb, and risked returning to the same pay phone for a quick follow-up that had just occurred to him. "One more thing," he said when he got through to her home number. "You know that flower arrangement I sent you? It would look good at a funeral, don't you think? Talk to you soon."

He thought he was done, but three blocks later he pulled into a supermarket parking lot and used his last thirty-five cents to call the KPTI switchboard again. The same operator answered. "Kris Barwood, please," Hickle said.

She let out a sigh. "I'm sorry, but Ms. Barwood—"

"Is unavailable. That's what you were going to say, right?"

"Yes, sir. I can take a message—"

"Would you, please? Uh, tell her Raymond called. Just Raymond, no last name. She knows me."

"Fine, sir, I'll do that."

"And one more thing? Hello?"

"I'm still here. What is it?"

"Tell her I hope a fucking rat crawls between her legs and chews out her fucking *cunt*."

He hung up. He had raised his voice at the end. A woman with a small child was staring at him from across the parking lot. He spat at her as he walked back to his car. She hurried away, and her little boy began to cry.

8

Hickle arrived home shortly after five o'clock. He parked in his assigned space under a carport and went inside.

The Gainford Arms, one of the oldest buildings in the neighborhood, was a relic of the era before garden apartments became fashionable—a rectangular brick pile, five stories high, with rows of small windows looking out on the dismal street in front and the parking lot in the rear. Iron fire escapes climbed the back of the building. Hickle sometimes sat on the fire escape outside his bedroom window and watched the sunset fade over the towers of more expensive real estate to the west.

In the lobby he checked his mail. There was a bunch of junk, a gas bill, and a reply from a TV station in Cincinnati. The station regretted to inform him that it had no photos of its former weekend anchorwoman available for public dissemination. It thanked Hickle for his interest.

He threw away the junk mail and the station's reply. A couple of months ago he had written to every TV station where Kris had worked, requesting her photo from the archives. So far the responses had all been negative. He supposed it didn't matter anymore.

He rode the rattletrap elevator to the fourth floor.

The elevator was slow. He passed the time reading graffiti on the walls.

His apartment, number 420, was halfway down the hall. He was fumbling for his keys when he noticed that the door to the apartment next door was open. A large, battered suitcase stood at the threshold. As he watched, a slender, dark-haired woman in a T-shirt and jeans stepped out of the doorway and picked up the suitcase.

She glanced at him and smiled. "Howdy, neighbor."

Hickle nodded.

She carried the suitcase into her apartment and shut the door. Must be moving in. He wondered who she was.

Once inside his apartment, he forgot her. This was his private place, his refuge from the world. Appraised objectively, it was a narrow, depressing hole. Cracks veined the plaster walls. There were no curtains anywhere; the windows were covered by sagging blinds, raised and lowered by pull-cords with paper clips at the ends. The carpet was a nauseous shade of gray-green, like mold, and its short-nap fibers had been stamped flat in the heavy-traffic areas.

Heat was supplied by an upright gas furnace against one wall, with a vent feeding into the bedroom. Nearly all furnishings were provided by the management. In the living room there was a battered sofa, the cushions flattened and misshapen; an armchair with a vinyl seat; chipped and mismatched end tables; undersized lamps with spotted shades. The landlord had also supplied the thirteen-inch TV with rabbit ears—no cable here—but Hickle had purchased the VCR that rested underneath. Lacking shelves, he had customized a few tables out of apple crates to fill up empty corners and undecorated walls. He had wanted to buy a computer but couldn't justify the expense, so he used the public terminals at the Goldwyn Hollywood Library on Ivar Avenue a mile away.

The kitchen area was a tiny alcove, equipped with a gas oven that had not been cleaned since he moved in, and a refrigerator that leaked on the linoleum floor. Two stained potholders hung forlornly from hooks under the cupboard. Empty soda cans and glass jars were assembled on the counter; he redeemed them for nickels at the local Safeway.

Sharing a wall with the kitchen was the windowless bathroom, smaller than a closet. A ribbon of rust ran down the wall from the medicine cabinet to the sink. More rust fringed the frame of the shower door, competing with a patina of mildew.

Finally there was the bedroom. The bed sagged. Some of the mattress springs were broken. One spring had punctured the mattress itself, its jagged end poking up like a weapon. When Hickle had informed the landlord of this problem, he had been told to flip the mattress. *Isn't it time to get a new bed?* he'd asked quietly. The landlord had answered, *Maybe it's time for you to get a new apartment. What do you think this is, the Ritz fucking Carlton?*

He had no air-conditioning; when the hot Santa Ana winds blew in from the desert, he sweltered like a beast in a cage. At night he was kept awake by the radios from cars moving in and out of the parking lot, where drug deals had been known to go down. A few months ago a dealer had been fatally shot by a rival.

The Gainford Arms was a crummy place, yet it offered him privacy. With the blinds pulled and the door locked and chained, he was as free as he could be from watchful eyes. He was free—

There was a knock on his door.

Hickle looked up, his head canted at an odd angle, his breath held. Momentarily he was baffled by the prospect of company. Nobody ever visited him. He had no friends, and the apartment building's outside doors were locked to keep out trespassers.

Could it be the people who were watching him? The people Kris had hired? Would they be so brazen as to approach him directly?

He crossed the living room, moving warily. Before opening his door, he peered through the fish-eye peep-hole.

It was the dark-haired woman, the one who'd said howdy.

He removed the security chain and drew back the deadbolt. This was an adventure—talking to an unfamiliar woman—and he felt his heart beating harder than it should.

The door swung ajar under his hand, and he was facing her. "Hi again," she said brightly.

He nodded, then realized a response was called for. "Hello."

"Sorry to bother you, but can you tell me where the phone outlet is?"

"Phone outlet?"

"Not the one in the living room. I found that. But there must be one in the bedroom somewhere. I've been crawling around on my hands and knees like a moron, but I can't find it."

"There isn't one."

"There's gotta be."

"Only one. All these apartments have the same layout. The only phone outlet is in the living room. If you need a phone in the bedroom, you'll have to get an extra-long phone cord."

She sighed. "Any other surprises the landlord didn't want to spoil for me?"

"Probably quite a few. There's not enough hot water in the mornings, so take your shower early. Don't hook up too many appliances on any circuit, or you'll blow a fuse."

"This gets better and better."

Hickle risked humor. "Not exactly a garden spot, is it?"

She rewarded him with a laugh. "That might be an understatement."

"So are you an actress?" Damn. He hadn't meant to say that. It had come out of nowhere and sounded strange.

She didn't seem put off by the question, though. "No. What makes you think I might be?"

Because you're so pretty—but what he said was "We've got a fair number of aspiring show-biz types in this building."

The explanation was lame, but she appeared to buy it. "Well, I'm not an actress. Actually, I'm not much of anything right now. I just came here from Riverside— you know, everybody's favorite desert hellhole. Spent last night in a Motel Six."

"No job?"

"I'll find something. I can type. I use all ten fingers." She held up both hands, as if to demonstrate that she really did have the full complement of digits. "How about you? What do you do?"

"I work at a restaurant." He wasn't sure why he had lied. Not lied, exactly. Exaggerated the truth.

"Really? A restaurant around here?"

"Beverly Hills." Another untruth.

She was impressed. "Wow."

"It's just a job." He looked for a way to change the subject. "So what's your name?"

"Abby Gallagher."

"I'm Raymond. Raymond Hickle."

"Glad to meet you, Raymond Hickle." She smiled. "It's good to have a nice neighbor."

This was too much for him. He had no idea how to handle anyone's kindness, and certainly not the kindness of an attractive young woman.

"Likewise," he said weakly. "Good luck getting moved in."

"Thanks. Bye."

He watched her walk away. When she was inside her apartment, he slowly shut his door.

She ought to be an actress, he decided. She was pretty enough. She had hazel eyes and smooth skin and dark brown hair in a cute pageboy cut, and she was fit and slim. *Nice*, she had called him. How often had a woman said that about him? Said it right to his face? And she had smiled.

Then he wondered if it wasn't a little odd that Abby Gallagher had come to him for help when the landlord was still on duty. She had found one phone outlet. She could have called the office to ask about an outlet in the bedroom. Instead, after making eye contact in the hall, she had knocked on his door.

Could she be . . . interested in him? Interested, the way women sometimes were interested in men?

New to the city. Friendless. Lonely.

"Impossible," he whispered.

Anyway, he had higher priorities. He had the shotgun and what he meant to do with it.

He had Kris.

Most nights Hickle dined on beans and rice, a cheap and nourishing repast. At 5:57, right on time, he ladled the pot's steaming contents onto a plastic plate and carried the plate to a card table, setting it down beside a can of diet soda, a spoon, and a paper napkin. He sat on the couch behind the card table and used his remote control to turn on the TV. It was always set to Channel Eight; he never watched anything else. His VCR was loaded with an eight-hour tape and set to record automatically at 6 and 10 P.M. every weekday.

"That does it for us," the male half of the 5 P.M. anchor team was saying. "Let's check in with Kris and Matt to see what's coming up at six."

Hickle leaned forward. It was always interesting to see what she was wearing. Today she had on a blue-green blouse, open at the collar to reveal the taut skin over her collarbone. She said something about a fire in Ventura, an arrest in a murder case, a good outlook for weekend weather. The words didn't matter. He studied her face. Was she thinking of him right now? Could he see fear in her eyes?

"All of that," her partner concluded, "is straight ahead on *Real News* at six."

Theme music. The faces of the anchors and reporters against a montage of news images. The Channel Eight logo. An announcer saying, "KPTI *Real News*, number one at six, with Kris Barwood and Matt Dale . . ."

Hickle sat and watched. When the camera was not on Kris, he lifted spoonfuls of beans and rice into his mouth, washing them down with soda. When she was on the screen, he did not move or even blink. There were so many details to watch for. Even after all this time, he had not yet decided on the exact color of her eyes. Were they blue or gray or some mysterious blend? She wore earrings today but not the ones he'd sent her. The shade of lipstick she was using seemed different than usual. A lighter, more natural shade, a good decision; it brought out the glow of her skin. She laughed during the weather segment. He saw the laugh lines at the corners of her mouth, the explosive flash of her smile.

He missed nothing. He wished the newscast had been all Kris, no one but Kris—she need not even speak, just sit before the camera, turning her head at different angles, posing like a model. In art classes female models posed nude while the students sketched. Imagine a class in which Kris was the model, naked on a pedestal, and he was the only student, free to stare.

Staring, however, would not be enough. For it to be perfect, she would have to descend from her pedestal and embrace him, and he would kiss her neck, her breasts—

He rose. With a sweep of his arm he flung the soda can against the wall, dousing the plaster with a spray of foam.

Then he stood with his hands on his knees, his head down, his breathing shallow and rapid. He didn't move for a long time.

His fantasy of lovemaking had brought him comfort once. But now he had accepted the truth. Maybe it was seeing her with her husband—maybe that was what had made things clear to him at last.

Whatever the reason, he knew that his fantasy was only a fantasy, and that he could not have her, ever.

Therefore no one would have her.

It was that simple and that absolute. Howard Barwood would not have her, and her audience would not have her, and this city would not have her, and the world would not have her.

Hickle raised his head. The newscast was continuing. It had reached the intro to the sports segment. Kris and her co-anchor were joshing with Phil, the sports guy. Making jokes about the Lakers' easy victory last night. Laughing.

"Laugh, Kris," he breathed. "Have fun. Enjoy life."

But not for long.

Because he was gaining proficiency with the shotgun. Soon he would be ready to lie in wait, a shadow among shadows. Ready to spring up and with a single trigger-pull erase her from existence, and where she had been, there would be nothing—no face, no voice, no eyes, no Kris.

He aimed an imaginary shotgun at the TV set, and when she appeared in a smiling close-up, he worked the pump action.

Blammo. Blammo. Blammo.

9

Back in her apartment, Abby removed a microcassette recorder from her purse and dictated her initial observations.

"Wednesday, March twenty-third. Made contact with Hickle. He's socially awkward but possesses basic interpersonal skills. Shy around women. He asked if I was an actress. The question seemed inappropriate. He claimed to work in a restaurant in Beverly Hills. Maybe he wanted to impress me. He's not a skilled liar, has a tendency to blurt things out. His defenses should be easy to penetrate.

"After talking with him, I visited his next-door neighbor on the other side. Hickle's apartment is a mirror image of mine; we share the bedroom wall. His other neighbor, in number four-two-two, shares the living room wall with him. She's an elderly lady named Alice Finley, and she was happy to give me the cup of flour I asked for. Mrs. Finley likes to gossip. She informed me that Hickle never has friends over to visit and almost never goes out at night. He's usually quiet, but at times she hears him shouting, and once or twice she's heard loud banging on the shared wall, like he was pounding with his fist. Her conclusion was that, quote unquote, he's not quite right in the head.

"Bottom line: Hickle is socially isolated, probably paranoid, and deeply angry. He suppresses his most antisocial responses when dealing with others but can be violently enraged when alone. He's a borderline personality, possibly schizotypal, but sufficiently well organized to hold down a job and pay the rent."

These notes were only partly for her benefit. In the event of her death, she wanted to leave a record that would allow the police to reconstruct what had happened. She was not entirely sure she could count on Travis to tell them what they needed to know. In her line of work, it was invariably necessary to break the law now and then, as Travis well knew. Faced with a police investigation, he would have to protect himself, quite possibly by denying all knowledge of her activities. A grim thought, but not unrealistic.

She switched off the recorder, then used her cell phone to call Hollywood Station, asking for Sergeant Wyatt. "Vic's not on duty tonight," she was told. "You can reach him at home."

She knew his home number. He answered on the third ring. "Wyatt."

"Hey, Vic. Guess who."

He made a sound like a chuckle. "Took you nearly twenty-four hours to call. I was starting to think you didn't need me after all."

"I need you. I'm a very needy person. There's a guy in Hollywood we have to talk about, but not over the phone."

"You had dinner?"

"Not yet."

"There's a place on Melrose that's not bad." He gave her the address. "Half hour?"

"I'll be there. Thanks, Vic."

"Don't thank me yet. I may not be able to help you this time."

"You're always able to help."

"But I may not want to. It only encourages you, and I'm not sure I should do that." He hung up without a good-bye.

Most people Vic Wyatt could figure out. A decade spent riding patrol in Hollywood Division had taught him everything he needed to know about human nature, and although his promotion to sergeant confined him to a desk more often than he liked, he still saw a greater variety of people, night after night, than the average working professional would encounter in a lifetime. He was sufficiently jaded to think he had seen it all. At least, he used to be—until he met Abby.

"Hope I didn't keep you waiting," she said as she slipped into the Leatherette bench opposite him.

He checked his watch. "You're right on time."

"Am I? That's a first."

She was wearing a T-shirt, jeans, and a vinyl zippered jacket bearing the LA Dodgers logo. It was not an outfit that ought to have flattered her, but Wyatt found himself taking note of the smooth fall of her hair, the shapely stem of her neck. She was twenty-eight, four years younger than he was, a fact he had learned by the simple expedient of looking up her DMV records shortly after they'd met.

He knew she never noticed him in that way. To Abby he was nothing but a resource. He had no chance with her at all.

"What looks good here?" she asked, reaching for a menu.

"I'm opting for the Matterhorn. Half-pound burger with Swiss cheese and pickles."

Her nose wrinkled. "You're clogging your arteries just by talking about it."

"You might prefer the Garden of Veggie Delights."

She surveyed the menu. "Sounds like the least damaging of the possible choices."

"It's funny, you being so concerned about health hazards." He leaned forward, studying her. "Something gives me the feeling you aren't so cautious when it comes to other hazards in your life."

"Me? I'm the original shrinking violet. I always play it safe." She was smiling.

He found that smile infuriating. He didn't know why he had agreed to meet her. Their meetings were always the same. She pumped him for info, then went off and broke the law in some obscure way he couldn't quite figure out—surveillance or undercover work or . . . something. She *used* him. At the same time she mocked him with her sweet smile and her evasions. She was polite about it, good company, very charming, but he couldn't trust her to level with him, ever.

After the waitress took their orders, Wyatt folded his hands and asked, "Who's the guy you want to ask me about this time?"

"His name is Raymond Hickle. He lives on Gainford. I'll give you his address. I don't think he has a record, but maybe you could ask around, see if any patrol guys have had run-ins with him or . . ." She trailed off, seeing his face. "You know something about him already, don't you?"

"Yeah."

"So give."

He didn't respond right away, and when he did, it was with a question. "How did you get mixed up with Hickle?"

"It's a case. I can't go into details."

"This is dangerous, Abby."

"I'm just doing some background research—"

"Shut up. Quit telling me that bullshit. It's getting on my nerves."

She was silent, chastened for the first time in their relationship. "I've met Hickle," Wyatt said after a moment. "Back when I was riding patrol, I went to his apartment twice, some low-rent place on La Brea."

"The La Brea Palms," Abby said. "South of Hollywood Boulevard. He lived there from 1989 to 1993."

"Sounds like you've done some checking on him already."

"Not me. The firm I'm consulting to. Employment history, residential addresses, things like that. But they didn't find anything about a criminal case."

"There was no case. Hickle was never charged. He doesn't have a rap sheet. It never got that far."

"How far did it get?"

"Like I said, I went to his apartment twice. Me and my partner, together. We were sent over there for a little intimidation session with Hickle. First time it didn't take, so we went back for an instant replay a couple weeks later. It still didn't take, but it did get Hickle evicted. The landlord didn't like having a tenant who was in trouble with the police."

"Why was it necessary to confront him at all?"

"Because he was harassing a woman who lived in the building. He was stalking her."

"What woman?"

"Her name was Jill Dahlbeck. She was in her early twenties, and she'd moved to LA from Wisconsin, planning, naturally, to be a movie star."

"An actress," Abby said.

Wyatt thought he heard a special emphasis in her voice but couldn't decipher its meaning. "She got a few small roles in TV shows, infomercials, and she did a lot of Equity-waiver theater work. Typical story. She was a nice kid. That was her problem. She was too nice."

"How so?"

"She made the mistake of smiling at Hickle, treating him like a human being. He misinterpreted it, or over-interpreted. Whatever. He decided she was meant for him. She had zero interest in the guy. I mean, they say men are from Mars, women are from Venus? Well, Hickle's from Pluto, and I don't mean the Disney version."

Abby nodded, unsmiling. In the darkness outside the coffee shop a kid sauntered by, rocking on his heels, shouldering a boom box that cranked out an obscene rap number. Abby waited until the noise had receded before asking, "What form did the harassment take?"

"Following her, sending letters, waiting outside her apartment. Finally she moved to a different address. He tracked her down. He was persistent. He kept saying she had to give him a chance."

"So she complained to the police . . ."

"And a couple of us—Todd Belvedere and me— were dispatched to have a talk with Hickle. Put a scare in him, make him back down."

He saw Abby shake her head slowly in disapproval.

"Not the way to handle it?" he asked.

"I'm afraid not."

"Yeah. Well, we found that out. You have to understand, we were treading on new territory here. The LAPD had established the Threat Management Unit only the previous year, and it was still limited to high-profile celebrity cases. And Jill, regardless of her movie-star ambitions, was definitely no celebrity, so we were pretty much on our own."

"I'm not blaming you. I'm just saying that a direct confrontation generally makes things worse. What Hickle wanted was some response from Jill. Your showing up qualified as a response—not the kind he was hoping for, but at least it showed he'd gotten through to her; he was on her mind. It cemented the connection between them."

Wyatt nodded. "And it made him mad. Subsequently he became a lot more aggressive in his pursuit. It was like his manhood was on the line."

"It was. Hickle was a loser with no career prospects and no social life, living in a run-down neighborhood. His self-esteem was precarious at best. When you came along, trying to intimidate him, it threatened what was left of his dignity. His manhood, as you said."

"Now you tell me. Where were you when I needed you? Anyway, we went back a second time for a more serious conversation, but it was like pouring gasoline on a fire."

"What happened to Jill Dahlbeck?"

"We finally had to admit to her that there wasn't a lot we could do. We couldn't protect her twenty-four hours a day, and we couldn't charge Hickle with anything serious. He stayed just inside the law. All Jill could do was get away. She moved back to Wisconsin."

The waitress returned, bearing a tray laden with a cheeseburger and a beer for Wyatt, a large salad and bottled water for Abby.

"Was Jill attractive?" Abby asked, lifting her fork.

"Very."

"Blond? Blue eyes? Nordic?"

"What hat did you pull that rabbit out of?"

"It was an educated guess. So if this all happened when Hickle moved out of the La Brea complex, it must have been 1993. He was twenty-seven."

"That sounds right."

"I'm surprised you remember the case in that much detail after all this time."

"Well . . . there was one thing that happened. Jill was attacked."

Abby looked at him. It occurred to him that she had beautiful eyes. They were calm and clear and the same shade of golden brown he had seen once on a trip to Nebraska, when the westering sun caught the wheat fields in a burnished haze.

"Attacked how?" Abby asked slowly.

"She was taking a class at some little hole-in-the-wall actors' studio near Hollywood and Vine. The place has closed down since then. Anyway, one night when she was walking to her car, somebody jumped out from behind a hedge and splashed her with battery acid."

"In the face?"

"That might have been the idea, but she spun away in time, and the stuff only got her coat. Her skin wasn't burned at all. The assailant fled. She never got a look at him. The street was dark, and it all happened in a second."

"But she thought it was Hickle."

"Obviously. And we did too. We went over to his new address and rousted him. Thing is, he had something close to an alibi. He was a stockboy in a supermarket, and he'd worked pretty late that night. Plenty of people saw him. He left only a few minutes before the attack took place. He might have had time to get there and lie in wait for Jill, but the time frame was tight."

"Search his apartment?"

"Yeah, he gave permission, but there was no acid, nothing that would tie him to the crime."

"Still, it had to be him."

"I don't know, Abby. This is Hollywood, remember. Lots of random craziness. Hickle's not the only nutcase. Anyway, Jill was rattled. That's why she left LA. She was gone the next day."

"Wise move," Abby said. "And she's still okay?"

"Far as I know."

"And Hickle was never charged."

Wyatt shrugged. "No way the DA could file with what we had. Nobody could prove a thing. Even so, whether Hickle did it or not, he *could* have done it. You know what I'm saying? He's capable of it. He's sick enough."

She was silent.

"Abby." He leaned forward, elbows on the table. "If you're mixed up in any way with this son of a bitch, you're taking a hell of a risk."

"What makes you think I'm mixed up with him? I'm doing—"

"Research. I know. Just be careful, whatever you're up to."

"I always am, Vic. Don't worry about me."

Wyatt picked up the check. Abby wanted to split the tab, but for reasons of masculine pride he insisted on paying. Outside, he offered to walk her to her car, but she said it wasn't necessary. "You sure?" he asked. "Lots of bad guys out there."

"I can take care of myself."

"I got that impression. But you know, there's a reason why patrol cops work in pairs. Sometimes you need a person to cover your back."

"I haven't needed one so far."

"Maybe you've been lucky."

"Well, let's hope my luck holds. 'Night, Vic. Thanks for everything."

He watched her walk away. His car, an ancient Camaro with a rebuilt engine, was waiting for him around the corner, but he didn't go it to yet. He lingered in the shadow of the coffee shop's awning, screened from the glare of the neon sign. Abby's footsteps faded with distance, and then there was the faint pop of a car door opening and a louder thump as it closed. A motor revved.

She'd made it safely to her vehicle. It looked as if she really could take care of herself, not that he'd had any doubts.

Something made him wait a minute longer in the dark. He heard her car pull away from the curb. Headlights flared into view, and a white subcompact shot past. He glimpsed Abby at the wheel, illuminated by the dashboard glow. She was driving a Dodge Colt, square and boxy, far from new. It had a dent in one side panel. The motor sounded peppy enough, but the Colt had seen some serious use. It must have racked up a hundred thousand miles.

His Camaro wasn't any newer, but it had been kept in perfect condition. It was a classic. There was nothing classic about Abby's rattletrap set of wheels.

Strange. Last night she'd told him she lived in the Wilshire Royal. Luxury building, where the parking garage was lined with Porsches. If Abby could afford that lifestyle, why was she driving a junkyard clunker?

He shook his head slowly, walking away. Something didn't fit, or if it did, he couldn't see it.

Or maybe he didn't want to see.

10

Abby parked in her assigned space under a carport at the Gainford Arms. When she killed the ignition, the little hatchback shuddered all over like a big wet dog.

The car, a Dodge Colt that she had bought from a used car dealer for two thousand dollars, was used strictly for undercover work. At home she kept her real car, a snazzy little Miata that let her negotiate the twists and curves of Mulholland Drive with the wind in her hair. Whenever she took that drive, she imagined herself back in the foothills south of Phoenix, riding one of her father's Appaloosas on the high, steep trails.

But she couldn't drive the Miata in this neighborhood without calling attention to herself, so the Dodge was her vehicle of choice at the moment. She locked it up and crossed the parking lot.

Music and laughter drew her attention. She followed the noise to the far corner of the lot, where she found a small concrete platform enclosed by an iron fence. The platform was the setting for an outdoor Jacuzzi, bubbling busily. A few young people were hanging out in the tub, drinking beer out of long-necked bottles, while a portable radio played a Shania Twain song.

The landlord had mentioned the spa area, the apartment building's only luxury feature. She hadn't quite believed him, though in retrospect there was no reason for doubt; this was LA, after all, where swimming pools and hot tubs were not unknown in even the least desirable neighborhoods.

The water looked inviting, but she had no desire to join the crowd. She was turning to go when one of the partygoers noticed her.

"Hey, you got a bathing suit?" he called out.

She smiled. "I'm not in the mood, thanks."

"We can put you in the mood," another guy yelled. He was drunk.

"Somehow I doubt that. Have fun. And try not to pass out in there, okay?"

She walked away. Behind her, the two men pled their case and, when that tactic failed, switched to wolf whistles and sexually suggestive grunts. Subtlety evidently was not their preferred method of romantic conquest.

She rode the elevator to the fourth floor. Outside Hickle's door she paused to listen, pressing her ear against the wood. She heard the TV in his living room. The time was nine o'clock, too early for the news. Maybe he kept the TV on just for the illusion of companionship it provided.

She unlocked her apartment and entered, deflating a little when she breathed in the musty smell and saw the cheap, worn furniture and the dingy walls. She had spent a great deal of time in places like this over the past few years.

Lying on the couch, she dictated what she had learned from Wyatt into her microrecorder. Then she fixed herself a cup of herbal tea and drank it slowly, sitting on the fire escape and watching the night sky.

Once, she saw a shooting star that traced a pale arc above the distant rooftops. It might be an omen—good or bad, she couldn't say.

Loud voices echoed through the parking lot below. The party crowd was leaving the spa area. She heard inebriated laughter, fading out.

The hot tub must be empty now. She decided to try it. She could use some R 'n' R.

Among the items of clothing she had packed, there was a one-piece swimsuit. She changed into the suit and took a large bath towel with her as she went downstairs to the lobby. She crossed the parking lot to the spa area. The gate was closed, but she discovered that the lock was broken, and she didn't need to use her apartment key. A sign warned that the Jacuzzi was to be used only by residents of the Gainford Arms and only between the hours of 8 A.M. and 10 P.M. She checked her watch. The time was 10:15. Well, there was nobody around to complain that she was breaking the rules.

The kids who'd partied here had left the place a mess. Empty beer bottles ringed the tub. Potato chips and pretzels were scattered around, and near one of the cheap lounge chairs lay the uneaten remnant of a Twinkie.

"Slobs," Abby murmured. She set down her purse and the towel on the lounge chair, then took off her wristwatch and her sneakers. Finally she eased herself into the tub. The water was still frothing and gurgling; the kids had neglected to turn off the jets when they left.

Eyes shut, she rested her head against the concrete rim of the tub and let the hot bubbling water massage the small of her back.

She had not rested, really rested, in much too long. The New Jersey case had been tricky, and then Travis had called her back to LA as soon as it had ended. There had been almost no downtime.

She wondered if she had been wrong to accept the TPS case. True, she desperately wanted to prove herself to Travis, make amends for the Devin Corbal disaster, if she possibly could—but she might be driving herself too hard. Fatigue was the real enemy in a profession like hers. Fatigue could be fatal.

After this one, she promised, she would take a vacation. Maybe head over to Phoenix and look up some old friends. Hike in the Superstition Mountains, ride a horse on a dusty trail, be a kid again.

Yes, she would do all those things . . . when this job was over . . .

She felt herself drifting into the alpha state on the threshold of sleep. Her thoughts fuzzed out and grew distant. All tension left her, and there was only a humming meditative sense of calm.

Then a sudden lurch forward, water over her head, the hot jets stinging her neck—

She was submerged in the tub, the surface only inches away but out of reach, because she couldn't rise.

Someone was holding her down with a strong hand clutching the top of her head, gripping her hair in tangled bunches.

She tried to grab the hand that held her, knowing she could inflict instant pain by bending back one of his fingers or squeezing the tender ball of flesh below his thumb, but with his free hand he deflected her attack.

If she could only see him—

But she couldn't, she was underwater, blinded by the lights ringing the interior of the tub, and above her was only darkness and she couldn't see anything, and there was no air.

She struggled to duck lower, pull free, but he had her by the hair and wouldn't yield. She braced both feet against the bottom of the tub and pushed hard, fighting to overcome the downward pressure that kept her submerged, but he had the advantage of leverage.

A cry of frustration burst out of her in an explosion of bubbles, blending with the jets of churning water.

The cry cost nearly the last of her oxygen. She would black out at any moment, and then he would simply have to hold her down until her lungs flooded with water in a final instinctive breath.

But she couldn't die this way, facedown in a Jacuzzi, surrounded by empty beer bottles and trash—

Beer bottles.

A weapon.

With her last strength she raised her arm out of the water and groped behind her, along the rim of the spa.

Her hand closed over the neck of a bottle.

She tilted it, smashed it against the concrete, then jabbed upward with the broken, jagged end.

Instantly the hand holding her down withdrew.

She stabbed again, blindly, not sure if she had made contact the first time—then surfaced with a hoarse, spluttering gasp.

Sucking air into her lungs, she spun in the tub, looking everywhere for her assailant, but all she saw was the gate clanging shut.

In the parking lot—running footsteps, fading out.

She leaned against the side of the tub, fighting to

control her breathing, then noticed that she still held the beer bottle in her hand.

She examined the jagged end for blood, found none. She saw no red droplets on the concrete surface of the spa area.

The bottle had merely scared him. She hadn't inflicted a wound. Too bad. Blood could be tested and matched to an eventual suspect. Besides, she would have liked to hurt the bastard after what he put her through.

She set down the bottle and climbed out of the spa, shivering in the cool air. With a towel wrapped around her, she considered the big question.

Who the hell was he?

She was quite certain her attacker had been male. Those hands had been decidedly masculine in their size and strength. But whose hands had they been? Hickle's? Was he on to her somehow, or had he simply equated her in his mind with Jill Dahlbeck, his earlier obsession?

He had asked if she was an actress, as Jill had been. Maybe there was something about her that had triggered the same feelings that might have led him to splash Jill with battery acid on a dark side street in Hollywood years ago.

Or maybe the assault had no connection with Hickle or this case. She remembered Wyatt saying, *This is Hollywood, remember. Lots of random craziness. Hickle's not the only nutcase.*

Then an absurd thought occurred to her. How well did she really know Vic Wyatt?

"Oh, come on," she said under her breath, "that's paranoid."

Of course it was paranoid. She was in a paranoid

business. She was trained to be hypervigilant. But the fact was, somebody had just tried to kill her, less than two hours after her meeting with Wyatt—and she didn't know Wyatt all that well.

He had bumped into her last night at the bar in Westwood. Suppose it wasn't a coincidence. Suppose he had been following her. Stalking her . . . She knew all about that kind of behavior, didn't she?

And suppose that tonight, after dinner, he had followed her to this building, and when he saw her enter the tub . . .

"Tried to kill me?" she asked herself aloud. "Why would he?"

She couldn't say, but she had to admit it was at least possible. The lock on the gate was broken; anyone could have entered the spa area.

She still didn't believe it. Wyatt had never struck her as the slightest bit unstable or hostile or obsessive.

Anyhow, there might be a way to eliminate him from suspicion.

She took the cell phone out of her purse and called Wyatt's home number. He lived in the mid-city district near La Brea and Washington. If he'd fled this location just minutes earlier, he wouldn't have had time to get home yet.

She waited through three rings, a small knot of worry forming in her stomach. She didn't want to suspect Wyatt. She didn't want the assailant to be anyone she knew and liked.

Four rings—

And the phone was answered. "Wyatt."

"Oh." She caught her breath. "Hi, Vic, it's me. Hope I'm not calling too late."

"No problem. I'm kind of a night owl, with the schedule I'm working lately. What's up?"

She couldn't very well tell him that she was calling to remove him from suspicion of attempted murder. But she hadn't had time to think of a cover story. She improvised. "I realized I forgot to ask if there were any other women Hickle went after. You know, in addition to Jill Dahlbeck. Anything in his past, any other reports, before or since."

"Not that I'm aware of. But I have a feeling you might know about somebody."

"Me?"

"Why else would a security firm be taking a fresh look at him?"

"Well . . . no comment."

"That's what I figured. And if I asked who his new object of affection might be?"

"No comment."

"You sound like a broken record. Anything else you forgot to ask?"

She almost said no, then changed her mind. "There is one thing. Any reports of drownings in the Hollywood district?"

"Drownings? You mean, like, little kids who fall in a swimming pool?"

"No, I mean adults . . . Any unsolved cases like that? An adult who drowned in a pool or a hot tub, that kind of thing?"

"What would that have to do with Raymond Hickle?"

"Probably nothing. Just a loose end I'm trying to tie up."

"Well, to answer your question—no, there haven't been any mysterious, unsolved Hollywood drownings. If there had been, I think the local news would have picked up on it, don't you?"

"Sure. Of course they would. Sorry I asked."

"No problem. I'm here to help. To protect and serve, that's my motto."

"I'll see you, Vic."

"Take care, Abby."

She ended the call. There was no chance he could have made it home that fast, and besides, she had detected no hesitation or fear when she asked about local drownings. He was in the clear.

That left one other suspect, one who was considerably more obvious than Vic Wyatt.

Abby went inside the building and rode the elevator to the fourth floor. Once inside her apartment, she slipped onto the fire escape, then crept close to Hickle's bedroom window.

The window was open. From his living room she heard the babble of his TV. Kris Barwood's voice. She checked her watch—10:40. The late local news on Channel Eight was still in progress.

She leaned over the railing of the fire escape and peered into the living room window two yards away. The venetian blind was open, and she could see Hickle clearly, seated on the couch, bare-chested, wearing a pair of ragged shorts, watching the TV in rapt concentration. He looked as if he had not moved in nearly an hour. Quite possibly he hadn't. When the news came on, it became the only thing in his world.

Abby retreated inside her apartment and considered the situation.

Wyatt was cleared. And she didn't think the assailant had been Hickle either.

Then who was it?

Random craziness, she decided, once again replaying Wyatt's comments on the subject. This was Hollywood. Plenty of nuts out there.

She had gotten careless and one of them had tried to take advantage. Maybe meant to kill her and steal her purse. When she fought back, he got scared and ran off. End of story.

The explanation didn't entirely satisfy her. She wasn't a big believer in coincidences. But Wyatt and Hickle were off the hook, and there was no one else to suspect.

Was there?

11

It was past midnight when Howard Barwood climbed the stairs to the bedroom. He'd been out later than expected. Kris was already home. He found her stretched on the bed in her nightgown and slippers. Her hair had fanned over the pillows, framing her face in a fringe of gold.

"Well, well," she whispered, her voice flat, "you're finally back. Out for another drive?"

He nodded, not looking at her. "Still breaking in the new Lexus. I took it all the way up to Santa Barbara and back."

"Quite a trip."

"Uh-huh." He didn't want to talk about this. He crossed to the window and peered out at the moonlit surf pounding the beach. "Look at those breakers."

"I'm too tired to look." Kris sighed. "You, on the other hand, don't seem tired at all."

"Why should I be?"

"All that driving would wear anyone out."

"It gets me energized." He wished he could change the subject.

She made a noncommittal sound. "You do seem a little . . . agitated."

"Agitated?" He wanted to sound casual, but the word came out raw and tense.

"Yes, I'd say so. Restless, jumpy, on edge. You didn't get in an accident, did you?"

"Of course not. Why would you even ask a question like that?"

"You strike me as kind of worked up, that's all."

"I'm fine. I like driving the new car. It's a kick. Maybe it takes me a little while to come down off the adrenaline high." He wondered if she could hear the lie in his voice.

Kris was silent for a moment. Then she whispered, "I guess anything is better than spending time here at the house—or with me."

He turned away from the window. "What are you talking about?"

"Lately you've been keeping your distance."

"That's ridiculous. I went with you to work yesterday, if you recall. I was at the studio. I was there all night."

"You were there. But you spent most of your time with Amanda." Amanda Gilbert was the executive producer of the six o'clock edition of *Real News*. "You two were inseparable, at least until she went home at seven-thirty."

In the stretch of stillness that followed, the roar of the surf was plainly audible even through the double-pane windows.

There were many things for Howard to say, but none seemed quite right. He settled on irony. "Paranoia's not a good look for you, Kris."

"It's not paranoia. I saw how you acted around her. And earlier that afternoon . . ."

"Yes?"

She averted her gaze. "Never mind."

He took a step toward the bed, then stopped. Distantly it occurred to him how absurd it was for a man to hesitate about approaching his own wife in their bedroom. "Come on," he said quietly. "Let's hear it. What mortal sin did I commit yesterday afternoon?"

"That woman Travis hired—she's about Amanda's age." The smile that flickered on Kris's face was one she never used in public. A sad, bitter smile. "Why is it always the young ones you can't take your eyes off? What's so special about youth anyway? Does a woman fall apart at forty the way a car does when it hits a hundred thousand miles? Or is it just that you always need this year's model even when the one you've got is still running fine?"

"I couldn't care less about Abby Sinclair."

"No? You were so vocal in your concern for her safety." Her voice slipped into a lower register. "Are you sure you won't get hurt? Aren't you taking an awful risk, you poor, brave thing?"

"I think her safety is a legitimate concern. Of course, I realize that in the larger picture it's only *your* safety that counts. The slightest threat to you is a national emergency—"

"The slightest threat?" She sat up straight, her hair falling around her shoulders. "Is that what you think Raymond Hickle represents, a *slight* threat?"

He wouldn't back down. "Under the circumstances . . ."

"You mean the circumstances of being stalked and harassed and terrorized night and day?"

"I mean the circumstances of being surrounded by armed bodyguards night and day."

"Devin Corbal was surrounded by armed bodyguards when his stalker shot him."

Howard spread his hands. "Well, if you don't trust Travis to protect you—"

"This isn't about Travis."

"So what the hell is it about?"

Abruptly she let her head fall back on the pillow. "What do you think?"

Finally he took the three steps that brought him to her bedside. He stood looking down at her. "What am I supposed to do, Kris?" he asked softly. "What do you want me to do?"

"What I want . . ." She rolled her head in his direction, swept a tangle of hair from her face. "What I want is for you to look at me the way you look at those other women. Younger women."

"I do, all the time." The words sounded false even as he pronounced them.

"Do you? When was the last time we . . . ?" Weariness overtook her. "Oh, never mind."

He knew that if he took no action now, she would hate him in the morning. She had asked him as plainly as she could, as openly as pride would allow.

"It's been too long," he murmured. It was the closest he could come to an apology.

She looked at him, wariness and hope mingled in her expression. "Yes." Her tone was neutral, giving him nothing.

Now was the moment for him to kiss her. Now was his opportunity to heal the breach between them.

He couldn't.

"It's this craziness with Hickle," he said dully. "Once that's past and things are back to normal, we'll be the way we were. We have to wait it out, that's all."

"Is that what we have to do?" Kris whispered.

"Just until this is all settled and we can breathe again."

She didn't answer.

"I think I'll fix something to eat," Howard said, though he wasn't hungry. "Can I bring you anything?"

She shook her head slowly. "I'm going to sleep."

"That's the best thing. Rest. Put everything out of your mind." He reached out and clumsily stroked her hair, his nearest imitation of affection. "It'll all be behind us soon."

She was silent.

Howard left Kris in the bedroom and went downstairs, wishing it was still possible for him to love his wife.

12

Hickle couldn't sleep.

He rolled over and stared at the glowing dial of his bedside alarm clock. The time was 2:19. He had to get up in three hours. His shift started at 6 A.M., and he was always punctual.

The smart thing to do was just close his eyes and relax. Sleep would come, if he let it. He was sure it would.

Instead, hating himself, he slipped out of bed and picked a pair of pants and a shirt out of his laundry basket, pulling them on. Then he removed the screen from his bedroom window and crept onto the landing of the fire escape.

His new neighbor's bedroom shared a wall with his own. The landing afforded access to her window. He approached, bending low. Her bedroom was dark, the window shut, the venetian blind closed. But the blind was old and warped, and through gaps in the horizontal slats he could dimly make out Abby Gallagher, asleep in her bed, limned by moonlight.

He knelt, pressing his face close to the window, watching her sleep.

She was pretty, all right. She reminded him of Jill.

Of course, they looked nothing alike. Jill had been taller and blond and almost severe in her beauty. She had looked a little like Kris, now that he thought about it. Funny how that had never occurred to him before.

Abby, smaller, dark-haired, was not at all like Jill or Kris in physical appearance. Still, she was not unattractive. Her eyes, he remembered, were hazel, and her skin was smooth. There were faint freckles on her nose and cheeks. Her mouth was a perfect shape—what people called a kissable mouth, he supposed.

No, she did not resemble Jill. Why, then, did she remind him of her? Maybe because, like Jill, she had been nice to him. She had smiled and made small talk. She had been friendly. Just as Jill had been—in the early stages of their relationship, at least.

Later, when he had tried to get serious with her, to express his feelings, Jill had rebuffed him. She had tried to give him the brush-off.

He wondered if Abby would do the same, if he tried to get to know her better. He hoped not. He wouldn't want things to get ugly with her, the way they had with Jill.

Toward the end, he had gotten a little bit crazy about Jill Dahlbeck. He had enough distance, enough maturity, to recognize that fact now. The business with the acid, for instance. That had really been uncalled for.

It was ordinary battery acid, which he had collected in a jar. He remembered waiting for Jill to leave her acting class, following her with his gaze as she separated from the other students and walked down the dark side street where her car was parked. Then when she was a few yards from the car, her keys jangling in her hand—

He'd leaped up out of hiding. Splashed the acid at her. He could still see the long fluid arc launching into space.

Her face had been the target. He had wanted her scarred, blinded. He had wanted to do something to her that was so terrible and so ineradicable that she could never forget.

But he'd failed. She had seen the flash of movement and instinctively pivoted away, and the acid had spattered her coat, ruining it but doing no further damage.

He had run, cursing his bad luck. For years afterward he had relived that moment, wishing he could have another shot at her. For a time he had considered tracking her down—he suspected she had returned to Wisconsin—and doing something to her. Kidnapping her, maybe, and taking her into the woods.

Now, however, he was past all that. He no longer had any feelings toward Jill. He had scarcely thought of her in the past year. Not since he had encountered Kris. She was the one for him, the only one. Jill could not compare. Neither could Abby, not by a long shot.

Still, Abby had smiled at him so sweetly . . .

He studied her, fascinated. She lay on her side, facing him. In the moonlight her skin had a porcelain quality. A wisp of hair draped her forehead, fluttering faintly in the breeze stirred by her breath.

In some ways she was even prettier than Jill. Of course, she wouldn't be so pretty with a cupful of acid searing the skin of her face.

He didn't expect it to come to that. He really didn't.

Still, you never could tell.

13

The first night in a new place was always the hardest. Abby woke at 6 A.M. stiff from the unfamiliar mattress.

Some noise from the parking lot had awakened her, she guessed. She lay still for a moment, adjusting to the reality of her surroundings. The sun was rising, and its glow through the slats of the venetian blind painted the bedroom in orange stripes. She saw cracks in the ceiling plaster, a furry patina of dust on the dresser, a cigarette burn in the short-nap carpet.

"Why aren't there any rich stalkers?" she wondered aloud. "This job would be more fun if I had to infiltrate a fashionable cul-de-sac in Bel-Air."

She rose from bed and looked out the window. Hickle's Volkswagen, which was normally parked under one of the carports on the opposite side of the parking lot from her Dodge, was gone. He must have left for the donut shop sometime earlier.

Lying on the floor, she performed a stretching routine, working her hamstrings and the muscles of her back, then limbered up her neck and shoulders with yoga exercises, and concluded the session with ten minutes of deep breathing. Then she considered the problem of how to search Hickle's apartment.

The job would be tricky. At first she contemplated breaking in through his bedroom window via the fire escape. But surely he had locked the window before leaving for work, and she doubted she could defeat the window latch without leaving evidence of intrusion. Better go in through the door.

After a breakfast of oatmeal, cinnamon toast, and a banana, she ran the shower, rinsing her hair in the thin, tepid stream. As Hickle had warned, hot water was scarce. She dressed in old jeans and a faded blouse.

She passed the time rereading the case file until after nine o'clock, when those tenants who had jobs were likely to have left for work, and the others had settled in for a day of soap operas and talk shows. Tool kit in hand, she stepped into the hall and looked around. Every door on the fourth floor was closed. A neighbor peering through a peephole might catch her in the act of a break-in, but she was willing to chance it.

Before Hickle's door she set down the tool kit and took out an electric pick gun and a feather-touch, coil-spring tension bar. The door was secured with a Kwikset pin-tumbler deadbolt lock. To turn the plug, it was necessary to free the pins, lifting them into the pin wells. She inserted the tension bar into the lower half of the keyway and the pick gun's blade into the upper half, then switched on the pick. It whirred like a dentist's drill until the row of pins popped free. The plug rotated under the pressure of the tension bar, and the deadbolt retracted with a metallic snick.

She stepped inside, shut the door, and looked through the peephole, watching for any activity in the hall. There was none. Evidently the pick gun's motor noise had aroused no concern.

Turning, she surveyed Hickle's apartment. The furniture was different from hers but of no better quality.

Although Hickle had lived in the building for years, he had not enlivened the decor with mementos or artworks or small, homey touches. There were no paintings on the walls, no framed photos resting on end tables. The place was as nondescript as a motel room.

She crossed the living room and closed the venetian blind, then turned on a light. The first thing she noticed was the VCR under the TV. Hickle must have bought the VCR himself; unlike the TV, it had not been bolted down by the landlord. She found the all-purpose remote and turned on both devices, then reviewed the on-screen programming menu. Hickle had set the VCR to tape Channel Eight every weekday from 6 to 6:30 P.M. and again from ten o'clock to eleven. Kris Barwood's two daily newscasts.

She turned off the machines, then inspected the kitchen. The fridge was stocked with several large plastic containers of rice and beans, Hickle's dietary staple. She found no snacks, no dessert foods, not even any sugar. At least he couldn't use the Twinkie defense.

Before proceeding with the search, she took care of one more item of business in the living room. She installed a surveillance camera.

The camera was an inch wide by an inch deep, with a 3.6mm pinhole lens that resembled a pen's ball point. The lens covered a ninety-degree field of view, and its light rating was .03 lux, permitting photography even in semidarkness. Soldered to the camera was an inchlong UHF crystal-controlled color video transmitter that broadcast 420 lines of video resolution without shakiness or drift. The transmitter had a range of three hundred feet and would send its signal through walls and any other obstruction except steel.

For extended use the unit had to be run off an external power supply. Fortunately there was a smoke detector mounted above Hickle's sofa, hard-wired into the main current. She took the smoke detector apart and found room inside for the camera-transmitter package, which she wired to the AC. Before replacing the smoke detector on the wall, she aligned the camera lens with one of the prepunched holes in the cover.

The camera was not equipped with a microphone. She considered installing an infinity transmitter in the base of Hickle's telephone—the device would pick up room noise along with both ends of his telephone conversations—but decided against it. Hickle, like many paranoids, might periodically inspect his phone for bugs. Besides, it was unnecessary to monitor his phone calls. The only calls that mattered were the ones he made to Kris Barwood, and TPS was already recording and tracing those.

Still, she wanted some audio surveillance. Mrs. Finley had reported that Hickle sometimes shouted when alone. No doubt he also talked to himself at times. Most people did. "Even me," Abby said, proving her point.

A simple hidden microphone would do the trick. She planted one inside the stove's ventilation hood. The microphone and its transmitter used less energy than the video camera and did not need to be hooked up to the main current. A single nine-volt battery would allow continuous transmission for more than a week.

The bedroom was next. Here was where Hickle truly lived, where he felt free to be himself. He had made the room a shrine to Kris Barwood. Her image was everywhere. The walls were papered with KPTI advertisements, photos of Kris from feature articles, and eight-by-ten glossies of Kris at various stages in her career.

"He really is her number one fan," Abby whispered. She snapped a series of still photos with a pocket camera.

She was disappointed that there was no computer in the room. Hickle had told Kris Barwood that he'd searched the Internet to obtain her home address. Presumably he had used a publicly available terminal. It seemed odd. Even on his income, he could surely afford a garage-sale computer. Maybe he was a technophobe or something.

The first thing she did was plant a second audio bug. This one she taped to the underside of his nightstand drawer. If he talked in his sleep, she would know.

Then she began her search. In a cabinet she found rows of videotapes, each eight hours long and carefully labeled with five dates in chronological order. Weekdays only. Kris's newscasts. The half-hour 6 P.M. show and the hour-long 10 P.M. edition added up to ninety minutes per day. Hickle recorded a week's worth of shows—seven and a half hours—on each tape. Thirty-six tapes in all. He'd been taping for roughly eight months, and by Abby's calculation he now had two hundred seventy hours of Kris Barwood. And he was still taping her, still adding new shows to his collection.

Two rows of books took up the cabinet's lower shelf. Some bore the labels of used book shops, while others were stamped "LIBRARY." The front row consisted of true-crime titles, many with photo sections. The photo pages were noticeably dog-eared. Hickle had spent time poring over black-and-white shots of stalkers escorted under guard after their arrest. Did he picture himself in the same circumstances, and if so, did the prospect bring him worry or satisfaction?

The second row leaned toward more practical subject matter, dealing mostly with the intricacies of finding confidential information in government archives or on the Internet. Blurbs on the dust jackets promised, *You can track down anybody!* Other books focused on tactics and strategy in guerrilla warfare. Passages concerned with the art of the ambush were copiously underlined.

The last few books, nestled in a corner, were of a different type. She brought them into the light and felt a chill run over the muscles of her back. They were Kris Barwood's high school yearbooks.

Abby looked at the most recent one, dated 1978. The senior class photos were in the front, in alphabetical order. Kris's picture was one of the first.

Kris at eighteen, a graduating senior. Her activities had included the school newspaper and the debate club. Her quotation was from Blaise Pascal: *The heart has its reasons, which reason knows nothing of.* Hickle surely must have agreed with that.

She examined the other yearbooks, which collectively provided a detailed record of Kris's teenage years. How had Hickle obtained them? Back copies might be offered for sale by the school itself, or perhaps he had gone all the way to Twin Falls and stolen them out of the school library.

After replacing everything in the cabinet, she focused on the bedroom closet, the last place left to explore and the one most likely to yield secrets. The closet had bifold doors, the knobs encircled by a short length of padlocked chain. Hickle wasn't taking any chances.

The padlock had four cams, each numbered with ten digits. That meant ten thousand possible combinations, from 0000 to 9999. There had to be some way to narrow it down. What would a person use for a combination? His birthday. The information was in the TPS report, but she'd left it next door, and she wouldn't go into the hall merely to retrieve it; the risk of being spotted by another tenant was too high.

Instead she used her cell phone, speed-dialing Travis's office, and pulled him out of a meeting. "Yes?" he snapped.

"What's Hickle's birthday?"

"What?"

"I need to know."

"For God's sake . . . All right, hold on." She waited until he came back on the line. "October seventh, 1965."

"Don't hang up. I need to try something."

She put down the phone and set the combination to 1007—October 7. No result. 1065? 0765? Nothing. Her gaze drifted to the walls covered with Kris Barwood's face, and the solution was so obvious she wanted to slap herself.

When she picked up the phone, Travis was practically shouting her name. "Abby, damn it, what's going on?"

"I'm back. Tell me Kris Barwood's birthday."

"Is this some kind of joke?"

"Yeah, right. April fool, a week early. Just do it."

Another interval of silence, and then grumpily he announced, "August eighteenth, 1959."

She set the combination to 0818, and of course it opened.

"Thanks, Paul. You've been a big help."

"What the hell are you—"

"Gotta go." She switched off the phone.

When she parted the closet doors, she saw a Heckler & Koch Model HK770 rifle, complete with telescopic sight, standing in a corner.

"Armed and dangerous," she breathed. She examined the gun. A light-emitting diode was installed in the trigger guard, wired to a pressure switch in the walnut stock. A laser sighting system. That kind of modification didn't come cheap. Neither did the gun itself. The whole package must have cost Hickle nearly a thousand dollars. Now she knew why he didn't own a computer. He had plowed all his savings into firearms.

A brown duffel bag lay on the closet floor. She unzipped the flap and found a Marlin Model 120 twelve-gauge shotgun and six boxes of ammunition. Two of the boxes were empty. The sportsman's plug had been removed from the shotgun, allowing it to hold four of the three-inch Federal Super Magnum shells Hickle favored. She turned the bag upside down. The bottom was encrusted with dark earth. He must have lugged it into some wooded area with the Marlin inside and used up two boxes of shells in shooting practice.

Most likely he'd purchased the rifle first, but he'd had trouble with his marksmanship. The scope and the laser sighting system had been an attempt to solve this problem. Later he'd realized that in the heat of battle he couldn't depend on steady aim. He needed a gun that could simply be pointed in the direction of its target, a gun that would spray a wide scatter of shotshell pellets to cut down anything in its path. The Marlin had replaced the HK.

He had given the killing some thought. He had assessed his limitations, his inexperience, and had selected the weapon best suited to his needs.

"I don't know about anybody else in the room," Abby said, "but I'm getting nervous."

She wondered if she ought to disable the guns, remove the firing pins or something. No, too risky. Hickle practiced with the shotgun and perhaps with the rifle as well. If either gun was tampered with, he would know it.

Standing on tiptoe, she scanned the shelf built into the top of the closet, where she found a large cardboard box. She took it down. Inside was paper, a lot of paper. Newspaper and magazine articles, bundled together, many dating back years. Some were clippings; others were printouts of material Hickle must have tracked down on the Internet or on microfilm. All the stories related to Kris Barwood.

She flipped through the articles, then paused on a copy of the birth certificate for Kristina Ingrid Andersen. Hickle had gotten hold of that too.

At the bottom of the pile she came across a photocopy of a zoning map that showed the layout of Malibu Reserve. One house on the beach was circled in red. He must have obtained the map from the county assessor's files, open to the public.

There was one other item in the box, a plastic carrying case with a Polaroid camera inside. Resting beside it was a stack of color photos bound with a rubber band.

They were Polaroids of Kris running on the beach.

"Not good," Abby whispered. "Not good at all."

14

At two o'clock Kris arranged her hair, smoothed her clothes, and asked Steve Drury to bring out the Town Car for the trip to KPTI. "We're leaving early today."

She found Howard in the game room, lining up a shot on the electronic putting green. "Good run?" her husband asked without looking up.

"I didn't go for a jog."

"No?"

"Wasn't in the mood. You know what that's like, don't you? Not being in the mood?"

This was the closest she had come to broaching the subject of their unconsummated liaison in the bedroom last night. She meant to wound him, but if she drew blood, he didn't show it. He merely tightened his frown of concentration as he tapped the ball into the hole with an expert touch. Tinny, synthesized applause issued from a hidden speaker. The playing surface automatically recontoured itself to simulate a different hole—an uphill putt this time.

Howard Barwood loved games. The game room had been his inspiration, and nearly all of its contents were his purchases—pinball machine, jukebox, virtual reality gaming system, foosball table, casino-style craps table, billiards table, and a fleet of radio-operated cars. He'd spent more than fifty thousand dollars on these and similar items, not to mention the sixty-five thousand he'd just paid for the new Lexus LS 400 sedan that he had taken on so many long, nighttime drives.

Expensive toys for a man who'd never fully grown up. His boyishness was something she had loved about him during their courtship. She was less charmed by it now.

"I'm on fire today," he said, lining up the next putt. "Those chumps over at the country club had better watch out."

Kris tried to find a smile but couldn't summon one. "Maybe you should join the seniors' tour."

"I just might."

"I'll have Courtney clear a space on the mantel for your trophy." She headed for the stairs, then turned back, remembering why she'd tracked him down in the first place. "I'm off to work."

He glanced up, neglecting his game for the first time. "So soon?"

"I have an errand to run before I go to the studio."

"Running errands is Courtney's job."

"This is personal." Under other circumstances she might have shared it with him, but not after last night. She had reached out to him, and he had rebuffed her. Well, he did grow tired of his toys when their novelty wore off. Even his costliest acquisitions lost their shine after a while.

The Town Car was idling in the driveway when she walked down the garden path. Steve let her into the backseat, then got behind the wheel and shifted into drive. "I'd like to take the surface streets today," she told him as they approached the front gates of the Reserve.

"Ventura Freeway's faster."

"No, let's go south, through the city. We have time."

He nodded, asking no questions.

Kris was silent until the Town Car reached Holly-wood. Then she requested a detour. "Take me past Hickle's apartment building."

She watched Steve's eyes in the rearview mirror. They narrowed slightly. "I don't think that's a good idea, Kris."

"I'm sure it isn't. Do it anyway."

"It's against procedure. I could get in trouble—"

"You won't."

"Travis would have my ass."

"I'll handle Travis if he ever finds out, which he won't because neither of us is going to tell him. Just do it."

"Okay . . . but why?"

"I honestly can't say."

Steve took Santa Monica Boulevard to Gainford, Hickle's street, and turned south. "That's his address," he said as the Town Car prowled slowly down the street. Kris looked at the Gainford Arms, a faded 1930s complex with glass lobby doors scratched by vandals, tiers of small windows that looked dirty, and un-adorned brick walls.

The street was lined with Indian laurel trees that had matured nicely. Otherwise it was bare of charm or beauty. She saw a tramp rolling a pushcart laden with old newspapers and other trash. He did not look out of place.

This was Hickle's world. She thought of Abby Sinclair living here for the next few days or weeks. Could she have gotten to know him yet? It seemed too soon. Probably it would take her a week simply to establish contact. How long before she learned anything of value? The scheme seemed hopeless, and Kris had agreed to it only out of desperation. Howard had worried about Abby's safety, but Kris was past the point of concerning herself with other people. What motivated her was survival, purely selfish. To save herself, she would underwrite any risk.

"Seen enough?" Steve asked as Hickle's building retreated.

"Plenty. Let's get on the freeway."

She took a last look at the block as Steve turned the corner. The neighborhood reminded her of places she had lived in the earliest years of her career. Hickle's neighbors would be loud and close, his plumbing would often fail, bugs would scuttle through his pantry. In the hot season of September and October, his apartment would broil, and he would lie awake in the sweltering darkness. Every day he would head off to his minimum-wage job knowing he had nothing to come home to.

She was sure he wasn't happy, and she felt glad about that.

"You don't have an appointment, Miss Sinclair." Travis's assistant, Rose, smiled up at Abby from behind her desk, relishing her temporary exercise of power.

Abby restrained herself from sidestepping the desk and simply barging into the office. "No, I don't. What I do have, however, is an important piece of information your boss needs to hear."

"Perhaps I could pass it along."

"Perhaps you could buzz him on the intercom and get his ass out here now."

Rose yielded. "I'll see if he's available," she said

tonelessly, adding as a final jab, "We really do insist on making appointments in advance."

Abby shrugged. "Looks like I'm breaking all the rules."

She waited impatiently for Travis to come out. Distantly she was conscious of being tired, but she wouldn't permit herself to acknowledge the feeling. There was too much left to do.

After leaving Hickle's apartment, she had set up the monitoring gear that received the audio and video signals from the bugs she'd planted. A late lunch, eaten while standing up in her kitchen, had revived her somewhat. At three-thirty she had left the apartment building and headed to Century City. She needed to be back before five. She had plans for the evening.

Finally Travis emerged from his office, wearing his trademark navy jacket, open-collar shirt, and tan slacks. "What's up? Need more dates of birth?"

"Not this time."

"What was that all about, anyway?"

"I had to open a combination lock."

"Oh. You could have explained that."

"I enjoyed leaving you in the dark. Am I interrupting anything?"

"Just my daily session with our chief financial officer. He's quantifying exactly how much red ink TPS is bleeding on a week-by-week basis. It's a meeting I can do without."

"Is there someplace we can talk?" She wanted to deprive Rose of the chance to eavesdrop.

Travis led her down the hall to a conference room. Paintings of seascapes and meadows ornamented the mahogany walls—safe, nonthreatening subjects, intended to soothe clients unnerved by whatever crisis had driven them here. She wondered how many times the glamorous and powerful had gathered in this room, seeking comfort from the man in the blue blazer and tan slacks, their protector.

Travis shut the door, and Abby sat on the edge of the long table, swinging one leg. The lacquered tabletop caught her reflection. Irrelevantly she wished she were wearing better clothes. Her faded blouse and jeans felt shabby in this room.

"Okay," she began, "here's the thing. The lock I opened was in Hickle's apartment. I was in there to establish audiovisual surveillance and to do a little snooping around. I found a bunch of Polaroids. Pictures of Kris jogging on the beach. Her outfit varied. He watched her a minimum of three times. I assume Kris jogs right outside her house?"

Travis didn't answer for a moment. He seemed to have trouble absorbing the news. "Yes, every day. She's accompanied by a bodyguard, but he usually hangs back a little."

"There was no bodyguard in these shots. He must have been out of frame. Doesn't matter anyway. A bodyguard wouldn't have done much good if Hickle had opened fire."

"Does he have a gun?"

"At least two. Twelve-gauge shotgun and semiautomatic hunting rifle. The rifle's equipped with a scope and a laser sighting system, but the shotgun seems to be his weapon of choice."

"A laser sight . . ." Travis moved to the wide windows and stood gazing out, shoulders sagging, head downcast. He looked more exhausted than she'd ever seen him. "So how serious do you think he is?" he asked quietly.

"I'm proceeding on the assumption that he's entirely serious. In fact, he may have already acted out his rage against another woman he was stalking."

"What?"

She told him about Jill Dahlbeck. "But we don't know Hickle was behind that attack," she added. "Even if he was, it doesn't seem to have been attempted murder, and he carried it out so badly that the only physical damage was to Jill's coat. Of course, the emotional damage is a different story."

"Yes," Travis said distractedly. She knew he tuned her out whenever the subject of emotions came up. "The important point is that if he did attack this other woman, it shows he's capable of going beyond fantasy, of actually taking action."

"He was younger then, maybe more reckless. He may be more cautious now. We don't know."

"But we do know he's at least gotten within striking distance of Kris." Travis expelled a breath. "How could he get that close? The Reserve has tight security. Perimeter fencing, a gatehouse manned by two guards, and two more guards in constant patrol."

"Have you checked the fence for signs of egress?"

"Sure. That was one of the first things we did. The fence is heavy-gauge steel wire topped with razor-wire coils."

"Wire can be cut."

"We didn't find any gaps."

"Have your people checked recently?"

"Daily." He moved away from the window, circling the room.

Her gaze followed the sweep of his reflection on the long table's glossy surface. "You'd better have them look again, more closely," she said. "Is there any other way into the compound?"

"The gate, but it's always guarded."

"How carefully do they screen delivery trucks, visitors, repairmen?"

"Most of the Reserve's security officers are retired cops. They're pretty sharp. And they've got Hickle's photo posted inside the guardhouse. I don't think he could get by them."

"What about the beach? It can't be completely sealed off. Below the high tide mark it's public property like all California beaches."

"True. There's a fence at the boundary, but it doesn't go far into the water, and anybody could step around it. But we've covered that angle too. We installed a hidden camera that feeds a live image of the beach access point to the Barwoods' guest cottage. The agents stationed there monitor the video at all times."

"Unless they screwed up, got careless."

"Once, maybe. Not three times."

"Well, however he did it, Hickle found a way in, and he can do it again. Next time he may bring a gun instead of a camera, and then . . ."

Travis looked away. "Devin Corbal, part two."

Abby winced. "That's not how I would put it."

"Sorry. You know what I mean."

"Yes. I know."

The air-conditioning system hummed, and somewhere far below, a siren fluttered past. Abby wondered if she ought to mention the other significant development of the past twenty-four hours—the attack that had nearly taken her life last night.

She decided not to. She had no idea how to make sense of that incident, no idea if it even tied into the

Barwood case. And she didn't want Travis second-guessing his decision to bring her in. She didn't want him to think she was in over her head . . . so to speak.

"It won't end up like the Corbal case," she said quietly. "I won't let it."

"I wasn't trying to imply . . ." His words trailed off.

She finished for him. "That I was responsible for what happened to Corbal?"

"You weren't, Abby."

"Maybe not. But the fact remains that he's dead, and you're meeting every day with your CFO to figure out how to keep this company running with a skeleton crew, and sometimes it sure as hell feels like it was my fault."

"I told you before, you're too hard on yourself. Look, forget I ever mentioned Corbal, all right?"

"Sure. Forgotten." But she knew it wasn't and couldn't be.

"Anything more to tell me?"

"Lots, but it'll have to wait." She hopped off the table and slung her handbag over her shoulder. "You'd better resume number crunching, and I have to get back to Hollywood. I have a big night planned."

"Do you?"

Abby nodded. "Hickle doesn't know it yet, but he's taking me out on a date."

15

Wyatt knew he ought to stop thinking about her. It was stupid, the way he couldn't get her out of his head. He wasn't the type to lose control over a woman. It wasn't like he was desperate or anything. He'd never had trouble with the opposite sex. In high school and college he'd played football, and he could vouch that everything ever whispered or imagined about the private lives of cheerleaders was true. He hadn't done too shabbily as a cop either. That cliché about how women preferred a guy in uniform—he had verified it. Repeatedly.

All in all, there was absolutely no reason for him to be tooling down Wilshire Boulevard at four-thirty in the afternoon on his way to Abby's condo.

Probably she wouldn't be home. Most people were at their place of employment during the day. They didn't get stuck on the night watch, working from 6 P.M. to 2 A.M.—his current schedule from Thursday through Monday. Still, he had a feeling Abby didn't keep regular hours, and he wasn't sure she had a place of employment to go to.

He parked his Camaro on a side street and walked past dainty one-story houses cowering in the shadow of the Wilshire Royal, then took a shortcut across the oval of manicured grass that bordered the Royal's driveway. The sky was blue and cloudless, reflected in fourteen floors of windowpanes, and a breeze from the ocean a few miles away flapped the flags in the forecourt.

As he approached the lobby, he found himself self-consciously brushing his hair with his fingers. He wondered if he looked okay in his civilian clothes. Then he wondered why it mattered. Come on, this was no big deal, right? He was just dropping by. He'd been in the neighborhood, and since he had some free time before work he would see if Abby wanted to grab a cup of coffee. That was his story, and he meant to stick to it.

The doorman nodded at him in a way that seemed disapproving. Wyatt ignored the guy. He focused on the two guards at the desk. One was young and had a shaved head. His partner was older and rumpled.

"I'm here to see Miss Sinclair," Wyatt said. For some reason he added, "I don't think she's expecting me."

The guards exchanged a glance. The older one answered, "Miss Sinclair isn't here."

"Oh." So he'd missed her. He should have figured. "Well, maybe I can leave a message."

"Don't know when she'll be back. She's out of town."

"She is?"

Shrug. "She travels a lot. Hardly ever see her."

The younger guy spoke up. "You're not in software, are you?"

Wyatt was baffled by the question. "Software?"

"Her gig. Thought maybe you were in the same line."

"I run a web commerce distribution center," Wyatt said smoothly, stringing words together with no particular regard to their meaning. "Abby's working with us on a project. Upgrading our server capabilities, developing some multitasking options."

"That's cool." The young man nodded as if he understood. Maybe he did. Maybe everything Wyatt had said actually made sense. "Hey, I'm always looking for freebies. You got any beta testing you want done, I'm there."

"Not right now, sorry. You, uh, get any freebies from Abby?"

"Nah. She said it was against company policy, which is weird, because she calls herself a consultant. What's the good of being a consultant if you gotta play by somebody else's rules?"

"I'm pretty sure Miss Sinclair plays by her own rules," Wyatt said quietly. "She been out of town long?"

"Left yesterday—"

His partner cut him off. "We can't give out that information."

You already did, Wyatt thought. "No problem," he said cheerfully. "I was just wondering. Thanks for your time." He headed for the door.

"Didn't you want to leave her a message?" the older guard asked in a mildly suspicious tone.

"I'll send her an e-mail. That's the best way to reach her. She spends most of her life online."

He escaped into the sunlight before the guard could ask a follow-up. Walking back to his car, Wyatt considered what he had learned. Abby wasn't home. She had been gone since yesterday. The building staff thought she was an independent consultant in the software field. They seemed to have the impression that she was on a business trip. Such trips evidently were frequent.

Except she wasn't on any trip. Wyatt had eaten dinner with her last night. She was in town, but not here, not at her home.

He thought about the old Dodge clunker she'd been

driving. It couldn't be her regular car; it didn't fit into this neighborhood. Still, there were parts of town where the Dodge wouldn't look out of place. East LA, Venice, Hollywood . . .

Hickle lived in Hollywood.

Wyatt stopped. He stood very still, putting it together. "No," he said aloud. "She wouldn't. She'd have to be nuts."

Across the street a woman tending her rosebushes cast an apprehensive gaze in his direction.

He drove into Hollywood, calling the dispatch center on his cell phone to obtain Raymond Hickle's address. Hickle's apartment building was the Gainford Arms. Wyatt knew the place. An old brick pile four stories high, ugly and dilapidated, the walls webbed with taggers' marks. He had answered many calls at that building when he was riding patrol. The lifestyle of the rich and famous was not lived there.

Wyatt reached the Gainford Arms by five o'clock. He pulled into the parking lot and scanned the rows of cars, looking for a white Dodge. There wasn't one. Maybe he'd been wrong, after all. Maybe Abby wasn't mixed up in anything as reckless and crazy as he'd feared. He hoped so.

He was circling the far end of the lot when he glimpsed a flash of motion in his rearview mirror. Another vehicle had entered the parking area—a white subcompact.

Wyatt parked in the nearest available space, safely hidden in a carport's shadow. Low in his seat, he watched the car cruise past. It was a Dodge Colt, and it had a dent in its side panel, and the woman at the wheel was Abby, of course.

She guided the Colt into a carport in a corner of the

lot, then walked briskly to the rear door of the Gainford Arms, checking her wristwatch. In a hurry, it seemed.

The rear door was locked. Abby had a key. She must be a resident. No surprise.

The door swung shut behind her, and Wyatt slowly sat up in his seat. A slow anger was growing inside him. He was tempted to barge into the landlord's office, show his badge, find out which apartment she was in. Bang on her door until she opened up, then demand to know what kind of game she was playing . . .

He told himself to cool off. He wasn't going to do that. Abby was obviously involved in something clandestine and dangerous. If he blew her cover, he would put her at risk.

After a few moments he composed himself. Calm again, he headed over to Hollywood Station, though he was off duty for another forty-five minutes. At an empty desk he called the phone company. It didn't take him long to determine that only one apartment at the Gainford Arms had established phone service within the past week. Number 418, rented to Abby Gallagher.

Hickle lived in apartment 420. Abby was his next-door neighbor.

Wyatt was suddenly worn out. He sank back in his chair, rubbing his face. One of the day-watch patrol guys, a training officer named Mendoza, sauntered past. "Rough day, Sergeant?" Mendoza asked.

"You could say that," Wyatt said.

"I bet it's a woman."

Wyatt had to smile. "How'd you know?"

"Only a woman can make a man feel that goddamn bad."

16

At five-fifteen Abby found Hickle in the laundry room of the Gainford Arms, unloading his clothes from the dryer. "Hi, neighbor," she said. "Fancy meeting you here."

Hickle flushed. "It's a small world," he managed.

She rewarded his effort at humor with a smile. Actually their meeting was no coincidence. After returning from TPS, she had rewound her surveillance videotape of Hickle's apartment and scanned it in fast motion. The tape was time-stamped, allowing her to determine that at exactly 4:27 he had left the apartment carrying a basket of laundry. Hastily she had stuffed some of her clothes into a plastic bag and headed down to the basement. She thought it would seem more natural to run into him there than to arrange another chance encounter in the hallway.

"How much do these machines cost?" she asked as she dumped the contents of her sack into one of the big washers.

"Seventy-five cents each."

"I'd better stock up on quarters. My wardrobe's pretty limited, and I have to keep washing the same items if I want anything clean to wear."

He didn't answer. He was collecting the rest of his clothes from the dryer, in an obvious hurry to depart. She knew he was nervous around her—around women in general. Still, she wasn't going to let him get away that easily. They had a date to go on, whether he knew it or not.

"I didn't spend a lot of time packing," she continued, as if his silence was the most natural thing in the world. "Lit out of town in a rush. Left most of my things behind."

This ought to tweak his curiosity, and it did. He looked up from the dryer. "Sounds like the move was kind of sudden."

"Extremely sudden. I threw some bare necessities into four suitcases, tossed 'em in the back of my car, and amscrayed."

"You're not on the run from the law, are you?"

He said it quite seriously, but she was sure he meant it as a joke, so she merely laughed. "On the run from my problems, I guess."

"You have . . . problems?"

"Doesn't everybody?"

"Sometimes I think I'm the only one."

"You're not. It only feels that way. Not a good feeling, is it?"

He looked away and mumbled, "No, it's not." He seemed embarrassed, as if he had revealed too much. He picked up the laundry basket and took a step toward the door. "Well . . . see you."

"Hey, you happen to know anyplace where a person can get a decent meal around here?"

Nonplussed by the change of topic, Hickle only blinked.

"I survived last night on crackers and cheese. Since you work in a restaurant, you must know the local dining scene. What I'm looking for is a tasty low-fat meal, something that won't drive up my cholesterol count to the stratosphere."

She waited, hoping he wouldn't panic so badly that his mind would go blank. She needed him to make a dining suggestion. Finally he came up with something.

"How about The Sand Which Is There?" he said. Abby asked him to repeat the name. He obeyed, speaking slowly to emphasize the pun. "It's in Venice, on the boardwalk."

"Great. Maybe we could go together, say, around quarter to six. I mean, who wants to eat alone?"

This possibility took him so completely by surprise that for several seconds he couldn't answer at all. She knew he was trying to find an escape hatch, a socially acceptable way to turn her down, because the prospect of spending the evening with a woman, any woman, would be terrifying to him.

Yet he did want someone to talk to. She could sense it. He had opened up a little already. She was giving him the chance to go further, if only he would take it. She waited.

"Well," he said at last, "okay. I mean, why not?"

She relaxed. "Great. I'll knock on your door around ten to six."

"Sure. Ten to six. No problem . . ."

He was already retreating, the laundry basket in his arms. He escaped out the door, and she heard his footsteps on the stairs to the lobby.

So far, so good. Abby smiled.

Having started the wash cycle, she might as well finish the job. She hadn't lied when she told Hickle she had only a few clothes with her. She had brought a total of four suitcases, and the two largest ones had been crammed with electronic gear and other tools of her trade.

The washing machine rattled and hummed, sloshing its contents against the porthole in the door. She watched her clothes as they were tossed around in a bath of suds. The shifting patterns reminded her of the colored glass fragments in a kaleidoscope. She'd had a kaleidoscope when she was a little girl; her father had given it to her. She remembered playing with it for hours, fascinated by the ever-changing patterns. Now she was an adult, but she still studied patterns—patterns of behavior, of body language, of verbal expression. Some patterns were obvious, like the selection of books in Hickle's bedroom, and some were more subtle, like the way he had asked if she was an actress when they met. Jill Dahlbeck had been an actress . . .

Wait.

She froze, suddenly aware of another presence in her environment.

Turning, she scanned the rows of washers and dryers, the windowless brick walls, the bare ceiling bulbs suspended from the low ceiling. She saw nobody. Even so, she was almost sure she was not alone.

She unclasped her purse and reached inside for her snub-nosed Smith, but hesitated. It wouldn't be a good idea to let one of the other residents spot her with a concealed firearm.

She left the gun in her open purse, within close reach of her right hand.

"Hello?" she called out.

Her voice rose over the rumble of the washer. No one answered.

Slowly she stood, then turned in a circle, studying every corner of the room. The place was empty.

If someone had been watching her, he had retreated from the laundry room. Perhaps he had gone upstairs—or perhaps he was hiding in the boiler room next door.

But who? Was it Hickle? Or her assailant from last night? Or merely the product of an oversensitized imagination?

She decided to find out.

Cautiously she approached the doorway. On the threshold she placed her hand inside her purse, wrapping her index finger around the Smith's trigger.

The stairway to the lobby was on her right. The boiler room lay to her left. The door was open, the overhead light off. Three large water heaters hissed inside.

She groped for a light switch inside the doorway. Couldn't find one. She entered in darkness. There was a flashlight in her purse but she couldn't take it out without releasing her grip on the gun, and right now the gun was more important to her.

The boiler room was large and musty. Concrete floor, brick walls, cobwebs in the corners. A man could crouch in one of those corners and not be seen.

"Hello?" she said again. "Anyone here?"

Nothing.

She advanced into the middle of the room. The water heaters were straight ahead. Big industrial heaters, gas-fired, probably holding eighty gallons each. She groped in front of her and touched the smooth surface of the nearest water tank.

She had thought that someone might hide behind the heaters, but as her eyesight adjusted to the gloom she saw that they were nearly flush with the rear wall, actually bolted to the concrete to prevent the gas supply lines from being ruptured in an earthquake.

There were hiding places on either side of the heaters, though. She took another step forward and something brushed her hair, and for a moment she was in the spa again, a stranger's hand pushing her down—

No. Not a hand, not an attack. Only the length of chain hanging from the ceiling. The pull cord for the overhead light. That was why she hadn't found a wall switch.

She tugged the chain, and the bare bulb directly above her snapped on, brightening the room.

She glanced around her, half expecting an assault, but nothing happened. There was no one in the boiler room. There never had been.

"God, Abby," she muttered, "get a grip."

She must have imagined the whole thing. Maybe it was some kind of posttraumatic reaction to her near-death experience in the hot tub last night. Or maybe she was just going crazy.

Abby left the boiler room. The washing machine had completed its cycle. Her clothes were soaking wet, but she decided she could dry them in the sink or bathtub of her apartment. She'd spent enough time in the basement.

Besides, she had to get ready for her big night on the town.

17

Hickle hated to miss the six o'clock news.

In the past year he had seen every one of Kris Barwood's broadcasts. Sitting in front of the TV each weeknight at six and ten was part of the daily rhythm of his life. When she'd taken a vacation last September, he had been seriously distressed. Yet tonight he was missing the show. He reminded himself that he was taping it and could view the tape later, and he was sure to be home in time for the ten o'clock newscast.

"Traffic's not too bad."

He glanced at Abby, seated on the passenger side of his VW. "Yeah, it's pretty light this evening," he answered, "considering it's rush hour."

"It's always rush hour in this city."

He could think of no worthwhile reply. "Yeah."

His face was hot, his palms were damp, and he wished he were safe in his apartment watching Kris on the news—the show would have just started—watching her and enjoying her presence in his home, even if it was only a magical illusion.

Instead here he was on Santa Monica Boulevard driving into the twilight with Abby Gallagher. She had changed into cotton slacks, a button-down blouse, and a nylon windbreaker. A nice outfit, better than the jeans and sweatshirt he'd thrown on.

He risked conversation. "I guess it's a lot different here from Riverside."

She raised her voice over the drone of the motor and the rattle of the dashboard. "LA's so big. I can't even find my way around. I'm lost."

"You'll get used to it." He forced himself not to retreat into silence. "I did."

"You're not from LA originally?"

"I moved down from the central part of the state a long time ago." He was no good at small talk. He decided to dare a more direct approach. "Mind if I ask you a question?"

"Go ahead."

"You said you were running from your problems . . ." He was sure she would tell him it was none of his business.

"Boyfriend problems," Abby answered, as unperturbed as if she'd asked his opinion of the weather. "Well, more than boyfriend. Fiancé. We were supposed to be married in May. Then I found him cheating on me. When I say *found*, I mean literally *found*. I walked in on him when he was banging her. In our bed. At one o'clock in the afternoon."

Hickle didn't know what to say, but for once he felt no awkwardness because surely no one would know what to say in this situation.

"So I screamed and threw things, the usual mature reaction of the woman wronged. Next day I drove out of town. Had to get away." A shrug. "That's my sad story."

The word *sad* cued him to the appropriate response. "I'm sorry."

"That's life."

"But it's awful, what he did to you."

143

"I guess you can't expect long-term commitment anymore. Even so, I really thought we were meant to be together. You know how that is?"

Hickle kept his voice steady. "I know."

"To find somebody who's everything you want, everything you're looking for—and then they go and do something like that . . ." Abby let her statement slide away unfinished.

"I know," Hickle said again, more firmly. "I know exactly what that's like."

"So it's happened to you?"

Because the car was stopped at a red light at Beverly Drive, Hickle could turn in his seat and look directly into Abby's eyes. "It's happened to me," he said. "Just recently, in fact—just within the past year—I found the perfect woman. Perfect. And she . . ." Abby watched him, no judgment in her expression. "She tore my heart out. She killed my soul. She murdered the best part of me."

There. It was said. Probably he should have stayed silent. The words had come out in a rush, desperate and angry. He was afraid Abby would think he was some kind of nut.

"I'm sorry, Raymond," she whispered.

Raymond. She had called him by name.

A horn blatted behind him. The stoplight had cycled to green. He was holding up traffic.

He motored through the intersection, continuing west, afraid to speak again and risk damaging whatever fragile intimacy he'd established.

Raymond. His first name. Spoken with such gentle understanding.

Raymond.

*   *   *

The parking lots that served the Venice promenade were filled to capacity this evening. Hickle navigated the maze of narrow side streets and alleys until he found an open slot at a curb two blocks from the beach. By the time he maneuvered the Rabbit into the space, the last of the twilight glow was gone, and darkness lay thick and smooth on all sides.

After his blurted confession in Beverly Hills, he had said little, and Abby hadn't prodded him. Although the present excursion was perhaps not technically a date, it came close enough to raise his anxiety level dangerously high. Once they were in the restaurant, he would loosen up, and she would learn what she had to know.

On every case Abby started out with a mental checklist, questions about the person whose threat potential she was assessing. The questions were simple and specific, and the more of them she answered, the nearer she came to a final evaluation. Already she had checked off several of the most serious questions about Hickle, each time with an answer in the affirmative.

Did he feel a deep personal connection to Kris Barwood? Yes. His unguarded comments in the car had confirmed it.

Did his obsession go beyond writing letters and making phone calls? Yes. After searching his apartment, she knew he had devoted enormous energy to researching Kris's life, tracking down her address, and photographing her from a distance.

Did his obsession show signs of escalating into violence? Yes. The books on stalkers and combat tactics were proof.

Had he obtained a weapon or weapons? Yes. Guns.

Two items on the checklist remained unresolved.

Did he believe he could successfully carry out an attack? Without that belief, he might fantasize and rehearse and plan but never act.

Would he be deterred by fear? Often fear functioned as a conscience of last resort.

Hickle struck her as a timid man. Possibly it was fear that had stayed his hand so far. Possibly the same fear would serve as a permanent brake on his most violent ambitions.

Hickle shut off the Volkswagen's motor and headlights, then fumbled the key free of the ignition slot. "We're here," he announced. "Well, not at the restaurant—we'll have to walk there—it's not far."

He was stammering like a high school kid. She would have felt sorry for him had she not seen the rifle and shotgun, the secret photos of Kris. "It's a nice night for a walk," she said cheerily. "The ocean air feels good."

They got out of the car, and Hickle locked it. "Yeah, it's one thing I've always appreciated about LA. Where I grew up, we were fifty miles inland. Not much chance for an ocean breeze."

"Desert country?"

"No, hills and farmland. My folks ran a grocery store. It was—what's the word? Bucolic."

"But boring."

"Yeah. Not exactly bright lights and big city." They started walking. "I guess you didn't see much of the ocean out in Riverside," Hickle said.

"Only in the form of a mirage, usually induced by imminent heatstroke. It gets to be a hundred-ten in the shade, and there is no shade. Sometimes I'd drive to the coast to get away from the desert heat. Never came to this part of town, though."

"It's . . . colorful."

"Why do they call it Venice?" She knew the reason but let him tell her as they approached the noise of a crowd.

"There are canals here," he said. "Only a few are left, but there used to be a whole network of them, like in Venice, Italy. The place was designed as a tourist attraction back around 1900 by a guy named Kinney. He was a visionary, they say."

She looked at the barred windows, the trash in the street, the gang markings everywhere. "Looks like his vision came up against a brick wall called reality."

"I'm afraid so. Santa Monica is nicer, but this is a good place to come when you want to hang out, see the people. It's like a street fair or a carnival."

"All the time?"

"Pretty much." He tried for levity. "LA, you know, is the city that never sleeps."

That's New York, Abby wanted to say but didn't.

Hickle escorted her to the beachfront promenade, crowded with every variety of human exotica—jugglers, peddlers, tramps, street musicians, tattooed bodybuilders. Loitering under a streetlight were a trio of bony, strung-out young women, probably hookers. On the nearby bike path kids on skateboards and Rollerblades yelled at the night. Down the walkway a band of Hare Krishnas banged tambourines. Hallucinatory murals covered the high brick walls of century-old buildings, serving as a backdrop to it all.

"See what I mean?" Hickle asked, checking nervously for her reaction. "A carnival."

Abby smiled. "As they used to say in the sixties, it's a scene."

They strolled along the concrete concourse that locals called a boardwalk. Stores passed by, made out of converted garage stalls, displaying racks of T-shirts and sunglasses and absurd curios. Above the general din a woman's voice became audible. She was yelling angrily in Spanish.

"You speak the language?" Hickle asked.

"A little. She's talking to her boyfriend, calling him a bastard, liar, cheat. Never wants to see him again. Wants him to get lost. She says: Go to hell." Abby shrugged. "Guess that's the end of one romance."

She was fairly certain Hickle would disagree. He didn't surprise her. "No," he said, "she's leading him on."

"Funny way to do it."

"It's a game women play. They say no when they mean yes. They tell you to go away when they want you to get closer. They yell and scream, and it's all part of the courtship dance."

"That ain't *my* style."

"Well, no, I didn't mean you. I was talking in generalities. For most women it's their nature to make the guy sweat. Deny him everything, let him beg. They get a kick out of it. Women are—" He cut himself off in midsentence.

"Are what?" Abby prompted.

"I don't know. Never mind. Nothing."

But she knew what he'd been ready to say: *Women are bitches . . . are cockteasers . . . are whores.*

The Sand Which Is There was a large, crowded, obviously trendy establishment, not at all what Abby had expected. There was a great deal of bamboo and wicker. Illuminated glass globes hung from the rafters, casting pools of lemon-colored light on lacquered tabletops. Ceiling fans spun torpidly, wooden blades beating the air in slow-motion whirls. A long teakwood bar lay on one side of the room, offering as much bottled water as alcohol. Facing the bar were the glass doors to a patio on the boardwalk.

The restaurant, evidently, was a hangout for aspiring stars—actors, actresses, musicians, models. Few had succeeded but all possessed the bare requisites of stardom: the telegenic face, the photogenic body. The room was a sea of lithe limbs and wild, untrammeled hair. Abby wondered how Hickle had ever come here.

A waitress escorted them to a corner table. Abby knew it would take Hickle a while to settle down. Their early interludes of conversation, while they ordered drinks and meals, were unproductive and shortlived. When the food came, Hickle consumed it ravenously, eating fast, saying little.

He didn't start to relax until he was working on his second beer. Abby could tell he was unaccustomed to alcohol. His speech acquired a slight slur, his breathing became more labored, and his eyes grew heavy-lidded and vague. He was a large, clumsy man, uncomfortable in his own body, and the double dose of Heineken only made him clumsier. Twice he overturned the saltshaker, and once he dropped his knife on the floor.

"How's your salad?" he asked finally, with his first authentic effort at initiating a dialogue.

"It rocks. Kale and portabella mushrooms—what's not to like? So do you come here often?"

"Hardly ever. Actually"—an embarrassed smile—"I've been here only once. It's not my kind of atmosphere."

"No?"

"Well, I mean, *look* at them." He propped his elbow

on the table and pointed an accusing finger at the room. "The way they move. Their faces. They're so *confident*. They own the world."

Abby followed his gaze, studying the other patrons. It was true. They were beautiful, women and men alike. The very distinction between male and female was all but lost in their unisex hairstyling and wardrobe. The men conveyed a sense of delicacy, of frail and sensitive soulfulness; the women looked hard. Hard-bodied after hours in the gym, and hard-featured, their faces untouched by makeup, eyes narrowed and stern.

"They own the world," Hickle said again, then wrinkled his brow. "Not that *you* need to envy them," he added in what was intended as a compliment but sounded like a reproach.

"I don't envy anybody." Abby twirled her salad fork, letting the tines catch the candlelight. "Green's not my color."

Hickle picked up his club sandwich and tore off a chunk with his teeth. "You don't envy them because you don't have to. You fit right in. You belong here."

"And you don't?" Though of course he didn't.

He waved his arm vaguely at the crowd in a loose, graceless motion that nearly upset his beer mug. "I'm not in their league."

"They're not that special."

"Oh, yes, they are. Can't you feel it?" He lowered his voice, leaning forward, shoulders hunched defensively. "There was a movie once with a strange title, *The Killer Elite*. Whenever I come to a place like this, those are the words I think of. The killer elite."

She noted the word *killer* and the fact that he projected it onto those around him, when it applied far more realistically to himself. "They're just kids out for a burger and a beer," she said mildly.

"Kids, yes, but not *just* kids. They have the look."

"The what?"

"The look," he said again, with peculiar earnestness. "You know how they say the world is divided into the haves and the have-nots? Well, it's true, but not the way most people think." He tipped the beer mug to his mouth and swallowed a third of its contents with a canine slurp. "It's not about money. Money is nothing; anybody can get money. Show up for work on time, display a modicum of intelligence, and in three months your boss will be offering you a promotion whether you want it or not."

"Why wouldn't you want it?" Abby asked, but Hickle didn't hear.

"What matters," he said, his voice too loud, his eyes too bright, "is the look. That's what the haves have and what the have-nots haven't got. You should know because you've got it. Every woman in this room has it. Every guy, too . . ." His hand closed into a fist, though he was unconscious of the gesture. "Except me."

His anger was growing dangerously large. She tried to contain it. "You're being way too hard on yourself."

"Just honest. See, in the end, brains don't matter. You can be the brainiest guy in the class, straight A's, but if you don't have the look, you can't get a date to the prom. Without the look you're nothing. You're either class clown or class . . . freak." He took a last, listless bite of his sandwich and set down the remnant wearily. "Hell, you're not going to understand. I'll bet *you* didn't have any trouble getting dates."

He was studying her with a lopsided smile that was

meant to look friendly but conveyed, instead, a cold and cramped malice.

Abby kept her tone light. "I was a tomboy, really. Not very popular. Certainly not a prom queen."

This surprised him. His expression softened a little. "Is that so?" he asked quietly.

"I was kind of a washout in most my classes. My mind had this tendency to wander. I was basically a loner. When I wasn't in school I spent most of my time hiking in the desert or grooming horses at a ranch. I was always dirty, hair mussed, no makeup. Mosquito bites on my arms, and a million freckles all over my face." Every word of this was true. "My dad called me a late bloomer."

Hickle considered her, and she felt his resentment cool. "Well," he said at last, "you've flowered nicely."

She smiled. "I'm a whole different person now. So I guess there really is life after high school."

"*Wrong.*" Hickle stamped the flat of his hand on the table, rattling the plates, then bit his lip in embarrassment. "Sorry, I don't mean to be overemphatic. But people are always saying stuff like that. I heard it the whole time I was growing up. Get out in the adult world, and everything changes for you. That's what they say."

"But it doesn't?"

"Not at all. High school *is* real life. It's real life without any pretense."

He took another gulp of beer, but it wasn't alcohol that was allowing him to talk so freely now. It was her questions, each as gently probing as a scalpel, and her calm, meditative gaze, and the silences she gave him in which he could say whatever he liked without judgment or reproach.

"Let me tell you about high school." He picked up a carrot stick from a side dish and toyed with it distractedly. "There was this guy in our class, Robert Chase. He wasn't particularly smart. Not an idiot, you understand, but no genius either, and not a good student. He cut class, got C's and D's, smoked dope in the bathroom, screwed around. But he had one advantage."

"Let me take a wild stab. Was it . . . the look?"

"That's right. Good old Bob Chase." Hickle's mouth twisted into an ugly shape. "The girls called him Bobby with that sigh in their voice, you know? He was tall, had thick curly hair and washboard abs, was a star on the basketball team. They all *loved* him."

She heard the stale envy in his voice. She said nothing.

"So a couple of months ago I'm reading the *LA Times*, and what do I see? Robert Chase from my hometown is chief of staff for a member of Congress in Washington, DC. He's an up-and-comer. They say he might run for office himself. He could end up as the goddamned—sorry—end up as President. Why? I'm smarter than he is. I got better grades. I didn't slam kids into lockers and sucker-punch them for laughs." Hickle snapped the carrot stick, tossed the pieces aside, and picked up another. "But I don't have the look. Be honest. Could I ever be President?"

In her mind Abby saw a convention hall, balloons, cheers, and in the spotlight the baffled, rumpled, shaggy figure of Raymond Hickle, black hair sloppily askew, neck red with acne, face drawn and fleshy at the same time—hollow around the eyes, meaty and thick at the jaw. She imagined him trying to make a speech, command respect, summon all his authority, and what she heard was a crowd's laughter. "Not everybody has to be President," Abby said gently.

Hickle waved off this reply as if irritated by it. "The President was just an example. People like Bob Chase are the winners in life. They can do whatever they want. They can have whoever they want. Anyone, anything." He turned his head, averting his gaze from the truths he was telling. "If they want money, it flows to them. Or fame . . . look at them on every magazine cover. Or, well"—he blushed—"sex, you know—if that's what they want, they get it."

Abby nodded, thinking hard. Years ago Hickle had fastened on Jill Dahlbeck, an aspiring actress not unlike many of the women in this room. Now his obsession was Kris Barwood, a more accomplished celebrity. Most likely there had been others, all famous or striving for fame. He was drawn to beautiful women, but beauty was not enough for him. There had to be stardom or the promise of it. Stars were golden people, and he desperately wanted to be one of them. He had not outgrown his adolescent longings for approval and admiration. For him, all of life was prom night, and he was the only one going stag.

"How about happiness?" Abby asked softly. "Do they get that too?"

"Of course. We just drove through Beverly Hills. Did you see the houses? Or go up to Malibu . . ."

Where Kris lived. Abby lifted an eyebrow. "Yes?"

"It's beautiful there. Have you seen it?"

"No."

"It's magical."

"You mean the beach? The seashore?"

"All of it. Malibu's a perfect place. How could anybody live there and not be happy? It's paradise."

Abby had in fact visited Malibu many times. For her, the town fell short of its reputation. The hills were sere and parched for half the year, afflicted by mudslides in the rainy season and chaparral fires in the hot, dry months. Beautiful homes could be glimpsed behind gated walls, but the main thoroughfare was lined with ramshackle surf shops and bike rental outlets. She would not have called it paradise. But to Hickle it was the Elysian Fields. It was where the prom queen and her consort would retire to act out their dreamlike lives.

She wanted to keep him talking about Malibu, but there was no way to do it without being recklessly obvious. Instead she said blandly, "People have problems everywhere, even in nice neighborhoods."

"Ordinary people. You know that writer who said the rich are different? He was right, except it's not just the rich. It's the killer elite. They have it all, and the rest of us . . ."

The second carrot stick snapped in Hickle's hands.

"Yes?" Abby asked.

"We get the table scraps. If we're lucky."

Abby tried to defuse his anger with a shrug. "I'll bet hardly any of these people here are rich or famous."

"Not yet. They're young. Give them time. Where will they be ten years from now?" His voice sank to a hush. "And where will I be?"

"I don't know, Raymond," she answered, her voice as low as his. "Where do you think?"

"I think . . ." Eyes downcast, he studied the table for a long moment. Then he looked up, meeting her gaze. "Actually, I expect to be quite famous."

"Do you?"

"Yeah. Everybody's going to know my name."

"You writing the great American novel or something?"

"Not exactly."

"So how's it going to happen?"

"It's . . . a secret."

"What good is a secret if you won't tell anybody? Give me a hint."

"I can't. Really."

"Pretend I'm not just Abby, I'm Dear Abby. People tell her everything. They tell her way more than she probably wants to know." Hickle smiled but shook his head. She wanted to press further, but instinctively she knew he wouldn't be moved. "Well, okay," she said. "Whatever it is, I hope it works out for you."

"Oh, it will. I'm very sure of that."

So there it was. She had the answer to one of her two remaining questions.

Did he believe he could successfully carry out an attack? Yes. He believed.

18

It was a crisis, as usual.

Every day at KPTI-TV's news division was an exercise in controlled hysteria. News people were adrenaline addicts; chaos was their normal operating environment; pandemonium was simply their way of getting things done.

This evening's red alert was occasioned by the rare birth of twin African elephants at the Los Angeles Zoo. News of the elephant calves' arrival came over the wire at 5:15 P.M. A news conference at the zoo was scheduled for six o'clock.

The sensible thing would have been to hold the elephant story until the middle of the newscast, but there was no chance of that. The elephant twins had to lead the show. They bumped a high-speed police pursuit in Pomona to second place, bumped the hospitalization of a soap opera actress to third, and bumped Channel Eight's exclusive interview with the mayor to fourth. Political stories were never a high priority in LA.

The live remote truck arrived at the zoo only minutes before the start of the 6 P.M. newscast. There was trouble establishing a microwave link. But when the show's opening theme music faded out and Kris Barwood announced the blessed event, the live feed from the news conference streamed in, and the transition to Ed O'Hern live at the scene miraculously went without a hitch. The crew even got video of the newborns taking a few wobbly steps, while "Baby Elephant Walk" played coyly in the background.

"What a mess," Amanda Gilbert said when she left the newscast's postmortem at seven-thirty. "Why couldn't little Dumbo and Dumber get born at a more convenient time?"

Her voice was loud enough for Kris to hear on the other side of the newsroom. She caught up with Amanda as the younger woman was heading for the exit, a briefcase in one hand and a thick sheaf of papers in the other. "I believe their names are Willy and Wally," Kris said.

"Whatever. They're cute, and they've got big ears and a certain Disneyesque appeal. Don't pester me with details."

"Anyway, you did a nice job pulling it all together."

Amanda shrugged. "It was touch and go for a few minutes, but hey, we got what we wanted. Smiling zoo officials, couple good bites, nice wrap-up from Ed. Only thing missing was a bunch of freckle-faced school kids toting Babar books."

Amanda Gilbert, executive producer of the six o'clock edition of KPTI's *Real News*, was thirty years old and talked very fast. She was high-strung and achingly thin and probably slept less than four hours a night. Assessing her with the maximum objectivity possible, Kris could not see what attraction this scrawny, bony, peppy young thing could possibly hold for her fifty-one-year-old husband. But of course there was no real mystery about it. Howard liked them young.

It wasn't Amanda's fault. Howard behaved the same way around secretaries, flight attendants, and the women stationed at cosmetics counters in department stores. Kris had found her husband's roving eye ruefully amusing at first. Not anymore.

"Kris? You still among the living?"

"What?"

"You drifted away for a second."

"Sorry. Just thinking."

"Yeah, I remember when I used to have the luxury for reflective moments. Now I hop on the ulcer express in the morning and don't get off till dark. Speaking of which, it's time for me to punch out. And time for you to review the rundown with Consuelo." Consuelo Martinez produced the ten o'clock newscast and the public affairs program that followed.

"I already did." Kris held up a loose collection of yellow script pages. "Got my lines right here."

"Until they're changed at the last minute. Which they inevitably will be. 'Night, Kris."

She started to walk away. Kris stopped her. "Amanda. I want to apologize for Howard. The way he was acting the other night."

"Howard? He's a sweetheart. He was fine."

"It seemed to me he was . . . sticking too close. Smothering you."

"He gets a kick out of the technical stuff, that's all. He's a big kid, asking me to explain how every button works. Okay, it can be a pain in the ass, but it's cute."

"I used to feel that way," Kris said. "But I think, in your case, he's interested in more than pushing buttons."

Amanda stepped closer. "What's that mean?"

Kris wondered how much she should say. She and Amanda were not exactly friends—their personalities were too contrary for true amity—but they had

159

worked together for two years, and two years in TV news was a time period measured on a geologic scale.

"The thing is," Kris said slowly after looking around to be sure no one was listening, "Howard's kind of unreliable."

Amanda frowned. "How am I supposed to interpret that?"

"The obvious way."

"You're saying he goes out dancing behind your back?"

"That's what I suspect."

"It sure doesn't seem like him. He strikes me as the old-fashioned sort."

"Appearances can be deceptive. He has a wandering eye, but I don't know if it's gone beyond that. It could have."

Amanda pursed her lips, not shocked, merely intrigued. "You mean he might be . . . you know . . . right now?"

"I can't say. It's just a suspicion."

"Based on?"

"Too many unexplained absences. Too much driving around aimlessly. He says he's breaking in his new car. It's possible. He does love his toys. But I don't know. And once I walked in on him while he was sending e-mail, and he shut down the program fast, as if it was something he didn't want me to see."

"E-mail love notes?" Amanda looked dubious.

"Haven't you heard of cybersex?" Kris shrugged. "It's a new millennium. People don't send sonnets anymore, or even regular love letters, I suppose." Except for Hickle, a voice at the back of her mind added.

Amanda shook her head. "Have you discussed this with him? Does he know you're on to him?"

"He doesn't know anything. Courtney, our house-keeper, is my informer. She confided in me after . . . after Howard came on to her."

"Right in your own house? Divorce the bastard."

"We can work it out."

"Not if you two don't start talking."

"We will when this stalker thing is over. When it's taken care of."

Amanda sighed. "I thought you two were a happy couple. You know, the kind who get a perfect score on the *Cosmo* compatibility test."

"I used to think we were. Now I don't . . . I . . ." She couldn't talk about this anymore. "Look, I just wanted to say I'm sorry if he was getting in your way last night."

"Forget about it." Amanda glanced at her watch. "I've gotta run, but tomorrow if we have time, let's talk, okay? Heart to heart?"

Kris smiled. "I never took you for the sob sister type."

"It's an unfamiliar role for me, but I can handle it." She gave Kris's arm a comforting squeeze. "Hang in there, kid."

Kris watched her walk away. She knew there would be no heart-to-heart conversation tomorrow, because there would be no time. In TV news there was never time for anything. That was all right. She wasn't sure she wanted to further unburden herself to a woman who, after all, was one of Howard's fantasy conquests.

She looked past the computers and gray metal desks to the row of wall clocks set to different time zones. California time was seven-forty-five. Better get moving. She needed to grab a late dinner and read the script and touch up her cosmetics and hair. Of these three items her personal appearance was the main concern. It seemed she spent a lot more time in the makeup room since turning forty.

"Funny how that works," she murmured. She must have a streak of masochism to have chosen a profession in which success was so utterly dependent on youth and beauty, then to have compounded her error by choosing a husband whose priorities ran along the same lines.

19

Hickle knew there must be something he could say to bring his date with Abby to the proper conclusion. In the movies people were always saying clever things. Why was it so much harder in real life?

He mulled over the problem as the elevator carried him and Abby to the fourth floor. Even when he escorted her down the hall to her door, he had not found a solution.

"Well," Abby said, "here we are."

This was his moment. He had to go for it. Be spontaneous.

"It was fun," he managed.

Damn, that was no good. Any jerk could have come up with that. But Abby surprised him by smiling in reply. "A blast," she said. "Your taste in restaurants is excellent."

"Oh, well . . . I work in a restaurant, remember?" He wasn't sure why he repeated his earlier lie.

"I remember. Maybe I'll drop by sometime for a free meal."

Caught, he had to think fast. "The owner frowns on that," he answered, hoping he sounded casual. "But you never know. We'll see." He decided to quit while he still could. "Good night, Abby."

" 'Night."

He wondered if he was supposed to kiss her. He had

Michael Prescott

never kissed a girl, except for Priscilla Gammon in the third grade, whom he had smooched on a dare. Priscilla had screamed and called him gross and wiped her mouth elaborately with her sleeve, and for the next two weeks whenever she had seen him she'd made retching noises. He doubted Abby would do anything like that. Still, he'd better not risk it.

"Good night," he said again, pointlessly.

Abby smiled, unlocking her door. "Don't let the bedbugs bite—which in this place is more than just an expression."

He nodded, not knowing what to say. He went on nodding until she disappeared inside her apartment. Then he found his keys and entered his living room. It occurred to him that he ought to check the VCR to be sure it had taped the 6 P.M. news, but somehow this didn't seem important, and he decided it could wait.

He wandered into the bathroom, not knowing why, and left without doing anything. He opened his windows, letting the night breeze filter through the swinging blinds. The cool air felt fine. In the kitchen he poured himself some water and drank it fast, belching pleasurably. He looked around at his apartment, and although it had always looked like a dump to him, tonight it seemed better, almost livable. He thought his life was pretty good, better than he had realized, and he wondered why he should be feeling that way.

Well, it was Abby, of course. They'd had a great time together. When the check had come, impulsively he'd insisted on paying it, though she had offered to pay half. He had wanted to treat her to the meal because that was the kind of thing a man would do, and it wasn't often he got to feel like a man.

Certainly Jill Dahlbeck had never let him feel that

way. He remembered summoning the courage to ask her out, and the strained, false politeness in her voice as she turned him down, giving some weak excuse. He had hated her in that moment and for years afterward. She had emasculated him, humiliated him, as women always did, because all women were bitches at heart, bitches and lying whores—

He calmed himself. Not all women, he reminded himself. Not Abby. She was different. She had to be.

The phone rang.

He looked at it, astonished. Nobody ever called him. It had to be a wrong number.

Unless it was Abby. Had she gotten his number? Was she calling to talk? He picked up the phone, his hand trembling a little. "Hello?" he said into the mouthpiece.

Silence for a moment, and then a female voice said, "You have mail."

Not Abby's voice. He wasn't sure it was even human. It sounded false, electronic. Baffled, he pressed the receiver closer to his ear. "Who is this? Hello?"

The voice said again, "You have mail."

Click. A dial tone hummed.

Slowly he set down the phone. He understood now. The voice had been a recording, the kind that greeted users of an Internet service provider when they logged on.

It meant the user had e-mail.

In her bedroom with the lights out, Abby sat curled on the floor watching closed-circuit, real-time coverage of Raymond Hickle's living room. The video image was crisp and stable on the seven-inch picture tube of a portable TV tuned to an amateur frequency. The TV—which Abby had brought from home, not trusting the antiquated set provided by the landlord— sat atop a VCR capable of recording forty hours of time-lapse video on a standard VHS cassette.

Audio from the two surveillance microphones was received on a stereo deck and recorded on a long-playing tape reel. Both audio transmitters operated at one of the standard frequencies for cordless telephones. Anyone who happened to intercept the signal and heard Hickle's mutterings would assume it was a stray, indecipherable telephone call.

Abby had set up the gear in her bedroom closet so that it could be easily hidden behind the closet door whenever she left. Not expecting her efforts to yield significant results right away, she'd been paying only desultory attention to tonight's broadcast until Hickle's telephone rang.

She saw him answer the phone, and via the surveillance microphone she heard him say hello and ask who was there. But she didn't know what, if anything, was said on the other end of the line. She found herself wishing she'd taken the risk of installing an infinity transmitter in the phone.

Hickle hung up and stood unmoving for a moment, then stepped into his bedroom, out of camera range. A minute passed before he emerged, carrying his duffel bag. The look on his face was grim. He left his apartment, moving fast.

"What the hell?" Abby was already on her feet, grabbing her purse. She ran to her door but hesitated. Hickle might still be in the hall. She peered out. At the far end of the corridor the elevator doors were closing.

She pounded down three flights of stairs. When she

reached the parking lot, Hickle's car was already gone. She tossed her purse into her Dodge and pulled onto Gainford. The street was dark in both directions. She went north to Santa Monica. There was no stoplight at the intersection; a left turn into the constant stream of traffic was impossible. If Hickle had come this way, he had headed east.

She shot into a gap in the traffic and accelerated, shifting from lane to lane as she scanned the boulevard for a white VW Rabbit. She didn't see one anywhere. "Where are you, Raymond?" she whispered. "Where are you going in such a rush? And what do you want the gun for?"

She had no idea what was happening, but her intuition, which seldom failed, insisted that it was big and somehow dangerous. Dangerous to Kris? she wondered. Or to me?

She didn't know.

Two blocks from Gainford, Hickle veered off Santa Monica, cutting south on Wilcox, then negotiated a maze of side streets and arterial boulevards until he reached Western, where he turned north. He checked his rearview mirror repeatedly.

There was a chance that Jack was following him, that the phone call had been a ruse to lure him out of his apartment after dark. It seemed unlikely, but Hickle had no way to fathom Jack's motives or the extent of his knowledge. To Hickle he was only a name on an e-mail account, untraceable, mysterious.

He remembered the letter that had arrived a month ago, bearing a downtown LA postmark and no return address. The letter had consisted of three lines of computer printout, unsigned. It had said that a ZoomMail account had been opened for Hickle under the name JackBQuick, with the Volkswagen's license plate number as the password. The note had advised him to check his mail regularly. It had concluded simply, *Destroy this letter.*

Hickle had obeyed the instructions, first burning letter and envelope, then visiting the library and using a public terminal to find ZoomMail's homepage, where he logged on as JackBQuick. There had been two messages in his Inbox. One was a note from ZoomMail congratulating him on selecting their free service. The other, according to the return address, had been sent by a ZoomMail client who called himself JackBNimble. It was right out of the nursery rhyme:

Jack, be nimble
Jack, be quick
Jack, jump over the candlestick

Whoever had made contact with him was someone who enjoyed playing games.

The e-mail message, though brief, had been dense with detailed information on the security measures that protected Kris. Hickle had read it slowly, pausing often to draw a breath. He'd learned that Kris employed a security firm called Travis Protective Services, that a bodyguard accompanied her at all times, that the bodyguard carried a 9mm Beretta and served as her chauffeur, that additional agents were posted in the guest cottage on the property. There had been more, a wealth of facts.

If they were facts. They might have been lies designed to ensnare him in some subtle way. He couldn't be sure. He could trust no one, not even his anonymous benefactor.

But if the message was what it appeared to be, then Jack was someone with inside knowledge of the TPS operation. A TPS employee, perhaps, or a member of the Barwood household. This person knew a great deal about Hickle—his address, his Volkswagen's plate number—and wanted Hickle to know a great deal about Kris.

The last lines of the message had been the most intriguing:

> The Malibu Reserve compound is securely gated and fenced, but a drainage pipe affords access to the property on the northwest side, sixty feet from Pacific Coast Highway.

Access to the property. JackBNimble@zoommail.com had wanted him to know this.

Hickle had replied to the message, typing one word:

> Why?

He'd reread Jack's note until it was committed to memory, then deleted it from his mailbox as the sender had instructed.

Hickle hadn't slept well that night. For the next few days he'd checked his e-mail account every afternoon. A week had passed before he received the next message. More security details, capped by a provocative closing observation:

> Kris is most vulnerable when she returns from work in her Lincoln Town Car shortly after midnight. An as-

sailant could lie in wait in the darkness and not be seen.
Think about it.

There had been no answer to Hickle's question.
Jack's motive, it appeared, was not for him to know.

Hickle had spent his next Sunday afternoon in the
brush near the Malibu Reserve, tracking down the
drainage pipe. It was narrow, but he could wriggle
through. Once inside, he was within sight of the Barwoods' house. Several times he had returned, snap-
ping Polaroids of Kris as she jogged on the beach in the
company of her bodyguard. He had watched the guest
cottage long enough to see men enter and leave.
Agents were indeed stationed there. Everything Jack
had told him had checked out.

There had been two more recent messages, different
from the earlier ones. Jack was growing impatient. He
goaded Hickle. The last message had been a childish
taunt:

Kris laughs about you. She thinks you're a joke. She's
told the TPS agents that you're no threat because you
don't have the guts to take action.

Crude manipulation. Hickle hadn't fallen for it. He
had come to distrust Jack. Something was going on
here, something complicated and mysterious. Maybe
TPS was sending the messages to prod him into com-
mitting some foolhardy arrestable offense. After the
last e-mail from Jack, he had sent a one-sentence
reply:

You can't make me your bitch.

He had not checked his Internet mailbox this week. He had expected never to hear from Jack again. Instead, for the first time Jack had made contact by telephone.

The call worried him, because he didn't know what had prompted it or what it might mean.

At this hour the library would be closed. To check his e-mail, he would have to use an all-night copy store on Western Avenue. The store was a block ahead.

Could Jack have anticipated that he would go to this store? Might he be waiting there, ready to spring some deadly trap?

"Seems doubtful," Hickle murmured, but as he eased into the right lane, he reached across to the duffel bag on the passenger seat and unzipped it, affording instant access to the shotgun.

If anybody opened fire, he would be ready. He would not go down without a fight.

Nobody shot at him. He guided the Volkswagen into a shadowy corner of the parking lot, where he could observe the store without being seen from inside. A neon sign blazed above a glass storefront framing rows of self-service photocopy machines and computers. A few people were running off copies or tapping at keyboards. The clerk behind the counter looked pale and drawn under the fluorescent glow.

Nothing out of the ordinary. Hickle stuffed the duffel bag on the floor of the passenger side, out of sight, then headed into the store to see what JackBNimble had to say.

20

Abby had lost him. After driving for twenty minutes on Santa Monica and adjacent streets she had caught no glimpse of Hickle's car. She pulled into a gas station and parked near the air hose to collect her thoughts.

The phone call was the key. She had to know its point of origin. There was a way. Pacific Bell offered call return service. Entering a three-button code on the phone's keypad provided the customer with the number of the most recent caller. A charge of seventy-five cents for the service would appear on Hickle's next phone bill, possibly tipping him off, but she couldn't worry about that now.

To use his phone she had to get inside his apartment. Picking the lock on his door was no good; the electric pick gun was too noisy to use in the evening when other tenants were around, and doing the job by hand would take too long. The only other means of entry was his bedroom window. She had seen him open both windows. He hadn't closed them when he left. He'd been in a hurry.

Abby pulled out of the gas station and headed back to the Gainford Arms, driving fast.

The copy store rented computer use by the hour. Hickle paid in advance and seated himself at the machine farthest from the counter, where he was least likely to be observed.

There was little activity in the shop. The tile floor and white countertops glowed under fluorescent lights. Folk music played on overhead speakers, drowned out when the big photocopy machines started to whir and drone.

Hickle focused on the desktop computer in front of him, which brought up a browser frame when he connected to the Internet. He found ZoomMail's homepage and typed *JackBQuick* and his password. There was one message in his Inbox. The sender was JackB-Nimble. The title was one word in capitals: URGENT.

Hickle felt a prickle of dread at the back of his neck. He opened the message. The first two lines appeared in the message window.

Your enemies are closer than you know. TPS is playing hardball. They've hired a spy.

The hard, rhythmic chugging in Hickle's ears was the beat of his heart. "A spy," he whispered.

One of the clerks at the counter glanced at him. Hickle realized he'd spoken aloud. Nervously he cleared his throat.

There was more to the message, but he would have to scroll down to see it. For a moment he did nothing, merely stared at the screen, unwilling to read further. A kind of superstitious fear held him paralyzed. If he learned nothing more, then maybe the news would not be real. Maybe he could pretend he'd never come here. Maybe he could go back to his apartment, carry on with his daily routine, have dinner with Abby again—

And then of course he knew.

His new neighbor, so friendly, always bumping into him, first in the hall, then in the laundry room.

The bottom seemed to drop out of his stomach, and he felt a wave of some indescribable feeling that was almost physical pain.

Numbly he read the rest of the message.

She moved in next door to you yesterday. Her job is to get close to men like yourself, learn their secrets, and report what she finds. She works alone, without backup. She is a threat to you and indirectly to me also. I hope you understand the gravity of what I am telling you.

The words ran together. Hickle couldn't concentrate. He was thinking that the story about her unfaithful fiancé had been a lie to win his empathy. He was thinking that she had never regarded him as a nice guy or somebody to have dinner with.

He shut his eyes, shoulders slumping. The computer hummed. Behind the counter one of the copy machines shut off, and the background music became audible again, Joan Baez singing about the night they drove old Dixie down.

His date tonight . . . the questions she'd asked . . . the things he'd told her. What had he said, exactly? Malibu—he'd mentioned how he liked it there. And he'd said he was going to be famous. How much could she determine from those clues? Enough to guess his intentions? Was she reporting to TPS now, telling Kris everything she'd learned?

He looked at the clock. Quarter past nine. Abby couldn't be meeting with Kris. Kris was still at KPTI preparing for the ten o'clock newscast. She would leave Burbank at eleven-thirty, arrive home soon after midnight.

He could get to Malibu well before then. The shotgun was already in his car. All he had to do was crawl through the drainage pipe, conceal himself near the beach house, and when Kris's car pulled into the driveway—

A pump of the shotgun, a spatter of brains and skull fragments.

The copy machine drummed again, churning out paper, and Joan Baez was lost in its noise.

He could do it. Do it tonight. Kill Kris—but first, detour back to the Gainford Arms and take care of Abby.

Jack had said she worked without backup. There would be no one to save her when he caught her by surprise and snapped her neck.

It would be easy. Almost too easy . . .

"Too easy," he whispered slowly.

No one heard him. The clatter of the copy machine swallowed every other sound.

He read the message twice more. He could be certain of this much—Jack knew that a woman had moved into apartment 418. Perhaps he even knew that Hickle had gone out with her tonight. He might have watched the building and seen them leave together.

For weeks he had been goading Hickle to strike. Had he decided to try a more subtle approach, convince Hickle that his new neighbor was part of a conspiracy against him, launch him into a homicidal rage?

Or was the information genuine? Was she really a spy?

He didn't know. His head hurt. He clutched his scalp and blinked at the light, which was suddenly too bright.

There was no one he could trust. Jack claimed to be a friend, but his identity and motives were unknown. Abby presented herself as a young woman fleeing a bad breakup, but how much did he know about her? She might be a TPS spy probing his secrets. Or maybe it was Jack who was the real TPS agent, playing mind games to push him over the edge and get him arrested. Or were they both in it together?

He read the message again. The words made no sense anymore. They spilled together and fell apart. Abby a spy? Ridiculous.

On impulse he clicked the Reply link, then typed a furious declaration:

I WON'T LET YOU PLAY WITH MY HEAD!

But he didn't send it. He stared at the crisp, explosive words, then deleted the text with a sweep of his mouse.

He couldn't assume Jack was lying. That was as foolish as blindly assuming he told the truth. He typed a new reply:

Are you friend or foe?

This was no good either. What was Jack supposed to say? What more could he say to establish his bona fides? He had already pointed Hickle to the drainage pipe and the agents in the cottage and the chauffeur who carried a gun.

He erased the second reply and stared at the screen. What was going on exactly? Was it simply that he didn't want to believe in Abby's betrayal? Maybe so.

He had pursued Jill Dahlbeck, only to be rebuffed

and humiliated and finally confronted by police officers warning him to back off. He had tried to reach Kris Barwood by every means available to him, but she would not meet with him or even acknowledge the reality of his feelings for her.

But with Abby, things had been different. She was not like Jill or Kris. She was kind to him. She treated him like a human being. She made him feel like a man.

But if it was all an act? If she was the enemy?

Pounding violence filled his skull. He wanted to scream and smash things. He lowered his head. Had to think. Jack could be telling the truth or lying. Abby could be what she was or a fraud. There was no way for him to gauge Jack's honesty directly. As for Abby . . .

He knew her. She lived right next door. She was not merely a made-up name on a computer screen, a collection of pixels that mocked him. She was real and close, and he could learn the truth about her.

He typed a third reply.

I'll check out your story and see for myself.

This was the right thing to say. He clicked Send.

He had no plan, but he would come up with one. He was smart. He would work something out. And if she had indeed deceived him . . .

He'd kill her. Yes.

First her, then Kris.

If she had deceived him. If.

Hickle clung to that word as he deleted Jack's e-mail message and signed off.

If.

Such a little word, but Abby's life hung on it.

* * *

Abby climbed onto the fire escape and stepped across the narrow landing to Hickle's bedroom window. The lights in his apartment were on, but because the blinds were drawn she couldn't see in. A glance at his empty parking space reassured her that he had not returned.

Although his window was open, the screen was still in place. From outside, it proved difficult to remove. She wished she had brought her locksmith kit, which contained a thin, flexible celluloid strip that could slip into the crack of a door and open a latch. It might have allowed her the leverage to work the screen loose.

She couldn't take the time to go back inside her apartment and get the kit. Rummaging in her purse, she found a Swiss army knife. Among its spring-loaded tools was a pair of wire cutters. She snipped through part of the screen, inserted her fingers in the gap, and lifted the screen out of the window frame, then climbed into the apartment.

The code for the call return service was the star key followed by 6 and 9. Abby punched the three buttons and listened as a synthesized voice gave her the most recent caller's phone number. It was a local number with an unfamiliar exchange. She dictated it into her microrecorder. Later she could look it up. She subscribed to an online reverse directory service that offered a comprehensive listing of residential and commercial phone numbers.

There was one more item of business in Hickle's apartment. She'd brought an infinity transmitter from her tool kit; it broadcast on the same frequency as the two microphones she had already installed. Quickly she wired the transmitter into the base of the telephone. Hickle could see it if he took the trouble to look, but this was a chance she'd decided to take. If the mystery caller phoned again, she wanted his voice on tape. A voiceprint could then be made for purposes of identification.

Done with the phone, she wiped off her prints. Mission accomplished. Time to blow this joint.

She returned to Hickle's bedroom, intending to make her escape through the window, then paused, noticing his laundry basket on the floor. It was still full to the brim. He had never put away his clothes.

Odd. He'd had plenty of time.

She knelt and rummaged through the clothes, not sure what she was looking for. Nothing was out of the ordinary, except that a few items seemed curiously damp, though the rest were dry.

Almost as if a wet article of clothing had been stuffed into the basket . . .

She touched the carpet and felt a wet spot, then another and another. The trail of drops led to the bathroom.

In Hickle's shower, hanging from the showerhead, dripping dry, was a pair of white high-cut Maidenform briefs.

Hers, of course.

When she'd sensed a presence in the laundry room, she had not been imagining things. Hickle had been watching her. He must have taken cover in the stairwell, and when she'd explored the boiler room, he had risked slipping past her and stealing this particular item right out of the washing machine.

His prize. His little piece of her, to touch and smell and kiss . . .

Abby shivered. She had a sudden urge to grab the

poor, wrinkled, soggy thing that hung on the shower-head and abscond with it, but she couldn't. If it was missing, Hickle would know she had been in here. She would have to leave it. And she would try not to think about what he would use it for.

She left the bathroom and braced herself against the bedroom window, preparing to climb through, and then she looked past the railing, down at the parking lot.

Hickle's car was there.

It was parked under the carport, headlights off.

Hickle himself was nowhere in sight. He must already be inside the building, maybe riding the elevator to the fourth floor.

Get out, a voice in Abby's mind yelled.

Hickle would be enraged to find her here. And he was armed; he'd taken the duffel bag. Her Smith & Wesson was a poor match for a shotgun. Unless she killed him instantly, he would have time to pump out a couple of shells, and at close range even a single shotgun blast would literally tear her apart.

"Oh, that's good, Abby," she hissed, scrambling through the window. "Keep thinking those happy thoughts."

She was on the fire escape. Her instinct was to scurry to the safety of her bedroom, but she couldn't leave until the window screen had been replaced.

Installing the screen from outside was harder than she'd expected. She got hold of it through the gap she'd cut in the mesh, then jammed the top of the screen into the frame, but the bottom stubbornly refused to snap into position. The panel was large and awkward, difficult to maneuver, especially with the venetian blind in the way, jangling and clattering.

She heard a squeal of hinges. Hickle's door, opening in the other room. He was home.

With a last effort she wedged the screen in place.

Footsteps inside the apartment. He was coming into the bedroom, probably to put away the duffel bag.

She ducked low. No time to crawl away. She hugged the wall.

The blind swung and rattled in the bedroom window. Hickle would surely notice. He did. She heard the complaint of the floorboards as he approached to investigate. She unclasped her purse and curled her finger over the Smith's trigger.

The blind opened, brightening the fire escape. She pressed close to the brick wall under the windowsill. Across the iron railing loomed Hickle's shadow, large and misshapen. His head tilted at a funny angle. He was peering out, surveying the night.

If he glanced down, he would see her. She waited, not breathing. She thought again of what a shotgun shell would do to her at this distance. Like a grenade going off in her chest.

He might have spotted her already. Even now he might be removing the shotgun from his duffel, preparing to fire, while she huddled like a child playing hide-'n'-seek. It took all her willpower to remain motionless.

His shadow shifted. She saw a movement of his arm as if lifting the shotgun—

Then there was a metallic clatter and a fall of darkness, and she realized he had merely reached up to pull the cord that closed the blind.

The tramp of his footsteps retreated. He had not seen her. He must have concluded that a gust of wind had set the blind swaying.

Close one, Abby thought. Kind of thing that really gets the blood circulating.

She slipped inside her apartment, then spent the next few minutes reacquainting herself with the experience of being alive and intact and ambulatory. Her throat was dry, and the back of her neck was stiff with tension.

When she checked the current programming on the closed-circuit TV monitor, she saw Hickle pacing his living room. He was agitated. He was angry.

She dialed up the volume, trying to catch the words he muttered under his breath. "Can't trust anybody," he was saying. "Can't trust him . . . or her. Can't trust either one."

Abby didn't like the sound of that.

21

Travis stepped out of the shower, throwing on his robe, and heard the chime of his doorbell.

Seven-thirty in the morning seemed early for visitors. He rarely had company anyway. He lived on a twisting dead-end street in the Hollywood Hills, in a ranch-style house cantilevered over a canyon—a good house for entertaining, but he preferred to pass his time alone.

He wedged moccasins onto his feet and padded down the hall, pausing in an alcove before a video monitor that displayed a view of the front steps. Abby stood there in a rumpled blouse and jeans. His first thought was that she looked different. There was something about her expression, something hard to define. Then he realized it was the first time he had ever seen her looking scared.

He shut off his alarm system and opened the door. "Hey," he said.

"Hey."

She entered without another word. She hardly seemed to see him at all. "Everything okay?" Travis asked, knowing it wasn't.

"Not exactly." Abby sidestepped into the living room and tossed her purse on the sofa but didn't sit. "Hickle may have an accomplice."

"Accomplice?"

"Or an informant. I don't know for sure. Actually I

don't know anything for sure." She paced, her Nikes squeaking on the hardwood floor. Sunbeams slanting through the deck's glass doors lit her trim, nervous figure.

She had been to the house many times over the years, though rarely without calling first. Travis was always struck by how well she fit in here. His decor was sleek and functional in a starkly modernistic style, and Abby suited it—Abby with her slender legs and narrow waist and supple, elongated neck.

"I think you should sit down," Travis said quietly. "You seem a little stressed."

She ignored him. "I should be stressed. I was up half the night. Couldn't go to sleep until Hickle did. I watched him on the monitor till finally he nodded off after three a.m.—"

"Okay, slow down and take it from the beginning."

She let out a rush of breath and made an effort to speak calmly. "Hickle got a phone call last night around eight-thirty. He left his apartment, taking his shotgun, and drove off. I lost him. I don't know where he went or who he might have made contact with. When he returned, he was obviously upset. The surveillance mikes picked up a lot of murmuring about not being able to trust anyone. It's possible somebody tipped him off."

"About you?"

"Yeah."

"You think he knows you're a plant?"

"He may."

Travis approached her slowly. "If he knows about you . . ."

"It could send him over the edge. I'm aware of that. See why I didn't sleep until he did? Even then I maxed out the volume on my audio gear so if he got up in the night, I'd hear him. I was afraid he'd do something extreme." She took a breath. "There's something else."

"Yes?"

"The night before last, I used the hot tub at the apartment complex. Somebody snuck up on me and pushed me under."

"Tried to *drown* you?"

She nodded. "I scared him off with a broken beer bottle. Never saw him. Don't think it was Hickle—he seemed otherwise occupied, from what I could tell. But maybe it was his accomplice. If there is an accomplice. I just don't know . . ."

"Why didn't you tell me about your near-death experience when we spoke yesterday afternoon?"

"I wasn't sure it meant anything."

"Somebody tries to kill you, and you think it might not mean anything? Come on, Abby, you can do better than that."

"All right, the truth is, I didn't want you pulling me off the case."

"I see."

She stared at him. "You're not going to do that, right, Paul? Right?"

He didn't answer. "Did you see Hickle this morning?"

"Yes, on the video monitor."

"How was he? Still agitated?"

"I think so. Can't be sure. He didn't hang around long. Left for work at five-thirty. I drove past the donut shop on my way over here and saw his car in the parking lot."

"If he hasn't varied his usual routine, maybe he's not as worked up as you think."

"Or maybe he's maintaining his routine to give himself time to think."

"Biding his time? Getting ready to strike?"

"Yes."

"Against Kris—or you?"

"Maybe both of us."

"All right. So tell me. If there is an informant, who could it be?"

Abby shrugged. "Someone with inside knowledge and a motive."

"Then we're looking for somebody who knows you're on this case. Somebody who can get in touch with Hickle. Somebody who would want to sell you out. And somebody who wants Kris dead."

"Right." She hugged herself. "I've gotta tell you, I hate this a lot. You know me, the original control freak. Now suddenly everything feels like it's out of control. I should be the one with all the secrets, but now Hickle has a secret I can't guess. It—it's got me kind of unnerved."

"Did you get any sleep at all?"

"Couple hours. Not good sleep. I kept having this dream . . . Forget about that. It's not important."

"A psychologist who says dreams aren't important?"

"I'm not a psychologist."

"Neither am I. Tell me anyway. It's not good to hold these things inside you."

"Well . . . I dreamed I was in the hot tub again, being held down, only this time I didn't find a way to fight back. I just struggled until my air ran out, and then . . ."

Travis put his arms around her. "It's okay," he whispered as he rocked her gently.

"No, it isn't. I don't like falling apart like this."

"You aren't falling apart."

"Well, wimping out, then."

"You're not doing that, either. But under the circumstances it might be best if we . . . altered our strategy."

"Took me off the job? Is that what you're saying?"

"It may be the only prudent solution—"

She pulled free. "No chance. I'm not running away. I signed up for the duration."

"If Hickle has been tipped off, you can't achieve anything useful anyway."

"Wrong. I can watch him the way I did last night. Besides, he may not even know about me. He may not know anything. And I'm not a quitter, Paul."

"We're talking about your life . . ."

"Right. My life. Therefore, my decision."

He studied her. "This isn't about Devin Corbal, is it?"

"I don't know what you mean."

"I mean trying to prove yourself to me. Or redeem yourself. Something like that."

"Don't get inside my head, please."

"I just want to know why you're so insistent on taking this kind of risk."

"Maybe I just like to live on the edge. Or maybe you're right about Corbal. What difference does it make? It's my job, and I'm doing it, and that's that."

She glared at him, defying him to disagree.

Travis relented. "Okay." He teased a strand of hair off her forehead. "You're stubborn, you know."

"It's a quality I pride myself on. Now, have you ever heard of a company called Western Regional Resources?"

"Should I have?"

"Probably not. They don't seem to do a lot of advertising. I traced the phone call Hickle received, then tracked down the number with a reverse directory. The call was made from a cell phone registered to

Western Regional Resources. I couldn't find it on the Internet or in Lexis-Nexis. Needless to say, they aren't in the Yellow Pages either."

Travis looked away toward the view of the canyon framed in the deck's glass doors. "We can find them."

"Could be tough. My guess is, it's a dummy corporation."

"That's my guess too," Travis said softly, still staring into the distance, and then he felt Abby's gaze on him.

"You know something," she whispered.

"I might. Follow me."

He led her to the rear of the house, detouring to pick up his notebook computer from the study. When he ushered her into the master bedroom, Abby shook her head in mock dismay. "You've got a one-track mind."

"Not today. This is all business." Travis opened the hinged double doors of a walnut entertainment center, revealing a TV set with a thirty-inch screen.

"There's nothing good on at this hour," Abby said.

"Watch and learn." He picked up the remote control and pressed the channel buttons in a seven-digit sequence. With a metallic snick, the front of the TV swung a few inches ajar on hidden hinges. "A safe," he explained unnecessarily. "State of the art."

"Very clever, but what if you want to watch Letterman?"

"The TV is fully functional. It's a flat-panel screen, four inches thick, with the circuitry imbedded in the frame. The rest of the unit is hollow."

"So what've you got in there? The family jewels?"

"I believe you know where I keep those." Travis opened the safe door fully, revealing racks of CDs in plastic sleeves. "What I store here are files. Highly confidential files."

"Background checks," Abby said quietly.

"How'd you guess?"

"I wondered about it sometimes. It seemed like a reasonable precaution. TPS is hired to protect people from a variety of threats. Not all stalkers are strangers. Routine background checks might come in handy in some cases. Anyway, it seemed plausible to me that you would cover that angle. Why not? You cover everything else." She smiled slyly. "You're basically an obsessive-compulsive, anal-retentive perfectionist."

"Flattery is cheap."

"So TPS digs up dirt on its own clients and the people in their lives."

"We prefer to think of it as gathering intelligence."

"Whatever. You investigate a client's spouse, business partners, personal trainer—anybody in a position to deliver harm. But you never tell them, because they wouldn't appreciate having their pals and loved ones put under a microscope."

"That's why these files are confidential and why they're kept in my home."

Abby approached the safe and peered inside. "CDs," she said. "Four dozen or so. That's, what, thirty gigs of data?"

"Not all the disks are filled to capacity."

"Even so, it's a lot of info."

"As you said, I'm thorough."

"Actually, what I said was that you're an obsessive-compulsive, anal-retentive—"

"I think *thorough* captures it adequately." He thumbed through the disks until he found one labeled "BARWOOD," which he lifted from its sleeve. "You're right, though. You can store a lot of information on a

CD. All seventy-five thousand articles in the *Encyclopedia Britannica*, for instance."

Abby nodded. "Or every detail of Kris Barwood's life and the lives of her friends, her relatives . . . her husband."

"Yes."

"Good old Howard." Her voice was low and thoughtful.

Travis frowned. "Once again you don't sound surprised."

"I was up most of the night reviewing the possibilities. And the husband is always a possibility. Please tell me that Howard Barwood set up a company called Western Regional Resources."

"I wish I could. That would make everything easy."

"And things are never easy. It would take all the challenge out of life. If he doesn't own that company, what made you think of him?"

"Let me show you." Travis placed his notebook computer on the bed and inserted the CD, bringing up its contents on the screen. A series of folder icons appeared. The first was labeled "BARWOOD, HOWARD." Others bore the names of various people connected to Kris—friends, coworkers, attorneys and managers, even her housekeeper.

He accessed Howard Barwood's folder. Inside were more folders, arranged alphabetically: BANK ACCOUNTS, CLIENT LIST, CREDIT HISTORY, FINANCES, INSURANCE, MEDICAL RECORDS, MOTOR VEHICLES, REAL PROPERTY, TAXES, TELEPHONE RECORDS.

Abby sat on the bed beside him, looking over his shoulder. She sighed. "There aren't any secrets anymore, are there?"

"Not many. It takes some effort to uncover all this, of course. A surname scan delivers the basic info: driver's license, vehicle registration, voter registration, and real estate holdings. The Lexis-Nexis property database supplies previous or secondary residences. We check employment history with an executive name search. Most of our information comes from the subject's credit history. It tells us where he travels, what he does for entertainment, where he likes to shop. Then there are insurance policies, medical records, phone bills, property tax filings, financial statements . . ."

"All technically off-limits to snoops and hackers."

"But accessible to those in the know." He opened the ASSETS folder. "When I first investigated Howard, the Barwoods' net worth was twenty-four million dollars. That was in 1994. Recently we took another look. This is the figure now."

Abby leaned close to the screen. "Twenty million," she said. "So either they've made some lousy investments or there's something funny going on."

"It's something funny." Travis scrolled through pages of spreadsheets, highlighting figures in the Date Sold column. "Howard has begun liquidating his assets."

"If the assets are held jointly, wouldn't he need Kris's approval?"

"Most of these accounts were set up so as not to require a co-signatory. It makes it more convenient for either asset holder to write a check."

"And also more convenient for one asset holder to move funds around without the other's knowledge. Where did the profits from the asset sales go?"

"Into a local bank account set up in Howard's name."

"His name alone. No Kris?"

"No Kris."

The bed creaked as Abby tucked her legs under her in a swami pose. "I'm beginning to see where this is going. The money didn't stay in that bank account, did it?"

"No, it didn't." Travis found Howard Barwood's statements in the BANK ACCOUNTS folder. Cash withdrawals had been made at irregular intervals. "Cashier's checks," he explained. "Fifty or a hundred grand at a pop. After that, the money trail runs cold."

"You have no idea where all that cash is going?"

"Yes and no."

"I thought you might say something like that."

"Did you? Why?"

"Because you still haven't explained how dummy corporations fit into all this."

"Good point. I haven't. There is another factor." He opened the REAL PROPERTY folder. "When we ran a property search on Howard Barwood, we found a house in Culver City." An address came up on the screen. "At first glance there's nothing odd about that. Howard owns a number of properties, small and large. But recently he sold this house, taking a loss. The buyer was something called Trendline Investments. They're incorporated in the Netherlands Antilles, if that means anything to you."

"A haven for offshore banking. Airtight secrecy laws."

"Very good. Now look at Howard's credit card statements." Travis opened the CREDIT HISTORY folder. "They include the purchase of round-trip airline tickets to Willemstad. It's the capital city of the Netherlands Antilles."

"So let me take a shot in the dark. Trendline Investments is a dummy corporation. Howard set it up. He sold the Culver City house to himself."

"I think so. Can't prove it, but his trip to the Antilles

is strong circumstantial evidence. He stayed for two nights, enough time for him to execute all the paperwork required to establish a shell corporation with its own bank account."

"When?"

Travis scrolled down to the hotel charge, dated November 22, 1999. "Late last year. Shortly before the transfer of the deed to the Culver City house, and shortly before the other assets started to mysteriously disappear."

"And Kris doesn't know?"

"There's no evidence that she does. Of course, financial records can tell us only so much."

"Seems like they're already telling us quite a lot." Abby thought for a moment. "Was the Culver City house deeded to Howard alone?"

"Yes."

"So even when he owned it openly, Kris may not have known the house existed?"

"Right."

"I see." She rubbed her forehead wearily.

"You get it, don't you?"

"You don't have to hit me over the head with a two-by-four. When a guy owns a residence his wife doesn't know about and goes to considerable lengths to keep it a secret, there's usually only one reason. Howard is cheating on his wife. He uses the house for the occasional secret rendezvous. He intends to get a divorce. He's going to say good-bye to Kris."

Travis nodded. "But California is a community property state . . ."

Abby untucked her legs and got off the bed. "Which means the Barwoods' assets will be divided down the middle. And that's a problem for Howard, because while his wife is extremely well off, he's worth much more than she is. He doesn't want to surrender half his wealth. To shield as much of it as he can, he's secretly transferring their assets overseas, hiding them under the umbrella of a shell company incorporated in a jurisdiction with extremely tight banking secrecy laws. That way, when the assets are divided, there'll be less to divide."

"All of which is perfectly legal," Travis said, "as long as he paid his U.S. taxes. There's no law against moving money overseas, even if the intent is to shield it from a claimant in a lawsuit or a divorce." He ejected the CD.

Abby shook her head. "You haven't told Kris?"

"Not a word. I'm fairly sure Howard's stealing her blind, but how can I say anything without revealing the background checks we've carried out?"

"Under the circumstances I hardly think she'd blame you for it."

"She would if it turns out I'm wrong. Most of this is supposition, remember. We don't know for sure that Howard owns Trendline or that he's conducting these transactions without Kris's knowledge. Possibly the two of them planned the asset diversion together. It could be some complicated tax shelter, only borderline legal. If it is, and I start asking about it . . ."

"You say good-bye to another client."

"Right. The one I can least afford to lose." Travis slipped the CD back into its plastic sleeve. "Besides, our job is to safeguard Kris's life, not her finances."

"It's her life I'm worried about," Abby said slowly. "If Howard is fooling around and wants a divorce, and if he's so desperate to keep his hands on his money—"

"Then he might have a motive to get rid of his wife in a more expeditious fashion."

"By providing inside information to the psycho who's stalking her. You think he would do that? Sell out Kris to her would-be assassin to get her out of the way?"

"It's cold, I grant you. But LA's not exactly a town known for its warmth and humanity."

"And if all this is true, then Howard might be my mystery assailant from the other night. He knew I was on the case. He might've been afraid I'd find out too much. If he was watching Hickle's building and saw me in the hot tub—"

"He could have decided it was a golden opportunity to get rid of you."

Abby frowned. "I knew I didn't like the guy. Is there any way we can discreetly find out if he's alibied for that night?"

"Sure. The security officers stationed at the guest cottage keep a log of all comings and goings. I can find out if Howard was out that night. Odds are, he was."

"What makes you say that?"

"He goes out nearly every night. Breaking in his new car, he claims."

"Or visiting his house in Culver City and whoever he's seeing there. And on the way home, maybe stopping at Hickle's apartment building to do a little mischief. It's all possible, but we have to nail it down."

Travis nodded. "We will. If Howard has set up one dummy corporation, there could be more, and one of them might be Western Regional Resources—in which case, Western Regional is probably incorporated in the Netherlands Antilles like Trendline. It might even be connected with Trendline. A shell within a shell, that kind of thing. I'll have my staff get on it right away."

"If they can establish a connection between Howard and Western Regional, we'll have to tell Kris."

"I know."

"And the police."

"Yes." Travis shrugged. "See, we've got options, leads. Things aren't as completely out of control as you thought."

She tried to brush off what he'd said with a wave of her hand. "It was a rough night, that's all. Left a bad residue."

"Feeling better now?"

"Considerably. Not that I came here to—well, I mean, I wanted to brief you on urgent developments. I wasn't looking to be . . . comforted."

He stood and drew her close. "But you wouldn't turn down a little comforting, would you?"

"Guess not." She looked down at his robe and smiled. It was her first real smile since she'd arrived. "You know, the last time we were together outside the office, I was the one in the bathrobe."

"I remember. Vividly."

"So do I."

He kissed her. It began as a tender kiss, and then the press of her body against his reminded him of how small she was, almost fragile despite her strength. He ran his fingers through her hair and kissed her deeply.

"Guess I'd better let you get dressed," Abby said, "or you'll be late for work."

"Work can wait."

"Can it?"

"Definitely."

He removed her clothes slowly, taking his time with each button and strap. Her body had always amazed him. Even before she had begun her training and conditioning, she'd had the supple, sinewy figure of an athlete, but without an athlete's unnatural hardness.

196

He did not take off his robe or even untie the belt. He simply swept back the flaps and entered her, his hands at her waist, lifting her as her back arched and he pushed deeper, and at the moment of release his eyes met hers in a frisson of contact.

When it was done, he kissed her smooth neck and one earlobe that poked out coyly from her tangled hair, and in her ear he whispered, "This time I think we both knew I would fit."

"Never doubted it," she breathed.

They lay there together in the morning sunlight, silent, exhausted. A long time later, but still too soon, he said, "I really do have to get to the office."

"I should go too," Abby whispered sleepily.

"No, you rest, catch a little shut-eye. I think you could use it."

"Ten minutes, maybe. A catnap."

"Sure."

"Wake me when you leave."

"I will."

But he didn't. By the time he was dressed, she lay fast asleep, and it seemed pointless to disturb her. He placed a spare key on the bureau so she could lock up when she left. Then he stooped and kissed her forehead. "Sleep tight, Abby."

Her lips formed a smile, and he felt sure she was dreaming of him.

22

In early afternoon, a few hours before the start of his shift, Wyatt drove to the Hollywood Reservoir, where Detective Sam Cahill was waiting for him.

"What'd you want to talk about, Vic?" Cahill asked after the usual manly clapping of shoulders and pumping of hands. Cahill had worked Hollywood Division before being bumped upstairs to Robbery-Homicide in Parker Center. He and Wyatt had gone fishing at Lake Arrowhead a couple of times, but since the transfer they hadn't seen much of each other.

"Remember the Emanuel Barth case?" Wyatt asked. It was in connection with Barth that he had first met Abby Sinclair. She had come to him, asking questions about Barth's past.

"Yeah, I remember." Cahill nodded slowly. He was a big man with bushy eyebrows that met in the middle, forming a single, furry line. "It's old news by now. Why bring it up?"

"I wanted to know how Barth got nailed the second time—you know, the arrest you handled. I was on vacation when it happened. Never heard the details."

"What's it been, a year? That was one of the last cases I worked before I moved downtown. What do you care, after all this time?"

"Humor me."

Cahill shrugged. "Sure, what the hell. I got nothing

better to do except fight crime." He looked out at the reservoir, its clear water reflecting the perfect blue sky. "Say, you think the city could stock this lake with bass? Wouldn't be a bad place to drop a fishing line."

"Why don't you raise the issue with the City Council?"

"Might just do that. Okay, Mr. Emanuel Barth. Well, he got nailed on account of outstanding detective work by yours truly, as usual."

"Save it for Ed O'Hern at Channel Eight. What's the real deal?"

"Dumb luck. We didn't have shit on Barth, weren't even looking at him, and then a nine-one tip comes out of the blue, telling us he's got a stash of stolen goods in his house."

"What kind of goods?"

"VCRs, PCs, jewelry, portable computers. You know how he had a prior for breaking into rich people's homes and vandalizing their stuff? Well, after he did his time, he went back to doing break-ins, only he got smart. He started wearing gloves to leave no prints, and taking the valuables instead of trashing them."

"What was the merchandise doing in his house? You'd think he would've fenced it."

"His MO was to accumulate a big haul, then fence it all at once. Maybe he got a better deal that way or he thought it minimized the risk, I don't know."

"So who gave you the nine-one tip?"

"Anonymous female."

"Any idea who?"

"Probably Barth's housekeeper. That's always been my theory, anyway. She came into his house twice a week to pick up after him. I figure she stumbled across the stuff while she was cleaning and realized it was hot."

"Why was it just a theory? Wouldn't she talk to you?"

"I never found her. She must've amscrayed out of town after making the phone call. I'm guessing she was worried the charges against Barth wouldn't stick, and he'd come after her. They stuck, though. He's tucked away safe and sound."

"Had she worked for him long?"

"The housekeeper? Just a month, I think."

"What was her name?"

"Hell, I don't know anymore. Wait a minute, it's coming back to me. You know, if my wife was here, she'd say an elephant never forgets. That would be in reference to a few pounds I've put on over the years."

"The name?" Wyatt prompted.

"Connie Hammond. Fairly common name, hard to track down. We didn't bust our asses trying to find her."

Wyatt nodded slowly. "Connie Hammond."

Cahill gave Wyatt a hard look. "You wouldn't happen to know Miss Hammond's whereabouts, would you, Vic?"

"Me? No."

"'Cause I'd still like to chat with her, just for the record."

"Never met the lady."

"Right. Sure you haven't. You don't know shit. And this whole conversation, dragging me out here on a Friday afternoon to this friggin' mud hole—it's all just an exercise in intellectual curiosity on your part."

Wyatt met his gaze. "Exactly, Sam. That's what it is."

They talked a little more, about fishing and Cahill's

wife and a homicide in the Valley that was taking up most of the detective's time. Then Cahill was on his way, and Wyatt was left alone, looking at the water.

The reservoir was a peaceful spot, a haven for joggers and power walkers and people who wanted someplace tranquil to visit on their lunch break. He came here fairly often to escape the grit and gridlock of the city, and to think. He had a lot to think about right now.

Abby had interviewed him about Emanuel Barth just a month before Barth went back to jail. Wyatt had always assumed it was no coincidence. At the time he'd thought that in the course of her research, she had uncovered some incriminating fact that she'd passed along to the police. He had never inquired about it. He hadn't wanted to know too much.

Later, as she involved herself in other cases, he began to suspect that she was doing more than research. Vaguely he'd imagined that she tailed a suspect or observed him from a distance. Surveillance work, maybe a few discreet payoffs to informers. Now he knew there was more to it than that.

A jogger chuffed past him, red-faced and sweaty. Somewhere a bird lifted off the reservoir in a clatter of wings. Wyatt watched it fly away into the deep azure of the sky, and briefly he wished he could follow.

Cahill's reading of the Barth case had made sense, with no more loose ends than any other criminal case in the real world. The housekeeper, Connie, had ratted on her employer and fled for her own safety.

It was logical but dead wrong. There never had been any Connie. There had been only Abby, whose DMV records, as Wyatt recalled, listed her middle name as Constance.

She had obtained work as Barth's housekeeper, probably a day or two after talking with Wyatt. Twice a week she had shown up, dusting and vacuuming, perhaps searching a different corner of Barth's house each time, until finally she had found the stolen items. The 911 call had followed. And Connie Hammond, who had never existed, had disappeared.

Abby hadn't merely studied Barth from a distance. She'd made herself part of his life. And now she was doing the same thing with Raymond Hickle, a guy who had a penchant for becoming obsessed with beautiful women, a guy who might have tried to splash acid in Jill Dahlbeck's face.

Wyatt wondered how often Abby had tried her skill at this kind of contest. It was amazing she was still alive. She must be damn good or damn lucky. Maybe both. But everyone made mistakes, and nobody's luck held forever.

Wyatt let out a slow breath. So what was he going to do about her? He didn't know. Maybe the best option was to walk away, leave her alone. She had told him she didn't want his help. *I can take care of myself*, she'd said.

But suppose she got in over her head. Would she admit it? Or would she plow onward, too stubborn and proud to back down?

He was pretty sure he knew the answer.

23

Abby woke in a bed that was not her own. She came alert instantly and knew where she was—Travis's bedroom. And she knew it was late, well past noon, and that Travis had let her sleep when he left for work.

She looked at the clock on the nightstand. The time was 3:47. She'd slept nearly all day. She ought to have felt guilty about it, but she knew she had needed the downtime. A body could run on adrenaline for only so long.

Hunger had awakened her. It urged her out of bed now. She went into the kitchen and raided Travis's fridge, finding a gourmet frozen pasta meal, which she microwaved and then ate out of the container while standing up. According to the package, the meal was only two hundred calories—not enough, but it would hold her.

When she was through, she returned to the bedroom, where she retrieved the spare house key Travis had left on the bureau. Then she took a long look at the TV that was really a safe. When Travis had punched in seven digits on the remote control, she'd been watching. She knew the code.

Feeling vaguely disloyal, she picked up the remote and pressed the necessary buttons. The safe's false front swung open. She looked inside. The CDs were arranged alphabetically. She flipped through them until she found the one she wanted. When she lifted it out, the disk flashed, catching the light. The label read "SINCLAIR, ABIGAIL."

She was not surprised. If Travis performed background checks on his clients' friends and business partners, it made sense for him to take similar precautions with his own associates.

Of course, she was more than an associate, wasn't she? She had been Travis's lover for four years, his protégée, his confidante. Yet her life, or as much of it as could be gleaned from databases, had been stored on this electromagnetic disk and filed away for safekeeping here in the same bedroom where Travis had made love to her, not only today but many times.

Perhaps she should have been outraged. But she knew how this business worked. No one could be trusted fully. Everyone had to be checked out.

"Even the people you're sleeping with?" she wondered aloud, but she knew the answer to that.

Especially the people you're sleeping with.

Those were the rules of the game. She had to accept them.

She replaced the CD and shut the safe, then left the house, wishing she could be naive enough to be angry. Anger would have felt good right now.

The house in Culver City was located on an unappealing side street off Sawtelle Boulevard. Decrepit garden apartments were interspersed with bungalows in the old craftsman style, houses that once had been comfortable starter homes for young families. Back then, the lawns had been neatly tended, the paint touched up every year. Now cars stood on cement blocks in weedy driveways, and graffiti decorated the brick walls that had been raised as ineffectual barriers to crime. Barred windows were everywhere. Although it was late afternoon, no children played in the street, and no one walked here. The only visible life was a stray dog nosing through the litter that lined the curb.

"Looks like the people at Trendline made one hell of an investment," Abby muttered as she parked down the street.

The address had come up on the computer screen when Travis reviewed the data with her. It had been visible long enough for her to commit it to memory. She'd had a feeling she would be paying a visit to the property.

She got out of her car and approached the bungalow. Unlike its neighbors, it was freshly painted, the lawn only slightly overgrown. A detached one-car garage lay at the end of a short driveway. She passed between the house and the garage into a small, unfenced backyard, pausing to look into the garage through a side window. No car. Most likely, nobody home.

The rear door was screened from the sightlines of neighboring homes by the garage on one side and a large fig tree on the other. She could work on the lock without fear of being seen. Her complete set of locksmith tools was back at the apartment in Hollywood, but in her purse she carried a picklock and tension bar. She inserted the pick in the keyhole and pressed the bar against the latch. In two minutes she had the door open.

No alarm went off. "Hello?" she called into the emptiness. She heard no response, no creak of floorboards, nothing to indicate another presence in the house.

Briskly she explored the place. It was a typical southern California bungalow—one-story floor plan, high ceilings, big windows. The living room had a fake fireplace. The kitchen was so tiny and ill-equipped that it would be more properly called a kitchenette. There were two bedrooms, one bath.

In the medicine cabinet she found a few personal items: a man's electric shaver, aftershave, and cologne, and a woman's toiletries and lipstick. There were bath towels on the racks and more towels in a linen closet. She checked out the bedroom closet, but only a couple of bathrobes hung there. The bed was comfortable, new, and of higher quality than the home's other furnishings. She poked around in a wastebasket and found a condom wrapper. "At least he practices safe sex," she muttered.

He. A safely ambiguous pronoun. She wanted to believe that Howard Barwood was the *he* in question, but so far nothing she'd found in the house could be tied to him.

Whoever made use of the bungalow evidently followed a simple routine. A romp in bed, then a quick shower to cool off. The place wasn't used for any other purpose. There were no foodstuffs in the pantry or the fridge other than some chocolate candies, a half-eaten block of cheese, and an unopened wine bottle. There were no books or magazines anywhere, no evidence of mail delivery to this address. Most likely the utility bills went directly to Trendline Investments and were paid out of the Netherlands Antilles bank account.

Abby searched the drawers of all the bureaus and cabinets, hoping to find some of Howard Barwood's stationery or a cell phone registered to Western Regional Resources. No such luck. Most of the drawers were empty. But in the nightstand beside the bed, she found a gun.

It was a Colt 1911 pistol, loaded with seven .45-caliber rounds. The pistol was an excellent firearm, sturdy and reliable, one of the few models that could be detail-stripped and reassembled without the use of tools, but the gun required care, which its present owner had neglected. It was in need of lubrication, and the extractor had lost some of its tension and should have been replaced. Abby frowned. She disliked the idea of a gun in the hands of an amateur, and a careless amateur at that. And if the amateur in question was Howard Barwood, and Howard was Hickle's accomplice, she liked the idea even less.

She moved to the second bedroom, which had been made into a study. The room had few accouterments— a thirteen-inch TV on a cheap stand, a worn sofa and armchair, built-in shelves that were depressingly bare, and a telephone.

Not a cell phone like the one that had been used to call Hickle last night. Still, it might tell her something. She lifted the handset and pressed redial. She counted four rings, and then the ringing stuttered as if the call had been transferred. A moment later a recorded female voice came on the line: "You've reached Amanda Gilbert's voicemail."

Abby hung up. The name Amanda Gilbert meant nothing to her. She hadn't seen it on any of the folder icons in the Barwood file. Possibly the man of the house had called Amanda at work, or Amanda herself had called to retrieve her messages. Either way, it was a fair assumption that Amanda's duties here had little to do with business.

Before leaving the study, she wiped her fingerprints off the phone, a procedure she had followed with every other item she had touched. She checked the other rooms and returned, at last, to the master bedroom. It had occurred to her that she ought to take a closer look at the bathrobes in the closet.

Persistence paid off. One robe, as she saw when she examined it in good light, was monogrammed HB. Of course there were plenty of HBs in the world—Halle Berry and Humphrey Bogart came to mind. But she couldn't see Halle Berry hanging out in this neighborhood, and Bogart was dead.

"Gotcha, Howard," she whispered. "You've been a naughty, naughty boy."

She replaced the robe, then spent a little more time in the bedroom. When she was done, she left the bungalow via the rear door. She drove around the block, parked across the street, rolled down the window, and slunk low in her seat, getting comfortable. She intended to wait awhile and see if Howard and Amanda showed up. Travis had said Howard went out nearly every evening to drive his new car. There was a good chance this address was his nightly destination.

There was no longer any serious doubt in her mind that Howard was the owner of the house, but the issue was too important to rest solely on a monogram. If Howard was indeed the HB in question, she would know three things with certainty: the house was still his, he was cheating on Kris, and he was the owner of the mysterious Trendline. And if Trendline could be tied to Western Regional Resources—well, she would have all her ducks neatly in a row.

She almost hoped it didn't work out that way. Kris had been hurt badly enough already. It would be better for her if neither Trendline nor Amanda Gilbert had any connection with her husband. But Abby wasn't betting on it. The world was not kind.

24

The production meeting for the six o'clock news broke up shortly after 5 P.M. Kris left in a rush, stuffing her yellow legal pad into her carrying case, and boarded the elevator with Amanda Gilbert. The two of them rode to ground level together.

"Another day, another nightmare," Amanda observed.

Kris smiled. "At least no more pint-size pachyderms came into the world at the last minute."

"Still a madhouse. Looks like we won't have time for that heart-to-heart we talked about."

Kris was surprised Amanda even remembered their conversation. Surprised—and touched. She had never imagined Amanda as the type to worry about feelings and personal crises. "Maybe after the show," Kris offered, just to have something to say.

Amanda shook her head. "No can do. I've got a . . . an engagement."

"A date? Is that what you started to say?"

Amanda looked away, embarrassed. This was Kris's second surprise. She had never imagined that Amanda could be capable of embarrassment on any topic.

"You do have a date, don't you? You, the workaholic?" Kris gave her a playful punch on the arm. "Who is he?"

"I'd rather not talk about it."

"You'll talk. This is big stuff. I want to hear all the details."

The elevator doors opened. Amanda got out first, in a hurry to leave. "Can't oblige you now. I've got a show to get on the air."

"Tomorrow, then." Kris stopped her at the door to the newsroom. "You tell me the secrets of your love life, and I'll tell you mine, okay?" She shrugged. "Who knows, maybe we have more in common than we know."

Amanda pushed open the door. "Stranger things have happened."

"Is it a deal?"

"Sure. Deal. Now I've gotta run." She vanished through the doorway.

Kris headed down the hall to her office, smiling. Her marriage was falling apart, but her executive producer had found a boyfriend. Maybe there was a cosmic balance to the universe, as her New Age friends said.

Her office was a large sun-streaked room cluttered with award certificates and statuettes, mementos from other stations where she'd worked, and framed snapshots of herself and Howard in happier times. Ellen, her personal assistant, was typing at her desktop computer. She glanced up when Kris entered. "Hey, boss lady."

"Hey. Stopped by to pick up my outfit."

"Linda dropped it off an hour ago." Ellen nodded toward the door to Kris's dressing room, adjacent to the office. "It's a new one, very snazzy."

Kris found her outfit hanging in the closet. It was a periwinkle blue suit with a cream-colored blouse, a good choice. That particular shade of blue always looked good on camera. Having been in the business for years, Kris knew what worked and what didn't. Solid colors were good; patterns, especially small, complicated patterns, were bad. Off-white tones were good; solid whites were bad.

She changed into the suit, checked herself out in the full-length mirror, and decided she looked quite elegant except for her flat-soled sneakers. Since she was always behind a desk while on the air, no viewer would ever see her footwear.

To complement her outfit, she selected a pair of earrings and a pearl necklace—costume baubles, large and ridiculously ostentatious. Small items of jewelry were distracting on camera; outsized items photographed better. With the jewelry stowed in a plastic bag for later use, she headed out of the office, then paused in the doorway. "How many calls?" she asked.

"Got a stack of message slips, but nothing urgent—"

"No, I mean voicemails . . . from him."

"Oh. Actually, none."

"No calls?"

"Not today." Ellen shrugged. "Maybe he's losing interest."

"I should live so long."

Kris proceeded to the makeup room down the hall. It was strange that Hickle hadn't called. Ordinarily by this time of day he would have left a couple of messages on her voicemail and one or two others with the switchboard. She should have been relieved by his silence. Instead she found it unsettling.

Julia, her makeup artist, and Edward, her hair stylist, were waiting by the barber's chair with impatient expressions. Edward went first. On Mondays he gave her a complete styling. For the rest of the week, a touch-up was all that was required. He did the job quickly, trimming and fluffing and spraying. "Done," he pronounced. "Though, you know, with a shorter 'do—"

"I'm not cutting my hair short."

"All I'm pointing out, Kris dear, is that after a certain age, long hair becomes unfashionable."

"I haven't reached that age." She picked up his scissors and clicked them menacingly. "Tell me that I have, and I'll cut *you* shorter—and I don't mean your hair."

Edward quailed. "I entirely see your point." He departed in haste.

Then it was makeup time. Kris sat patiently, reviewing script changes, as Julia applied a thick coat of Shiseido foundation to every exposed inch of her skin, even the insides of her ears. The blush followed. It seemed that the reworking of her face became more elaborate every month. Soon she would do the news from behind an inch-thick mask of cosmetics, looking as stylized as a geisha. No one would recognize her. She could change her name, move to another city, continue doing the news—and Hickle would never find her.

She tried to smile at this fantasy, but there was nothing funny about Hickle. He hadn't called her at work. Strange . . .

"Julia."

"Mmm hmmm."

"Bring the phone over here, would you? I need to make a call."

Julia obeyed, sulking; like any artist, she resented interruptions. Kris called her home number. When the machine answered, she asked one of the TPS agents to pick up.

"This is Pfeiffer," one of them said.

"Hi, it's me. I wanted to know what the tally is. You know, his phone calls to the house."

"It's zero, ma'am."

"Zero?"

"He hasn't made a peep."

"He hasn't called my work number either. Does that strike you as peculiar?"

"You can never tell with these guys. Tomorrow he could call twenty times."

"I suppose you're right. Okay, thank you." She switched off. Julia asked what that was all about. "My stalker seems to have varied his routine," Kris said.

"Is that bad?"

"I'm not sure."

Julia applied the last cosmetic touches. "You know, I used to think it would be cool to be famous," she said. "Now I have to wonder."

"It has its ups and downs."

Even after her makeup was complete and Julia was gone, Kris remained seated in the chair, thinking about Hickle and his unnatural silence.

"Kris." The floor manager was at the door. "Ten minutes."

"Thanks." She hadn't realized airtime was so near.

She almost left the room, then changed her mind. She picked up the phone and called Travis.

Her fear might be groundless, but it didn't feel that way.

25

Abby passed an hour watching the bungalow in silence. After six o'clock the sky began to darken. By six-thirty a sunset flamed over the rooftops. She thought about leaving. She should get back to Hollywood and see if Hickle was home, but as long as Kris was at KPTI, there was no immediate danger. She decided to wait a little longer.

To use her time more productively she fished her microrecorder out of her purse and dictated notes. She reported her visit to Travis's house, tactfully leaving out the steamy stuff but including everything else, then her unlawful entry to the bungalow and what she'd learned. If she died, she would at least leave an up-to-date record of her activities.

In the hot tub she'd come close to cashing it in, and if things had gone a little differently when she was escaping from Hickle's apartment last night, he might have unloaded his shotgun on her at point-blank range. She had cheated her own mortality twice already. Third time's the charm? she wondered ruefully, and then headlights flared in her rearview mirror.

She sank lower in her seat and watched a black Lexus roll by. As it eased past her car, she glimpsed the driver's profile, lit by the glow of the dashboard. It was Howard. No surprise.

The Lexus pulled into the bungalow's driveway,

and Howard got out to lift the garage door, then parked in the garage. He entered the house via the front door. Lights came on a moment later, but the curtains remained shut.

Abby had seen all she needed to see, but she lingered, curious about Amanda Gilbert, who was sure to show up before long.

At seven-fifteen a white BMW parked at the curb a few doors down. The woman who hurried to the house was slim, almost bony, and quite young. She started to unlock the bungalow's front door with her own key, and then the door opened from inside and Howard ushered her in.

Abby got out of her car and took a stroll, partly to stretch her legs and restore the circulation to her tush, but mainly to check out the BMW. She noted the license plate number and, resting on the dashboard, a parking permit for KPTI stamped with the words *March* and *Employee*. Amanda Gilbert worked at Channel Eight. She was one of Kris's colleagues, and if her car was any indication, she didn't occupy an entry-level position.

Driving out of the neighborhood, heading toward Hollywood, Abby activated her cell phone. She obtained the number of KPTI's switchboard from Information, then called the station. "I have some correspondence for Amanda Gilbert," she said when the receptionist answered. "May I have her exact title, please?"

"Executive Producer," she was told.

"News Division?"

"Yes, that's right."

"Thanks very much." Abby ended the call.

So Amanda was Kris's executive producer. All of a sudden Abby found her dislike of Howard Barwood rising to uncomfortably high levels. She supposed the identity of his illicit paramour shouldn't have made any difference to her assessment of him. Yet it did, because intuitively she knew that it turned him on to be balling Kris's boss, that in doing so he obtained a sense of power and control over his wife that no call girl or receptionist could have provided.

She pulled into a mini-mall and found a pay phone. Her next call was too sensitive to entrust to a cellular transmission. She dialed Travis's office, expecting him to be working late. He answered the phone personally; his assistant had gone home.

"The bungalow is Howard's love nest," she reported, keeping her voice low to be sure she wasn't overheard. "He meets his girlfriend there."

"Who is she?"

"Does it matter? If not, let's leave her name out of it. What's important is that Howard owns the bungalow, which means he owns Trendline, which almost certainly means he's funneling assets overseas without Kris's knowledge."

"Which means he has a motive for getting Kris out of the way."

"True. Marriage has become inconvenient for him. He seems ready for a fresh start. I doubt he's capable of arranging Kris's murder on his own, but when Hickle came along, he may have seen an opportunity." Abby blew out a tired breath. "You remember how concerned he was about my safety, asking if I had backup or if I was on my own? I thought he was being chivalrous or sexist, depending on how you look at it. But maybe not. Maybe he wanted to assess my vulnerability so he could attack me."

"He may have had the opportunity. The guest cottage logs show that he left Malibu at six o'clock on Wednesday evening and didn't return until shortly after midnight—later than usual."

"I was in the hot tub around ten o'clock, ten-thirty."

"It fits. When he failed to finish you off personally, he may have decided to rat you out to Hickle and have him handle it."

"Was he out last night? The phone call reached Hickle around eight-thirty."

"Howard was out from six-thirty to eleven."

"Okay, then he might have spent the first part of the evening at the bungalow. After that, he called Hickle, using his Western Regional phone because he didn't know if Hickle's phone was tapped, and he figured it would be harder to link the cell phone to him. Speaking of which—"

Travis cut in. "We're still trying to nail down a connection between Western Regional and Trendline. Nothing so far, but I've got two of my computer jocks burning up their high-speed modems. They're pros. They can nose out anybody's secrets."

Even mine? Abby wondered, but what she said was "How about Hickle? Any escalation in his attempts to contact Kris?"

"Just the opposite. A total shutdown. No phone calls to her home or office all day. Kris is worried."

"She should be. You'd better tighten her security."

"I will. Where are you now?"

"Heading back to Hollywood. Don't try to stop me."

"I wouldn't dare." She heard him sigh. "Good luck, Abby. And watch yourself, all right?"

"Always do," she said.

The lights in Hickle's apartment were on when she reached the Gainford Arms, and his Volkswagen was in its assigned space, at the opposite end of the parking lot from her own. She was glad he was home. At least he wasn't in Malibu, lying in ambush outside the Barwoods' house.

She rode the elevator to the fourth floor. As she was fumbling with the key to her door, Hickle emerged from his apartment next door. "There you are," he said.

The first thing she noticed was that his right hand was positioned awkwardly behind his back, concealing something. Her mind inventoried the possibilities: shotgun, handgun, jar of battery acid.

She still hadn't unlocked her door—she was trapped in the hall, Hickle two feet away—and the .38 Smith in her purse was not instantly accessible.

Hickle was smiling, but it was a tight, false smile. "I've been waiting for you," he said.

"Really?" She shifted her purse, placing two fingers on the clasp.

"Yeah. I've got sort of a surprise." He stepped forward, his right hand swinging into view.

She saw what he'd been concealing, and it wasn't acid or a gun or a weapon of any kind. It was a bulky paper sack emblazoned with *"Shanghai Palace."*

"Hope you haven't eaten yet," Hickle said. "I ordered Chinese."

26

Abby kept smiling as she admitted Hickle to her apartment, and she emitted the appropriate exclamations of delight when he removed the food from the bag and filled the kitchen with its medley of aromas. "Sweet and sour pork," he announced, "almond chicken, and—because I know you like veggie meals—broccoli with black mushrooms."

"Sounds great," she said, still smiling, smiling. But she didn't like this situation, didn't like it at all. Hickle was a profoundly antisocial man, not the type to press for close friendship with anyone. He was too insecure, too scared of women, of people in general, to take the initiative so boldly unless he had a compelling, hidden motive.

Maybe he was planning an attack in the privacy of her apartment. Or he might have doctored the food—the veggie dish, the one he'd bought for her. Might have put poison in it, or a sedative.

One thing was certain. This was no casual get-together. It was a chess move, a tactic in a deadly serious contest of strategy, and she had a sense that it was perilously close to the endgame.

"Still warm," Hickle said, touching the sealed containers. "I hope it wasn't presumptuous of me to order this stuff without asking you."

"Not at all."

"I just thought . . . well, I enjoyed our dinner last night."

"Me too."

"I guess I don't get out as often as I should."

"I don't know if dinner in my apartment exactly constitutes getting out."

"Is it a problem, eating in here? We could use my place if you want."

She thought about taking the opening he had offered, but if he had trouble in mind, he could strike as easily in his place as in hers. "*Mi casa es su casa*," she said. "Let me get the windows open, okay? It's gotten stuffy."

She raised the windows in both rooms, checking to be sure her surveillance gear was safely concealed behind the closed door of the bedroom closet, then deposited her purse on the coffee table by the sofa. She hated to be separated from her gun, but it wouldn't look natural to hold on to her purse while at home. Anyway, it was within close reach.

"Now I'll get out some plates"—she nudged him aside to reach the cabinet—"you set 'em up on the coffee table, and we'll chow down."

"Sounds like a plan." He seemed lighthearted, almost droll, which worried her because she knew it was an act.

Rummaging in the cabinet, she became aware of her deficiencies as a hostess, at least in these temporary quarters. She lacked napkins, china, glassware, and metal utensils, as well as any beverages other than bottled water.

"I'm afraid we'll have to dine picnic style," she told him. "Styrofoam plates, plastic cups and forks, paper towels as placemats and napkins. And if you want anything to drink besides water, you'll have to grab it from your fridge. Sorry."

"Water's fine with me."

"I'll try a little of the pork and chicken if you don't mind." She spooned the meals onto the plates. "I'm not a strict vegetarian. And why don't you take a little of the broccoli?" If he had tampered with the veggie portion, he might find a way to decline the offer.

"That'll be great," Hickle answered calmly.

Maybe the food was okay, then. She sat next to him on the sofa, balancing the picnic plate in her lap. For a few minutes there was nothing to say. Ordinarily Abby was a skilled mechanic when it came to fixing a stalled conversation. She knew how to lubricate the gears and recharge the battery and get things moving again. Tonight her mind seemed frozen. She knew why. She was not in control of this encounter. She was not the only one keeping secrets this time.

She ate the meat dishes exclusively until she saw Hickle sampling the veggie meal. He seemed to have no reservations about eating it. She saw him chew and swallow. Her fear of poisoning receded. Even so, she wasn't very hungry.

"Anything on TV?" Hickle asked.

"I don't think so."

"You watch it much?"

"A little."

"Like what?"

"Nothing special. Sometimes one of those magazine shows, you know, like *Dateline*." She had never watched *Dateline* in her life, but she had the impression that it was on nearly every night, so it must be popular. "How about you? You have any favorite shows?"

He hesitated. "I like to watch the local news."

She was almost sure he was studying her reaction. She played it cool, showing a slight frown of distaste. "The news? Isn't that depressing?"

"I think it's good to, uh, stay informed—you know, about the community."

Yes, she thought, you're very civic-minded. "But there's so much crime."

"Crime is part of life. Without people who break the rules, where would we be?"

"The Garden of Eden?"

"Maybe, but what's the point of living in paradise if you're not really living? Know what I mean?"

She speared a chunk of broccoli with her plastic fork. "Tell me."

"Okay, here's the thing. Adam and Eve were only going through the motions, see. They were content to just exist. They didn't strive for anything. They never sought out their—well, their destiny."

"Do you believe in destiny?"

"Yes, I do."

"What is destiny, do you think?"

"Destiny . . ." Hickle drew a slow, thoughtful breath. "Destiny is like what happened with Dante and Beatrice. You know that story?"

"Not really."

"Dante became a great poet, but his destiny was set when he was nine. That was when he saw a girl from afar, a girl his own age. Her name was Beatrice. He fell in love, dedicated his life to her. Years later, when he was in his forties and Beatrice was dead, he wrote an epic poem in tribute to her. She lives on through his art. She was his destiny, I think—even though they were never lovers, never even friends. Still, she was meant for him, and finally she was his, not in life, but in death."

"I see," Abby said softly.

He must have heard doubt in her tone. "You don't agree with me, do you? You don't think it's destiny?"

"I think . . ." Abby calculated the risk of honesty, then looked directly at him. "I think it sounds like a kind of madness, Raymond."

He stiffened but forced himself to smile. "The kind of madness that breaks all the rules," he said evenly. "So I guess we're back where we started."

"Crime, you mean." Abby looked away, breaking eye contact. It was not good to challenge him. "Where there's crime, there's usually punishment."

"Some people aren't afraid of punishment."

"Maybe they should be."

He was silent, pensive. She forced herself to eat another few bites of her dinner. It had been a gamble to raise the issue of punishment. She had no idea how he would react. With violence, maybe, or simply by withdrawing into a sulk.

She thought she was ready for anything, but when he spoke, his question surprised her. "Did you really come here from Riverside?"

"Sure," she said, holding her voice steady.

"And you had a fiancé who cheated on you?"

"Yes, I did." She didn't like being interrogated. She tried to turn the tables. "Why would you ask?"

"Sometimes I have the feeling you're not what you seem."

Not good. How to respond? With a smile. "Then what am I?"

He smiled also, but it was a smile without humor.

"An image. An illusion. Or maybe what I said the first time we met: an actress."

"I told you, I'm a girl trying to get her head together after a bad breakup. Nothing more complicated than that."

"Everything is more complicated than that." He studied her openly, his food forgotten. She knew he had more to say, and she waited for it. "Do you know how it feels," he asked finally, "to want to believe in something . . . or someone . . . when you're not sure you can?"

She saw what looked like anguish in his face and almost pitied him. "I know how it feels. But there are times when you've got to believe."

"Why?"

"Because relationships are built on trust." She thought of Travis when she said it, Travis with his stash of CDs.

Hickle shifted closer to her on the sofa. She could feel him trembling, but whether it was a signal of fear or rage or some other feeling she couldn't guess. "You trusted your fiancé," he said, "and he lied to you."

"Not everybody lies."

"I think they do."

He leaned toward her, and she felt the heat coming off his body and knew his pulse was racing. He might be preparing to strike. She almost tensed in anticipation of a fight, but if she did, he would sense it.

"I think," Hickle said slowly, his voice dropping to a whisper, "everybody lies all the time. We all put on an act. We hide from view."

"Including you?" she asked.

"Yes."

"And me?"

224

"I think so, Abby."

"So you don't trust me." She put no judgment in the words.

"I'd like to, I really would."

"But you don't."

"Should I?"

"Of course you should. I'm trying to be your friend."

"What else are you?"

"Nothing else."

She saw the intensity building in his gaze. "Who are you, really?" he whispered.

Her purse was on the coffee table, but to reach it she would have to spring forward, and with Hickle pressed against her, she wasn't sure she could. "I'm your friend, Raymond." She knew he wasn't buying it. "Just your friend." If he had any kind of weapon, she was dead.

"My friend."

"Yes."

"I hope so," he said, leaning nearer, closing the distance between them, and he kissed her.

It was the briefest kiss, a gentle meeting of the lips, and Abby knew it was unplanned, an act of impulse. She did not resist or respond. Hickle was the one who pulled back in a violent recoil that upset the plate in his lap.

"Sorry," he mumbled. "I shouldn't have—didn't mean to—"

Abby didn't know whether to feel relieved or embarrassed, but she was suddenly sure he posed no immediate threat. "It's okay, Raymond," she said soothingly. "Forget about it. It's okay."

He looked away, his face flushed scarlet, and then he

saw the multicolored stain painted on the sofa by his spilled chicken and pork.

"Uh oh," Abby said, following his gaze. "Looks like it's wet cleanup time."

"I'll take care of it."

"We'll do it together. Wait here." She busied herself in the kitchen, wetting paper towels under a stream of tap water. When she returned to the sofa, she saw Hickle standing near the coffee table, nervously shifting his weight like a boy who had to go to the bathroom. Whatever his intentions had been in coming here, kissing her had not been on the agenda.

He took the towels from her and blotted up the mess. "I'm sorry," he said again.

"Don't worry about it. The furniture's not even mine. Besides, it looks like you got rid of the stain."

"I think so." Hickle put down the towels and began edging toward the door. "Guess I'd better be going. It's late."

"Only nine." Suddenly she didn't want him to go. He'd reached out to her in his clumsy way. She wanted to explore the new path he'd opened for her.

"I'm kind of tired." He put his hand on the doorknob.

She tried stalling. "There's some leftovers for you to take."

"You keep them. It'll make a good lunch." He fumbled the door open and stepped into the hall.

"Raymond, if you ever want to talk to me . . . about anything . . . drop by, okay?"

He didn't look back. "I'll keep that in mind. Thanks."

Then the door was shut and she was alone. Abby wished he hadn't fled. There had been a chance for a dialogue, a breakthrough. It was an opportunity that might not present itself again.

Hickle stood unmoving in the hallway for a long time, thinking of one thing only.

He had kissed her. Kissed her mouth.

He hadn't meant to. Nor had he meant to ask most of the questions he'd asked. He'd simply been unable to stop himself. It was as if he'd been carried along on a current of energy that flowed between Abby and himself, with no willpower of his own, no self-control.

He let himself into his apartment, then paced the living room. After a while it occurred to him that he was hungry. He'd managed to eat only a few bites with Abby so near to him on the couch. In the kitchen he fried up some beans and ate them out of a bowl, washing them down with Coca-Cola. Eating calmed him.

He had made a fool of himself, but she hadn't seemed to mind. She had smiled kindly and offered to be there if he needed to talk. She had said she was his friend. He wished he could believe her. But the words from last night's e-mail message still scrolled through his memory: *Her job is to get close to men like yourself, learn their secrets, and report what she finds.*

He finished his meal, wandered into the bedroom, and sat on his bed, shoulders slumping. He still didn't know if Abby was his friend or his betrayer. But he could find out. It was easy now, as easy as the press of a button.

Hickle reached into his pants pocket and took out the item he had snatched from Abby's purse.

There had been other things in the purse, things he'd barely had time to notice in his brief, frantic rummaging. A lightweight revolver—suspicious but not conclusive; in LA many women armed themselves. A wallet containing a driver's license that bore the name Abby Gallagher and an address in Riverside—it meant nothing; ID could be faked. A pair of small tools, their purpose unidentifiable.

The last item he'd found had been the one he wanted. He had slipped it into his pocket and backed away from the coffee table just before she emerged from the kitchen with the wet towels. He held it now in the palm of his hand.

A microcassette recorder with a tape inside, partially used. He touched Rewind, and the tape began to run back.

If she was keeping secrets, he would find them on the tape. Her ruminations and reminders, her notes to herself. All he had to do was listen.

The tape kept rewinding. It made a low hiss as it turned.

He wondered if he wanted to play it. Maybe he would be better off not knowing. If he could accept Abby as what she claimed to be, if he could put away all doubt and suspicion, wouldn't he be happier?

He weighed the tape recorder in his hand, as if weighing the choice it represented. Then his finger pressed the button marked Play.

From the small speaker came Abby's voice, faint as a whisper. Hickle stretched out on the bed, the tape recorder inches from his ear, and listened.

27

"Where is this going to lead?"

Howard Barwood paused in the act of pulling on his pants. He looked at Amanda, naked in bed. "I told you," he said, "I intend for us to be together."

"When?"

"When Kris is out of the picture."

"I'm a cynical big-city gal, Howie. And I'm starting to wonder if that's ever going to happen."

"It'll happen." He tugged his pants up around his waist and fastened the buckle. He hated it when she called him Howie.

The bedside lamp was the only light in the room. It was fitted with a three-way reading bulb, but the two higher wattages had burned out, and only the lowest setting was still functional. The bulb cast a wan, sallow glow over half the bedroom, leaving the far corners in shadow.

"You know," Amanda went on as if he hadn't spoken, "I'm starting to sense a certain proclivity toward procrastination on your part. You've had months to tell her."

"There are other considerations."

"Such as?"

"The timing of certain financial transactions." It seemed safe to tell her that much.

"Sounds very mysterious," Amanda purred, "and disturbingly nonspecific."

"Let's just say we're not going to be poor."

"Was that ever an issue?"

"Poor is a relative term. Poor by my standards might be rich by somebody else's. We'll have all we need."

"And what will Kris have?"

Howard turned away. "You don't have to worry about Kris."

He found his shirt and shrugged it on. He felt better when he was not bare-chested. As a younger man he had been proud of his muscular torso, but now his pecs were sagging and his abdomen had loosened as his waistline expanded. He was out of shape. He didn't like to look in the mirror anymore. Or maybe there were other reasons why he preferred not to look at himself.

Outside, the siren of an emergency vehicle—police car, ambulance, fire engine—caterwauled down some nearby street. Sirens were a constant background noise in this neighborhood. Howard thought of the crash of the surf on the Malibu sand, the only noise he ever heard from the deck of the beach house, and briefly he wondered what he was doing in this place.

Well, it was a little late to be asking that question, wasn't it? Already he had set in motion a chain of events that would free him from his marital obligations and his life in Malibu. At times he might regret the course he'd taken, but he could not undo what he had done. There was no turning back.

"What?" Amanda asked.

He realized he had spoken the last thought aloud. "Nothing," he said, buttoning his shirt.

"Okay, be secretive. It's irritating, but manly in a reserved, nineteenth-century sort of way."

She rolled onto her side, showing her back to him. Tattooed above the left cheek of her buttocks was a red rose. Howard had been fascinated the first time he'd seen it. He had been with many women, but never one with a tattoo. It had seemed exotic and arousing. Now he regarded it with indifference and the faintest touch of condescension. He wondered if he regarded Amanda herself the same way.

No, of course not. Where had that thought come from? He was serious about Amanda. She was exactly what he needed. She was young. She had energy, ambition, confidence. She talked fast and proposed a thousand ideas an hour. And she was—what was the word?—adventurous. Sexually adventurous, not to put too fine a point on it. She did things with enthusiasm, things Kris would have been reluctant or unwilling to do at all.

He remembered his first night with Amanda—how she had teased his pants down around his knees and taken him into her mouth, drawing him out to full extension with her tongue, and in that moment he had been twenty years old again, not a man in middle age with hair on his earlobes and a potbelly that left him winded when he climbed a flight of stairs.

Not that their whole relationship was about sex. Far from it. They had conversations. Take tonight, for instance. He had talked with her for most of the evening over an anchovy pizza and a bottle of Merlot. Only afterward had they retreated into the bedroom for a different kind of intimacy. What he was doing with Amanda was no cheap fling. It was an affair of the heart. It had to be.

Yawning elaborately, Amanda slipped out of bed and brushed past him into the bathroom. She poured a glass of water and drank a long swallow before fussing with her hair. Unlike him, she had no problem with mirrors. He liked the trim economy of her body, her small breasts with their stiff nipples, her tight thighs and the tight space between them, a space he had grown to know well over the past six months.

He had met her during a visit to KPTI, months ago. He had flirted, she'd responded. He was incapable of resisting temptation. Sometimes he told himself that Kris must have been familiar with his weakness, and if she had chosen to marry him anyway, she had known what was she getting into. As a rationalization it was not much good, but it was the best he could do.

The truth was that he had loved Kris once, but the feeling had ebbed. He supposed she'd been right when she said that for him, a woman's novelty wore off and she became another discarded toy. But there were always more toys to be bought if a man had the money . . . and if his previous possessions didn't weigh him down.

"She suspects, you know," Amanda said from the bathroom.

Howard, who had been hunting for his shoes amid the tangled bedspread on the floor, looked up in bewilderment. "What did you say?"

"She thinks you may be having an affair. She told me so."

The world seemed to freeze around him, or maybe it was simply that his breath froze in his chest. "When?"

"Yesterday. It was True Confessions time, at least for her." Amanda smirked, then turned grave. "I shouldn't find it funny. After all, she is my friend in some sense of the word."

She stood nude in the bathroom doorway, hips

cocked, arms akimbo. Her collarbone stood out against the pallor of her skin. She was not as pretty as Kris, Howard thought irrelevantly. But she was young. "Why didn't you tell me before now?" he asked.

An insouciant shrug. "Slipped my mind."

"Well, what did she say, exactly?"

"She thinks you're fooling around. I promised her a heart-to-heart talk, but I didn't follow through. It would be like a cat playing with a mouse. There might be a certain sadistic pleasure in it, but it's not the sort of entertainment calculated to raise your self-esteem."

"No." His voice was flat. "I guess not."

"I'm not saying she knows anything for sure. She has a hunch, that's all—feminine intuition or whatever. Anyway, it's good, isn't it?"

Good. What a word for her to use. "Is it?"

"It makes it easier for you to tell her about us." A frown pinched her face. "You *are* going to tell her, aren't you, Howie?"

"At the appropriate time." He knew it sounded perfunctory, and that she would be angry.

She was. "I sincerely hope you're not getting the proverbial cold feet. I've taken a serious risk, you know. Your wife has more clout with the station than I do. She's the bionic newsbabe, the six-million-dollar girl. What I'm trying to say is, she could get me canned, and if I don't have anything to fall back on . . ."

He held up a placating hand. "You'll have plenty to fall back on. And you won't be fired. It's not going to work out that way."

"So how is it going to work out?"

"For the best." Howard sighed, suddenly tired. "By the way, you're not the only one who's taken a risk."

"No? What have you ever done, besides show up with a bulge in your trousers?"

"I've done more than you know. More than you need to know. Now where are my goddamned shoes? I have to get—" *Home,* he almost said but caught himself. "I have to get going."

The time was almost ten o'clock, and it would take him an hour to get to Malibu from here. Kris would arrive at the beach house around midnight, and he wanted to be there well before she arrived. It had been awkward the other night, when he had come home later than usual, and she had already been there.

She had asked him questions then—questions about his imaginary drive up the coast, and about how restless and agitated he seemed. Of course she suspected him. It was obvious now, though at the time he hadn't allowed himself to see it.

Well, it didn't matter. It was too late for her, no matter what she suspected. Things were moving quickly to a conclusion, and soon everything would be resolved once and for all.

He found the shoes in one of the dark corners the lamplight couldn't reach. When he bent to slip them on, involuntarily he grunted, an old-man noise. He hated making noises like that.

Amanda was his ticket to youth. Or if not Amanda, then some new companion, younger still and lacking any tattoos.

But not Kris. Kris was the past. Kris was a dead weight dragging him down.

He had to be rid of her. He would be.

Soon.

28

After Hickle left, Abby opened her bedroom closet. The VCR and audio deck had been recording continually, but the TV was off, the audio console muted.

She turned on the monitor and speakers, then sat on the floor in a sloppy lotus position, resting her back against the bed, watching the monitor. She saw Hickle pace his living room before fixing a meal in the kitchen. She wondered if eating was a response to stress or if he simply hadn't had enough dinner.

He ate standing in the kitchen, almost out of camera range. When he was done, he left the cookware in the sink and went into the bedroom. She checked her watch. It was 9:40. Kris's newscast would start in twenty minutes. She assumed he wouldn't miss it.

But he didn't emerge from the bedroom. The surveillance microphone picked up no sounds of activity. She waited, feeling a new, prickling intimation of trouble.

Another glance at her watch. Nearly ten o'clock. Still no sign of him. Strange. Ominous. If any part of his daily routine was sacrosanct, it was the ritual of watching Kris at six and ten.

"What's going on, Raymond?" she whispered. "What are you up to?"

She increased the volume. Dimly she made out a

sound, something low and regular and ongoing, hard to identify. A murmur.

Was he running an electric fan? She didn't remember seeing one. Anyway, this sound had a different quality than a motor noise. It wavered, fluctuated.

She leaned close to the speakers, maxing out the volume, but the noise floor—the ambient hiss that was part of any acoustical environment—rose to a high, steady sizzle, and the murmuring sound was barely more distinct than before.

"He fastened on Kris because she represents his feminine ideal, what he calls *the look*. She exists in Hickle's mind as a mature, perfected version of Jill Dahlbeck, who was also a blue-eyed blonde. But this time he's chosen a woman unlike Jill in every other respect—a celebrity, married, rich, famous, older than he is. He wants her to be unattainable. He wants to pursue her and fail, because his humiliation will give him the excuse he needs to destroy her and destroy himself . . ."

Supine on the bed, Hickle listened. Pain cramped his belly. Slowly he rolled on his side and contracted into a fetal curl.

"What is Kris Barwood to him, really? She's his fantasy lover, his dream wife, and not to get all Freudian about it, his mother too—an older authority figure who has a home and a husband. She represents all aspects of the female presence in the world, from erotic temptress to domestic companion to nurturing parent. And she's big enough to play all these roles—larger than life, in fact. Her face appears on TV sets, billboards, magazine covers. She's everywhere. She is Woman. Lashing out at her, Hickle will strike at the archetype of the other sex, the sex he hates and fears. No *vive la difference* for him."

Abby's voice, coolly analytical, dissecting him. No, vivisecting. That was when the surgery was performed on a living body. Sometimes it was done without anesthesia—nothing to deaden the pain.

"He has zero concern for Kris as a human being, because to him she's not a human being, only a symbol. Hickle lives in a world of symbols and images and fantasies, connected to society only through the TV set and *People* magazine. I guess he's not much different from a lot of us these days, and I might even feel sorry for him if he didn't pose a measurable threat . . ."

Feel sorry for him. Feel sorry.

Who was she to say that, to pass judgment on him? She was the one who ought to be ashamed of who she was and what she did. She was the one who made up stories about a failed relationship and bumped into him in the laundry room and got him to talk about the TV news. She was the one who burrowed her way into other people's lives and poked around and uncovered secrets. She was a liar and a snitch and a sneak and a conniving little whore, and what she deserved . . . what she deserved . . .

The shotgun.

That was what she deserved, yes, the shotgun, absolutely.

Hickle sat up, ignoring the cassette as it continued to play.

She was a goddamned bitch. She had deceived him, manipulated him, served as a tool of his enemies, spied on him and reported to Kris. And she had done it so skillfully that if not for his friend JackBNimble, he might never have known.

His anonymous informer hiding behind a nursery-rhyme name was the only person he could trust, the only person who had been honest with him all along. Every item of information Jack had passed on had proven true. Every word of advice had been sound. And he had told Hickle what to do, hadn't he? Hadn't he?

First Abby, then Kris.

The two of them—dead.

Now, without further delay.

He got off the bed and unlocked his bedroom closet. He took out his duffel bag and unzipped it, removing the shotgun. He checked to be sure it was loaded.

Blammo. No more Abby.

Blammo. No more Kris.

Everything would come to its proper end tonight. He would win, and they would lose.

The tape kept playing, Abby's voice a whisper amid the folds of his bedspread, but he didn't need to hear it anymore.

To isolate the mystery noise, Abby first used the lowpass filter on her audio deck to remove all frequencies higher than eight kilohertz. This cut off part of the hiss but not enough. She fiddled with the ten-band graphic equalizer, pulling down the sliders on the higher frequencies while boosting the midrange tones.

She tried to minimize the hiss without losing the murmur. It was hard. The two sounds were at similar frequencies. But as she made fine adjustments, the murmur came through a bit more sharply, and she identified it as a voice.

Was Hickle muttering to himself under his breath?

She didn't think so. Maybe he was listening to the radio, but she didn't recall seeing a radio in his bedroom.

Then she heard new noises. She paused, kneeling on the floor alongside the console, her ear close to the speakers.

Creak of the bed, thump of footsteps. A door opening. Something being dragged briefly on the floor.

"What are you up to, Raymond?" she breathed.

Footsteps again. She glanced expectantly at the monitor, but he did not enter the living room.

Then a rattle of activity, a thump that was not a footfall . . . and silence except for the lingering room-tone hiss and, behind it, the murmuring sound that might have been a voice.

The frequency of the human voice falls mainly between 1.5 and 2.5 kilohertz. She boosted this range, rolling off the higher frequencies, and the background hiss dropped away, leaving the mystery sound isolated and distinct.

It was her own voice.

". . . all depends on whether or not he has the nerve to follow through on what has been, until now, only a detailed fantasy of violent revenge . . ."

The thoughts she'd dictated into her microrecorder.

Hickle must have taken the recorder, stolen it.

He was listening to the tape.

He knew everything.

Abby's gun was in her purse, and her purse was in the living room. She twisted upright, spun away from the closet—

Too late.

Framed in her bedroom window was Hickle. On the fire escape, shotgun in his hands.

He swept the barrel toward her. She ducked behind the bed, denying him a clear shot, but she'd bought herself no more than a couple of seconds. The window was open. He only had to punch through the screen and climb in.

Distantly it occurred to her that the last question on her mental checklist had been answered.

Would fear deter Hickle from taking action?

It would not.

Prone on the floor, she heard the crunch of the wire mesh, the rattle of the screen as it fell out of the frame. The unidentified noises from his bedroom—she understood them now—rattle of the screen being removed, thump of the screen as it fell. He had slipped through his window onto the fire escape.

Now he was climbing into her bedroom. She heard the rustle of his clothes.

Had to get past him, reach her revolver in the living room. If she left cover, he would kill her with one shot.

Okay, so crawl under the bed. She might have time to wriggle out the other side before he figured out where she'd gone.

Good plan, except the bed was too low—she couldn't squirm under it.

She was trapped, and he was coming, his footsteps vibrating through the floorboards.

Her only chance was to fight. She had been trained to respond to an attack from a position of disadvantage, and if her current circumstances didn't qualify as a position of disadvantage, nothing would.

As Hickle came around the bed, she sprang to her feet and ducked under the shotgun's barrel, then brought up her right arm with her hand closed to the second finger joint and aimed a straight blow at his larynx.

He dodged, she delivered a glancing strike to the side of his neck, and he stumbled back, raising the gun.

She snapped a kick at his right arm. It caught him near the elbow.

His fingers splayed. The shotgun fell.

Before he could pick it up—finish him.

She let out a yell of rage and drove her open palm at his face, but he darted sideways, the strike missed, and now she was off balance.

He seized her by the hair and flung her onto the bed, then dipped out of sight and came up with the shotgun in his hands.

She tried to scramble clear, but already he was on top of her, the shotgun muzzle in her face.

"They'll hear you," she gasped. "Fire one shot and everybody in the building will hear."

The words had come out of nowhere, and she didn't think they had reached him.

There would be a flex of his index finger, and her life would be gone. She braced for it.

He didn't shoot.

The shotgun withdrew a few inches.

She waited.

"That's a good point, Abby," Hickle said so softly that she could barely hear him above her roaring pulse. "If that's your real name. Is it?"

"Yes."

"Good. That's one thing you didn't lie about."

"We have to talk, Raymond."

"So talk."

She licked her lips. She smelled lubricant on the

shotgun's muzzle. Absurdly it made her want to sneeze. "Could you put that thing down? I think I'm allergic to it."

He took a step away from the bed, shifting his grip to hold the gun by the barrel, not the stock.

"Okay," she said. "It looks like you found me out."

"Looks like."

"You're smart, Raymond. I underestimated you."

"Yes."

"Now that I know how smart you are, things will be different. I can be straight with you."

"Go ahead, tell me what's going on."

"I will. I'll tell you everything." She was starting to get matters under control. She'd had a bad moment there, but it had passed, and now she had options, possibilities.

She sat up, choosing her next words with care, and Hickle slammed down the shotgun on the back of her skull.

29

Abby fell off the bed and collapsed on the floor. She shuddered once, then did not move again.

"No more lies, whore," Hickle whispered.

He stood over her, wary of a trick. She could be playing possum, though he doubted it. The shotgun's buttstock had clipped her pretty good. Even so, he kept a tight grip on the gun as he crouched beside her and peeled back one eyelid. Her eye was rolled up in the socket. She was out cold. Breathing, though. Still alive. Well, not for long.

She'd been right about firing the shotgun in a crowded apartment building. Had he been thinking more clearly, he would have recognized the danger himself. But there were other ways to kill her. Cut her throat with a kitchen knife. Yes, that would do it. He was halfway out of the bedroom before he remembered that all her eating utensils were plastic.

Break her neck, then. He knelt and gripped her by the throat, tensing for a lethal twist of his wrists, but something in him recoiled from the hands-on intimacy of the act. There had to be another way.

Suffocation. He could smother her.

He turned toward the bed, reaching for a pillow, then stopped.

Beyond the bed was the closet, the door standing open, a cache of electronic gear inside. In the frenzy of his attack and its aftermath, he hadn't even noticed the stuff.

It seemed odd to have audiovisual equipment set up in a closet, and what was odder still was that the image on the TV screen was his own living room.

How could his living room be on TV?

Then he understood that he was looking at a closed circuit broadcast. The TV must be receiving a signal from a camera Abby had planted.

But that meant she had been inside his apartment. She had broken in, bugged the place. Then she had sat and watched him when he thought he was alone.

"Watched me," he breathed. It seemed horrible, obscene.

Stiffly he approached the closet. Beneath the TV was a VCR, recording the live video feed. Next to it, an audio console, tape reels turning. When he'd talked to himself as he often did, she must have recorded his voice. She knew his every thought. She hadn't simply invaded his life in the obvious ways. She had intruded on his most private moments, his solitude. She had watched and listened and recorded it all.

A new thought struck him. An awful thought. When exactly had she been in his apartment? Before or after he'd sneaked into the laundry room? Because if it was after . . .

Then she would have seen the thing he stole out of the washing machine. The white high-cut panties that had once been worn on her body. Her panties.

She would have seen them, would have known he'd taken them, would have guessed what he wanted them for.

Or maybe . . . maybe she didn't need to guess. Maybe she had set up a camera in his bedroom as well.

Maybe it had an infrared lens, so she could watch him in the dark.

Had she watched him late last night, when he had taken those panties into his bed, when he had used them the way other men used pornographic pictures? Had she seen that? Had she gotten it on tape?

Rage seized him.

He pawed at the VCR's Eject button, cracked open the cassette, pulled ribbons of tape off the spool in tangled handfuls.

Maybe she had recorded the sound effects too—the creaking of his mattress springs, the low shudders of his breath.

He wrenched loose the audiotape reels, unwinding them, spewing tape everywhere until the reels dropped from his shaking hands.

Useless. He'd accomplished nothing. Somebody could wind the tape back onto the spools and view the video, hear the sound.

Objectively he knew it didn't matter what anybody saw or heard. There was a good chance he would die in his assault on Kris. Even if he lived, he would be arrested, his guilt undeniable.

Still, he couldn't stand the thought of strangers having a window into his most personal moments. Watching him like an exhibit at a sideshow. Laughing at his perversity. Or worse, feeling sorry for him, feeling pity for the sick, lonely freak.

No. He would make sure that nobody ever saw or heard the tapes. He would get rid of the goddamned things, erase them or something.

But first he would remove the bugs she'd planted. He couldn't let anybody see what she had done.

He confirmed that Abby was still unconscious, then

returned to his apartment via the fire escape. He searched his living room first. The TV camera's vantage point had clearly shown that it was stationed above the couch. He pried loose the smoke detector and found a lens and transmitter, but no microphone. He stomped the camera under his heel and scanned the room for a microphone's likely hiding place. The telephone? He turned the phone upside down, saw what might be a bug of some kind, and battered the phone to pieces against the kitchen counter.

There could be other bugs in the room. He peered behind the couch, behind the TV, in his kitchen cabinets, in the refrigerator. He didn't even know what he was looking for. An eavesdropping device might be in front of his face and he wouldn't recognize it. The tricky little bitch might have planted a dozen microphones or a hundred. He had no way to know.

He stumbled into the bedroom. Had she planted a mike in here too, or had she listened through the shared wall with a stethoscope? And what about that second camera? There could be a hidden lens peering at him through a pinhole in one of his pictures of Kris. He tore down the pictures. No camera. No microphone. There had to be something. She wouldn't have bugged one room and not the other. He must have overlooked it. He searched under the bed, behind the nightstand. He unscrewed the base of his table lamp. Nothing.

"Where is it? Where did you hide it, you whore?" His voice was an octave higher than normal.

Given a day or two, he could find everything she'd planted. But he didn't have a day or even an hour. He had to strike against Kris tonight. Delay would wreck his chances. When Abby failed to report, her colleagues would know something was wrong. They would come after him. Even if he evaded arrest, Kris would be protected behind additional layers of security, and he would never be able to reach her.

It was nearly ten-thirty. Kris would leave the KPTI studios in an hour or so. She would arrive home after midnight. He had to be there when her car pulled into the driveway of the beach house. To stay on schedule, he must leave soon. But he hadn't debugged his apartment. He hadn't erased the tapes.

"There's no time." Hickle spun in circles. He couldn't undo all that Abby had done. But neither could he leave it for the police to find.

Destroy it, then. Destroy it all—everything in both apartments—every trace of it.

"All right," he whispered, regaining some measure of self-control as a plan took shape in his mind. "All right, yes, it'll work, it'll be fine."

Before leaving his apartment, he gathered all the items he would need for that night's work, both there and in Malibu. He removed his duffel bag from the closet and stuffed his rifle inside. With its scope and laser sighting system, the HK 770 had been a costly investment, and he intended to have it with him as a backup should the shotgun fail.

What else was required? Extra ammo for both firearms. A flashlight. A jacket—the night was cool. He shrugged on his navy blue windbreaker. The dark color would provide camouflage.

And the padlock and chain that had secured the closet. He took those with him, along with the duffel. He left his apartment, climbing through the window, never looking back.

The TV monitor in Abby's bedroom was now a sheet

of static. Abby remained unconscious. Hickle nudged her with his foot. She didn't stir.

He knelt by her for a minute or two, then turned his attention to the bedroom windows. The screen had been ruined by his forced entry, but the glass pane was intact. He closed and locked the window, then sealed the living room window as well.

The apartment was now airtight. Crouching, he checked the furnace's pilot light and saw its blue flame.

Now for the hard part. Muscles straining, he wrestled the oven away from the kitchen wall until he heard a metallic pop and a hiss of gas. The coupling on the gas inlet pipe had ruptured. Gas was flooding in from the main supply line. It smelled like rotten eggs. The gas was a bomb. The pilot light was the fuse. When the gas reached critical concentration . . .

"Blammo," Hickle whispered.

Half the fourth floor would be obliterated. Abby's apartment and his own place next door and, with luck, nosy Mrs. Finley in apartment 422—all gone in a white-hot explosive flash. He had wanted to erase the tapes. This was one way to do it. As a bonus, he would erase all vestiges of his former life . . . and, oh yes, Abby too.

He added his shotgun to the duffel and headed into the hall, shutting Abby's door behind him. Quickly to the elevator, then down to the lobby and across the parking lot, running hard.

One thought galvanized him as he ran. He was doing this, really doing it. After months of delay he'd found his nerve.

Hickle stashed the duffel on the passenger seat of

his VW, slipped behind the wheel, keyed the ignition. The dashboard clock glowed 10:59.

At this very moment the late news on Channel Eight was ending, and Kris Barwood would be signing off for the last time.

30

Kris saw Travis across the soundstage as she and Matt Dale wrapped up the ten o'clock news.

Travis had not come to KPTI in months. His presence rattled her, and she stumbled during her closing remarks. Matt saved her with a joke, allowing both of them to beam smiles at Camera One while the theme music came up and the set faded to black.

"You okay?" Matt asked, removing the Telex from his ear.

"Got distracted. It appears I have a visitor."

Matt followed her gaze. "That's the TPS guy, isn't it?" After the furor surrounding the Devin Corbal case, Travis was recognizable to any media person in LA.

"The very same."

"He seems to be putting the 'personal' back in personal protection."

"Maybe that should be his slogan." Kris got up from behind the curvilinear shell of the desk. "I'd better find out what he wants. See you Monday."

"Have a nice weekend."

She wished she could. Somehow she found it unlikely.

Quickly she made her way past the cameras, away from the small set with its video wall and its photographic backdrop of LA at night, complete with artificial city lights that glittered like stardust. Lit with klieg lights and photographed through a layer of diffusion, the set was a magical island, but up close it was cheap, almost tacky. The desk was a false front, the swivel chairs were uncomfortable, and the backdrop had been torn and hastily repaired, leaving a ragged seam like a fault line. At full power the lights were harsh and hot, though the studio itself was cold in deference to the balky equipment that cluttered the floor.

Travis smiled at her as she approached. That smile worried her. It seemed calculated to convey reassurance. "What's up?" she asked guardedly.

"I thought I'd ride along with you tonight in one of our staff cars."

"What's wrong with my car?"

"If you don't mind, I'd like you to use our vehicle right now. I chose a Town Car from our fleet—same model as yours."

"If it's the same, why can't we take mine?"

"This car has added features." Travis paused until a pair of stagehands had sauntered past. "Bullet-resistant glass, armor plating, the works."

"Why exactly do I need this extra level of protection? Because Hickle varied his routine by not calling today?"

"That's part of it."

"What's the rest?"

"Abby's found out a few things. I can't go into detail right now." Travis placed a hand on her arm, lowering his voice. "There's a chance he may be close to taking action."

"There's a nice euphemism. Trying to kill me is what you mean."

"It could be a false alarm. Anyway, Steve Drury will be driving, and I'll ride in the back with you. The detail posted at the house has been put on alert. The guards at the Reserve's gatehouse have been notified, as well as the KPTI security staff. Every precaution is being taken. You'll be fine, Kris. You'll be fine."

He was still touching her arm. Gently she pulled away. She didn't want his reassurances. He found it easy to be calm. Dealing with threats was his job. He reduced the problem to a set of procedures, an action plan. He enjoyed it. To her it was only a nightmare without logic or clarity, offering no escape.

She looked back at the set. From a distance its magic was intact. At this moment she wanted only to return to her fake desk under the lights and continue reading off the TelePrompTer and smiling into the cameras. She felt safe there, enclosed in a protective circle, doing what she did best. But the show was over, and all she could do was go away into the dark and hope Travis and his people kept her safe.

"Okay." She felt Travis deserved a smile for his kindness, but she couldn't summon one. "Let me scrub this makeup off. I'll meet you in my office. You know where it is."

"Kris—I'm sorry about this. We could be wrong in our assessment, but we can't take the risk."

She said she understood. And she did. The rational part of her understood perfectly well, but there was another part of her, less sober and composed, that wanted to scream that it was unfair and she was tired and why couldn't Hickle leave her alone and harass somebody else?

In the dressing room she bent over the sink, removing her makeup with a towel. When she was done, she studied herself in the mirror. The face she saw was beautiful and haughty and scared. It was not her face. Her face never showed fear, and this one did.

Hickle had stolen everything from her now. Her peace of mind, her daily routine, her comfort, perhaps her marriage. Even the face in the mirror wasn't her own anymore.

There was nothing left for him to take—except her life.

Howard parked in the garage of the beach house at 11:15, later than he'd expected, because before leaving the bungalow he had decided to smooth things over with Amanda, a process that had taken some time and further disarranged the bed sheets.

But things had worked out all right. He had beaten Kris home by at least a half hour.

He walked around to the guest cottage, where he was met by the two TPS staff officers on duty. Their names were Pfeiffer and Mahoney, though he never could recall which was which. The men seemed unusually alert tonight. Even as they greeted him, they were scanning the darkness on the far side of Malibu Reserve Drive. "Anything wrong?" Howard asked.

They assured him the situation was normal. He didn't find their protestations entirely convincing. Something was up. His suspicion was confirmed when one of them mentioned that Kris would be arriving in a TPS staff car tonight.

"A staff car? Why?"

"Routine precaution," Pfeiffer or Mahoney said.

"If it's routine, why haven't you done it before now?"

"It's just standard procedure," his partner, who was either Mahoney or Pfeiffer, replied. Both men kept their gazes fixed on the shadowy foliage across the road.

His answer was no answer at all. It was, in fact, just another way of saying the same thing. Howard thought of pointing this out but decided against it. Kris was Travis's client. The TPS people would tell her whatever she demanded to know. They rarely extended the same courtesy to him.

He said good night to Pfeiffer and Mahoney, then proceeded down the garden path to the house. Courtney opened the door for him as he climbed the steps. She must have heard the TPS agents buzz him in. " 'Evening, Mr. Barwood."

He acknowledged the housekeeper with a nod, noticing how she backed away when he stepped into the foyer. Courtney had been keeping her distance from him since the day, several months ago, when he'd reached out in the game room to stroke the dark sheet of her hair. It had been an impulse on his part, stupid and thoughtless. She had recoiled and started to cry, and he'd felt bad, but not so bad that he hadn't resorted to threats to ensure that she kept quiet about the incident, particularly where Mrs. Barwood was concerned.

Now he wondered if she had kept quiet after all. Maybe she had said something to Kris. Maybe that was why Kris now suspected his affair.

Courtney shut the door. "How was your ride?" she asked.

"Terrific. I went all the way to Santa Barbara. That car hypnotizes me."

He said it as jauntily as he could, but she merely murmured, "Sounds like fun."

She didn't believe him. She knew he hadn't been out

cruising the coast road. She could guess what he'd been up to. And so could Kris. It was obvious now. Perhaps, to a more perceptive man, it would have been obvious all along.

"I think I'll unwind out on the deck," Howard said. "It's a beautiful night."

"Sure is." She seemed relieved to be rid of him.

He walked to the rear of the house, thinking he'd been insane to think he could fool either his housekeeper or his wife. Women had a sixth sense about these things. They could tell when a man was fooling around, the way dogs could sense an earthquake before it hit. It was uncanny, the way women's minds worked. They should all be detectives and fortune-tellers and shrinks.

Still, Kris hadn't guessed all his secrets, had she?

Hickle had sped from freeway to freeway, taking the 101 to the 110 to the 10, in a desperate rush for the coastline. Now he was traveling through West LA on the Santa Monica Freeway, the gas pedal on the floor, the needle of the Rabbit's speedometer pinned at eighty-five.

Time was his enemy. He had to be in position outside the beach house by 11:50 at the latest.

He checked the dashboard clock. The readout glowed 11:21. He was still four miles from Pacific Coast Highway. It was going to be tight.

He pulled around a slower car, passing illegally in the right-hand lane, not giving a damn, and then in his rearview mirror he saw the blue-red sparkle of a lightbar.

CHP unit. After him.

Disaster.

He could not afford a speeding ticket. Simply being pulled over would take five or ten minutes, costing him any chance of reaching Malibu in time. Worse, the cops might want to know what was inside the duffel bag. Possession of the guns was legal, but he was sure the authorities would find an excuse to hold him for questioning—and while they did, a report would come in about an explosion at his address.

No.

He had failed at everything he'd ever tried. But tonight he would not accept defeat. Tonight nothing would stop him. Tonight, just this once, he would win.

Hickle accelerated, veering from lane to lane, whipping around slower traffic. The CHP car accelerated in pursuit, and an amplified voice came over a loudspeaker, giving orders that he didn't even hear.

"Fuck you," he breathed. He had taken orders all his life. He had submitted meekly to the demands of carwash proprietors and supermarket managers and Mr. Zachareas of Zack's Donut Shack. He had been quiet and punctual and reliable, and he had never talked back. Well, he was talking back now, talking back to the whole goddamned world.

The cops were trying to keep up as he skidded from lane to lane, but they had to worry about the safety of other drivers, and he had no worries at all. The dome light shrank in his rearview mirror, and directly ahead he saw an off-ramp.

Swerving into the exit lane, cutting off traffic with a blare of horns, Hickle veered onto the surface streets.

The cops would want to follow, but when he'd last seen them, they'd been in the fast lane, and he doubted they could cut over to the exit in time.

Even if they did, they wouldn't find him. He was

too smart to travel in a straight line. He detoured down side streets, swung through residential neighborhoods, drove along alleys, until he was sure the patrol car had been left behind.

31

Her first awareness was of pain.

Blinking, Abby raised her head, then shut her eyes against new agony. It throbbed from the back of her skull to the bridge of her nose. It pulsed behind her eyes.

"Man," she muttered, "this is one bad hangover." The words came out raspy and blurred. Her tongue was an immense cotton wad blocking her throat.

She was sprawled on the floor alongside her bedroom bureau, and there was a bad smell in the air, a smell like two dozen kinds of garbage blended together on a hot day, a smell like a swamp. She'd been knocked out—couldn't remember how. Her last memory was of Hickle.

Looming over her, the shotgun in his hand.

Had he shot her? She didn't think so. She wasn't aware of any holes in her body, but somehow he'd rendered her unconscious and left her here. And that sour, brackish smell . . .

Gas. The apartment was filling with gas.

Natural gas had no smell of its own, but the gas company added an odorant as a warning agent in the event of a gas leak. Gas leaks could be dangerous, could be fatal. Any spark or open flame could ignite an explosion.

Open flame. The furnace pilot light.

She saw it then—exactly what Hickle had planned for her.

What she had to do was obvious. Open the windows, shut off the gas. Simple, except she couldn't move. Every muscle in her body had gone slack. Her pulse was rapid and faint. Swooning ripples of dizziness ballooned through her head.

She tried to prop herself up, but her arms would not support her, and she collapsed, gasping. There was no air to breathe, only the swamp stench. Natural gas was an enemy of respiration. It inhibited the blood's ability to carry oxygen. The more she inhaled, the more labored and irregular her breathing would become. Her muscles, starved of oxygen, would lose all remaining strength. Her awareness would flicker and fade out. Well, no. She doubted she would last that long. The explosion would kill her first.

"That's me," she groaned. "Always looking on the bright side."

The longer she waited, the weaker she would get. She had to take action now, had to raise the bedroom window, draw some air into this death trap. But she couldn't stand. All right, crawl. The window was only six feet away. A baby could crawl that far.

She started to roll onto her belly. Something stopped her—a tug of resistance. Her left ankle had been fastened to a leg of the bureau by the chain and padlock from Hickle's bedroom closet. He'd anchored her in place so that even if she regained consciousness, she couldn't escape.

Nice touch, but the joke was on him. She knew the combination. Bending at the waist, she reached the padlock and lined up the numbers, then tugged on the shackle.

The padlock didn't open.

But it had to. Unless . . .

Hickle had changed the combination.

Abby shut her eyes. "I take it back, Raymond. Looks like the joke's on me."

The greatest danger, Hickle knew, was that the cops had read his license plate during the chase. If they had, his plate number and a description of his Volkswagen would already have been radioed to other CHP units and to LAPD and Santa Monica PD patrol cars. He could outrun one car but not a dozen.

He reached Ocean Avenue and turned north into heavy traffic, typical on a Friday night. Bikers and low-riders surrounded him. Rough crowd, the sort that drew a lot of cops on patrol. He scanned the sea of car roofs for a lightbar. Couldn't see one, but that didn't mean police units weren't out there—maybe behind him—maybe closing in.

Panic started his heart racing. He thought he might throw up.

The traffic thinned a little as he entered a better neighborhood. On his left was the park on the palisades, busy with tourists and teenagers. Hotels and restaurants and condominium towers rose on his right. It occurred to him that soon, even if things went exactly as planned, he would be either dead or in custody. He would never again walk in a park or eat at a restaurant. He would not see the moon, which hovered over the ocean beyond the palisades, unless he saw it through the barred window of a cell.

But if he lived, he would see Kris in his memory. She would be with him every day, bloodied and torn, his victim, his sacrifice. Every time he closed his eyes, he would see her. He would give up the moon for that. And if he didn't survive . . .

With death came immortality. He would be remembered. His name, his face, would be known. He, not Kris, would be on the covers of magazines. He, not Kris, would stare out at a world of television viewers from a million picture tubes. And who could say? Maybe there was a life after this one, when all destinies were fulfilled. If so, he would be with her forever, as he deserved.

But only if he killed her first. To do that, he had to get to Malibu, and time was ticking down.

Ahead was the incline to the coast highway. He eased into the turn lane, then got stuck behind a line of cars at a red light. A minute of waiting followed. He was helpless. If a patrol unit spotted him now, there was nothing he could do except go down shooting.

Finally the stoplight cycled to a green arrow. He followed the traffic downhill, breathing hard, his chest heaving with strain. There was sweat on his face, sweat pasting his shirt to his armpits and his underpants to his crotch. He smelled bad. But he'd made it at least this far.

He pulled into the fast lane, racing between the pale cliffs and the sea. Fear of attracting attention competed with the need to make up lost time. Urgency won.

Hickle accelerated—sixty-five miles per hour, seventy, seventy-five—breaking the speed limit as he hugged the curving shoreline of Santa Monica Bay on his way to Malibu.

Okay, think, Abby. Think.

Plan A had proven unsuccessful. Time to go to Plan

B—if there was a Plan B, other than just lying here till the whole place went kaboom.

She shook her head, rejecting pessimism. There was always a Plan B, and if that failed, a Plan C and D and so on through the alphabet for as long as she lasted. Never give up, that was the spirit.

Plan B was to try variant combinations based on Kris's birthdate—August 18, 1959. Abby moved the four cams to 0859, 1859, 5918, 5908. No luck. How about Hickle's birthday? Travis had told her. It was October 7, 1965.

The cams seemed to be getting slippery. No, it was her fingers that were slick with perspiration. She wiped her shaking hands on her blouse and spun the disks. 1007, 1065, 0765, and reversals of all these sequences. Nothing happened.

The gas odor was worse than before. Her stomach coiled. Nausea threatened.

All right, Plan C. Kicking off her shoe, she tried to slip her foot through the chain. No use. The circle of steel links dug like small teeth into the skin above her heel, gripping fiercely. Either the chain was too tight, or her darned foot was too big.

Something like panic welled up inside her. She pushed it down. Mustn't freak out. Freaking out was not a survival tactic.

Time for Plan D. So what was it? Well, she could pound the floor, scream for help. Trouble was, she didn't think she could get enough air into her lungs to force out a decent scream, and if she banged on the floor, the downstairs neighbors would either ignore the noise or call the cops. And the cops would take hours to respond to a low-priority call in this district, if they responded at all.

She didn't have hours. The gas was thick. Before long, it would reach the critical mass necessary to set off an explosion and a flash fire. The temperature in a flash fire could hit 1300 degrees. That was hot enough to fry her up pretty good.

"Damn it, Abby." She blinked sweat out of her eyes. "You're supposed to be smart, right? And highly trained, with all these advanced skills . . ."

Skills. She did have skills. Among them was the skill of picking locks.

She had no tools, but maybe she didn't need any. She pulled the shackle taut, then fingered the cams. The second one had tightened; it turned with difficulty. That was the one to work on first. Carefully she dialed the cam through its ten-digit range. On 6 it loosened. The second number in the combination was 6.

Her heart fluttered. Her vision was blurring in and out. Her general condition was not good, and the prognosis was poor. On the menu tonight, rotisserie Abby, served charred.

Quit it. She needed to concentrate. Easier said than done. Her head was squeezed in a vise of pain, and the bedroom had begun to imitate a carousel, and there was the stench of week-old diapers in her nose and mouth.

Maintaining pressure on the shackle, she tested the other three cams. Now the first one resisted turning. She worked it slowly, trying not to think about the gas and the pilot light and what 1300 degrees would feel like. Hotter than Phoenix in July, if such a thing was possible.

The cam loosened when it was set to 8. That was the first number in the combination. Six was the second. Eight. Six. Put it together, Abby. Eight. Six.

Channel Eight. The news at six . . . and ten.

The last two digits were 1 and 0. 8610 was the combination. Had to be. She set the cams in that sequence, and the padlock released. She was free.

Now get the window open. Hurry.

Prone on her stomach, she crawled across the floor. Her breathing was awful to hear. Her chest heaved, and she couldn't get oxygen into her lungs, and her head was sizzling, and there was pain like a crushing pressure at the back of her eyes. Sometimes, she thought, I really hate my job.

She came up against the bedroom wall. The window was just above her. Close, but she couldn't reach it, couldn't raise herself off the floor. Too weak. Come on, she chided silently, you can do a pull-up, can't you?

With one arm extended, she got hold of the windowsill and, using it as leverage, lifted herself to her knees.

The window was locked. Hickle, the bastard, had actually taken the time to secure the latch. She fumbled at it, but her fingers, glazed with sweat, couldn't find a grip. This whole situation was starting to get on her nerves in a big way. Nothing was easy. And time was running out.

Finally she got the latch open. Okay, lift the window. She put both hands on the sash bar and strained. Nothing happened. She had no strength. She battered the glass with her fists. Her blows fell like sighs. A kitten could have done more damage.

Again she tried to raise the window. Still no luck. Weakness overtook her, and she lowered her head, coughing. God, she was tired. She wanted to sleep . . .

Plenty of time for rest later. Eternal rest, if it worked out that way. At the moment she was still alive. She would not waste whatever time she had left. The explosion could come at any moment. She had to dilute the fumes with clean air, or she was dead. Open the damn window. Do it now.

She put everything she had into a final effort, pushing upward with her last strength, and the window cracked open a few inches.

Success.

She rested her head on the sill and tried to draw a breath, but her throat had closed. There was air coming in, pure air, and she couldn't breathe it. What the hell was wrong with her lungs?

But it was simple, really. Her vision was graying out, and her ears hummed, and she was going to lose consciousness. She had driven herself to the point of collapse, and although she had forced the window ajar, it was not enough to save her.

"Nice try, girlfriend," Abby murmured, "but no lollipop."

The floor rushed up, and she fell away into the dark.

32

"... vehicle is a VW Rabbit wanted for felony evading, license plate ..."

Wyatt heard the call on his radio as he cruised back to Hollywood Station after supervising a crime scene on Highland—drugstore hold-up, nobody injured. The suspect had taken a hundred bucks out of the cash register and three packages of Trojans. Apparently he had a big night planned.

It was nothing major, and Wyatt had passed the time pondering what to do about Abby. He had decided on a confrontation tomorrow. Call her, arrange a lunch meeting, then demand to know what she'd gotten involved in. And once she told him? He didn't know. His planning hadn't made it that far.

At 11:40 he had been relieved of responsibility for the crime scene by the arrival of a bored detective, accompanied by an equally bored forensic photographer. Now he was driving down Melrose, listening to the dispatcher report a CHP stop gone awry on the Santa Monica Freeway, miles away, twenty minutes ago. He wondered why the BOL was going out over a Hollywood Division frequency. As he turned onto Wilcox, he got his answer.

"... registered to a Hollywood resident ..."

That explained it. There was a fair chance the suspect would be stupid enough to return home. Patrol units in Hollywood were advised to watch for a VW Rabbit with the reported plate number, and to keep an eye on the suspect's residence.

". . . address, 1554 Gainford . . ."

Wyatt stiffened. The Gainford Arms.

". . . name, Hickle, Raymond, that's Henry Ida Charles . . ."

It was Hickle who had been speeding on the freeway, Hickle who had fled a traffic stop. Wyatt had no idea what this might mean, except that Hickle was out of control and dangerous and crazed.

"Abby," he breathed, a cold feeling in his gut.

The time was 11:48 when Hickle abandoned his car in a small beach parking lot off Pacific Coast Highway. He'd made it. He was in Malibu, on Kris's territory. The police had not intercepted him.

The access path to the public beach was never closed. He lugged his duffel down the dirt path, then headed into the woods that bordered Malibu Reserve, his flashlight probing the foliage.

Midnight was close, the time frame tight, but he no longer feared failure. He was destined to succeed. He could feel it. Kris had messed with him, and she would pay, as Abby had paid.

Thinking of Abby made him wonder if she was dead yet. Fifty minutes had passed since he'd released the gas. By now she must have been asphyxiated or blown to bits.

Now it was Kris's turn to die.

Not far from the Reserve's perimeter fence, he located the mouth of the drainage pipe. The pipe was two feet in diameter, jutting out of a mound of earth under a eucalyptus tree. There was a small brackish pond nearby, and evidently the pipe had been laid down as a flood control device, its purpose to channel overflow from the pond away from the path and into the ravine that ran through the fenced compound.

On hands and knees Hickle bellied inside, dragging the duffel after him. The bag got stuck in the opening, and briefly he was afraid it wouldn't fit—he'd never brought weapons on his previous outings, only the Polaroid camera—but when he turned the bag sideways it slipped through. He crawled over leaves, twigs, candy wrappers, and other detritus washed in by storms. Beetles skittered out of his path. Some backtracked and flitted over him, tickling like light fingers. He didn't mind. He had come this way before, and there were always bugs.

He'd never made the passage at night, though. His flashlight traced pale loops and whorls on the pipe's soiled interior. Past the light there was only darkness, not the reassuring glow of sunshine that had drawn him forward on past occasions. He guessed he had come halfway, which meant he was under the fence. Inside the Reserve.

Kris had surrounded herself with a fence and a gatehouse, a bodyguard at the wheel of her car and other bodyguards stationed in her guest cottage, yet all these precautions had proven useless against him. He was unstoppable. He was a force of nature, a man of destiny.

He crawled faster.

Wyatt parked by a fire hydrant outside the Gainford Arms and mounted the front steps two at a time. The lobby door was locked, and he didn't have a master key. He buzzed Abby's apartment, got no answer. He went around to the rear door, locked also. He scanned the parking lot and saw her white Dodge Colt in its assigned space.

She was home. She wasn't answering the buzzer. And Hickle, the man she'd been spying on, was running from the police.

With his side-handle baton he smashed the glass panel adjacent to the rear door, then reached in and released the latch. Inside, he stabbed the elevator call button, but when the elevator didn't instantly arrive he gave up on it and ran up the stairs. At the fourth floor he exited, slowing to a walk. There was a remote chance Hickle had already come back and was waiting to ambush the first cop who arrived. Might have been a good idea to check the parking lot for Hickle's Volkswagen or call for backup. A little late for either plan now.

He drew his service pistol, approaching Hickle's apartment. He tested the door. Locked. He heard no movement inside. Even so, he ducked low, dropping below the peephole, as he passed by.

Abby's apartment was next. Number 418. He rapped his fist on the door, then frowned. He smelled something. "Oh, shit," he whispered.

He tried the knob. It turned freely. He stepped into a den of fumes, moving fast, unafraid of an ambush now. Hickle wasn't here, wasn't coming back. He'd made Abby's apartment into a giant bomb and fled before it could explode.

The stench was overpowering. The gas must be nearly at critical mass. Any spark could set off a detonation. Wyatt advanced into the room, grateful that the lights had been left on; he wouldn't dare flip a light switch now.

He saw the dislodged oven immediately, the ruptured inflow line spewing gas. He cranked the shutoff valve, sealing the pipe, then got the living room window open. Leaning on the sill, he took a deep breath of fresh air to dispel any dizziness. He was shaking. It seemed okay to shake. He was standing inside an apartment that had been converted into a large-scale explosive device. It could still go off at any moment.

In the bedroom he found Abby. She lay unmoving in a twisted pose before the window, which was unlatched and a few inches ajar.

Hickle hadn't left it open, that was for sure. Abby must have raised it. The effort had exhausted her, but by bringing in a small quantity of clean air and diluting the lethal concentration of vapors, it had also saved her life.

If she was still alive. Wyatt didn't check until he had raised the window fully. Then he knelt, feeling her carotid artery. His fingertips detected the flutter of a pulse.

He hauled Abby through the window onto the fire escape and set her down. She was barely breathing. He tilted her head back to open her airway, pinched her nostrils, sealed her mouth with his and blew air into her lungs. He did it a second time, then paused, studying her chest, waiting for an exhalation. None came. He repeated the procedure, expelling air down her throat, forcing her chest to rise. Still she wasn't breathing. He did it again. He would not give up. He would not let her die.

33

Hickle struggled out of the drainage pipe, toting the duffel bag, and scrambled through a shallow ravine, emerging near Gateway Road. Gateway was two lanes of pitted macadam lined with eucalyptus trees, the only way for vehicular traffic to get in or out of Malibu Reserve. The guardhouse with its lowered gate lay at the end of the road, the coast highway beyond.

He needed to cross Gateway, a risky endeavor if the guard happened to be looking in this direction. He took a breath and scurried across, the heavy bag slapping his hip with every step. At the far side of the road, he disappeared into the woods, sure he had not been seen.

Fast through the trees, heading toward the smell of the sea. He could hear the crash of breakers. Malibu had been named for that sound; the Chumash Indians had dubbed it *the place where the waves are loud*. But tonight there would be something louder than the surf. There would be gunshots. And screams.

Hickle reached Malibu Reserve Drive, which intersected with Gateway and ran parallel to the beach. The Barwoods' house lay on the far side of the street, one of a row of beachfront homes built close together, most fronted by guest cottages and elaborate entryways.

He hunkered down behind a tuft of weeds and studied the house. The lights in the guest cottage glowed, and there was restless movement in the windows. As he watched, a man in a dark blazer and turtleneck stepped out of the cottage, looking around. A moment later the man went back inside, but he kept the door open.

This was bad. The two security agents stationed in the house seemed to have been put on alert. Was it possible TPS had already been notified of the explosion in Hollywood? He doubted that the news would travel that fast. More likely, Abby's earlier reports had triggered a higher state of readiness.

His idea had been to cross the road and hide in the bushes alongside the Barwoods' driveway, then fire at the Town Car when it pulled up. Now he wasn't sure the plan would work. He might be spotted as he approached the house or when he took cover close to the cottage.

He checked his watch. Midnight. Kris could arrive at any time. If he was going to rethink the ambush, he had better do it fast.

The TPS man slipped out of the doorway again, casting another wary glance up and down the road. That decided things. There was no chance of success if he stuck to his original plan. He had to improvise.

Hickle slipped through the woods, moving parallel to Malibu Reserve Drive, until he reached the intersection with Gateway. After entering the compound, Kris's Town Car would proceed down Gateway, then turn left on Malibu Reserve Drive, heading for the beach house. It was a sharp turn, forcing the driver to cut his speed. When the car slowed and the driver was turning the wheel, Hickle would strike.

He squatted in the tall grass. To his right he saw the dim glow of the guardhouse four hundred yards away. The guard would come running when the shots were fired, as would the two security agents in the cottage, but nobody would reach the scene in time to save Kris.

Hickle set down the duffel bag and took out the shotgun, dumping extra shells into the pockets of his windbreaker. He wondered how long he would have to wait, how long Kris had left to live. He did not hate her now. He was past hate. He merely wanted to set things right, out of a sense of justice.

At the far end of Gateway—headlights. A car pulled up to the gate. He couldn't tell if it was a Lincoln.

Hickle crouched low, the shotgun gripped in his cold, steady hands.

There was air in her lungs, and she was breathing. The smell of rotten eggs was leaving her nostrils. She felt a flicker of returning strength in her arms and legs.

These were the first reports that reached her as Abby swam upward out of bright light and found herself on the fire escape with Vic Wyatt bending over her.

"You'll be all right, Abby," he said. "You'll be fine."

She had no idea how he had come here. He might have been a dream. But the cold iron grillwork beneath her was real enough, and so was the pulsing pain in her head.

Later she would find out how he'd rescued her. Right now there was something else she needed to deal with. Something urgent, if only she could remember what it was.

An image flashed in her mind: Devin Corbal motionless on the floor of the nightclub. Was it Corbal who was in danger? No, it was too late to save him. She saw the lake of blood spreading under his body. He was dead, and it was her fault, no matter what anyone said. She had to make up for it somehow. Couldn't lose another one. Couldn't lose Kris . . .

Kris.

And Hickle. Ambush in Malibu. Tonight.

With a jolt of panic she tried to sit up.

"Rest, Abby," Wyatt said.

Couldn't rest. Had to tell him. She tried to force out speech but produced only a dry cough that racked her abdomen with spasms.

"Abby, lie still, okay? You had a close call."

She wouldn't listen. She gulped air and found a way to make words.

"Phone," she gasped. "Get me a phone . . ."

The car was a Lincoln. Hickle could see it clearly as the gate lifted and the guard waved the driver through.

Kris's car. He was sure of it.

The Lincoln rolled forward, moving slowly, headlights fanning across the cracked macadam. Hickle sank lower on his haunches, tensing for the moment when he would leap upright and open fire.

Side windows first. Kris rode in the backseat. Kill her with multiple shots to the head and upper body. No need to aim, just point and shoot. He knew what shotshells could do to a human being at close range. Each disintegrating shell was like a miniature shrapnel bomb, flinging a cloud of lethal debris. Kris would be ripped apart. She would have no time to react, no chance to duck or hide, and even if she tried, there was no place for her to take cover in the Town Car's rear compartment.

She was sealed in a box, and killing her would be, quite literally, like shooting fish in a barrel.

"You should've answered my letters, Kris," Hickle whispered.

34

As soon as the Town Car stopped at the Reserve's gate, Travis shifted into hypervigilance.

He was seated beside Kris in the backseat. Inside his jacket, strapped to his left shoulder, he carried his 9mm Walther. He unbuttoned the jacket and let his right hand rest on the lapel, ready to draw the gun if necessary.

When the gate rose, Kris seemed to relax a little. No doubt she felt safer inside the compound. She didn't know about the photos in Hickle's apartment, the ones that showed her running on the beach. She didn't know there was no safety here. Quite the opposite. This was the time and place of maximum jeopardy. If Hickle planned to strike, this was where he would do it.

The Lincoln advanced along Gateway Road, Steve Drury driving at a cautious pace. In the rearview mirror his eyes were visible, ticking back and forth.

Halfway down Gateway now. The intersection with Malibu Reserve Drive was two hundred yards ahead.

"Almost home," Kris breathed.

He glanced at her, silhouetted in profile against the foliage on the left side of the road. It occurred to him, not for the first time, that her face had the perfect bone structure. Probably she worried about getting old, losing her looks, but what she didn't understand was that a beauty like hers was not a matter of smooth skin and ripe complexion, but of the underlying architecture of her strong frontal bone and well-defined zygomatic arches. She would be beautiful when she was eighty, if she lived that long.

One hundred fifty yards to the intersection. Still no trouble. Kris sighed, relaxing a little more—the amateur's mistake. Proximity to home only increased the danger. Hickle would wait until the car had slowed to a crawl, as it would when it turned into the driveway.

Drury had not relaxed, Travis noted. Good man, well trained. He wore a Kevlar vest under his jacket; Travis had brought it for him. He had brought no vest for himself. He'd been afraid Kris would see it and panic. Sometimes it was necessary to take certain personal risks to maintain the client's confidence. Anyway, Travis was fatalistic about such things. He always estimated the risks of any undertaking before proceeding with it. Once committed, he put all danger out of his mind. All danger to himself, at least. The threat to Kris was a different story. Nothing could be allowed to happen to her.

One hundred yards to Malibu Reserve Drive. The interior of the car was quiet except for the thrum of tires, the muffled vibration of the engine, and Kris's breathing, slow and steady.

Then a new sound, startling—a loud, insistent chirp. His cell phone. Who would be calling him at midnight?

He whipped out the phone and held it to his ear, his gaze fixed on the dark roadside. "Travis," he barked.

"Sir, it's Hastings." One of the TPS computer jocks tracking down Trendline Investments and its possible connection to Western Regional Resources. "You told us to call if we found anything definitive."

"Did you?"

"Yes, sir. I'd say we did."

"Give it to me fast," Travis ordered, still watching the darkness. "I don't have much time."

Abby had propped herself to a sitting position on the fire escape when Wyatt returned, climbing through the bedroom window with her purse in his hand.

She took the cell phone from her purse and powered it on. In the glow of the liquid crystal display she found the menu button and navigated to the first number stored in memory, the number of Travis's mobile phone. She speed-dialed it.

Wyatt crouched beside her, saying nothing. She knew he had many questions to ask, and she loved him just a little for not asking them yet.

Busy signal.

She hissed a curse and terminated the call, then redialed.

Still busy, damn it.

"What's the matter?" Wyatt whispered.

"Can't get through." She forced the words past gritted teeth.

"You can dial the operator, have the phone company break in on the call."

"It'll take too long." She called again. Busy. "Come on, Paul, clear the line."

"I'll cut to the chase." Hastings's voice crackled in Travis's ear. "We started with Trendline Investments. Trendline, as a corporate entity, sits on the board of directors of something called ProFuture Opportunities, also incorporated in the Netherlands Antilles. There are three other companies on ProFuture's board—all dummy corporations, as far as we can tell. One of them is named GrayFoxx Financial. You following this?"

Travis nodded, his gaze never leaving the blur of shadows at the edge of the road. "Go on."

"Here's the link. GrayFoxx is the largest shareholder of Western Regional Resources."

"Bang," Travis said softly.

"You got it. Essentially, GrayFoxx owns Western Regional, and GrayFoxx and Trendline jointly own ProFuture. Our guess is that Mr. Barwood—"

"Owns all of them," Travis finished.

"Right. He set it all up as shells within shells, very complicated, hard to trace. But we nailed him." There was pride in Hastings's voice. Travis supposed he was entitled to it.

"Good work. Now get some rest." Travis ended the call.

Twenty yards to the intersection. The Town Car slowed in preparation for a sharp left turn.

"What was that about?" Kris asked.

Travis couldn't tell her now. Later was the right time. Later, when she was safe.

"Some other case," he said. "Don't worry about it."

She frowned at him, her reporter's instincts evidently disputing his answer, but before she could ask anything further, the phone chirped again. Was it Hastings, calling with additional details? For a moment Travis considered shutting off the phone to silence it.

Ten yards.

Oh, hell. He took the call. "Travis," he snapped. "This had better be—"

He didn't finish. On the other end of the line was a hoarse, desperate, anguished voice, Abby's voice, and she was screaming.

"Code Red, Paul, you hear me, *Hickle is Code Red!*"

35

The Town Car was turning onto Malibu Reserve Drive when its brakes squealed, and suddenly the car was reversing fast, and Hickle knew they were on to him.

He sprang out of the foliage, the twelve-gauge in both hands. From this angle he didn't have a clear shot at the side windows so he opened fire on the windshield, hoping to take out the driver. The glass starred but didn't shatter. Behind the web of fractures he saw the driver spinning the wheel as he backed onto Gateway. Once lined up, the Lincoln could reverse straight to the gate, where the guard must already be dialing 911.

Hickle fired two more shots at the windshield, emptying the Marlin, but although the glass buckled, it still did not give way. The shots distracted the driver long enough for the car to skid partially off the road at a crazy angle. For a moment the Lincoln was stuck, its right rear tire mired in dirt.

Hickle ditched his duffel bag and charged the car, reloading on the run. He saw movement in the backseat, two figures. One of them was Kris.

The driver shifted out of reverse and plowed forward, but by the time he was back on the road, Hickle had run alongside. He fired three shells at the car's side panel, hoping to blow it apart. No good. The car absorbed the shots with only superficial damage.

Armor plating. Bulletproof glass. JackBNimble had never mentioned anything about that. Either he hadn't known, or this was some kind of setup. Hickle had no time to puzzle it out. The Lincoln was executing a clumsy K-turn as the driver tried to orient the car toward the exit. Hickle fired one shot at the front tire, puncturing it, but it didn't go flat. Even the tires were bullet-resistant.

He dug in the pocket of his windbreaker and reloaded. As the Lincoln completed its turn, he leaped onto the hood, face to face with the driver. Over the ringing in his ears he heard a male voice from the backseat shout, *"Get down!"*

Hickle pumped the Marlin and fired a shot into the windshield at point-blank range. Charred shell wadding blew back in his face. He shut his eyes against the debris. When he opened them, he saw a hole in the windshield, exposing the Lincoln's interior. He swung the shotgun into the hole and fired twice, not aiming, hoping for a lucky hit or a ricochet.

The Lincoln slammed on its brakes. He thought he must have hit the driver until, with a scream of tires, the Town Car snapped into reverse. Inertia rolled him off the hood. He flopped onto the pavement, and the Lincoln stopped. One headlight was dark. The other pinned him in its glare.

He knew what was about to happen even before the car shot forward, trying to run him down.

Reflexes saved him. He plunged off the road, taking refuge in the trees. Behind him, the pursuing car slammed to a halt at the edge of the woods. Hickle threw himself prone on the ground, below the cone of glare from the one intact headlight. By a miracle the shotgun was still in his hand, and now he had a clear view of the Lincoln's underbelly.

He fired a single shot, targeting the chassis.

Sparks and broken metal showered the earth, and he knew that one part of the vehicle was not armored.

The Town Car retreated onto the road, but Hickle was already scrambling after it, cramming more shells into the gun. He fired four times, aiming low. The Lincoln veered away, skidding on something wet and shiny, which was gasoline. He had ruptured the fuel tank.

"Fuck you," Hickle gasped, "I got you now!"

He reloaded, tramping through pools of gasoline, and fired again and again, pursuing the wounded car as it reversed down Gateway. The sedan wobbled on damaged tires and bent wheels. It accelerated, still backing up, and for a moment he thought it would get away.

Then the gas caught fire.

Abruptly the entire front section of the Lincoln was burning—tires, chassis, gas-soaked chrome. The Town Car careened to a stop, and Hickle plucked the last shells from his pocket and loaded them as he loped toward his quarry with death in mind.

Inside the Lincoln there had been chaos and terror from the moment Travis heard Abby's warning and shouted at Drury to back up. Kris had looked at him with an unvoiced question as the first shots crackled out of the darkness. Shotgun fire.

The TPS staff car was shielded by panels of aramid fibrous armor, lighter than steel and nearly as impenetrable, lining the doors, roof, quarter areas, and pillar posts. All the glass in the vehicle had been replaced by bullet-resistant sheets of multilayered transparent composite, a lamination of glass and polycarbonate. The tires were fitted with antiballistic runflat inserts that allowed them to hold their shape even when ruptured. The level of protection these features offered was moderately high, but there were points of weakness. The ballistic glass could stop handgun rounds and other small arms fire, but repeated blasts from a heavy-gauge shotgun might penetrate. The armor plating provided perimeter and roof protection, but the floor and the underside of the chassis were unshielded, vulnerable to attack from below. A fully armored vehicle offered greater protection but, because of the increased weight, less maneuverability. Tradeoffs had been made.

Travis wondered if those tradeoffs had been advisable as the first two shotshells chipped and splintered the Lincoln's windshield.

After that, there was no time to wonder about anything. The range of his thinking narrowed to the immediate concern of keeping Kris alive. He told her to get down, but the words didn't register with her. There was stark panic on her face, every muscle drawn taut. When the Town Car blundered partly off the road and was briefly stuck in the dirt, Travis actually felt the shiver of pure fear that rocked her in her seat. Then they were back on the road but no longer positioned to go either forward or back, and Drury had to spend a few desperate seconds hauling the car around in a ragged turn. That was when Hickle opened fire on the side of the car, trying to punch through the doors. Kris screamed. Travis saw the door panel cave inward a few inches under the impact of the multiple hits. But the armor held, and the Lincoln straightened out. As Drury accelerated, Hickle threw himself onto the hood.

Travis saw the shotgun kiss the weakened glass, and he knew the next blast would open up the car to a direct assault. He seized Kris and shoved her to the floor as two explosions from the shotgun echoed inside the car.

Exactly what happened next Travis didn't know. Bending to cover Kris with his body, he was aware only of a succession of stops and starts, the car braking, then reversing, then flying forward and braking again, and then another shot, this one striking low, and more low hits as the Lincoln backed off and screamed in reverse toward the guardhouse four hundred yards away.

The low hits scared Travis most of all. He was thinking of the unshielded underside of the car. He was thinking of the fuel tank.

He held Kris tight and heard her whispering the same words over and over in a hushed, urgent monotone: "God help us . . . God help us . . . God help us . . ."

Then there was fire.

Travis heard the whoosh of igniting gasoline even before the sudden orange glare lit up the front windows. By luck or skill Hickle had punctured the gas tank, and sparks from successive shots had set the gas ablaze.

The Lincoln would be enveloped in fire within seconds. The car might not blow up—gasoline was less combustible than Hollywood movies liked to pretend—but it would certainly burn to cinders, as would its occupants.

He pulled Kris upright and yelled at Drury to evac-
uate the vehicle. The car stopped at a crazy angle
halfway down Gateway Road, and Drury got out, or at
least Travis thought he did. He couldn't be sure, not
when his full attention was focused on prying open
the rear door and dragging Kris out of the car and
away from the spreading flames.

He pulled her into the bushes at the roadside, then
drew his Walther and turned in a crouch, scanning the
dark for Hickle, who had to be out there somewhere,
because if anything was clear and obvious in the midst
of this insanity, it was that Hickle would not give up
until Kris was dead.

The car was a flaming pile. It threw off a moist heat
that slapped Hickle in the face as he sprinted closer,
the shotgun gripped with both hands. He became
aware that he was favoring his left leg. Must have
turned his ankle when he rolled off the hood onto the
pavement. It didn't matter. He was still mobile, and
the car had been abandoned. Kris was outside, unprotected. Only one shot was needed to finish things.

Kris had been riding in the back of the Lincoln. The
rear passenger door hung ajar. Hickle ran toward that
side of the road and saw her on the roadside, a huddle
of fear and shock. With her, a man Hickle didn't recognize. Not her husband. A man with a gun.

Hickle saw the gun come up fast and flung himself
to the ground, taking cover behind the wreckage of the
Lincoln, then sensed movement nearby and turned in
time to see the driver taking aim with a pistol from behind the open front door. Hickle fired the shotgun, and
the man went down. Hit? Hard to tell. Hickle darted
around the door, preparing to fire again, but it wasn't

necessary. The driver was alive but out of commission, writhing on the pavement, his pistol dropped and forgotten. Hickle ignored him. He had no interest in delivering a coup de grâce. The man meant nothing to him. It was Kris he wanted.

He scrambled to the rear of the Lincoln, staying low. The air was brutally hot. Alongside the rear bumper he peered out and saw Kris and her defender retreating farther into the foliage. He jerked the Marlin's trigger twice, blowing sprays of shot at them, and saw them go down, but he didn't think they'd been hit. They had dived for cover.

Muzzle flashes from the foliage. Kris's bodyguard was shooting back. Hickle snapped off another shot, then retreated to the front of the Lincoln, moving fast. He had a plan now. They thought he was positioned at the rear of the car. They wouldn't expect him to charge from the front.

He sprang out from behind the car and instantly collided with something—somebody—who fell in a heap at his feet.

Kris.

She had panicked and run. Run right into him.

She looked up and saw him, and the look on her face was the most priceless gift he had ever received. It was a look of stark fear, of total resignation and final submission. It told him that he had won and she had lost, that he was the master and she the victim.

All of this lasted less than a second, no longer than it took for him to swing the shotgun toward her, the muzzle stamping its cold kiss on her brow. He pulled the trigger.

Nothing happened.

The gun was empty.

He registered this fact, and then a pistol's report rang out from the roadside, the bullet slicing past him, inches away.

The man with the handgun. Coming.

Hickle turned and fled.

He had no choice. There were no more shells in his pockets.

Another crack of pistol fire behind him. He reached the far side of the road and dived into the woods, stumbling over something that got caught up in his feet. His duffel bag.

There might be more shells in the bag, but he had no time to dig for them. There was the rifle, fully loaded, but he couldn't pull it out and take aim, not with an armed man pursuing him.

Anyway, he had lost his chance. Even if he could kill Kris's protector, the other TPS agents must already be rushing to the scene, and so was the guard, and the police too—everybody.

It was finished.

Hickle slung the duffel over his shoulder and charged through the trees, head down, panting hard.

He tried not to think about what had happened, how close he had come, how badly he had failed. He knew that if he thought about it, he would simply stop running and fall on his face and cry like a child, because the world had cheated him and life was so terribly unfair.

36

Travis pursued Hickle a few yards into the woods and saw him disappear among the eucalyptus trees and the deep drifts of weeds. Briefly he considered following, but looking after Kris was his highest priority. He doubled back and found her kneeling, dazed, on the pavement, her face streaked with tears, eyes wide and unblinking.

"God damn it," he snapped, anger overcoming compassion, "why the hell did you leave cover? What made you do that?"

She didn't answer, and of course she didn't have to. He knew what had made her scramble away from him when the bullets started flying. She had lost her nerve. She had heeded the blind impulse to put distance between herself and gunfire. In consequence she had blundered into Hickle and had nearly gotten killed.

Travis steadied himself. Gently he clasped her shoulder. "You okay, Kris?" he asked in a softer voice.

She looked at him. "I thought I was strong," she whispered.

He understood. She was a veteran of the news business. She had covered earthquakes, gang wars, sadistic slayings. She had believed she could handle anything. But tonight when the gunshots were aimed at her, when she was at the center of the story, she had cut and run like a panicky child. She wasn't as tough as she'd imagined. It was a painful lesson, but she would survive, and to Travis her survival was all that mattered.

Not far away he heard sirens. The local residents and the guard at the gatehouse must have called 911 when the shooting started. Malibu contracted its law enforcement services to the LA County Sheriff's Department. The nearest sheriff's station was miles away in Agoura, but evidently a couple of squad cars had been in the area.

He looked up and down the road. The two TPS staff officers stationed at the guest cottage, Pfeiffer and Mahoney, were approaching fast. Every light was burning in the homes that lined both intersecting streets. Nothing like a little midnight gun battle to wake up the neighborhood.

Circling the car, Travis found Drury sprawled on the macadam, his knees twisting slowly, blood soaking through the left sleeve of his jacket. Hickle had unloaded the shotgun at the driver, but most of the spray had gone wide. A few steel pellets had caught Drury in the arm and shoulder. There was blood loss but no arterial spurting. The angle of the arm inside the jacket suggested broken bones, possibly a shattered elbow.

"It's okay, Steve," Travis said, knowing the man couldn't hear. "You'll be fine."

The sirens grew louder, then whirred to a stop. Travis saw the gate rising to admit a pair of sheriff's cruisers.

"Status?" That was Pfeiffer, arriving with his Beretta unholstered, his eyes glassy with an infantryman's thousand-yard stare. Mahoney came right behind.

"Hickle ambushed us and fled," Travis said crisply. "I don't think he'll be back. He scored a lucky hit, incinerated the car. Nailed Drury in the shoulder. Mrs. Barwood is okay, just shaken up. Where's the husband?"

"We told him to stay put," Mahoney answered. He lowered his voice to add, "He didn't need much persuading."

Travis nodded, unsurprised that Howard Barwood was reluctant to throw himself in the line of fire.

A few yards from the smoking wreckage the squad cars rolled to a stop. Two deputies, each riding solo, got out with guns drawn and eyes wary. Travis met the men and summarized the situation. "RA coming?" he asked. Rescue ambulance.

"En route," a lanky red-haired deputy answered. His nameplate read Carruthers. He couldn't have been older than twenty-five. His gaze kept darting to the shrubbery at the roadside.

Travis knew he was worried that Hickle would return for a second try, but there was little chance of that. Hickle had taken his best shot and failed. Now he was heading for some dark corner where he could console himself and lick his wounds. But he hadn't had time to go far.

"Either of you men care to join me in pursuit of an armed suspect?" Travis asked. "I think we can pick up his trail."

Carruthers wanted in on the action. The other deputy, less enthusiastic, elected to remain at the scene and wait for the paramedics.

Travis drafted Pfeiffer to complete the posse. "Mahoney, you stand post over Drury and Mrs. Barwood. See if you can find some blankets for them. Drury looks like he's shivering."

"Nice kid, Drury," Pfeiffer said.

"He'll be all right. Let's move."

The three of them set off together, Travis in the lead, Pfeiffer and Carruthers close behind. "What kind of firepower this son of a bitch packing?" Carruthers asked.

"He used a shotgun in the assault. My information is that he also owns a rifle with a telescopic sight and laser sighting system. You wearing a vest, Deputy?"

Carruthers snorted. "I wish. Thing is, this duty's usually pretty quiet, and that vest gets hot."

"Pfeiffer?"

"Yeah, I got on my Kevlar. How about you, Boss?"

"Left mine at home." Travis snapped a new magazine into his Walther. "Let's hope Raymond doesn't put up a fight."

Hickle ran blindly, lugging the duffel like a heavy load of guilt. Behind him there were sirens. He never looked back. He was afraid he would see a whole squadron of cops rushing after him.

This was bad. This was a complete mess. In his imagination he had always carried out the attack perfectly. Yes, he had been arrested afterward, but only once Kris was dead and his immortality was assured.

It was JackBNimble's fault. In all his e-mail messages Jack had said not one word about armored plating on Kris's car or bulletproof glass.

"Not one goddamned word," he gasped, furiously indignant, and then he blundered into a steel fence topped with razor wire.

It was part of the fence that encircled the Reserve. He had reached the perimeter of the compound.

Panic screamed in him. He was trapped.

He could turn around, try hiding in the woods, but

they would find him before long. There had to be another way. Think.

The fence ran down to the water's edge but no farther. He could slip around it onto the adjacent public beach, then use the access path to get back to his parked car.

Limping on his bad ankle, he ran along the fence toward the sea. The last house on Malibu Reserve Drive loomed on his right. The space between the home's side wall and the fence was narrow, but he crabwalked through, pulling the duffel after him. The shotgun, he noticed, was in the duffel now. Sometime during his run he must have stuffed it inside the bag to free his right hand. He couldn't remember doing this. He was operating on instinct like any hunted animal.

On the verge of the beach Hickle paused, afraid of the open space where he would be exposed and unprotected. If the police had anticipated his escape route, somebody might be watching the beach even now. But he saw only white sand, the fringe of the surf, and above the water a few scattered rocks glistening with kelp. He risked going forward, kicking up sand as he ran. Where the fence ended, he sloshed into the tide and staggered ashore on the public beach.

As he climbed a hill of damp sand above the low tide mark, it occurred to him that he was leaving tracks.

He looked back. A line of shoe prints receded into the water. There must be a similar line on the other side of the fence and in the loose dirt of the woods. His enemies could follow him easily.

As if on cue, a glow of flashlights appeared in the shadows between the last home and the fence. They were coming. At least two of them, maybe more.

He ran for the path that led to the parking lot, but at the end of the path, beyond the trees and the dark roof of a ramada, danced a flickering glow of red and blue—the domelight of a police car.

Cops had pulled into the parking lot already. They'd found his car. Hickle reversed course, retreating up the path toward the beach again.

The flashlight beams were nearer. The pursuers who'd followed him from the Reserve were closing in, following his shoe prints in the sand.

His every escape route was cut off—except one.

The lagoon.

It lay on his left, a dark spread of mudflats and low shrubs bordering two shallow ponds fed by Malibu Creek. Forty acres of wetland, Malibu Lagoon State Park. A nature preserve, a nesting spot for migrant birds . . . and for him, a place to hide.

Hickle left the path and started running again. He wondered if he would ever be able to stop.

"He went into the lagoon." Pfeiffer stood where the beach met the dirt path, staring down at a confusion of tracks. "He ran for the parking lot, must've been spooked by the cop car, came back, and took cover in there."

His flashlight beam picked out a zigzag line of shoe prints that vanished among the tall cattails and pickleweed, their roots sunk in the muddy soil.

Travis and Carruthers stood beside him, guns and flashlights drawn. "Might be hunkered down," Carruthers said nervously, "drawing a bead on us right now."

"This guy is too rattled to draw a bead on anyone," Travis answered. "He's a scared rat on the run." He looked at Pfeiffer, who had a good eye for a trail. "Can we track him?"

"Don't think so, Boss. He must've trampled the foliage, but it looks to me like it's already springing back. And what with storm surges and careless hikers, there's enough damage to cover whatever tracks might be left."

Travis surveyed the ranks of cattails, then pointed at the bridge over Malibu Creek. "He's heading that way. He'll go in the water, cross under the bridge, and get out on the opposite side."

Carruthers frowned. "How can you be sure?"

"I know how these guys think. I was right about the car, wasn't I?" Travis had suggested the possibility that Hickle left his car in the beach parking lot. Carruthers had passed on the alert over his radio, and a CHP unit in the vicinity had taken the call. The highway cops had found Hickle's Volkswagen Rabbit a couple of minutes ago.

"You were right," the deputy conceded. "Well, if the bridge is where our boy is going, we better stop him." He unclipped the radio from his belt and, via the dispatcher, relayed a message to the CHP officers in the parking lot, reporting that the armed suspect had entered Malibu Lagoon and might attempt to make egress under the Cross Creek bridge. He really did use the words *make egress*. "If those guys are done securing his vehicle," he told the dispatcher, "we could use 'em on the bridge to keep an eye out."

"Good idea," Travis said when the transmission was over.

"Yeah, if you're right about where he's headed. If you're wrong, then we're watching the bridge while he circles back to the beach and hightails it out of here in any of three directions."

"So how do we proceed?" Travis asked. He had to defer to Carruthers because the kid was the only law enforcement officer on the scene.

"We split up, cover the whole lagoon. If he's hiding in there, we flush him out."

Travis nodded. "It's a plan."

"Who checks out the creek under the bridge?" Pfeiffer asked.

"I do." Travis shrugged. "My theory, so I get to prove it."

"Watch your back," Carruthers said.

Travis sketched him a wave and headed into the lagoon, holding his flashlight down at his side to conceal its beam.

37

Hickle crawled through the ranks of high, waving cattails, dragging the duffel. His elbows and knees were slimed with mud. Gnats buzzed at his ears. Twice he had blundered close to nesting waterfowl, which had flapped their wings at him, squawking angrily. He didn't know if his pursuers could pinpoint his position from the noise.

The ground turned softer. He smelled brackish water. One of the ponds was just ahead. He scrambled forward, sloshing up thick clumps of ooze, and finally burst out of the cattail forest into the open space at the edge of the estuary.

The pond joined the mouth of Malibu Creek, which flowed under the bridge that was part of the coast highway. Bridge traffic flashed past with a rattle and hum.

On the far side of the highway no one would be looking for him.

This thought impelled him off the muddy bank into the pond. He stayed low, bending almost double as he slogged through the shallow water, kicking up swirls of silt. Mud sucked at his waterlogged shoes, sending jolts of pain through his bad ankle. He kept going, his attention fixed on the bridge and the safety beyond it.

The duffel bag was an increasingly difficult burden, but he would not relinquish it. He might need the guns. As the water deepened, he hoisted the bag higher to keep it dry. He couldn't afford wet ammunition.

The bridge was close. When a faint current moved against him, he knew he had left the pond and entered Malibu Creek. The creek wound inland through forest and scrub. He could follow it as long as he liked, exit whenever he felt sure he'd shaken off his pursuit. Then he would need a car. He would steal one. He knew how to hot-wire an ignition. He had seen it done on television a thousand times. One of Kris's newscasts had detailed the procedure in a report on auto theft.

He hated to think of Kris. It stirred up too much anger and pain. He consoled himself with the thought that at least Abby was dead.

Under the bridge now. Traffic thrumming overhead. No moonlight or starlight reached into the concrete grotto. Dark water sloshed fitfully against the pylons, its wet slaps repeated in a train of soft echoes. He could hear his own breathing, amplified by the peculiar acoustics of the place.

He was nearing the far side of the bridge when he heard a car stop directly above him. Instinct froze him in place. A moment later a spotlight snapped on, sweeping the water straight ahead.

The car was a patrol unit, maybe the same one from the parking lot, and it was angling its spotlight down into the creek. He couldn't go forward. If he left the cover of the bridge he would be seen instantly. Had to retreat, conceal himself in the lagoon until the way was clear.

He headed in that direction, then stopped as a flashlight beam shone down from the bridge on that side, panning the water.

There must be two cops. Highway patrol officers,

probably; they rode in pairs after dark. Between them, they had both sides of the bridge covered. He was safe only as long as he stayed hidden underneath.

Trapped.

He backed up against one of the rusty pylons and huddled there, a scared animal. Minutes earlier he had been the predator lying in ambush. Now he was the prey, hiding from those who hunted him.

With trembling hands he removed the shotgun from the duffel, then felt inside the bag until he found a box of ammo. He fed four Federal Super Magnum shells into the gun. If the cops figured out where he was, he would open fire. The twelve-gauge was a better weapon than the rifle at close range. He might kill one of them, at least, before the sound of gunfire led his other pursuers to the bridge.

He hoped it wouldn't come to that. If Kris had died, his own fate would no longer matter. But as long as she lived, there was still a purpose to his life.

Travis saw him there, under the bridge.

The poor son of a bitch was pinned between one highway cop's downcast flashlight beam and the spotlight from the CHP car itself. He couldn't leave without being seen. All he could do was brace himself against a pylon and sit tight.

Crouching on the mudflat, his flashlight off, Travis considered his next move. Carruthers and Pfeiffer were too far away to see him. The highway patrol cops were within hailing distance, but he would be invisible to them as long as he stayed in the high bulrushes and sedges along the bank.

Carefully he pocketed his flashlight, then made his way through the foliage, keeping his head down and relying on the tall plants for cover. He advanced step by step, waiting for a gust of wind to shake the sedges and mask the disturbance his passage caused. As he drew close to the bridge, he timed his moves to coincide with each new rush of traffic, letting the roar of a Harley's unruffled motor or the rattle of a camper drown out the noise of his progress.

It had been a long time since he had been involved in the pursuit of an armed assailant. He found himself enjoying it. He almost wished he were an employee of Travis Protective Services, assigned to field duty, rather than the founder and proprietor, condemned to spend most of his time behind a desk.

He proceeded to within five feet of the bridge, and still the cop with the flashlight hadn't spotted him. Travis could see the patrolman leaning over the side, casting the beam into the waist-deep water, then exploring other parts of the creek and pond. Behind him the CHP car's lightbar threw blue and red pulses over the scene.

Travis was wondering how he would get past the drifting glow of the flashlight when his problem was solved for him. The patrolman abruptly lifted the flashlight and turned away, his attention drawn by the rising whine of two ambulance sirens.

The fire station was practically next door to Malibu Reserve, and the paramedics must have arrived almost immediately. The nearest hospitals were in Santa Monica and West LA. To get there, the ambulances had to cross the bridge, heading south on PCH. The patrol cops had paused in their surveillance to slow oncoming traffic and wave the emergency vehicles through.

It would take less than a minute for both ambulances to pass, but that was all the time Travis needed. He entered the creek, holding his gun high, and with one hand he cut the water with a strong stroke, gliding under the bridge.

When the first ambulance screamed overhead, he risked propelling himself forward with a strong kick. He was sure Hickle couldn't hear the splashing above the din from above.

Behind a pylon Travis paused, only his head and the Walther above water. Hickle, he saw, had turned toward the far side of the bridge. He was watching the spotlight, which had stopped moving. The duffel was strapped to his shoulder, and the shotgun was in his hand.

The second ambulance blew past with a cacophonous wail. Travis used the covering noise to glide forward, eel-like in the slippery water, moving from pylon to pylon until Hickle was within reach.

At the last moment Hickle seemed to sense another presence in the dark, but it was too late. Before he could turn, Travis pressed the Walther's muzzle to the back of Hickle's head. "Don't move, Raymond."

Hickle stiffened. Travis knew he was thinking of the shotgun, calculating odds and risks.

"I know you want to do something heroic," Travis whispered. "Something crazy. Don't. Just listen to me. Will you do that, Raymond? Will you listen to one thing I have to say?"

"So say it," Hickle breathed, tension bunching up the muscles of his shoulders.

"Okay, here it is, Raymond. Here's what I came to tell you."

Travis leaned close, pressing his mouth to Hickle's ear, and smiling in the dark, he recited the words of a nursery rhyme.

"Jack, be nimble . . . Jack, be quick . . ."

38

The gas was off. The furnace's pilot light was out. The windows in the bedroom and living room were open. Abby had not yet risked turning on an electric fan to expel the gas—any spark might ignite an explosion—but already the air was clearing.

"We've got to get you to a hospital," Wyatt said for the third time. The rover radio clipped to his uniform belt crackled with unintelligible crosstalk; he ignored it.

"I told you," Abby said, "I'll go when I'm through here."

"Through with what, exactly?"

"Damage control." She tried giving him a sharp look, but the effort of focusing her gaze spun ripples of vertigo through her skull.

She knew he was right about the hospital. It wasn't the inhalation of gas that worried her as much as the head trauma she'd suffered when Hickle knocked her out. She still had a raging headache centered behind her eyes, pain that she could no longer attribute entirely to the gas. She was less steady on her feet than she ought to be, and the nausea in her belly had not completely vanished even after she'd started breathing fresh air.

So, yes, she would go to a hospital, but not until she had tied up a few loose ends. The police—by which she meant officers of the law other than Vic Wyatt—

would arrive before long to check out Hickle's apartment and look in on his immediate neighbors. This was standard investigative procedure, and it would be triggered by Hickle's attack on Kris Barwood.

Abby knew there had been an attack. On the phone she'd heard Travis yell an order to a driver. Kris's voice had been briefly audible, asking what was wrong. Then, gunfire. The shotgun, from the sound of it. Several shots, Kris screaming, Travis yelling at her to get down—

And silence. The connection had been lost.

Anything could have happened after that. Desperate to know, Abby had redialed Travis's cell phone twice. No answer. She'd considered phoning 911 before remembering that TPS had stationed security agents at the beach house. They must have heard the shots, as had Kris's neighbors.

So the police were definitely involved. Whatever the outcome of the attack, there would be a thorough investigation. The Hollywood side of the case would focus on Hickle's apartment. Nice men in suits would be banging on every door on the fourth floor very soon. But by then she would be gone.

She made her way somewhat unsteadily into the kitchen and took out a pair of rubber gloves. As she was pulling them on, she heard Wyatt's low-top boots on the linoleum floor. "I'm not sure I want to know what those are for," he said wryly.

She saw a frown of disapproval pinching his mouth. "Then you'd better not follow me when I go into Hickle's apartment."

"His apartment?" The frown deepened, and he folded his arms across his chest, the blue sleeves of his jacket straining taut. "Sounds like tampering with a crime scene."

"Going to arrest me, Sergeant?" His silence was an eloquent reply. "Okay, then."

Taking her cell phone in case Travis called back, she hustled into the bedroom, where she picked up the padlock and chain. Then she climbed onto the fire escape and lifted herself into Hickle's bedroom window.

"You took a blow to the back of the head," Wyatt said from behind her.

His voice surprised her. He had followed her so silently that she hadn't been aware of his presence. She paused, straddling the windowsill. "Yeah, Hickle clipped me," she admitted, self-consciously fingering the bump he had seen. There was no laceration, no bleeding, only a large, swollen knob, tender to the touch.

Wyatt leaned close and patted the injury also, drawing a wince from her. "How?" he asked, worry in his eyes. "What did he use, his fist or a weapon?"

"I don't know. I've got a little memory gap. I remember fighting him . . . then coming to."

"You lost consciousness from the blow? Hell, Abby, you've suffered a grade three concussion. We have to get you to an ER. You need a neurologic exam—"

"I need to take care of business. The ER can wait."

She tried to complete her unlawful entry into Hickle's apartment. Wyatt grabbed her hand to stop her. "You have any idea how serious a major concussion can be?"

She raised her head and met his eyes, experiencing another swoon of vertigo. "I think I do. Let's see, when my brain sloshed forward, I could have suffered a contre-coup injury—contusion of the frontal and temporal lobes. Or I could have ruptured some blood vessels, in which case I have a nice little subdural hematoma building up pressure in my skull. Maybe I've formed a blood clot, and if I receive another blow it'll be jarred loose and I'll have a stroke, possibly fatal. So yes, Vic, I have a vague idea of how serious a concussion can be, and the sooner you let me do what I have to do, the sooner I can get medical attention. Okay?"

She shook free of his grip and finished climbing through the window. She knew she had been sharp with him. Irritability was one symptom of head trauma.

The air in Hickle's apartment was clean. He hadn't set a similar death trap in his own place. "Don't touch anything," she instructed Wyatt when he followed her inside. "You were never here."

She wiped off the padlock and chain, tossing both items on the bedroom floor, and proceeded into the living room. The first thing she saw was that Hickle had pulled down the smoke detector. Scanning the carpet, she discovered the camera's crushed remnants. She put them in her pocket.

"What was that?" Wyatt asked.

"Surveillance camera. In pieces, but the crime scene guys would still be able to identify it."

"Camera? One of yours?"

"It's just a tool of the trade, no big deal, except it's illegal."

"Yeah, except for that."

Abby retrieved the infinity transmitter from the smashed telephone, then found the bug in the oven's ventilation hood, which Hickle had overlooked. She returned to the bedroom. The place was a mess. Hickle had torn down most of the photos; they littered the floor like a drift of faces. Abby wondered if Wyatt noticed that the subject of every photograph was Kris Barwood. If so, he didn't mention it.

As she was groping underneath the drawers of Hickle's nightstand to recover the other microphone, she heard Wyatt say, "You think you can disappear, is that it?"

"Possibly. I've done it before."

"You mean when you were Emanuel Barth's housekeeper?"

"How'd you guess?"

"I didn't, until Sam Cahill gave me the details. He's the detective who handled the case and put Barth away the second time."

She looked at him. "You talked with a detective about me?"

"Your name never came up."

"Even so, you must've raised his suspicions."

"Sam's a friend. He'll be discreet. You can trust him."

"I don't seem to have a choice," she snapped.

"You know, for someone who just cheated death, you're in a pretty foul mood."

Abby found a smile. "Sorry. I just don't like people knowing my secrets, that's all."

"Even me?"

"Even you, Vic. Even though you saved my life. It may be irrational, but that's the way I am. Anyway, you're right about the Barth case. I was Connie Hammond."

"And you disappeared."

"It was easy enough. Nobody was looking very hard for Connie. This time there are complications. Hickle knows the truth about me. Someone else may know also. If either of them ends up in custody and wants to talk, I could have some explaining to do." She pocketed the second mike, then picked up her micro-cassette recorder, which Hickle had left on the bed.

"Sounds like you're in a lot of trouble, Abby."

"No, I *was* in a lot of trouble. Now I'm fine, thanks to you. And I do mean thanks. I was wrong, you know, the other night."

"Wrong about what?"

"When I said I didn't need any help, that I could handle myself and I didn't need anybody watching my back. I was wrong." It was difficult for her to say this. Self-reliance and self-sufficiency had been the basic credo of her life.

"Yeah, well"—Wyatt shrugged—"we all make mistakes."

The last thing Abby took out of Hickle's apartment was the Maidenform briefs he'd stolen from her laundry. She noticed Wyatt eyeing the underwear with a puzzled look, but he didn't ask any questions, and she didn't feel like talking about it.

They returned via the fire escape to her apartment. By now the gas had largely dissipated, and Abby felt ready to risk a spark. She turned on a table fan, blowing the rest of the fumes out the living room window. In her bedroom, she removed the monitoring gear from the closet and arranged it on the bureau.

"More spy stuff?" Wyatt asked.

"Not anymore. Now it's your garden-variety TV and VCR."

"And an audio deck with long-playing reel-to-reel tapes."

"Quirky, but not particularly suspicious. I doubt

anybody will even notice it on a casual walk-through. Can you get me a trash bag from the kitchen?"

While Wyatt fetched it, Abby went into the bathroom and poured a long drink of water. God, her throat was so sore. She was tempted to take aspirin, but she knew it would thin her blood and exacerbate any internal bleeding. At least her head no longer was beating like a bongo drum. Now it was more like a snare drum. That had to constitute an improvement.

She checked her eyes in the mirror. The pupils looked evenly dilated, a good sign. Maybe her injury wasn't as bad as she'd feared. Had she dodged the blow at the last instant, receiving only a glancing impact rather than a direct hit? Had her reflexes saved her from a skull fracture and brain injury? It was possible. She didn't remember how she had reacted or even what Hickle had hit her with. She didn't remember the moment of impact at all.

"You're hurting," Wyatt said when she emerged from the bathroom. He had been watching her.

"It's nothing a little fresh air and exercise won't cure." She took the trash bag from him and stuffed it with the wrecked video cassette and audio reels, as well as the Maidenform briefs, which she sure as hell wasn't going to wear again.

Wyatt grunted. "Maybe. But you're still going to the ER, if I have to drag you there by your hair."

"How Neanderthal of you. But entirely unnecessary." She added the camera, microphones, and transmitters to the bag, along with the rubber gloves. "I'm going of my own volition. See?" She held up the trash bag. "All packed."

In the living room she picked up her purse and checked to confirm that her gun was still there. She put her microrecorder and cell phone inside, pausing as she wondered if she should try Travis's number again.

Wyatt saw her hesitate. "He still hasn't called back—whoever you reported to."

"Maybe he can't. Maybe the alert came too late. Maybe"—she hated to say it—"maybe he's dead, and the client too."

"Kris Barwood," Wyatt said. So he had noticed the photos.

Abby nodded. This time her head did not reel from the effort, and she took some comfort from that.

They left the apartment together and rode the elevator to ground level. Wyatt said he would drive her in his squad car, and she said, "Yes, of course." In her present state she was unfit to sit behind the wheel of an automobile. If she had suffered any serious craniocerebral trauma, she could black out at any time. "But," she added, "we have to move my Dodge out of the parking lot so your pals in blue don't find it."

"Why?"

"So if I'm interviewed, I can say I drove myself to the hospital." As he walked her to the Dodge, she explained more fully. Talking was good. It kept her alert. "See, I'm trying to keep all my options open until I know how things work out. I'd prefer to have Abby Gallagher disappear forever, like Connie Hammond. But if Hickle or someone else identifies me to the police, I'll have to come clean. At least, reasonably clean."

"How clean exactly?"

"I won't admit to any illegalities. No electronic surveillance, no breaking and entering. I was hired to move in next door to Hickle and keep an eye on him, that's all. He found me out and attacked me. When I came to, I was confused and disoriented. I drove myself to the hospital in a daze and didn't remember my obligation to talk to the cops until my memories came back at a convenient time."

"Weak."

"But undisprovable."

"That's not a word."

"It is now."

"Hickle will tell them about the bugs in his apartment. How are you going to explain that?"

"Explain what? The paranoid ravings of a homicidal stalker?"

"And if Hickle is never caught and your cover isn't blown?"

"Then farewell, Abby Gallagher, wherever you are."

He looked at her with admiration. "You've got it all worked out, haven't you?"

"This is nothing. You should see me in action when my brain hasn't been batted around like a beach ball."

Wyatt moved the Dodge to a side street, then escorted her to his cruiser. He asked which hospital she wanted. She ran through the options in her mind and decided that on a Friday night any emergency room in this part of town would be a war zone. "I don't suppose you could chauffeur me all the way to Cedars-Sinai," she said. It was in West Hollywood, a better neighborhood.

"No problem."

"It might be a problem for you if the watch commander starts to wonder where you've been for so long."

"I'll tell him I stopped at a donut shop. That's always plausible for a cop, right?"

Abby smiled. "No comment."

Three blocks from the Gainford Arms, Wyatt detoured into an alley and discarded the trash bag in a Dumpster. As he pulled onto Santa Monica Boulevard, heading west, Abby fished her cell phone out of her purse and speed-dialed Travis's number. Still no answer.

"It'll be all right," Wyatt said quietly.

"Sure. I know. The good guys always win, don't they?" She sank back wearily in the passenger seat and shut her eyes, repeating the words as a mantra. "The good guys always win."

39

"A re you really him?" Hickle breathed. "Are you JackBNimble?"

"I'm him. You still thinking about using that twelve-gauge?"

The tension eased out of Hickle in a shaky expulsion of breath. "Guess not."

"Glad to hear it." Travis stepped back, lowering the Walther. "You can turn around. No reason we can't talk face to face. We're partners, after all."

Hickle turned, the water rippling around him. Overhead a burst of crosstalk sounded from the squad car's radio, the volume high. The flashlight winked on again, and the spotlight resumed probing the creek waters. The two cops had returned to their task.

"We're both trapped in here now," Hickle whispered.

"No, I'll get us out. You'll go inland while I distract the two Smokies on the bridge."

"Distract them how?"

"Don't worry about that. We have a lot to discuss and not much time. Do you know who I am?"

Hickle studied him in the gloom. Travis took the opportunity to assess Hickle's face. He had never seen the man in person. He had small, suspicious eyes, a rodent's eyes. His skin was pasty, his hair greasy and wild. He belonged here under the bridge in the fetid water, amid the flotsam of fast-food containers and cigarette packs.

"No," Hickle said finally. "Should I?"

"I think so, if you've watched the news." Travis allowed himself a brief smile. "And I know you never miss the news."

The small eyes narrowed. The bloodless line of Hickle's mouth pinched in a frown. "Hey," he whispered, "you run the security firm. You're Paul Travis. You're famous in this town."

Hickle seemed almost honored to be meeting a celebrity, even if the encounter had to take place in a dark creek during a police pursuit. And why not? Fame was his obsession.

"You're the one who's famous now," Travis said. "In a few hours your name will be all over the newspapers and the TV, radio—everywhere."

Hickle nearly brightened, then twisted his mouth in a pout. "As a failure."

"For the moment." Travis sighed. "You know, you really should've killed her when you had the chance."

"Don't you go blaming me for that. It was the car, the Lincoln. It was bulletproof—"

"That's not what I meant. I'm talking about Abby."

"Abby?" A beat of silence as Hickle took this in. "She's—she's still alive?"

"Unfortunately, yes. But she doesn't have to be." Travis's words returned in a wave of echoes.

"What do you mean?" Hickle's voice, very soft, produced no echo at all.

"I know a way for you to get Abby, really get her this time, no mistakes. You'd like that, wouldn't you?"

The glimmer in Hickle's eyes was pure malice. "I'd like Kris more."

"She'll come later. Abby first. It only makes sense. Security around Kris will be tight for a few days. Not just TPS security—police protection too. But Abby won't have any protection at all."

Hickle processed this, then nodded. "How do I do it?"

"I can tell you where she lives. Her permanent address, not the apartment she rented next door to you. With that rifle of yours, you can nail her easily. I've got it all worked out."

"Yeah, sure, you've got it all worked out." Hickle took a step toward Travis in the deep water, launching concentric circles of ripples that sloshed against the pylons. "So why the hell didn't you ever mention the armored car and the bulletproof glass? Why—"

"Keep your voice down." Travis glanced upward at the underbelly of the bridge. "They may hear."

"Don't tell me what to do," Hickle said, but he did lower his voice. "You're the one who messed up everything. Or maybe it was all a setup. Is that it? You were in the car with her. You're the one who protected her from me. You never wanted me to kill her. This is all some kind of game—"

"No game, Raymond."

"So explain it." Hickle was close now. Travis could see the wildness in his eyes. To control him, Travis would have to handle this next answer just right. He wished he were more skilled at reading people. That was Abby's special talent. Absurdly he regretted that she wasn't here to help.

"Raymond," he said quietly, "I had no choice about what happened tonight. Kris insisted on using a TPS staff car, one of our armored vehicles. And she insisted that I ride shotgun. I couldn't refuse either request without raising her suspicions. It all happened fast; I had no chance to e-mail you an update."

The story sounded plausible, Travis thought. He waited while Hickle's eyes ticked back and forth, his brain probing the story for weaknesses. "Why would Kris want special protection tonight of all nights?" he asked finally.

Travis was ready for that one. He fixed Hickle with a reproving stare. "Because you varied your routine. You didn't call her today."

A beat of silence, broken only by the sizzle of radio crosstalk overhead. "You're saying," Hickle breathed, "it's my fault?"

This was precisely what Travis was saying, but he chose to be magnanimous. "What's done is done. It's nobody's fault. Just one of those things."

"But you protected her. You helped her find cover after I blew up the car."

"I wasn't protecting her. I was defending myself. You would have killed us both. A shotgun isn't a discriminating weapon."

"You fired at me even after she broke away from you. You popped off two shots right at me."

"And missed both times. I'm a skilled marksman, Raymond. I didn't have to miss." He paused to let that statement register. "For that matter, I don't have to be telling you any of this right now. I could have alerted the cops on the bridge—or shot you in the back of the head when I swam up. Instead I've taken you into my confidence. I've revealed my identity. Don't I deserve a little trust in return?"

Nicely done. Travis was pleased with himself. Even Abby couldn't have manipulated the man any more expertly.

"Well," Hickle muttered, "maybe. But I can't figure your angle. Kris is your client. Abby's your employee or business associate or something. Why would you want either of them dead? Why would you be helping me when it's your job to stop me?"

"Good questions. I wish I had time for an in-depth discussion. But you see, there are other men combing the lagoon. One of them will see us soon. We need to wrap this up."

His point was punctuated by a sudden clatter of wings in the lagoon—a bird startled into flight. Either Carruthers or Pfeiffer must have blundered into a nest not far away.

"Hear that?" Travis said. "They're closing in. Now, do you want my help or not?"

Hickle hesitated only a moment, then nodded. "I want it."

"Okay, first things first. How were you planning to get out of Malibu?"

"Head upstream to where there are houses and ranches, then steal a car out of somebody's driveway. Or if I can't find a car, I'll hide in the woods till the heat dies down."

"No good. Either way it'll take too long, and time is not on your side. You're underestimating the gravity of this situation. You're big news, Raymond. Let me tell you what's going to happen within the next fifteen minutes. First the choppers will arrive. Sheriff's department aerial units. TV and radio helicopters too. One of them will spot you in the creek or the woods. If they don't find you, the dogs will. K-nine units. You've seen them on the news, right? Those dogs will be sniffing for a scent on both sides of the highway. The creek won't cover your scent, either. That's a myth. Smells carry just fine over water."

Clearly Hickle hadn't thought about dogs, choppers. He licked his lips.

"So," Travis continued relentlessly, "you're screwed any way you look at it. Stay in the creek or hide in the woods, and the dogs will track you down unless a chopper spots you first. Take cover in a house, and the police will figure out where you are once they start conducting house-to-house searches. You'll be surrounded by a SWAT team, and your only choice will be whether you kill yourself or let them do it for you."

"All right, all right." Hickle was even paler than before. "I won't hide out. I'll steal a car, like I said."

"That's right, you will, but you have to do it fast. There'll be roadblocks set up before long. Highway patrol units and sheriff's cruisers, checking every car that goes through. The one thing that's working in your favor is that Malibu is relatively isolated. It takes time to deliver manpower and other resources out here. That's why there are only three patrol units on the scene so far. You have to make your move before it gets any more crowded. That means you don't have time to go far inland. You grab the first car you see. This creek runs past a parking lot behind the little shopping center across the street. Even at this hour, there's a good chance you'll find some sort of vehicle in that lot. If there's anything you can drive, take it. And go north."

"Not south? There's more traffic that way. I might blend in better."

"South is too obvious. There may already be a roadblock south of here. Your odds are better if you cut through Topanga Canyon to the Ventura Freeway. They won't block off the freeway, so once you're on it you'll be reasonably safe. Connect with the north-bound 405. You know where San Fernando Road meets the Golden State Freeway?"

"North end of the Valley."

Travis nodded. "High-crime district, lots of auto theft. That's where you'll ditch your vehicle. Leave it unlocked, motor running. With any luck someone else will take it for a joyride, and by the time the police find it, they won't know where you abandoned it."

"Then what do I use for transportation?"

"Steal another car. Cars get stolen in that part of town every night. The crime probably won't be linked to you at first, which means it won't be a high priority. Drive south into LA but avoid Hollywood. They'll be expecting you to return there. Where you want to go is Westwood."

"Because that's where Abby is," Hickle breathed.

"Or where she will be, eventually. She lives in a condo tower called the Wilshire Royal." Travis gave the cross street and the address. "Her unit is ten-fifteen. It's at the front of the building, fourth window from the right, facing Wilshire."

"How do I get inside?"

"You don't."

Travis explained in detail. Hickle listened, nodding now and then to signal either agreement or under-standing.

"Got it?" Travis asked when he was through.

"I got it. Now how about Kris?"

"I told you, she'll come later."

"When?"

"I'll be in touch. Once you've nailed Abby, hole up somewhere safe. Get access to your e-mail account at a library or someplace and log on once a day. I'll contact you as soon as I can. Trust me."

"I'm still not sure I should."

"But you have to. Right now, Raymond, I'm the only friend you've got."

Hickle gave him a cool, perceptive stare. "I bet Kris and Abby think you're their friend too. Don't they?"

Travis didn't answer.

40

The Emergency Department at Cedars-Sinai Medical Center had been recently renovated and expanded, and to Abby it felt more like a hotel than a hospital. Then again, at a hotel she would not have been sitting on a wheeled mechanical bed that doubled as an examination table, reading a poster about flu season while holding an ice pack to her head.

Wyatt had dropped her off at the entrance. She'd declined his offer to accompany her inside, knowing that it was best for both of them if they weren't seen together. The nurse at the semicircular admitting desk had listened to Abby's story of a blow to the head delivered by a racquetball partner's errant swing. If the nurse wondered why anybody would be playing racquetball at midnight, or where the partner had gone, or why Abby wasn't wearing workout clothes, she didn't ask. Obviously she assumed the story was a lie, and that Abby's boyfriend or husband had struck her.

The ER was not excessively crowded even on a Friday night. It didn't take long for a physician to perform an initial baseline evaluation, which included an eye exam and tests of her reflexes, as well as gentle probing of the goose egg on her head. "Any vomiting?" he asked. "Amnesia? Drowsiness? Headache?"

She answered no, yes, no, yes but it was getting better.

He gave her a nonaspirin painkiller and an ice pack. His diagnosis was an uncomplicated concussion, full recovery anticipated. He wanted her held overnight for observation. She could sleep, but a nurse would wake her periodically to monitor her alertness. She would be moved out of the ER shortly. "Meanwhile, relax," he said, adding that someone else would drop by to check on her before she was moved upstairs. A domestic violence counselor, Abby figured.

Now she waited restlessly, shifting on the bed and swinging her legs. Really, she wasn't sleepy at all. There was too much adrenaline roaring through her system after her near-death experience. And there was fear. Travis still hadn't called.

Gazing around the room, she saw what resembled a TV hovering at the end of a mechanical arm alongside the bed. Closer inspection established that it really was a TV—a color TV, in fact. She wondered if it got cable. "Next vacation," she decided, "I'm booking a room here."

She was debating whether or not to turn on the TV and search for a news update when her purse began to chirp. It took her a moment to understand that a call was coming in on her cell phone. Fumbling one-handed with the purse, she got out the phone and answered the call on the fifth ring. "Yes?" she gasped, praying to hear Travis's voice.

"Abby—it's me."

A knot of tension unraveled in her gut, and she let herself breathe deeply for the first time in more than an hour. "Paul. Are you okay?"

"Just fine. You?"

"Never better," she lied. "What happened in Malibu? How's Kris?"

"Not a scratch on her. We had a close call, though."

"On the phone I heard gunshots."

"Yes, our friend mounted an assault with his shot-gun. Fortunately we were riding in a shielded car from the TPS fleet. Even so, he found a weak spot in the armor. The driver suffered superficial wounds, but he'll be all right."

"And you?" She knew she had asked him already, but she needed to hear his answer again.

Travis chuckled. "The only damage was to my pride. I got wet. Soaked through."

"Wet?" She didn't understand.

"I pursued Hickle into the lagoon next to the beach. Thought I saw him under the bridge. Tried to sneak closer and ended up falling into the damn creek. There were two highway cops on the bridge who got a good laugh out of it."

"And Hickle? Was he under the bridge?"

"Nobody was there. What I saw was a trick of the light. I humiliated myself for nothing."

"So he got away?"

"Evidently. The police are combing the area, and they've put up roadblocks on PCH, but I think it's a case of locking the barn door after the horse is gone. There's a report of a car stolen from a shopping center across the highway from the lagoon. It's a safe guess Hickle took it. Even so, with all the media attention, he won't get far."

Abby wasn't so sure, but she didn't pursue the issue. "I tried calling you again and again—"

"Lost my phone in the attack. It probably melted when the car caught fire."

She hitched in a breath. "Caught fire?"

"It's a long story."

"Were you burned?"

"Not at all. Stop asking for health updates. I'm fine."

"Where are you now?"

"The Barwoods' guest house. Some of the TPS staffers keep spare clothes there, and Mahoney's just my size. My suit was soaked through; I had to change before I caught pneumonia. Next on the agenda is a visit to the sheriff's station in Agoura. I have to give a heads-up to the captain who runs the show."

"About Howard?"

"Right. I'll keep you out of it for as long as I can. You're not still in Hollywood, are you?"

"No, of course not. I had to make myself scarce."

"That's what I figured. Back in Westwood, then? My advice is to stay put in your condo for at least—"

"I'm not in my condo."

"You're not?" There was an odd note of disappointment in his voice.

"Actually, I'm staying overnight at Cedars. Got a minor bump on the noggin."

"Oh. I see. Hell, I thought you said you were unhurt." He sounded more angry than concerned.

Abby shrugged. "It's nothing. I'm here as a precaution, that's all. My brain's my livelihood; I don't like to take chances with it."

"Well, it sounds like you need your rest. I'd better let you go, but I'll visit you first thing in the morning. You check in as Abby Sinclair?"

"That's right. I'm back to my old self."

"Take care, Abby."

"Paul?"

"Yes?"

"It's good to hear your voice."

"Yours too, Abby. Always."

She ended the call and sat very still, the ice pack in one hand, the phone in the other. She sensed a peculiar tautness in the muscles of her face. At first she didn't understand it. Then she realized she was smiling. Until now she hadn't permitted herself to know how scared she had been.

There was nothing to fear any longer. Paul had survived. And Kris.

The good guys really had won after all.

41

Abby did her best to sleep once she was moved to a room on the third floor, but relaxation would not come. When she closed her eyes, her mind was crowded instantly with a confused rush of images—Hickle with the shotgun, Wyatt kneeling beside her on the fire escape, photos of Kris torn and scattered on Hickle's bedroom floor. At times Travis entered her thoughts, and she imagined him flailing in the creek while the cops on the bridge kidded him and laughed . . . but it wasn't funny, because dimly in the distance a slouching, raggedy figure that must be Hickle was slipping away unseen.

This made no sense. She was overtired, her brain making irrational connections. She wished she could quiet her thinking. At home she would have brewed some valerian tea, but she was sure the hospital stocked only conventional medicines. Anyway, the nurses wouldn't give her any tranquilizers; they needed to monitor her mental clarity at two-hour intervals.

Past 6 A.M., as dawn was brightening her window, she found a way to sleep. She expected bad dreams, but there were none. Her mind had shut down at last, and she drifted weightless in the humming dark.

And woke to see Travis gazing down at her.

"Sorry," he whispered. "Did I wake you?"

She sat up quickly, noting in a detached way that she experienced no vertigo after the change of position, and that her headache was entirely gone.

"No," she said. "I mean, yes, I guess you did, but it's all right. What time is it?"

"Eight-thirty."

"In the morning?" she asked stupidly.

Travis smiled. "Saturday morning, March twenty-six. How are you feeling?"

"Not so bad, just drowsy. Didn't get much sleep last night. How about you?"

"No sleep. Spent all night at the sheriff's station. The captain in charge of the Malibu-Lost Hills station was extremely interested in what I had to say, as were two of his detectives."

"You sure it's not too soon to make an accusation? We don't have any hard evidence—"

"We do now. Our computer techs found a link between Western Regional Resources and the company that owns the bungalow in Culver City. However, I didn't approach the subject that way with the captain. I left the bungalow out of it for now. Didn't want to raise any questions about unauthorized activities."

"You mean, like the fact that I illegally entered the place and searched it?"

"Exactly. All I said was that we'd learned Howard Barwood has at least one dummy corporation, Western Regional Resources, and we have reason to believe he may own a cell phone registered to that company. I suggested that if in fact Howard is Hickle's informant, then Howard might have used that phone to talk with him or arrange a rendezvous. I suggested they check the cellular carrier's records."

"Did they?"

"Yes. They found the Thursday night call made to Hickle's apartment. That was when they started taking a serious interest in Mr. Barwood, though he doesn't know it yet."

"Where's Howard now?"

"Scheduled for a talk with those two detectives I mentioned. They'll be handling him with kid gloves, giving him the OJ treatment. He's well-connected, and they don't want to do anything rash until they know what's going on."

"Just be sure they keep an eye on him. If they give him too long a leash, he may flee. Then you'll have to tell them about the bungalow."

"Why? You think he'd go there?"

"It's possible. He keeps a gun in his nightstand. He might want to pick it up, especially if he has any plans to rendezvous with Hickle."

"A gun? You never mentioned that."

"It didn't seem too important at the time. A little Colt forty-five, like the malt liquor."

One of the nurses appeared in the doorway, telling Travis he'd been allowed only five minutes with the patient, and his time was up.

"I was just leaving," Travis said with a smile.

The nurse was not charmed. "See that you do. Miss Sinclair suffered a nasty concussion in a racquetball game." She squinted at Travis suspiciously. "You wouldn't happen to be the one she was playing with?"

"Abby and I never play games," Travis said. "At least not with each other."

The nurse frowned, aware that some sort of veiled joke had been told but unable to see the punch line. "Well, say your good-byes, and let the patient sleep."

When the nurse was gone, Abby smiled at Travis. "See how well protected I am?"

"I should hire her for TPS. She'd make a good body-guard. As for Howard, you don't have to worry about him. Men of his social standing seldom run. They stick around and hire smart lawyers. They always think they can beat the system. Half the time they're right."

"I guess so."

"But I'll keep the bungalow in mind. If he flees, I'll tell the police." He touched her hand lightly, then pulled away. "Better get going before Nurse Ratched returns. Besides, there's another stop I have to make on this floor. Kris is here."

"Kris? Right down the hall?"

He nodded. "She showed symptoms of neurogenic shock. The paramedics brought her in."

"Saint John's would have been closer, or UCLA Medical."

"Her regular physician is on call at Cedars, so this is where she wanted to come. And you don't say no to Kris Barwood, especially now. If you thought she was big before, you should see the coverage of this case."

She understood what he was thinking. "Then maybe TPS will make a comeback?"

"Here's hoping."

"And maybe . . . maybe I can let it go." She said the words softly, half to herself.

"Corbal?" Travis asked.

She nodded. "I know I told you I wasn't trying to prove anything or redeem myself. I lied. It's all I've thought about for the past four months. The way I screwed up . . . and what I could do to try to make it right."

"You did everything you could," Travis said gently,

"and then some. Now get some sleep. You've earned a good long rest."

"I will. Thanks, Paul."

She let her head fall back on the pillow, drowsiness washing over her. She was closing her eyes when Travis leaned down and kissed her forehead, a tender act, unusual for him.

"A good long rest," he repeated softly.

She was asleep before he left the room.

42

Their names were Giacomo and Heller, and they greeted Howard Barwood at the sheriff's station with smiles and handshakes, saying how much they appreciated his taking the time to clear up a few minor details about the case. He scarcely listened. He'd slept little, having spent most of the night at Cedars-Sinai with Kris. He was tired and hungry; Courtney had fixed him breakfast, but he'd had little appetite. Above all, he was burdened with guilt.

He regretted his every hour with Amanda. He regretted every thought of leaving Kris. He regretted being a bad husband. What made it worse was that he knew this was only a mood that would pass, and before long he would be sneaking out for more liaisons with Amanda or some new young thing. His good intentions never lasted.

Preoccupied with these thoughts, he let Giacomo and Heller usher him into a small office, where they offered him a seat at a battered wooden table. They sat opposite him. Heller took out a notepad and a pen. Giacomo placed a cassette recorder on the table and said something about a need to record the interview to ensure an accurate transcript. "Fine," Howard said indifferently.

Giacomo did most of the talking. He began by speaking into the recorder, giving the location, date, and time of the interview. Howard noticed he used military time—oh-nine-hundred thirty-five hours. "We're here with Mr. Howard Barwood," Giacomo said, asking for Howard's birthdate. Howard rattled it off without thinking, his voice alien to him, coming from far away.

"Now, Mr. Barwood, I'm going to give you your constitutional rights. It would be good if you would listen carefully—"

For the first time Howard roused himself. "My rights?"

Giacomo said yes, and Heller nodded, both men smiling in a way that seemed too friendly.

Howard blinked. "Am I a suspect or something?" The idea seemed bizarre, incomprehensible.

"Actually, Mr. Barwood, we're mainly interested in eliminating you as a suspect."

"But . . . a suspect in what? Hickle attacked Kris. People saw him. I was in the house—"

"Of course you were. There are witnesses who support everything you just said. And nobody doubts that Raymond Hickle ambushed that car."

"Then what . . . ?" He couldn't finish the question. Nothing was making sense.

"There are always a lot of angles in a case like this," Giacomo said. "We need to tie up some loose ends, that's all."

Angles, loose ends . . . Howard was baffled. "You never said anything about viewing me as a suspect."

Heller spoke. "We don't view you that way. Truth is, we hate to even waste your time with this. What we'd like is to get it over with so we can all go home."

"It's been a long night for everybody," Giacomo said.

"I'm beat," Heller added.

Vaguely Howard understood that something was taking place that was not necessarily to his benefit. But the two detectives were right about one thing. It had indeed been a long night. He was reluctant to walk out of the interview now, only to return later and go through all this rigmarole again. And if he did walk out, he'd have to contact Martin Greenfeld, his attorney. Martin would never let him talk to any detectives or waive any rights. Martin believed in handling every situation as if it were an adversarial contest played for the highest stakes.

Howard imagined the consequences of refusing to talk. The story would leak to the media. People would suspect him of complicity in the attempted murder of his wife. And if his relationship with Amanda came out . . .

On the other hand, if he simply kept Martin and all other lawyers out of it and did as the detectives asked, he could be done with this interview in thirty minutes. No suspicions, no rumors, no damaging publicity, no journalists digging up dirt.

"Fine," he said evenly. "Let's proceed."

Giacomo recited Howard's rights. Howard said he understood them. Yes, he wished to give up his right to remain silent. Yes, he gave up his right to have an attorney present. Yes, yes, yes.

Then there were questions about his activities last night. He told his story about taking the Lexus for a long drive up the coast. The detectives didn't interrupt or challenge him. He began to think this really was a routine interview. By the time he narrated the climax of the story—the moment when, standing on his beachfront deck, he'd heard gunshots—he was relaxed and confident. He didn't need Martin to hold his hand. He could take care of himself. "So that's the way it happened," he finished.

"Great, Mr. Barwood." Giacomo spoke in the tone of a man adjourning a meeting. "I guess you drove that Lexus of yours here today, didn't you?"

"I drive it everywhere. I love that car."

"Maybe when we're done here, Kevin and I could take a look at the odometer."

This froze Howard. "The odometer?"

"Just to note the number for our records. If you've been driving up to Santa Barbara on a regular basis, you must have logged some serious miles."

"Well . . . I may have exaggerated the number of trips I took. And it's a new car, quite new. There aren't a lot of miles on it yet." He was starting to babble. He shut up.

Heller wrote something in his pad.

"Okay, well, we'll talk about that later," Giacomo said blandly. "Now I wonder if you could tell us anything about this company of yours, Western Regional Resources."

Western Regional. How the hell could they know about that? How was it possible? Why would it even come up? "I don't think my business holdings are relevant," he said stiffly, playing for time.

"Oh, you're probably right, Mr. Barwood." Giacomo would not stop smiling. "It's another of those loose ends we told you about. You do own a company called Western Regional Resources, don't you? Or are we wrong about that?"

By all logic Howard knew he should stop the interview and get Martin Greenfeld on the phone, but stubbornly he still believed he could talk his way out. He was a good talker. He had developed parcel after parcel of prime Westside real estate on the strength of his facility with words, his charm, his self-possession. He called on those faculties to rescue him now.

"I own it," he said slowly, punctuating the admission with an insouciant shrug. "Western Regional Resources is a corporation I established in the Netherlands Antilles. All perfectly legal. There are sound reasons—tax-liability reasons—for setting up such an entity. As I say, it's all within the bounds of the law."

Giacomo said he was sure it was. "And in the course of setting up this offshore, uh, entity, you presumably set up a few other things? Like a bank account?"

"Yes."

"And you arranged for someone to oversee the account and handle any legal issues for the company, right?"

"A bank officer in the Antilles does that for me, yes."

"And I suppose you might have acquired, say, a residence in the Antilles for business purposes."

"No residence. I used a hotel the one time I went there."

"How about other acquisitions? A car, a phone, a club membership?"

"Nothing like that. Western Regional Resources is— well, it's a legitimate corporation—I mean, it's legal in every way, but—but it has no tangible assets, it's not a going concern, it's—"

"A dummy corporation?" Giacomo asked.

Heller was writing in his pad again.

"It could be described that way," Howard said.

"A tax haven?"

"It's all legal," he repeated for what felt like the fiftieth time. The hell of it was, the goddamned arrangement really was legal. But he wouldn't expect these two ruffians to understand that. They could hardly relate to his problems, his priorities. If he claimed he was hiding money from the IRS, they wouldn't sympathize. And if he admitted the truth—that he was executing an end run around California's community property laws to smooth his way through an upcoming divorce—well, they would think he had a motive for getting rid of Kris . . .

And in fact, he did have such a motive, didn't he?

Didn't he?

"Do you have any other business entities offshore, Mr. Barwood?" Giacomo asked. He put a slight, disdainful emphasis on the word *entities*.

"I don't think I'm under any obligation to discuss the details of my financial situation with you," Howard said.

Heller's pen scratched again.

"Okay, that's fine." Giacomo was still smiling. He must smile in his sleep. "We're trying to tidy things up here, that's all. I guess you were over at KPTI the other night."

The change of subject startled Howard, but he was happy to drop the issue of his business dealings. "That's right."

"What night was that? Tuesday, wasn't it? March twenty-second?"

"Yes. How'd you know?"

"Some people who work there mentioned that you were around. It's nice to share an evening with your wife at her place of work, isn't it?"

"Yes," Howard said warily.

"Though I understand you weren't with her the

whole time. You spent a good part of the night with the producer, Miss Gilbert—isn't that her name?"

Howard focused all his willpower on the task of holding his face expressionless. "Amanda Gilbert," he said.

"Amanda, yeah. She a friend of yours?"

"Why would you say that? She works there, that's all. She works there—"

"Hey, hey." Giacomo held up both hands. "Take it easy. It's just that some folks at the TV station seemed to think you and Amanda were pretty friendly with each other. Maybe a little less friendly when your wife was around."

"What are you implying?" Howard breathed, as if the question needed to be asked.

"Not implying anything, Mr. Barwood. How does Amanda feel about those offshore accounts? She like the idea?"

"I never told—" He caught himself. "She doesn't know anything about my private affairs." Damn, *affairs*—the wrong word to use. "She's Kris's business associate, that's all. We have no personal relationship—"

"Funny." That was Heller, finding his voice for the first time in a long while. "She told us something different when we talked to her a couple of hours ago."

There was silence. The detectives stared at him. Howard stared back, his gaze ticking from one interrogator to the other. He had no way of knowing if they had actually talked to Amanda or were merely hoping to elicit some incriminating response. But if they hadn't interviewed Amanda yet, they soon would. And she would break. She was weak. Any woman who needed to assert her individuality by having a tattoo stamped onto her butt, for God's sake, was weak by definition. And what had he ever found alluring about that ridiculous tattoo anyway?

"Mr. Barwood?" Giacomo ventured.

Howard looked at him, then widened his field of view to take in the table, the fluorescent light panel overhead, the bare walls, the short-nap carpet, the metal wastebasket in the corner. It was real to him finally—where he was, whom he was facing, what was happening here. This was a sheriff's station, and these men were cops, and they thought he was mixed up in the attack on Kris. They thought he had a motive. They thought they had the goods on him.

"Mr. Barwood," Giacomo said again, not making an inquiry.

"I have nothing more to say," Howard whispered. "I want to consult with my attorney."

Heller closed his notepad.

"Okay." Giacomo shrugged. "That's your right, as we informed you." He placed a hand on the tape recorder. "We're terminating this at ten-hundred forty-six."

He shut off the recorder. He and Heller stood up. Howard noticed they weren't smiling anymore.

"You're in trouble, Howard," Giacomo said, not bothering to call him Mr. Barwood any longer. "You conspired with that psycho Hickle to ice your wife. You know it. We know it. And we're going to prove it."

They left him alone in the room to think about that.

43

Although Travis hadn't had any sleep in more than twenty-four hours, he was curiously alert. An uninterrupted adrenaline rush from midnight onward had supercharged his nervous system, replenishing his energy whenever his strength began to flag. He had not felt this good in years.

Part of it was the excitement of the final round. His strategy, conceived months ago, had reached its climax. In a day or two, everything would be settled. The game would be over. And he could sense that it would end in his favor. Despite unanticipated setbacks, despite twists of fate that had required creative improvisation on his part, he had persevered and won.

At 11 A.M. he parked in front of the bungalow in Culver City and got out of his car. The street was deserted. No doubt most of the residents were at work or engaged in their daily chores. Even if someone was watching from a window, he wasn't overly concerned. It was unlikely that any of the neighbors had ever seen Howard Barwood up close, and from a distance one well-dressed, middle-aged white male looked basically like another. He could pass for the owner of the house.

And he had a key. Months earlier, when he had done his research on Howard and learned of the bungalow's existence, he had anticipated the possibility that he might require access to the house. He had thought of planting the cell phone here—the phone he'd purchased himself and registered in the name of Western Regional Resources—although as things had turned out, he had been able to place the evidence in an even more incriminating location.

In any event, wanting to be prepared, he had come here late one night when the house was empty. Working in the glow of a pencil flashlight, he had used an impressioning file and a key blank to produce a new key for the front door.

That key was in his hand now. He used it to enter the bungalow.

The house was still, the air heavy. He moved quickly down the hall to the master bedroom. Abby had told him that Howard kept a gun in his nightstand.

And yes, there it was in the sock drawer, a neat little Colt .45.

Travis picked it up with his bare hand. He had no worries about fingerprints. The gun would be thoroughly wiped before he left it for the police to find.

He was pleased to see that the serial number had not been filed off. The gun was traceable. There was every reason to believe that Howard Barwood had bought it legally and that it could be easily linked to him. Presumably Howard had purchased the .45 for the same reason he had installed bars on the bungalow's windows. In a high-crime neighborhood he had wanted to feel safe.

Travis pocketed the gun after confirming it was loaded. Soon enough he would have a use for it. He would send Hickle an e-mail arranging a rendezvous in a secluded spot—perhaps one of the trails in Topanga State Park. At dawn, say, when no one was around. When Hickle arrived, Travis would sidle up next to him conspiratorially, and then—bang—one bullet to the head. He would wipe the gun and leave it in Hickle's dead hand. Easy.

But first Hickle had to take care of Abby. Well, she ought to be going home later today. She would face a one-man welcoming committee.

The police could be trusted to put it all together the right way. They would say that Hickle had killed Abby, then had shot himself in the woods. They would say that Howard Barwood, a real estate developer with ready access to property assessment records, had given Abby's home address to Hickle sometime in the previous two or three days, just as he had supplied Hickle with other inside information. They would say that Howard had even gone so far as to arm Hickle with a handgun he himself had purchased.

Howard would deny everything, but no one would believe him. It was all very tidy, no loose ends. The only person who might have been able to see through the charade was Abby. She was intuitive about these things. She was also a few hours away from being dead.

He only wished he could have contrived a way of killing her personally. Sadly, the idea wasn't practical. He must content himself with arranging the hit, pulling the strings as Hickle's puppetmaster. It was not all he wanted, but it was enough.

Abby had to die. She had failed him, after all.

And failure was the only sin he recognized.

Travis left the house, locking the front door. The sun was high and bright, and he blinked at its glare, keeping his head down as he walked to his car.

There had been a time when he loved southern California's sun. Lately he preferred the dark. He wasn't sure why.

44

In midafternoon Abby woke for good. She knew she had recovered from the concussion. Her headache was gone, and she felt no aftereffects of her head trauma. After lunch she informed the nurse of her diagnosis. The nurse smiled and suggested that a second opinion might be required.

"Fine," Abby said, but once the nurse had left, she dressed herself in yesterday's outfit, preparing for her departure.

There was a rap of knuckles on the open door. She turned and saw Kris Barwood in the doorway. Abby almost said hello, then hesitated, struck by the wildness in Kris's eyes.

"Kris," she said uncertainly.

"Abby." The word was less a greeting than a dulled acknowledgment.

Abby looked her over. Kris was fully dressed, evidently ready to leave. In the hallway a TPS officer in a sport jacket and open-collared shirt stood post. "Going home?" Abby asked.

"In a minute or two. Mind if we talk first?"

"Of course not."

Kris shut the door for privacy, leaving the TPS man outside. "I guess you've heard," she said.

"Heard?"

"It's been all over the radio and TV—with my loyal friends at KPTI leading the charge."

"I've been asleep," Abby said gently. "Why don't you sit down?"

Kris looked at the visitor's chair in the room and took a moment to study it, as if trying to decide what it was for. Then she sat. Abby assumed a lotus position on the unmade bed.

"It's Howard," Kris said, her voice hushed.

Abby nodded. From the look on Kris's face she had already guessed that word of Howard Barwood's probable involvement in the crime had been leaked to the media. "What about him?"

"Well"—Kris lifted both hands, palms up—"he's disappeared."

This took Abby by surprise. "Disappeared?"

"Yes."

"When?"

"An hour ago. He—he ran away. He ran away." She needed to repeat the words in order to make them real.

"Kris, what happened exactly?"

"What happened . . ."

"Tell me the who, what, where. The bare essentials. The time line." Abby hoped an appeal to the woman's journalistic training would prod her to organize her thoughts.

The tactic worked. Kris straightened, her gaze clarifying. "All right, here it is. Howard was with me for most of the night. This morning he left for an interview at the sheriff's office. It was supposed to be routine. I expected him to return, but he never did. Finally I reached him at home. He was in a meeting with his lawyer, he said. He promised to call back."

"But he didn't?"

"No. Half an hour ago I called again. This time Martin Greenfeld answered. Howard's attorney. He said—well, it's just incredible what he said."

"Take it easy. Go slow."

"He said detectives had arrived with a search warrant for the house. *Our* house. They'd searched and found something. They seemed excited about it. Martin saw it in a clear plastic evidence bag. It looked like a phone, he said. A cell phone."

Abby knew it had to be the phone registered to Western Regional Resources, the phone Howard had used to call Hickle's apartment. "Where did they find it?" she asked.

"Martin wasn't sure. It could have been in a closet downstairs, but why? Howard and I have three cell phones, but we don't keep any of them in a closet."

"And after this," Abby prompted, "Howard disappeared?"

Nod. "He said he had to use the bathroom. Must have slipped out of house via the rear deck. He went to Terri and Mark's place down the road and asked if he could borrow one of their cars—they've got three. Claimed he had to visit me here and his Lexus wouldn't start. They gave him the keys. He got out of the Reserve without being spotted. Now he's gone, just gone. And it's on the news, every channel. They're saying he's a suspect in the case, and he fled. Martin won't give me any details, and I'm afraid to call anybody in the news business—I can't talk openly with them. They're my friends, but they won't hesitate to screw me if they can get a jump on the competition. I'm about to go home now, and I still don't know what's going on."

Her last statement was a plea. Abby knew she had to

answer it. "Travis told you I was here?" she asked, stalling a little.

"Yes, he mentioned it."

"But he didn't say anything else, anything about Howard?"

"Not a word."

"Well . . . he should have." Courage was a quality Abby prided herself on possessing, but she felt it desert her as she met Kris's earnest, beseeching gaze. She steeled herself for honesty. "All right, here's what I know. Hickle had an informant who ratted me out. We don't know exactly who it was, but . . ."

Kris shook her head in automatic denial. "No. Oh, no, impossible."

"There's evidence."

"What evidence?" Kris got up, paced the room. "The phone? Is that it? The cell phone they found?"

"I think so."

"What could a phone possibly mean?"

Abby answered with a question of her own. "Has Howard ever mentioned a company called Western Regional Resources?"

"No."

"On Thursday night Hickle got a call at his apartment, probably to arrange some kind of rendezvous. I traced the call. It was made from a cell phone registered to Western Regional Resources. Travis found evidence that the company is something Howard set up offshore—without your knowledge, apparently."

"No, it can't be true. Why would he want to help that man? What conceivable motive could he have?"

"Well, this is only speculation . . ."

"Say it," Kris snapped, losing patience.

"Western Regional Resources isn't the only such corporation Howard established. He owns several. He's been moving his assets—your assets—into secret accounts offshore."

A beat of silence in the room while Kris took in this statement and its implications. "Hiding our assets," she said finally. "That's what you mean, isn't it? Hiding them from me?"

"It looks that way."

"So he can leave me and . . . when we split the estate . . ."

"Exactly."

"Then it's true." Kris turned away, staring blankly at nothing.

"What's true, Kris?"

"That he's been unfaithful to me. I suspected it. But I couldn't quite believe . . ." Her voice dropped to a whisper. "I wonder who she is."

Abby didn't answer. This was one blow she could spare Kris. "We might be wrong," she said weakly.

"About the transference of assets, the corporations he's set up?"

"Well, no. That part is pretty well nailed down, but it doesn't prove he's Hickle's accomplice. Not absolutely."

"Not absolutely," Kris echoed, then added in the same faraway voice, "I wonder if he thought I was unfaithful too."

"Why would he think that?"

"I've been offered the opportunity. I turned it down. But Howard might not have known that. He might have thought I went through with it." She looked away. "It's even possible he wanted us both dead."

Abby couldn't see what Kris was getting at, but she

asked no questions. Sometimes it was better to just let a person talk.

"No." Kris shook her head after a moment's reflection. "That doesn't make sense. Howard couldn't have anticipated that Paul would be with me in the car last night, could he? It was the first time he'd ever accompanied me home."

Paul.

Abby sat very still, but under her the bed seemed to shift as if in a small earthquake, or perhaps it was her world that had shifted off its foundation.

In the same moment Kris came back to herself, realizing what she had revealed. "Oh, God, I didn't mean to say all that."

Abby found a smile somewhere inside her and brought it to the surface. "It's okay, Kris."

"Did you know? Did he tell you about his . . . his interest in me? I mean, you work so closely together."

Closer than you know, Abby thought—but not quite close enough. "He didn't have to tell me," she answered, her voice steady, her face an emotionless mask. "I guessed."

"Oh." Kris was relieved. "Of course. You're intuitive about people, aren't you?"

"Nearly always," Abby said lightly, putting the slightest ironic emphasis on the first word. "So Travis suggested having an affair?"

"He didn't put it quite that crudely, but, well, he made it clear he was available. He's not seeing anyone now, apparently."

"When did the idea first come up?"

"Oh, I guess around the time when I was threatening to leave TPS. He was very persuasive in getting me to stay. At first I thought the rest of what he said was just part of his sales pitch. Later, when he restated his intentions, I began to realize he was serious."

"You must have seen him fairly often."

"He would drop by the house every week or so. Almost always when Howard was out playing golf. He's quite a golfer, my husband. Paul would update me on the situation. It was mostly business, but then there would be a more personal touch. He knew I was unhappy with Howard. He said we would be good together. But he was a gentleman about it. No pressure at all."

"Did anything happen?"

"No. I may be the last person in the greater LA area to still honor my marriage vows. I won't say I wasn't tempted. He can be a charming man. And who knows? Maybe we would be good together, as he said. But we never did anything. It was all very civilized."

"Do you think he's still interested?" Abby asked, already knowing the answer.

"I know he is. I think, in some odd way, he's a lonely man. He told me once that the women he's been with have never meant much to him. They're merely—well, diversions, I guess. Novelties. Like with Howard and his toys."

"Toys," Abby echoed. There was a stillness within her that felt dangerous, like the hush before a storm.

"I doubt the women were to blame for that. Paul's a fascinating man, but he keeps his feelings close to the vest. He doesn't open up, and he's not easy to open up to."

"But you got him to open up."

"Emotionally? Yes. We just connected, I think. Even though we never did more than talk, it seemed to mean a lot to him. To me too. I needed somebody to talk to, somebody who wouldn't treat me like a paranoid fool because I worried about Hickle all the time. Somebody who would show me some respect. Howard never respected my feelings at all."

"How do you think Paul felt about your time together?"

Kris smiled. "He told me it was like coming alive at the age of forty-four. As if he'd been numb for years, withdrawn and tight, until . . ."

"Until you."

"I know it sounds silly—"

"No, it doesn't. What about Howard?"

"Howard?"

"You seemed to think he suspects you of actually having an affair."

Kris pursed her lips. "I think I was being hysterical. The truth is, I doubt Howard has a clue that Paul has ever looked at me as anything other than a client. He's too wrapped up in his toys and cars and . . . maybe this plot against me."

"If he is Hickle's accomplice . . ."

"Yes?"

"You'll be free of him."

"I suppose I will."

"And Paul will still be there."

"You're asking if I might hook up with him?"

Abby nodded. "It seems to be what he wants. And from what I can tell, it's what you want too."

Kris laughed sadly. "Oh, hell, I don't know what I want. You know, everybody's life is such a mess, isn't it? We're so screwed up, all of us." She fixed her blue gaze on Abby. "Except maybe you."

"Me?"

"You're one of the few truly self-sufficient people

I've run into. I'll bet you wouldn't get your love life tied up in knots like this, would you?"

"Don't be so sure."

Kris lifted an eyebrow. "So you have your blind spots too?"

"Maybe just one. But it's a big one."

"Well, I'm glad we have something in common."

Abby was silent. She didn't know what to say.

"It's good you told me all this," Kris added. "I wouldn't have wanted to find out from the police or our lawyer."

She took a step toward the door. Abby stopped her. "You never answered my question."

"About Paul? A future with him?" Kris canted her head to one side, an unconsciously glamorous pose, her blond hair falling across one shoulder like golden smoke. "You know, it's funny."

"Is it?" Abby wasn't finding anything funny right now.

"Before last night I would have said no. But now . . . well, Paul Travis saved me. He pulled me out of that car and dragged me to cover with shotgun shells flying. He saved my life." She emitted a short laugh like a sob. "Howard didn't even come out of the house."

Abby nodded slowly. She'd heard everything she needed to hear. "Thanks, Kris."

"What for?"

"This talk."

Kris shrugged, honestly bewildered. "I'm the one who should thank you for all you've done. And just now . . . for listening."

"I'm a good listener." Abby smiled. "Everybody tells me so."

They said good-bye. Abby sat on the bed and listened to Kris and her bodyguard walk away down the hall. Their footsteps faded out, and Abby was all alone. Still she didn't move. She thought it was possible she would never move again. Maybe she had experienced too many poundings, physical and psychological, over the past twenty hours. She was worn out. She'd thought—she had honestly thought—

"I thought he loved me," she whispered, saying the words aloud to hear them in her own voice.

She had always been wary of love and intimacy. She had protected herself from hurt. Yet it seemed all the barriers she had raised had not saved her. Or perhaps it was the barriers that had been the problem. Had she been too vigilant or not vigilant enough? Or was it wrong to blame herself when what mattered was Travis's dishonesty, his betrayal?

Eyes shut, she wondered if she had loved Paul Travis, imagined a life with him. It seemed ridiculous to plan a future with a man who wouldn't even kiss her in public for fear of exposing their relationship. Why, then, had she continued to see a man who gave her so little? Perhaps because he demanded so little in return. It was a relationship that had seemed to suit them both. Some people had marriages of convenience. Theirs had been a love affair of convenience. She could see the plain truth now, but never before. The mind was capable of phenomenal feats of self-deception. And the heart . . . the lover's heart . . .

"The heart has its reasons," she murmured. She had read those words someplace—where? Oh, yes. In Kris Barwood's yearbook, in Raymond Hickle's bedroom.

The heart has its reasons, which reason knows nothing of. Hickle's heart, and Kris's, and Howard's, and Travis's—and hers too, she guessed. Hers too.

45

The doctor took his time coming to see her, but by 5 P.M. he had given Abby a clean bill of health, and at 5:30 she was in the backseat of a cab, riding toward Hollywood. She watched the streets flow past in a grainy smear. The orange sun burned through the taxi's rear window and pressed against the back of her head.

After her talk with Kris, she had turned on the TV to follow the news coverage. Hickle had achieved the status he'd always longed for; he had become, in some sense, a celebrity. His photo, several years out of date and taken apparently from an employee identification badge he'd worn on one of his various jobs, was flashed on the screen whenever any local station interrupted its Saturday afternoon programming for another pointless news update.

Howard Barwood was no less famous. A photo of him at a charity function was broadcast with almost equal regularity. Both men were still missing. The only new development was that a car stolen last night from Malibu had been found, abandoned in the Sylmar district of the San Fernando Valley. Since the car had disappeared around the same time that Hickle made his escape, he was presumed to have taken it. How long the car had been in Sylmar, and where Hickle was now, nobody could say.

The cab dropped Abby near the Gainford Arms. Her Dodge was still parked on the side street where she and Wyatt had left it. She unlocked the door and keyed the ignition.

Home was where she wanted to go, but first she had a stop to make. She drove to Hollywood Station, arriving after 6 P.M. By now Wyatt ought to be on duty.

She hated entering a police station; the fewer cops who saw her face, the better. But she had two questions to ask, which Wyatt might be more inclined to answer if she spoke with him in person.

She left her gun and locksmith tools in the glove compartment so she wouldn't set off the metal detector in the station house. At the entryway she paused to look again at the swollen, westering sun. Having slept for much of the day, she found it odd that the darkness was coming on so soon. She wondered what the night would bring.

In the lobby she asked for Sergeant Wyatt. The desk officer spoke into the phone, then said the sergeant would see her in a minute or two. As it turned out, she waited more than ten minutes. When Wyatt appeared, he led her into an office down the hall. He didn't speak to her until the door was closed.

"Abby, how are you doing?"

She lifted her arms to demonstrate that all her parts still worked. "Made a full recovery."

"You ought to be home resting."

"I'm on my way home now. Did you just come on duty?"

"Yeah, that's why you had to wait awhile. I conduct a briefing at the start of the watch."

"You mean like on *Hill Street Blues*? 'Be careful out there'?"

He smiled. "I just tell 'em to watch their ass." The smile faded. "Maybe I should start telling you the same thing."

"I can take care—" She stopped.

"Of yourself? I know you can, most of the time."

"Okay, last night was an exception. I couldn't have made it without you. And I guess if you want to tell me to watch my ass, I can't argue, since you already saved it for me. That fair enough?"

"Fair enough." Wyatt dropped into a chair. "So why are you here, Abby? I have a feeling you don't pay a visit to your local police department very often."

"I want to know something."

"Why am I not surprised? Go on, ask."

"Hickle apparently stole a car in Malibu and ditched it in Sylmar. That much is public knowledge. What isn't public is the make, model, and plate number of the car he replaced it with."

"What makes you think we know what car he's driving now?"

"I'm not saying you know anything for certain. But come on, Vic, we're talking Sylmar on Friday night. Auto thefts aren't exactly uncommon in that district. My guess is, you've got at least a couple of grand theft autos that occurred in the appropriate time frame— say, one to three a.m."

"Okay, we do. Three of them, in fact."

"I want info on those vehicles. One of them is probably Hickle's new set of wheels."

Wyatt studied her with narrowed eyes for a long moment. "You don't plan to go looking for him, I hope."

"No."

"Then why do you need that information?"

"He tried to kill me once. He may try again. If he's looking for me, I'll stand a better chance of spotting him if I know what vehicles to watch out for."

"How could he come after you? He knows only your Hollywood address, and you're not going back there."

Abby shrugged. "Haven't you been watching the news? Howard Barwood is suspected as Hickle's accomplice. Don't you think Howard could find my home address if he wanted to? He knows my name. He used to be in real estate."

Wyatt looked away, his face pained. "I never thought of that. Which makes me feel pretty goddamned stupid."

"You've probably had a few other things on your mind. So can I have the info?"

"Yeah, hold on, I'll get it."

He left the office and returned with a BOLO sheet. "Until we can nail down which vehicle he lifted, we're not releasing these details to the media. We don't want some hothead opening fire on a teenager who took one of these cars for a joyride."

"I don't intend to open fire on anybody." Abby copied the details from the Be on Lookout form into her notepad. The stolen vehicles were a '96 Civic, an '87 Mustang, and a '92 Impala.

"I'm sure you don't," Wyatt said, not sounding sure at all. "But if you see any of these cars, call me. No heroics, please. Not this time."

"I hear you." She flipped her pad shut and handed back the sheet. "One other thing. Do you know if Culver City PD is watching Howard Barwood's bungalow?"

"They've put an unmarked car across the street. If

Barwood shows, they'll grab him. Did you tip them off?"

"Travis did. I asked him to, if Howard fled."

"How'd you—" Wyatt dismissed his own question. "No, don't tell me how you knew about the bungalow. I don't want to know. So it sounds like you anticipated he'd run."

"It occurred to me. He's weak, I think. Like a kid who's never grown up. A crisis would shake him. He'd panic. That's my reading of him."

Wyatt nodded. "It comes back to what we were talking about in that bar the other night—how there aren't too many grownups in LA. Except I don't know too many overgrown kids who try to have their wives knocked off by a stalker."

"People are complicated," Abby said softly, thinking of Travis and his attempted seduction of Kris. "They can always surprise you. Even the ones you think you know best."

46

It was fully dark, nearly 7:30 P.M., when Abby reached Westwood. A block from the Wilshire Royal she turned onto a side street and cruised through the hilly residential neighborhood, looking for any of the three stolen cars. Nonresident parking was prohibited on most of the streets, and there weren't many vehicles for her to look at. None matched any entry on the list.

She wondered if she was being paranoid about this. Hickle might not know her home address. Even if he did, he might have higher priorities at this moment than revenge. His survival was at stake. He was a hunted animal. By now he could be across the border or holed up in a motel in the desert.

Then she shook her head, recognizing this train of thought for what it was—a dangerous rationalization. She was tired and wanted to rest. She was trying to convince herself that it was safe to let down her guard, safe to go home and curl up on her sofa and listen to soft music. It was what she badly wanted to do, but what she wanted and what she needed were not necessarily the same thing. Intuition had saved her life on other occasions. She could not afford to ignore it now.

Her intuition insisted that Hickle had not forgotten her. He had learned where she lived. He was close.

*   *   *

The condominium board of the Wilshire Royal had been displeased when plans were announced to raise a sixteen-story office tower directly across the street. The building, the board members correctly prophesied, would be an eyesore. It would block the views from all the units facing Wilshire. It would reduce property values.

Their petitions and protests had been ignored. The building had gone up, a charmless monolith with dull black walls and narrow slits of windows. The Black Tower, people had inevitably called it. Then when the building was nearly completed, the developers had unexpectedly filed for bankruptcy. Work had halted. And those residents of the Wilshire Royal with northern exposures had been left to stare at a lightless, lifeless hulk.

But tonight the Black Tower was not lifeless. There was body heat inside. There was breathing. There was the slow beat of a patient heart.

Hickle waited, caressing the hammer-forged barrel and walnut stock of his Heckler & Koch 770.

He had arrived at the building last night. In the trunk of the stolen Impala, he'd found a tire iron, with which he'd pried open the locked gate at the construction site. He had climbed nine flights of stairs, guided by his flashlight, lugging his duffel with the shotgun and rifle inside. On the tenth floor he had made his way along a dark hallway to the front of the tower, where bands of plate glass windows overlooked the rushing traffic on Wilshire Boulevard. Directly across the street was the Wilshire Royal. Travis had told him that Abby's apartment was number 1015, fourth from the Royal's western end. Hickle had taken up a position opposite her window. Her lights were off, the curtains shut. But she would be home eventually.

Among the scattered tools left by the workmen were a glass cutter and a straightedge. With them, Hickle had cut a rectangular hole in the plate glass window. Through it, when the time came, he could fire.

To pass the hours, he had tested the rifle's laser sighting system, throwing a long beam of reddish-orange light along the target-acquisition line. Its glowing pinpoint was brilliant in the variable-power scope. He could direct the beam at any spot on Abby's balcony or on the curtains behind the glass. And where the beam alighted, a bullet would be sure to follow, racing at twenty-two hundred feet per second across a distance of thirty-five yards.

Periodically he had checked the flags in the Royal's forecourt. He didn't think windage would be a serious factor at this distance, but he was prepared to adjust his aim by a few inches if a strong gust kicked up. The flags had been limp throughout the day and evening. There was no breeze.

Most of his time was spent simply waiting. He never rested, never shut his eyes. Now and then he shifted his position, easing the strain on his muscles. He tried standing and squatting, then sitting on a rough work table he'd dragged close to the window. Reluctant to leave his post even for a minute, he had ignored hunger and thirst and the need to urinate. After a while these bodily urges had faded. Now it was eight o'clock on Saturday night, and he felt nothing. He was numb.

The only thing that still worried him was a flare-up of his nerves. He would have to hold the rifle steady, and he wondered if his body would betray him at the critical moment. He didn't think so. He had failed to kill Abby once. By a miracle he had been offered a second chance. He did not intend to squander it.

Abby checked the area north of Wilshire. There were more parked cars here. Many, belonging to UCLA students, were older models. Several times she thought she spotted one of the wanted vehicles, but always the license plate proved her wrong.

Passing a house with dark windows and a FOR SALE sign on the lawn, she noticed a car in the carport. The car might be a Chevy Impala; at a distance it was hard to be sure. She parked down the street and returned on foot, carrying her purse with the gun inside. At the foot of the driveway she studied the car. It was parked facing out, which meant the driver had backed into the carport, an awkward procedure. And the front license plate frame was empty. California drivers were issued two plates and usually mounted both.

She switched her attention to the house, which looked empty. She made a show of studying the FOR SALE sign, her performance for the benefit of anyone watching from a neighboring residence. Having established her bona fides as a prospective buyer, she approached the front door. The short, curved walkway allowed her to pass close to the bay window. The curtains were open, and although the living room was dark, she could see well enough in the glow of the streetlights to know that the furniture was gone. Whoever was selling the place had already moved out. So why was there a car in the carport?

She rang the doorbell. No answer. She rang again without result, then entered the carport, her purse open, her index finger on the trigger of her Smith & Wesson.

These precautions were unnecessary. The carport was empty.

She checked out the car. It was indeed a Chevrolet Impala of the right age and color, and the rear license plate matched the number on the BOLO sheet. Hickle had parked here, off the street, and had removed the front plate to reduce the risk of the car's discovery.

The possibility that Hickle had stolen one of the other cars on the list, and that this one had been ditched by some other thief, wasn't worth considering. She had learned not to think in terms of coincidences where her safety was concerned. The Lincoln had made its way from Sylmar to a carport within a few blocks of her home. That meant Hickle had left it here. He knew where she lived, and he had come for her.

Abby went around to the side and rear of the house, inspecting every door and window. She found no sign of entry. Hickle must have used the house only to ditch the car. He was hiding somewhere else. In her condo, maybe, or in the condo building's garage. Security at the Wilshire Royal was tight, but the same could be said of Malibu Reserve. Hickle had penetrated that compound. He could get inside the condominium building if he wanted to. He might have been there since early this morning, lying in ambush for more than twenty hours by now.

It seemed just plain rude to keep him waiting any longer.

47

Headlights.

They splashed into the ramp that fed into the Royal's underground garage. A small white car paused at the gate, and an arm extended out the driver's side to feed a passcard into the slot.

Hickle leaned close to the window. The car was a white subcompact, not new. It looked out of place in this neighborhood. He peered through the rifle's scope and glimpsed dark hair, a pale forearm. It could be Abby. He wasn't sure. Her car had not been parked near his at the Gainford Arms, and he'd never seen it.

The gate lifted. The white subcompact rolled down the ramp into the garage.

He had a funny feeling it was Abby. The car was too beat-up to belong to the typical resident of the Wilshire Royal. It could have been a maid's car, but why would a maid be arriving for work at 8 P.M. on Saturday? And the driver's dark hair had looked familiar.

It had to be Abby. Just had to be.

"She's home," Hickle whispered.

Abby guided the Dodge up to the access gate to the Wilshire Royal's underground garage. She knew there was a fair chance Hickle was lying in wait nearby, ready to open fire with the shotgun when she stopped to use her passcard. Though she could try to return fire, she would be in a vulnerable position—and her Dodge, unlike Travis's staff car, wasn't armored.

She fed the passcard into the slot with her left hand, while her right hand gripped the .38 Smith. She almost wanted him to try something.

The gate opened without incident. She steered the Dodge inside, heading down the ramp to the condominium building's underground garage.

The garage was the next possible location for an ambush. Hickle might have concealed himself behind one of the reinforced-concrete pylons or in somebody's vehicle. He might be waiting for her to emerge into the glow of the overhead fluorescent lights.

She parked in her reserved space, then slung her purse over her shoulder, holding the Smith down at her side, and got out of the car quickly. She let a moment pass after she shut the car door, listening to its echoing thud. Slowly she came out into the open, her eyes big, her gaze ticking from shadow to shadow.

No shadows moved. No gunshots sounded.

She remained alert as she crossed yards of concrete to the elevator and pressed the call button. The elevator carried her to the tenth floor. She put the gun in her purse but kept her finger on the trigger.

The elevator doors hissed open. She scanned the hallway before proceeding to her apartment. The likeliest place for Hickle to hide was her own living room. She kept her head low, away from the peephole, and cautiously tested her doorknob. Still locked—a fact that proved nothing, but if the door had been unlocked, it would have proven a great deal. She looked closely at the knob and detected no sign of tampering. In her search of Hickle's apartment she'd found no locksmith tools or books on picking locks. She had no reason to assign him any expertise in that area.

Nonetheless, she tensed herself for violence as she found her key and unlocked her door. She removed the Smith from her purse and held it in front of her. If one of her neighbors stepped into the hall in the next few seconds, she would have some explaining to do.

The most dangerous part was what came next. Going in, she would be most vulnerable. She had no idea what sort of greeting she might expect inside.

Hickle aligned the rifle's muzzle with the hole in the glass, keeping the barrel inside to muffle the shot. Carefully he sighted the balcony, the glass door, the curtains.

He would wait for her to open those curtains. It shouldn't take long.

When she stood in plain view, large in the scope, he would depress the trigger—gently, gently—and one-twentieth of a second later, there would be no more Abby in the world.

Abby went in fast, throwing open the door and pivoting inside, then ducking into a crouch so any shots aimed at her head would go high.

No shots. She closed the door but didn't touch the wall switch near the frame. Her living room was in darkness; trusting the Royal's security, she never bothered with putting her lights on timers. She was glad it was dark. If Hickle was hiding and she was exposed, light was her enemy.

In her purse she carried a mini-flashlight with a surprisingly bright beam. She found it by feel and held it in her left hand, well away from her body, before turning it on. If the light drew fire, she wanted the shots aimed away from her vital organs.

She swept the light over the living room, picking out the familiar shapes of her sofa and armchair, her stuffed animals, her stereo equipment and TV. Nothing had been moved or damaged, as far as she could tell.

Into the kitchen, then down the short hall to the bedroom. She shone the flashlight into closets and behind doors, into the shower stall in the bathroom, and under the bed. She returned to the living room and checked behind the couch and the chair.

Hickle was not here. He had never been here.

She ought to be glad about that. Not having a psychopath in one's home was ordinarily cause for celebration. But she knew something was wrong. She stood in the dark, her flashlight angled low, the gun still drawn and ready, and pondered the situation. Hickle hadn't staked out the garage entryway or the garage itself, and he hadn't gained access to her condo and waited for her return.

So where was he?

She tried to put herself into his mind. He was angry and desperate. He had the shotgun and was itching to use it. His fantasy of squeezing the trigger and blasting Kris into hell had been unfulfilled. He wanted a second chance.

But the shotgun had not been his first choice of weapon, had it? He'd bought the rifle first. Fitted it with a scope and a laser targeting system. Last night when she'd entered his apartment to debug the place, she hadn't seen the rifle in his closet. He must have taken it with the shotgun. He must still have it.

The shotgun was good only at close range, but the

rifle was made for longer distances. For marksmanship. With the scope and the laser, it was a sniper's gun.

Sniper . . .

Her gaze moved to the curtains over the balcony door.

48

Hickle was losing his patience. If it had been Abby's car he'd seen, she should have arrived in her apartment by now. But no lights had come on inside, and the curtains had not opened.

"Come on, you bitch," he muttered, blinking away a bead of sweat that trickled into his left eye. "Show yourself. I only need one shot, Abby. One shot."

Abby considered the curtains. If she had not suspected that Hickle was in the neighborhood, what would she have done upon entering her condo? When she and Hickle shared Chinese food the other night, what was the first action she had taken?

She had opened the windows to let in some air.

She understood then, not in words but with a pair of bodily sensations—the prickling of the short hairs at her nape, the sudden tightening of her abdominal muscles.

She pictured herself parting the curtains, sliding open the glass door. For a few seconds she would be framed in the doorway. Visible from outside. From a vantage point across the street. And across the street was an unfinished, unoccupied commercial building—a perfect hiding place for a man on the run.

Abby switched off the flashlight and approached the glass door. Kneeling to make a smaller target, drew the curtains an inch apart. She stared past the railing of the balcony at the black, looming mass of the office tower. She waited, her gaze fixed on the row of windows opposite her own.

Some time passed, maybe a minute, maybe five or ten. She didn't move, barely breathed.

When a dim red light flickered in one of the windows, she knew what it was. Hickle, restless, testing the laser sighting system.

"You're so sly," Abby breathed, "but so am I."

She saw the beam alight on the balcony railing, then jerk a few inches higher, pressing a faint dot of light against the glass door a yard to her left. The dot crawled toward her. Carefully she closed the curtains and let the red dot slide over the fabric, some of its glow bleeding through to stamp a pale tattoo on her face.

After a moment the light winked out.

Hickle was now sure he had been wrong about the car. It must have belonged to some maid or some teenage kid—anybody but Abby. She had not come home yet.

But she would. Soon.

He simply had to wait. He would not give up. This time he would not fail.

Abby left the condo, locking the door. As she rode the elevator, she took a quick inventory of the contents of her purse. Gun, spare ammo in a speedloader, microrecorder, mini-flash, cell phone.

On the ground floor she bypassed the lobby and ducked into the small gym, empty on a Saturday night. The gym's rear door opened on the street behind the Royal, which Hickle couldn't see from his firing site. She headed down a side street, intending to cross Wilshire a few blocks away and circle around to the tower.

As she walked, she fished the phone out of her purse and, after a moment's hesitation, speed-dialed the second number in the unit's memory.

Ringing at the other end. Two rings, three, and the click of a pickup.

"Hello?" Travis said. She had reached him at home.

"Paul, I've located Hickle. He's in Westwood. He's—well, he's stalking me. Nice turn of events, huh?"

"Abby, slow down—"

"No time to slow down. I've *found* him, Paul, I've found him . . . and now I'm going to need your help."

49

Travis arrived in Westwood fifteen minutes after Abby's call and saw her standing, purse in hand, on a back street behind the office tower. The building loomed over her, sixteen floors of unfinished commercial space, untenanted except for one very temporary occupant.

He couldn't decide whether to be angry or pleased. True, he had expected Hickle to take care of this job. Travis's instructions had been explicit, and even an amateur ought to have been able to fire a laser-sighted rifle accurately at a distance of a hundred feet. Something had gone wrong, though in their brief phone conversation Abby hadn't revealed any details. Still, she was alive when she ought to be dead, and this fact disturbed him.

On the other hand, things hadn't worked out so badly, had they? He had been given the opportunity to take care of matters personally. He expected to enjoy it.

Travis parked his Mercedes down the street, then patted himself to be sure neither of the handguns he was carrying had printed against his jacket. In his shoulder holster was a Beretta 9mm, the gun issued to most TPS personnel. If Abby noticed the Beretta, it was no big deal; under the circumstances she would expect him to be armed. The second gun was the one he couldn't let her see.

Tucked inside his waistband near his spine, hidden by the jacket's flap, was the Colt .45 from Howard Barwood's bungalow.

He got out of the car, closing the door quietly, and approached Abby at a brisk walk. "Where is he?" he asked, keeping his voice soft, as if he had no idea that Hickle was on the tenth floor of the tower, well out of earshot.

Abby glanced at the building. "Up there."

"You sure?"

"I saw him sighting me with the laser beam on his rifle. He's staking out my condo, planning to make like a sniper."

"How could he—" Travis knew it was a mistake to play dumb. "Of course. Barwood's in real estate. And he knows your last name. He passed along your home address."

"Looks that way."

"You said you actually saw the laser? Then Hickle must have seen you."

"No, I kept my place dark and peeked through the curtains. I don't think he's fled yet."

"Why didn't you call the police?"

"And tell them what? That I think a strange man is aiming a laser beam at me from the building across the street? They'd send out the men in white coats with the butterfly nets."

"You could've told them it's Raymond Hickle."

"Sure. How many reports about Hickle do you suppose they've received since this story hit the airwaves? My bet is, he's been spotted everywhere from Oxnard to La Jolla." She looked at him, her face upturned in a streetlight's glow, her expression hard. "The only way I could convince them to take me seriously is if I explain my involvement in the case. And that's more than I want them to know."

"They'll know it anyway, once Hickle is in custody and starts to talk."

"But maybe they'll be inclined to go easy on me, overlook some of the various felonies I've committed over the past few days—if I'm the one who brings him in."

A minivan burred past, headlights sweeping the pavement. Neither of them spoke until was it gone. Then Travis said, "You want to capture him? Personally?"

"I was thinking more along the lines of us. As in you and me together. We go up into the building, and we find a way to make Hickle come along quietly."

"We're not vigilantes, Abby."

"Speak for yourself. Besides, it's a citizen's arrest, that's all. We get the jump on Hickle, disarm him, and drive him to the West LA police station."

"Unless he gets the jump on us first."

"It's a risk, admittedly." She puffed her cheeks and blew out a jet of breath. "Everything I've done in the past few days is a risk. So how about it? You with me?"

Travis made a show of indecision, though of course there was nothing to debate. On the drive over, he'd plotted gambits to get Abby inside the tower, where he could deliver the fatal shot with no risk of being heard by anyone but Hickle. Now she was volunteering to go in, even insisting on it. It was perfect.

"Oh, hell, I'm with you," he said finally. "Of course I am."

50

Kris was glad she lived at Malibu Reserve. The gated complex had not protected her from Hickle, but tonight it served the almost equally important function of keeping out the crush of reporters stationed beyond the fence.

As a reporter herself, she understood the desperation that drove her colleagues to camp out on the shoulder of Pacific Coast Highway, or dial her home number sixty times an hour until Courtney disconnected the phone, or buzz overhead in helicopters taking footage of her deck, or slip onto the beach and focus long lenses on her windows. She had done such things herself during the earlier stages of her career when she had delivered reports from the field.

She risked opening the vertical blind on her bedroom window far enough to see a slice of the moonlit beach and the pale, restless tide. She supposed she couldn't complain too loudly about her present circumstances. She was, after all, alive. Her heart still pumped, and her face in the mirror had lost some of its haunted, harried strangeness. She had begun to feel almost like herself again. The strain of waiting for something to happen had finally been relieved. Now there were only the broken pieces of the aftermath that had to be picked up and put together.

She wondered where Howard was.

The police had confirmed what Abby had told her—he'd been hiding their joint assets in overseas accounts. The accounts had been opened in the Netherlands Antilles. It was possible Howard had made his way to the islands already. Of course he need not go there. He could travel anywhere in the world and still be within reach of his money. Martin Greenfeld, Howard's lawyer, had speculated that he might have headed south to Mexico, but Kris couldn't picture her husband in a Third World country. He was too accustomed to the good life.

She doubted he'd ever planned an escape. He had fled out of sheer panic. He would be caught before long. Her husband had his areas of competence, but running from the law was not likely to be among them. Luckily for her, in conspiring with a stalker to have her killed, he had proven equally inept.

"To have me killed," she whispered. It still didn't seem real. An extramarital affair she could believe all too easily. But to plot her murder . . . to rendezvous with a man like Hickle, a lunatic, a fanatic . . .

Her husband, the overgrown child with his toy trains and radio-controlled model airplanes, was a killer. Or a would-be killer anyway, foiled only by Travis's foresight.

"Kris?" That was Courtney, calling from downstairs.

Kris left the bedroom and leaned over the railing in the hallway to gaze down at the living room. "Yes?"

"They just talked to me over the intercom. The guys in the cottage."

Travis's men, still on post until Hickle was caught. "And?"

"They said Mr. Barwood's come back."

These words were so strange that Kris couldn't absorb them. "Come back?" she echoed.

"He's here with some police. They're letting him in for a minute. I don't know why." The doorbell chimed. "That's him."

There was silence while Kris tried to sort this out. "Well, let him in," she said finally.

Slowly she descended the stairs while Courtney opened the door for Howard and four other men. One was Martin Greenfeld, two others were uniformed patrol officers, and the fourth was a man in a business suit who must be a detective.

At the foot of the stairs Kris stopped, staring at her husband from across the room. She saw fear in his face and something more, something that might have been a desperate, faltering effort at courage. He was not handcuffed, she noticed. They had granted him that much dignity. "Howard," she said.

"Hello, Kris." Even from a distance she saw the heavy swallowing motion of his throat. "It's not true."

"What isn't?"

"All the crap they're saying on TV. The charges and allegations. I never talked to Hickle. I never gave him any help. I never wanted to see you hurt."

"Then why did you call him on that cell phone?"

"I didn't. It's not even my phone. I never bought it."

"Then how did it get into our downstairs closet?"

"I don't know. It's a frame. It has to be."

Kris had done enough interviews with the guilty to know that nearly all of them said they had been framed. "Then why did you run?" she asked tonelessly.

"I got scared. I figured these sons of bitches planted the phone to hang me. I figured there was no way to fight them."

The man who must be a detective spoke Howard's name in a low tone of warning. He and the two patrol officers hadn't liked being called sons of bitches. Howard didn't seem to notice.

"I came back," he said. "That's what you have to understand."

"You got caught."

"No, I turned myself in. I walked into the West LA station and surrendered. I didn't have to. I was halfway to Arizona when I turned back."

"Arizona? What's there for you?"

"Nothing. That's what I realized. That's why I had to come back. I called Martin"—he glanced at the attorney as if reassuring himself that Greenfeld was still there—"and he worked out a deal. I would turn myself in, and in exchange I'd be brought here."

"Why?" She tried to sound hard, though the effort was exhausting her. "Did you forget your toothbrush?"

"I wanted to see you . . . here, in our home. I had to tell you what I just told you—whether you want to hear it or not."

Kris was quiet for a moment. "That was the deal? Just to be escorted home?"

"Yes."

"Then what?"

"County jail, until Martin can work things out, however long that takes."

Despite herself Kris almost smiled. "A night in stir? I'll bet you'd rather be in Arizona."

"No. Right here is where I have to be. All I want is for you to believe me."

"You did transfer our assets overseas, didn't you?"

"Yes."

"And you've been having an affair?"

"Yes."

"With whom?"

To his credit Howard did not avert his gaze. "Amanda."

Kris blinked, appalled as much by his bad taste as by anything else. "Amanda at work? Anorexic Amanda?"

"I'm sorry, Kris."

She thought of Amanda Gilbert's sympathetic cooing when told that Howard might be unfaithful, her promise to sit down for a nice heart-to-heart. She made a mental note to have the bitch fired. "You could have done better," she said simply.

"I already did. I was too stupid to know it."

Kris knew he was hoping for some encouragement or forgiveness. She would not give it to him. "I think you should go," she whispered.

"I didn't do it," Howard said.

Martin advised him not to say anything more.

The two patrolmen were easing him toward the door when he turned back, grief written on his face. "I never even wanted her. It's just that she was available and, well, she was—"

"Young," Kris said. It sounded like an epitaph.

He left with the others. Before Courtney shut the door, Kris heard the whir of a chopper overhead. Somebody was getting first-rate footage of Howard Barwood as he was led down the garden path to the police car.

It would lead the late news on some local station. Kris hoped it wasn't KPTI.

51

The office tower was hemmed in by cyclone fencing, but the side gate had been forced open, allowing access to the grounds. Abby led Travis directly to it, explaining that she'd already reconnoitered the area and found the way in.

Travis silently admired her diligence. Except for her one blunder in the Corbal case, she really was quite good at what she did. It would be almost a shame to lose her.

But even one blunder was more than he would permit.

The lobby of the office building was two stories high, enclosed by wide windows, one of which had been smashed. Travis stepped through, kicking away wedges of glass that clung to the frame. Abby followed.

The glow of streetlights penetrated only a few feet into the building. The rest of the lobby was dark.

"Bring a flash?" Abby whispered.

"No." He should have thought of it, but he'd had other things on his mind.

"I've got one."

She rummaged in her purse and removed the miniflash. Its beam swept the room, highlighting a quarry-tile floor, curved metal-lath walls partially finished in plaster, and a high coffered ceiling. Dropcloths, ladders, and worktables on sawhorses were distributed throughout the cavernous space.

"No Hickle," Travis said.

Abby shrugged. "If he were down here, we would have been dead the minute we stepped inside."

The beam found a doorless opening in an alcove, with a steel staircase visible inside. She led Travis to the stairwell and played the beam up the shaft, illuminating the concrete walls and steel landings.

"Empty," she said, "at least as far as I can see."

"Then up we go."

"Just a minute." She shifted the flashlight to her left hand and reached for her purse. "I'm starting to feel a little naked without my thirty-eight."

He couldn't allow her to get the gun in her hand. He had to make his move now.

"Don't do that, Abby," he whispered.

His tone stopped her for a moment, which was all the time he needed to pluck the Colt from his waistband and press it into her rib cage.

Abby's gaze ticked down, registering the gun in her side, then rose to his face.

Travis studied her expression. He expected to see shock, fear, anger. He was looking forward to it.

But she disappointed him. What he saw was only a look of sad reproach.

"So it really was you," Abby said quietly. "I'm sorry, Paul. I was hoping I was wrong."

52

Abby watched Travis's eyes narrow as his mouth formed a bloodless line. "You knew?" he whispered, his voice returning in soft echoes from the corners of the stairwell.

"I suspected," she said calmly. "I wasn't sure. I guess I didn't want to believe it."

The muzzle of the gun was a hard circle of pressure against her ribs. She felt the pistol trembling slightly, perhaps with her own breath or with Travis's pulse. She waited for whatever he would do next.

"Hold your hands up," he said finally. She obeyed, her movements deliberately slow, like the subtle progressions of a t'ai chi exercise. "Now give me the flashlight."

She let him take it with his left hand. He took a half step back, the gun shifting to the spot between her shoulder blades.

"All right," Travis said, "let's go."

"Where?"

"Up."

"Is there some advantage to killing me on a higher floor?"

"As a matter of fact, there is. Now get going."

Abby climbed the stairs, guided by the flashlight and the gun in her back.

"I'm betting that gun isn't silenced," she said.

"True."

"When it goes off, the report will echo through the building. Hickle will hear it. He'll panic and flee, maybe take a different stairwell."

"And I may not be able to intercept him. Very good. You get an A plus."

"I'm not your student anymore, Paul."

They reached the third-floor landing and continued higher. Abby noticed that the fire doors on the landings had not yet been installed. Dark halls lay beyond the doorways. They looked like the narrow passageways of a pharaoh's tomb, the kind of place where ghosts walked. But there were no ghosts here. Not yet.

"It's Howard Barwood's gun," she said quietly, "isn't it? You stole it from his bungalow this morning, after you left the hospital."

"That's right."

"Was that before or after you planted the cell phone in the beach house?"

"Oh, I took care of that chore several weeks ago, during one of my visits to Kris to update her on the case. The phone, of course, is registered in the name of Western Regional Resources, though poor Howard never knew anything about it."

"If you planted the phone back then, how did you use it to call Hickle on Thursday night?"

"I didn't. I used a different phone, which I'd programmed with the identical code. It's not hard to do. Some people make a nice living by stealing cell-phone codes."

"What happened to this other phone?"

"It's at the bottom of the canyon behind my house. I threw it off the deck earlier this evening. I had no further use for it."

"Just as you have no further use for me ... or Hickle."

"You catch on so fast. It's what I've always loved about you."

They had passed the fourth-story landing.

"I guess pretty soon you'll have everything you want," Abby said. "I'll be dead. Hickle will be dead. Howard will be in jail or running for his life. And if your luck really holds, you may get to marry Kris."

Travis was behind her, and she couldn't see his face, but from his tone of voice she knew he had registered another small shock. "You even figured out that part of it?"

"It didn't take any major intuitive leaps. Kris told me you've made yourself available. She's under the impression you haven't been seeing anybody. I didn't disillusion her, by the way."

"That's good of you, Abby. I appreciate your discretion."

On the fifth-floor landing now. Halfway to Hickle's firing site.

"I'm sure you do," she said quietly. "It would ruin that part of your plan if Kris found out she's not your one and only. She wouldn't be so receptive to your proposal of marriage. Not that marriage is an essential ingredient in the scheme. More like icing on the cake, correct?"

"Correct."

"You wouldn't mind having her money, her lifestyle, her connections, and with Howard out of the picture, you'd have a pretty good shot at all that. But the main thing has always been rescuing the reputation of TPS. And with the Barwood case, you saw a way to do it. When did you first get the idea? When you did the background check on Howard?"

"That's right. From what I learned, I could see it was obvious that he was fooling around and preparing for a divorce. That's when it occurred to me that if Hickle was believed to have an accomplice, Howard would be the logical suspect."

"You made your move on Kris . . ."

"Just to lay the groundwork for future possibilities. The icing on the cake, as you called it." They were above the sixth-floor landing. "Then I started contacting Hickle via e-mail, feeding him information, prepping him for the attack."

"Did you know about the incident with Jill Dahlbeck?"

"No. If I had, I might have hesitated to use Hickle. I knew he was potentially dangerous, but I didn't realize he was that unstable, that impulsive. I wouldn't have wanted him splashing acid on Kris."

"Or shooting her in the head, for that matter. You couldn't afford to let him succeed."

"Of course not. I wanted Hickle to make his attempt—and fail. Kris had to survive unharmed, or the whole plan would be ruined. Despite everything, her safety really was my highest priority. That's why I switched to the armored staff car and rode shotgun— to be sure Kris was fully protected."

"Then in the aftermath, TPS gets a media makeover. Now you and your staff are the heroes of the hour, a fact that Channel Eight will exploit to the max on their top-rated newscast—thus canceling out the Devin Corbal story, reviving your prospects, and making you the golden boy all over again."

"Something like that. But we needed a scapegoat. If

Hickle had been captured alive, he would have revealed the existence of an informant with inside information. Even if he had been killed in the attack, the police might have found evidence of the e-mail account I'd set up for him, and they would have known he was working with somebody. I couldn't afford any suspicion falling on TPS itself, and certainly not on me personally."

"So Howard was framed as the accomplice."

"Why not? He was the perfect candidate—cheating on Kris, out every night with no good alibi, hiding her assets, preparing for a divorce. When they catch him, he'll never be able to talk his way out of it. Especially when the police find Howard's own gun in Raymond Hickle's cold, dead hand."

"And a bullet from that gun—in me."

"Exactly. And one of your bullets in poor Raymond. Bang bang. You went after Hickle on your own. He shot you, and you shot him. Two corpses. End of story."

They'd reached the seventh floor. Each flight consisted of eighteen stairs; she'd counted. Fifty-four stairs to go.

"Not quite the end," she said. "You haven't explained why you brought me into the case."

"Can't you guess? There were two reasons. The first was of a practical nature. I had to do something to set Hickle off. I'd tried goading him, pushing his buttons, but he kept hesitating. I needed a way to make him crazy—even more crazy than usual. I knew he was paranoid. If he found out the new woman in his life was a spy . . ."

"He'd snap."

"So I sent you in . . . and set you up."

"Nice. But you said there were two reasons. Mind if I take a stab at the second one?"

"Be my guest."

"Devin Corbal."

"Bingo."

"You told me a hundred times that it wasn't my fault."

"I lied. That night four months ago, you fucked up. You *fucked up*, Abby."

She heard the surge of raw hostility in his voice, and for a moment she was reminded of Hickle inveighing against the people he hated, the people with "the look." They were not so different, Paul Travis and Raymond Hickle. Both knew all about hatred and little else.

"You had a job to do," Travis was saying, "and you failed. In one moment of carelessness you jeopardized everything I've worked for, brought me to the edge of bankruptcy. I started in a Newark housing project, and I made it this far—and you nearly took it all away. And you expected me to *forgive* you? To say it's okay, don't worry your pretty head about it? You're supposed to know all about people, Abby. Didn't you know me?"

"Not as well as I'd thought," she said quietly.

"There's no forgiveness in matters of this kind," Travis breathed. "That's one lesson I learned on the street a long time ago. Nobody fucks with me. Nobody takes what I have. And if they fuck up, they pay. *They pay.*"

Eighth floor. Abby's shoulders were getting sore from the strain of holding her arms above her head. Well, it wouldn't be a problem much longer. Two flights of stairs—thirty-six steps—and it was the end of the line.

"Is that why you went after me in the hot tub?" Abby asked.

Travis made a small affirmative sound. "I hadn't planned it. It just happened. I was watching Hickle's building to see if you'd established residency yet. I saw you enter the spa area. And—well, it just looked so damn easy. I would push you down, and in a minute you'd be dead."

"You weren't worried about the consequences?"

"What consequences? Most likely it would have been ruled an accidental drowning. If it wasn't, I could pin the blame on Howard. He was out nearly every night. He would have no alibi except the word of his mistress, hardly a credible source."

"But I wouldn't be around to push Hickle over the edge."

"There were other ways to motivate him. But I wasn't thinking of that. I was thinking—"

"You weren't thinking, Paul. Not at all. You were caught up in rage, a child throwing a tantrum."

"I almost got you," he muttered sullenly. "If you hadn't grabbed that damn beer bottle . . ." He sighed. "I couldn't afford to let you cut me. I couldn't afford to leave any blood at the scene. But it doesn't matter. I've got you anyway. I've got you." They reached the ninth-floor landing, and suddenly the gun pressed harder into her back. "Okay, this is your last stop."

"You've lost count. We want the tenth floor."

"My math is fine. You'll die right here. I'm close enough to Hickle now. And I'd rather have the police find you one story below—like he got the drop on you while you were coming up. Now turn around slowly."

Abby obeyed, wishing they'd climbed one story higher. She'd wanted a little more time.

"I'm impressed, Paul," she said softly. "I didn't think you'd have the nerve to face me."

The flashlight illuminated his features from below, casting the hollows of his eyes into harsh relief. He was smiling. "On the contrary, I've been looking forward to it. So do you want it in the head or in the heart? Considering our relationship, I think the heart would be more appropriate."

"You're not going to shoot me," Abby said softly.

"No? What's stopping me? Sentiment? Affection? I don't traffic in those weaknesses. If you didn't know that by now, you'll have to learn it the hard way." He studied her, a connoisseur admiring a prized acquisition, then lowered the gun to target her left breast. "In the heart, then."

He squeezed the trigger.

Nothing happened.

No shot, no recoil, not even the click of a misfire.

"Sorry, Paul. That gun isn't any good." In one smooth motion Abby lowered her hands, plucked the Smith from her purse, and aimed it at his face. "This one, on the other hand, works just fine."

53

Hickle crouched by the window, his muscles stiff with tension, his gaze still fixed on Abby's balcony.

She wasn't there, and he was beginning to think she would never be there. Maybe she was spending the night someplace else. Or maybe he'd misunderstood Travis, maybe he'd been watching the wrong window all along, in which case he had failed again . . .

"No way," he whispered angrily.

His voice came back at him from the far corners in a ripple of echo, and then behind that echo he became aware of other sounds.

Voices.

Faint but unmistakable, drifting through the vacant corridors to reach him where he crouched.

He was not alone.

Travis pulled the trigger again and again, willing the gun to fire.

Abby watched him, a sad smile on her lips. "Are you done, Paul?" she asked finally.

Slowly he lowered the pistol. He blinked, and for a moment he found it difficult to form words. "How'd you do it?" he whispered. "How'd you—what did you—" He couldn't complete the thought.

"It's simple, really." The .38 in her hand never wavered. It was targeted at his chest. "I knew if you'd framed Howard, you'd want to use his gun tonight—a gun traceable to him. I gambled that it was the one you'd bring."

The one he would bring. The one . . .

But he'd brought two guns. There was the Beretta in his shoulder holster—

Even as he thought of it, Abby shook her head in a warning. "Don't try, Paul. I know you're carrying a backup, but you can't draw fast enough. You've seen me at the firing range. I'm quick when I have to be. And I *will* shoot you."

He studied the hard set of her mouth, the coldness in her eyes. She wasn't lying.

"Anyway," she went on as if there had been no digression, "when I found that gun in the nightstand, I had a bad feeling about it. Thanks to you, I had Howard Barwood pegged as Hickle's accomplice. It didn't seem like a good idea to leave him with a fully functioning deadly weapon, so before I left, I took the gun apart. The Colt 1911, you know, is one of the few models that can be detail-stripped without the use of tools. When I put it back together, I left out the firing pin."

Travis heard everything she said but couldn't quite make sense of it. "You didn't disable Hickle's guns," he whispered.

"No, because the next time he used them for target practice, he would have discovered the tampering. But Howard's gun wasn't being used at all. He hadn't even lubricated it." Abby smiled. "At the hospital, I intended to let you know what I'd done, but that nurse interrupted us. Lucky for me, huh?"

"Lucky," Travis echoed.

"I've always been a fortunate gal. Now, shall we go downstairs?"

Travis was suddenly too exhausted to move. "What for? What's down there?"

"Nothing yet, but after I call a friend of mine at the LAPD, we'll have some company. Go on, Paul."

"Why don't you just shoot me right here?"

"It's a temptation. But I think I'd rather turn you over to our system of justice, risky as that can be in LA. I actually look forward to visiting you in prison. But don't get your hopes up. They won't be conjugal visits."

A surge of helpless anger shook Travis like a fever chill. "You bitch. Fucking *bitch*."

Abby frowned. "That's not very nice. I may have to edit that part out."

"Edit . . . ?"

"I've been running the recorder in my purse ever since we entered the building. Switched it on when I was rummaging for my flashlight. I've got your whole confession on tape."

On tape. She'd thought of everything.

"Get moving," Abby ordered, but Travis still did not obey. The full reality of what she'd done, how she'd handled every detail, was finally real to him.

"You set me up." He said it slowly, almost in righteous indignation. "You *played* me. Asking for my help, telling me how we couldn't call the police, getting me to talk. You put on an act and sold it to me, sold it all the way."

Abby shrugged. "That's my job, Paul. It's what you trained me for—or did you forget about that?"

"No." Travis's anger was spent. "No, I didn't forget." Then his gaze drifted upward, and in a softer voice he added, "But maybe there's something you forgot."

On the upper landing, amid the shadows, the long barrel of Hickle's rifle was slipping through the bars of the banister to draw a bead on Abby's back.

54

Abby saw Travis's gaze tick upward and the almost imperceptible change in his expression. He said something, but she didn't register the words, because she was too busy processing what her eyes had shown her and seeing all the implications as clearly as if she could see the red stamp of Hickle's laser on her back.

The rifle cracked a split second later, but she was no longer in the bullet's path.

Diving for the floor, she hit the concrete hard as the shot flew over her head and clanged on the steel handrail of the banister. A second shot was coming, but before Hickle could adjust his aim she snap-rolled through the landing's open doorway into a dark ninth-floor hallway.

The rifle barked again. Abby scrambled half upright and flung herself into the deeper darkness of the hall until she was out of Hickle's line of sight.

Not Travis's, though. The hall was illuminated suddenly with a fan of light from the flashlight in his hand. Three shots crackled behind her. Small arms fire. Travis had unholstered his Beretta. She spun and snapped off two rounds, then ducked into the nearest doorway.

She found herself in a dark, windowless inner office. From what she'd seen in the sweep of the flashlight, she believed that the office was situated at the intersection of two halls, the short hallway from the stair-well and another, wider corridor running perpendicular to it. Somewhere along the far wall there might be a second doorway, which would open onto that other corridor. She groped her way toward it, her hands sliding blindly over sheets of gypsum wallboard.

She had messed up. She should have made Travis head downstairs sooner, should have anticipated that Hickle might leave his firing site and approach the stairwell. If she died tonight, the fault would be hers. Okay, blame assigned, responsibility accepted. Now shut up about it and stay alive.

She advanced in darkness, feeling her way toward an exit that might not even exist, and then outside the office there was movement. Two sets of footfalls pounding hard. The beam of a flashlight flickered through the doorway she had used. Travis and Hickle were coming after her, hunting her together.

Huddled against the wall, she lifted her .38. If they were reckless enough to burst into the room, she would open fire.

They didn't enter. She saw the flashlight's glow slide past the doorway, and a new brightness dawned a few feet from where she crouched. There was indeed a second exit, and she'd been close to finding it, but Travis, aided by the flash, had found it first.

She pressed her ear to the wall. It was cheap plywood screwed into wooden studs, and it conveyed sound fairly well. She heard faint whispers, the words unintelligible. The two men evidently had stationed themselves at the outside corner of the office, where they could cover both halls and both doorways. If she tried to leave via either exit, they would gun her down.

It was two against one. They had her trapped. Now they were discussing strategy.

Abby liked to think of herself as an optimist, but right now she had to admit that things did not look good.

"Where the hell is she? Where did she go?"

"Calm down."

"God damn it, *where is she?*"

"She ducked into that office. We've got her boxed in. Just breathe easy, Raymond. Breathe easy."

Hickle's ears were still ringing from the flurry of gunshots, his own and Travis's. Every report had been amplified in the echo chamber of the stairwell, the sounds reverberating off the steel staircase and the concrete walls. Even now, in the aftermath, he could hardly hear Travis's low voice over the din in his ears. But he knew the man was right. Keep calm—yes, that was the right thing to do. Keep calm and kill Abby.

They stood together at the intersection of two hallways, where Travis had led him on the run. Instinctively Hickle had yielded to Travis's expertise in this situation, but he couldn't resist pointing out that Travis had not always been in command.

"She had you, man," Hickle whispered. "I saved your ass back there."

"Yeah, you saved me." Travis's face, lit harshly by the flashlight, was all hollows and crevices and bright, staring eyes. "I owe you for it. Maybe later I can buy you a beer. At the moment we have more immediate issues to deal with. Abby's trapped but not defenseless. She carries a thirty-eight Smith, five shots, and a five-shot speedloader in her purse."

"How do you know what she's got in her purse?"

"Because I know her. It's what she always carries. She's wasted two rounds already, so she's got eight left. How's your ammo holding up?"

"Eight rounds to go."

"No spares?"

"Not with me. I left my duffel upstairs."

"Eight shots is plenty. Just conserve ammo. My Beretta was fully loaded—sixteen rounds in the clip, plus one in the chamber. I fired three times, so I've got fourteen shots left. Between us we have twenty-two shots, and she has eight. If we play this smart, we can get her to use up her remaining ammunition. Then she's helpless, and we move in and put her down."

Hickle licked his lips. "Okay, how do we do it?"

"Cover the first doorway. I'll cover the second. We take turns firing one shot apiece into the office. If we're lucky we might nail her. There can't be much cover in there; from what I can tell, it's an empty room. Even if we don't hit her, she'll have to fire back. We count her shots. When she's used all eight, she's history."

"Why not go in after she's fired three shots? She'll be reloading."

"Probably she's already replaced the rounds she wasted. Play it safe. Don't take any chances. Not with her." Travis switched off the flashlight, darkening the hall. His voice reached Hickle like the whisper of a ghost. "Remember, one shot at a time. Save your ammo. The whole point is to outlast her."

"I got it, I got it," Hickle breathed, teeth gritted. He was impatient to get started. Here and now he hated Abby more than he hated Kris. It would be so damn good to make her dead.

55

Working by feel, Abby had found the speedloader in her purse and fumbled two rounds out of it, dumping the two expended shells in the Smith's cylinder and tamping in the replacements. She had five shots again, but five shots didn't amount to much against two armed men.

Her purse also contained a cell phone, but calling for help was not an option. If her pursuers heard her voice, they could pinpoint her position in the office and fire through the wall. Anyway, the police would never get here in time to save her. She was on her own. Ordinarily she valued her independence, but not tonight.

In the hall the flashlight winked off. She heard movement outside. It sounded as if her two adversaries were splitting up. She listened, bent almost double to make a smaller target, her heart beating in her ears. She wished she had light. The wish was irrational, since she couldn't use any light without exposing herself to enemy fire. She wished for it anyway. She didn't want to die in the dark.

Through the first doorway, a purple muzzle flash and a cough of rifle fire. Hickle, coming in. She fired twice at the doorway and scrambled across the floor to a new hiding place as Travis's handgun spit out a single shot from the second doorway. She whirled on him and fired once more, then bolted to another corner and waited, the gun shaking in her hands.

They hadn't entered. She had been sure they were mounting an attack. Now she saw it differently. They'd fired in order to panic her into using ammunition. It had worked. It would continue to work. She had to return fire, keep them out of the doorways, or they could shoot at will until a lucky hit took her out.

She removed the three cartridge cases from her Smith and replaced them with unexpended rounds from the speedloader. Five shots, all she had left.

From the first doorway the rifle cracked again. This shot landed close. She heard it puncture the drywall a yard from where she knelt. She scurried to her left and fired once, not at Hickle but at the second doorway. There was a chance that Travis had stepped into the doorway to take his follow-up shot. She might get lucky.

She didn't. The Beretta fired at her, Travis targeting her muzzle flash, but she was already rolling into another corner of the office, and the shot missed.

She had four rounds now. The odds were stacked high against her. She needed to even things out. There might be a way.

"Raymond!" she yelled. *"He'll kill you next!"*

Even as she said it, she was on the move again, knowing that her voice would draw their fire.

56

Hickle was about to squeeze off another round when he heard Abby's shout. From the connecting hall Travis called, "Don't listen to her."

There was a shot. Travis had fired. Hickle had missed his turn. Still he hesitated, thinking about those words: *He'll kill you next.*

Travis seemed to guess what he was thinking. "She's playing with your head," he said in a loud, calm voice. "She's a shrink, you know."

"A shrink?"

"She's been studying you up close like a lab specimen. She thinks she knows what makes you tick."

That sounded right. Sounded just like Abby. "Fuck her," Hickle said, and he leaned through the doorway and fired once.

There was silence for a moment. He allowed himself to think he'd hit her, or maybe Travis had. Then Abby shouted again. "He never wanted Kris to die. He's framed Howard Barwood—"

"Don't pay any attention to her bullshit," Travis snapped.

"—and he's setting you up as the other fall guy. Raymond, he's not your friend, he's *using* you!"

Two more shots from the Beretta. Hickle knew Travis was rattled. Travis had insisted on not wasting ammo, taking only one shot at a time. Now he was violating his own rule.

"What's going on, Travis?" Hickle yelled.

"Don't let her get to you. You can't trust her, God damn it. You know that."

Hickle did know it. But maybe he couldn't trust Travis either. "You never told me why you did all this," he called out. "Why you jeopardized your own client, your business associate. You never said what it was all about."

"Take your shot, asshole. We've got her right where we want her—"

"What's in it for you, Travis? *Tell me!*"

Travis hesitated long enough for Hickle to know he was improvising some lie.

He had no time to use it. Abby answered first. "He has to keep Kris alive in order to save TPS. And he wants her husband out of the way so he can marry her, Raymond! So he can *marry Kris!*"

And with a crash of terrible insight Hickle knew it was true.

Travis had never wanted Kris dead. He had wanted the attack to fail. That was why he had requisitioned the armored sedan, why he had ridden with her. The whole thing had been a setup, and what he wanted . . . what he really wanted . . .

Kris as his wife. Mrs. Paul Travis. He would get her money, and more than money—her lifestyle, her circle of glamorous friends, her world. He would have everything Hickle had dreamed of and fought for, everything that should have been his, as Kris should have been his, because she had always been his destiny.

"Motherfucker," Hickle breathed.

With a roar of rage he charged for the connecting hall, pivoting around the corner, firing twice with the rifle, both shots aimed at the doorway, and then the flashlight snapped on, unexpectedly close, its glare catching him in the eyes, dazzling him for a crucial split second, and erupting through the glare a shapeless burst of violet like an afterimage of the sun, and another and another and noise everywhere.

Hickle's knees buckled. He staggered backward into the first hallway and slumped against a wall, the rifle leaving his hands as he clutched at the smooth unpainted wallboard. Slowly he slid down, leaving a track of blood, and sat in a spreading red puddle, trembling all over.

Travis crouched by him, the flashlight sweeping the damage done to Hickle's body by the volley of shots. "You're a born loser, Raymond." He did not say it unkindly. He was even smiling. "You can't do anything right. You couldn't kill Abby. Strike one. You couldn't kill Kris. Strike two."

Hickle wanted to say something, utter some protest or excuse, but he had no more excuses, and anyway, there was a lot of blood in his mouth.

"And you couldn't kill me." Travis bent closer, and his gun felt sleek and smooth as it slid gently under Hickle's chin. "Strike three. You're out."

Blammo, Hickle thought numbly.

The last thing he ever saw was Travis's cold smile.

57

Abby heard the coup de grâce delivered outside the office wall.

Her plan had worked. It was no longer two against one. She had gotten Hickle killed. She ought to have felt good about that, but all she felt was nausea, cold and burning at the same time.

Think about it later. There was still Travis to deal with. If she wanted to survive, she had to take him out too.

"Nice job, Abby," Travis said, his voice clear and close through the wall. "I'll bet Raymond was thinking of you when he died."

She didn't answer. Talking would only betray her position, and she knew she couldn't manipulate Travis the way she had played with Hickle. Travis was too smart and knew her too well.

"You've helped me out, actually. I was wondering how I'd explain one of my nine-millimeter rounds in your body. The police would ask questions about that. Now it won't be an issue. You want to know why?"

She wouldn't be goaded into giving a reply. She waited.

"Cat got your tongue? I'll tell you anyway. See, when the police find you, the Beretta will be in your hand. My prints won't be on it. It's not my personal weapon; that gun was confiscated by the sheriff's department for ballistics tests after the little dust-up in Malibu. This Beretta is one I got from the TPS supply room. Only, when the police look at the sign-out sheet, they're going to see your signature. I can forge it."

She was sure he could. He had many talents, some of which she'd never guessed until today.

"They'll think you weren't satisfied with your five-shot Smith, so you stopped by TPS and checked out a backup that packs more firepower. Then you went on a vendetta against Hickle. Tracked him down, and there was a running gun battle, slugs deposited everywhere—rounds from his rifle and your Smith and your new Beretta. There'll be no way for the evidence techs to ever piece it together and no reason for them to try very hard, since the bottom line will be obvious. Double homicide. I'll be inconsolable when I hear the news."

None of that mattered, except for one thing. He had told her he would be using the rifle now. It was the only way he could kill her and pin the blame on Hickle.

The rifle had to be nearly empty. She had lost count of the rifle shots, but there must have been at least six or seven by now, and Hickle's Model 770 had a ten-round magazine. Hickle might have carried spare mags in his pocket, but it was equally possible he kept the ammo in his duffel, and she doubted he had lugged the duffel with him on the run. There was a fair chance Travis was down to only three shots. He couldn't blast wildly. He would have to get close. If she ran, he would pursue until he had a clear shot.

"Abby," Travis called, "did I ever tell you how much I love you?" He was laughing.

She ignored his words. They meant nothing. But from the direction of his voice, she knew he was closer to the second doorway than the first. It was all she needed to know.

58

Travis held the rifle in both hands, ready to fire. The flashlight was lashed to the long barrel with a strip of his shirtsleeve; its glow moved wherever the muzzle pointed. The Beretta was holstered again, to be wiped clean and left with Abby once she was dead.

He was ready. He would enter the office, and then it was a simple matter of kill or be killed. Either Abby would get him, or he would get her. He couldn't hope to flush her out of hiding, and he could no longer force her to waste her ammo. Even if he had been willing to use the Beretta, he could not fire through one doorway while covering the other exit. That was a job for two men, and he was alone.

Still, he had the advantage. Abby's survival instinct was strong, but her conscience was stronger, and it was her conscience that would make her hesitate for an instant before shooting him. He, on the other hand, would not hesitate at all.

He drew a few quick, shallow breaths, overbreathing like a diver preparing to submerge, then readied himself to go in.

In the adjoining hall—running footsteps.

She'd fled, using the first doorway.

He sprinted around the corner, the glow of his flashlight swinging down the hall and spotlighting a blurred, disappearing figure. He almost fired but didn't trust his aim, and then she spun and shot at him once, driving him back behind the wall. When he looked out again, she was gone.

There was only one exit she could have taken. The door to the stairwell. She was trying to get out.

She'd made a mistake. He knew it. He charged down the hall, the flashlight bobbing with the rifle in his arms.

Heading downstairs, she would be an easy target. He would have the high ground. He could fire on her from the landing and finish her before she could take cover.

He reached the stairwell. Professional caution made him hesitate on the threshold of the landing. He swept the rifle downward, and the flashlight's beam picked out a small, familiar shape on the stairs descending to the lower level.

Abby's purse. She'd dropped it as she ran.

No, wait. Too obvious.

She hadn't dropped the purse. She'd thrown it there to mislead him into thinking she'd gone down, when actually—

She'd gone up.

Ambush.

Hugging the doorway, he aimed the rifle straight overhead and fired twice, gambling that she was in the doorway directly above him, leaning out to take her shot.

A cry, a clatter of metal on metal—Abby's .38, clanging on the steel staircase. He'd nailed her.

He burst onto the landing and took the steps two at a time to the tenth floor, expecting to see Abby's fallen body, but she wasn't there.

His flash swept the area and found no blood spatter.

He hadn't scored a hit after all. But she'd lost her weapon. She was disarmed, defenseless. She was finished.

Travis proceeded down the dark hallway at a run. The game was nearly over. The tenth floor would be the killing ground.

59

Abby had liked to believe she was lucky, but that was before Travis saw through her ambush and literally shot the gun out of her hands. She didn't think she'd been hit, but the gun was lost, and now she was out of options and almost out of time.

She ran along a tenth-floor corridor, away from the stairwell into a wider hall that fed into an open floor plan occupying the front half of the building. Bands of plate glass stretched from floor to ceiling along the far wall. Through the windows came the glow of streetlights, starlight, the luminous haze of the city. The light allowed her to orient herself and to dimly see the space around her. When the tower was finished, where she stood would be a large work area partitioned into cubicles. Now it was an open expanse of concrete floor without walls or furnishings.

Nowhere to hide. She ran toward the windows, seeking light. Dying might be a little easier in the light.

In the corridor behind her, there were footsteps, charging hard.

She reached the windows. Past the glass lay Wilshire Boulevard and her condo building. By one of these windows Hickle had waited for the long-distance kill that had never come. Waited with the rifle in his hands, the rifle Travis was carrying now.

Ahead was a worktable, indistinct in the gloom.

Hickle must have dragged it near the window to have a place to sit. She'd found his firing site.

"*Abby!*"

Travis, bursting into the room, the flashlight attached to his rifle like a bayonet, the beam stabbing the darkness as he pivoted from side to side.

He hadn't spotted her yet. She ducked low and kept running, thinking she could use the worktable for cover, buy herself a few more seconds.

The beam swept toward her, rippling across the broad sheets of glass. She dropped to her knees and crawled under the worktable to hide.

The flashlight probing, licking the room's far corners, then drifting back to alight on the table and illuminate her small, huddled shape.

"You're dead, you bitch," Travis breathed, his voice eerie in the dark, and he was coming her way.

She scrambled out from beneath the table and collided with something shapeless and heavy on the floor.

Hickle's duffel bag. Not empty. Something was inside.

He had used the rifle in the stairwell. But the shotgun was his weapon of choice at close range. Why hadn't he used it? Because he'd left it here—left it in the bag.

Her shaking hands unzipped the flap, touched the sleekness of the shotgun's barrel.

Travis sprinting. Light expanding at her back.

She jerked the long gun free of the bag, braced the butt against her chest and spun in a crouch, pumping the action once. Her finger groped for the trigger, and the flashlight found her.

She couldn't see Travis, only the blinding glare. It was easier that way.

She fired at the light.

The recoil upset her precarious balance, blowing her backward onto her tailbone. The room spun in curlicues of yellow glare. She thought she was suffering some extreme onset of vertigo, then realized that what she saw was only the smeared beam of the flashlight as it spun with the rifle across the concrete floor.

The gun and the flashlight attached to it came to rest against a wall, by chance casting the beam at Travis, sprawled limp on the floor.

Abby knew he was dead even without taking a close look. She had fired at him from six feet away. The shotgun shell had cut him almost in half. She couldn't see his features and didn't want to. She imagined that the last look on his face had been one of surprise.

He had never thought he could lose to anyone and certainly not to her. He was her mentor, after all, and she was only the gifted protégèe.

She got to her feet, leaving the shotgun where it had fallen after she fired. She didn't need it any longer. There were no more bad guys to kill.

Her first step was shaky, and she almost sank to her knees before steadying herself. On her way out of the room she stooped to pry the flashlight free of the rifle. Its beam guided her to the stairwell. On the stairs below the ninth floor she found her purse with her cell phone inside.

She took out the phone and sat on the steps, taking a moment to compose herself before calling Wyatt at the Hollywood station.

"Hickle's dead," she said when he came on the line.

"And somebody else too. But I'm okay. I just wanted you to know."

"Abby, what the hell are you talking about? Where are you?"

"It doesn't matter where I am. I'll be calling nine-one-one after I'm through talking to you. Everything will be taken care of. But you have to stay out of it, all right? I mean completely out. Don't visit me, don't call me, at least for a while. I don't want your friend Detective Cahill putting things together—and he will, if anybody connects you with me."

"You still haven't told me what happened."

"Do you promise to keep your distance?"

"Yes, damn it, I promise. Now what's going on?"

She let her head fall back against the cold concrete wall. "It's nothing, Vic, really." She sighed. "Just another day at the office."

She ended the call before he could ask her anything more.

60

Paramedics delivered Abby to UCLA Medical Center, where she was checked for injuries and released. There were two detectives waiting for her outside the examination room. They asked her to accompany them to the West LA station. She was relieved to learn that neither of them was named Cahill.

The first interview was brief. She was too tired to give more than a bare recitation of the facts, carefully edited. But she gave the detectives a present—the tape in her microcassette recorder. It was a fresh tape, which she had loaded immediately before Travis's arrival in Westwood; it contained his confession and nothing else.

The police allowed her to leave by 8 A.M. She had not seen her condo in daylight for a week. She slept until two in the afternoon, then fixed a meal. At three the guards in the lobby said two men from the LAPD were here to see her.

This time she gave the detectives the full story, staying close to the truth but not too close. Fatigue made lying easy; it was as if her body was too worn out to register any of the usual discomfort that a lie detector or a trained observer could catch.

"Travis hired me to move in next door to Hickle. I was there to track his movements, make note of when he came and went. We wanted to get a feel for his daily routine. That was what I was told, anyway. But in fact, I was being set up. Travis told Hickle I was spying on him, and it drove Hickle over the edge. He tried to kill Kris. After he failed, Travis gave him my home address in Westwood. I guess you know what happened after that."

They asked what had led her inside the office building. She said she had begun to suspect Travis. Suspecting an ambush, she'd checked out her neighborhood and found evidence of illegal entry to the office tower. She'd thought Hickle might be inside.

"That's when you should have called the police," the older of the two detectives said in an almost fatherly tone.

"I wasn't sure Travis was guilty. I wanted proof. I wanted it on tape."

The younger detective, less sympathetic, pointed out that her words on tape and the condition of Howard Barwood's gun, recovered from Travis's body, served as evidence that she had broken into Barwood's Culver City bungalow and tampered with his property.

Abby admitted to this. "If Mr. Barwood wants to press charges against me, he's entitled." She allowed herself a sweet smile, aimed mainly at the older cop. "Think he will?"

"Considering that you've cleared him on multiple felony counts, ma'am, I think he'll give you the damn gun if you ask for it, and the bungalow too."

The younger detective wouldn't give up. "On the tape Travis seems to hold you responsible for the death of Devin Corbal. What have you got to say about that?"

"Travis hired me to follow Sheila Rogers, Corbal's

stalker, and report her movements. That particular night, I lost her. I didn't know where she had gone, and so I wasn't able to give Travis's men a heads-up when she entered Lizard Maiden, the club where Corbal was hanging out. Travis never forgave me for it."

"But you weren't actually present at the scene of Corbal's death?" the younger detective asked.

"No."

"Suppose we were to round up some of the people who were in the club that night and show them your photo. What do you think they'd say?"

"Probably that the club was crowded and dark, and it's been four months since the incident, and under the circumstances their memories aren't likely to be reliable. That's what a defense attorney would say, don't you think?"

The younger detective had no answer to that. He and his partner left shortly afterward. Before they left, Abby made them promise that her name would be kept out of the media.

They returned twice in the next two days, asking her to fill in details. At first Abby thought they were leading her on, pretending to believe her version of events while preparing charges against her, either in the Travis shooting or in the Corbal affair. Eventually she realized that the truth was somewhat different. They didn't entirely believe her, but they had no clear idea of how badly she had misled them, and they didn't particularly care.

On Wednesday morning, they paid their last visit and informed her that they were closing the case. Her identity had not been made public. "There was a close call," the younger cop said. By now he was friendlier. He had grown to like her, at least a little. "Channel

Eight got hold of your name through a departmental leak. They were set to run with it, but the story got killed. I think we can guess who did you that favor."

"Probably not Amanda Gilbert."

"Amanda Gilbert is no longer with the station. But Kris Barwood's still there."

All of the following day, Abby lazed around, listening to soft music and fixing simple meals. She did a little redecorating. After some deliberation she took down her print of *The Peaceable Kingdom* and put it in her closet. It no longer amused her to see the lion snuggle up to the lamb.

On Friday morning she drove to Travis's house.

She parked her Miata a block away and walked to the house, lugging a light backpack. Outside the house she waited a few minutes until a Lincoln Town Car arrived, Kris at the wheel. She was driving again—no need for a bodyguard now.

"Abby," Kris said when she got out of the sedan, "I just want to say—I mean, I know everything you did for me—well, maybe not everything, but enough . . ."

"It's okay, Kris."

"Thank you. That's what I'm trying to say. Thank you so much."

Abby smiled. "You may not quite understand this, but all the things I did—I didn't do them for you. I did them for me. No gratitude is required."

"You have it anyway. So why did you call me out here?"

"There's something in Paul's house you need to see. And something I need to see, also."

Kris looked at the yellow police ribbon strung across the driveway. "It's illegal to violate a crime scene, you know."

"So we're Thelma and Louise, breaking all the rules. Come on."

Nobody saw them when they ducked under the ribbon and headed to the front door. Abby had brought her locksmith tools in the backpack. It was easy enough to get inside and equally easy to disable Travis's alarm system; she had watched him punch in the code on numerous occasions. She didn't bother wearing gloves; the police had already been here.

"How are things in your life?" she asked Kris as they headed down the hall to the rear of the house.

"Improving. I've filed for divorce."

"I assumed you would."

"Howard may not have tried to kill me, but he did plan to steal me blind, and he's hopelessly unfaithful. I can do better."

"No argument here." She led Kris into the master bedroom. The bureau drawers had been opened and emptied, the walk-in closet cleaned out, but as Abby had expected, the Scientific Investigation Division technicians had overlooked the TV set. On casual inspection it would never have been identified as a safe.

She tapped the combination into the remote control. The front of the TV swung ajar, revealing the array of compact disks. The first one that interested her was the Barwood disk. She handed it to Kris.

"Your life story is on there," she said, "and Howard's too. The assets he tried to hide from you— you'll find some leads in tracking them down. Get a good accountant on the case."

Kris handled the disk in its plastic sleeve. "Travis had been investigating our background?"

"Not just yours. Everybody's. Including mine."

Abby found the disk with her name on it. "This is what I wanted to see."

The other item in her backpack was a portable computer. She switched it on and loaded the disk labeled "SINCLAIR, ABIGAIL."

"Maybe I shouldn't look at this," Kris said as Abby began navigating through the data.

"Don't be shy. We have no secrets from each other. Travis tried to use us both. It's only fair that we see what he was up to."

The disk contained dozens of scanned articles on the Corbal case. Travis had obsessively collected them. He seemed to feed his frustrations on every insult and innuendo directed at TPS.

The articles held little interest for Abby. She was looking for photos. She found them in a folder marked "JPEG," a standard photo-compression format. When she opened the folder, dozens of thumbnail images appeared in a checkerboard pattern.

Images of her.

There she was, leaving the lobby of the Wilshire Royal to go for a walk. There she was, dining at a coffee shop in Westwood Village. There, visiting a park in Beverly Hills. There, playing tennis on a Sunday afternoon. And more: washing her car, shopping at a mall, strolling on Santa Monica Pier, hiking in Will Rogers Park. Standing on the balcony of her condo—a shot taken from the office tower across the street, the same vantage point Hickle had chosen.

No wonder Travis had been able to guide Hickle to the tower. He had been there himself. Watching her. Photographing her, just as Hickle had snapped Polaroids of Kris jogging on the beach.

"He was stalking you," Kris whispered. "Like Hickle stalked me."

Abby nodded. She was not surprised. Travis had said he'd been watching her on the night when he tried to drown her in the Jacuzzi. She'd had the feeling it wasn't the first time his obsessive hatred had drawn him close.

He had taken photos with a long lens, probably using a digital camera, then had simply stored the images on the CD. His private collection. She remembered the dozens of photos of Kris that Hickle had cut out of magazines and newspapers and tacked to his bedroom walls. Travis had been doing much the same thing, driven by the same compulsion.

"He could have taken a shot at you whenever he liked," Kris said. "When you were on the balcony . . . or walking in the park . . ."

"I'm sure he was tempted more than once. But he was cautious by nature. He was waiting for his best opportunity. He was biding his time."

"Like Hickle," Kris breathed.

"They were more alike than different, it appears."

"But why? Why did he hate you so much?"

"Because I failed him. He had trained me, mentored me, and then I made one mistake and nearly cost him everything he had. This house with the canyon view, his office suite in Century City, his glamorous friends, the A-list parties—he saw it all slipping away, and he blamed me."

Kris shook her head slowly. "We both know how to pick 'em, don't we?"

"Maybe next time our luck will be better." Abby smiled. "It can't get much worse."

Before leaving, Abby gathered up the remaining

CDs, dumping them into a plastic garbage bag. She took them with her when she said good-bye to Kris outside the house.

"Thanks for keeping my name out of the news," Abby said.

"It's the least I can do. And I mean that literally. Thanks, Abby. And . . . take care, will you?"

"I always do. It's how I've stayed alive this long."

On her way home Abby stopped in an alley in West Hollywood and buried the bag at the bottom of a trash bin. There were secrets on those disks no one had any right to see.

That evening she took a walk in Westwood Village, window-shopping aimlessly. When she saw the bar that served good piña coladas, she went inside. The piña colada remained her one weakness. At least she liked to think it was her only one.

She sat at the bar, the glass raised to her lips, thinking of Travis and his secrets.

"Buy you a drink?"

She looked up. It was Wyatt, off duty, in street clothes. He slid onto the stool next to hers and ordered a beer.

"This is the second time you've encountered me here," Abby said with a slow smile. "You're not stalking me, are you?"

"If I were, I'd expect you to know it. You're the expert."

"I used to think so," Abby said, remembering the photos on the disk.

Wyatt's beer arrived. They passed a few minutes sipping their drinks, not speaking.

"Truth is," Wyatt said eventually, "I've been hanging out here a little more than usual. Hoping I might run into you."

"It worked—just as long as you weren't followed."

"I wasn't." He swiveled on his stool to face her. "So how are you doing, Abby?"

"Never better."

"Not sure I believe that."

"Well, I'm alive and fully functional. How are things with you?"

"No complaints."

"And no heat from your friend Cahill or anyone else?"

"Zero heat. There's no reason for anybody to link the Hickle case to Emanuel Barth. And no reason anybody would link me to you."

"Unless somebody at Hollywood Station remembers that I paid you a visit a few hours before the excitement started."

"Nobody remembers. Hollywood's a busy place. People come and go. So we're okay, Abby. The case is closed. It's over."

"It's over," Abby echoed. The words felt good to say.

Wyatt looked away. "I understand how you wanted to keep things out of official channels, but I wish you'd confided in me. When you came to see me at the station, you already suspected Travis, didn't you?"

"Yes."

"You should have said something."

"I wanted to handle things myself."

"Yeah."

"Typical of me. Right?"

"You said it. I didn't." He tipped the beer mug from side to side, sloshing the foam in the glass. "You know, I'd like to keep seeing you."

"Absolutely. You're my main resource in Holly-wood. I depend on you."

"What I mean is—not on business."

"Oh." Abby was quiet for a moment, staring into the mirror behind the bar, where her face gazed back at her, calm and contemplative. "I don't know, Vic."

He studied her, his expression showing more bewil-derment than hurt. "We get along pretty well, and you wouldn't have to keep any secrets from me, so . . . why not?"

"Maybe because of what you just said—I can't keep secrets from you. See, I don't like to be with people who know me too well. I like staying hidden. I like having my space. It's been like that for me since I was a kid. I keep my distance, always."

"That's no way to live, Abby."

"But it's a way to survive."

He let his hand rest gently on hers. "I won't pressure you. If you change your mind, call me. Think it over, okay?"

"I will. I promise."

They parted a short time later. Abby was first to leave the bar. When she looked back from the door-way, she saw Wyatt sitting alone at the bar.

The sun was setting when she returned to her condo. On her balcony she watched the red glaze of the sky. She remembered sitting with her father before another sunset, years ago, and asking if her aloneness, her need for solitude, was a good thing. He'd said it would be, if she could make it work in her favor. His words were like a riddle she had never solved.

Call me, Wyatt had said. She wondered if she would.

In the living room, her phone rang. She left the bal-cony to answer it. For some reason she expected to

hear Wyatt's voice, but it was Gil Harris on the line—
the New Jersey security consultant who'd brought her
in on the Frank Harrington case. "Abby, how you
doing?"

"Fine, Gil. I'm great." She carried the cordless phone
back onto the balcony.

"I take it you've recovered from your latest run-in
with a crazy man," Gil was saying.

She wondered how he could know about Hickle,
then realized he was referring to Harrington. "Sure,"
she said easily. "It's amazing what ten days of rest and
relaxation will do for you."

"Well, I hope you've had enough vacation time, because I've got something that's definitely up your
alley. Interested?"

She hesitated only a moment. "When do you need
me?"

"Soon as possible."

"I'll catch a flight first thing tomorrow, be at your office by late afternoon. Deal?"

"Works for me. Oh, and I should warn you—this
one could be kind of tricky."

"They're all tricky, Gil." She leaned back against the
railing and smiled. "Although I have to admit, some
are a little trickier than others."

After the call she lingered on the balcony, watching
the last of the sunset. She felt her old friend, adrenaline, pumping through her body, and she knew it was
what she needed. Wyatt could wait. Her personal life,
whatever there was of it, could wait. In the end it was
the job that kept her alive and sane. The job was what
she lived for. The job was who she was.

People were always reaching for what they didn't
have—fame or wealth, youth or love, some final vic-

tory or vengeance. They chased after the prizes that would sum up their lives, seeking to complete themselves. It was so easy to get caught up in the chase. Easy but unnecessary, at least for her, at least right now.

If you can make it work in your favor, her father had said.

When the sun was gone and there was only darkness, Abby went inside to pack.